THE
GIRL
IN THE
ROAD

THE
GIRL
in +HE
ROAD

Monica Byrne

CROWN PUBLISHERS
NEW YORK

Published in the United States by Crown Publishers, an imprint of
the Crown Publishing Group, a division of Random House LLC,
a Penguin Random House Company, New York.
www.crownpublishing.com

Crown and the Crown colophon are registered trademarks of
Random House LLC.

Library of Congress Cataloging-in-Publication Data
Byrne, Monica
The girl in the road / Monica Byrne. — First edition.
pages cm
1. Women—Fiction. I. Title
PS3602.Y764G57 2014
813'.6—dc23

ISBN 978-0-8041-3884-0
eBook ISBN 978-0-8041-3885-7

Printed in the United States of America

Book design by Ellen Cipriano
Jacket design by Christopher Brand
Jacket photography by Eduardo Jose Bernardino/Et/Getty Images

1 3 5 7 9 10 8 6 4 2

First Edition

For my mother and father,
the two greatest loves of my life.

THE
GIRL
in the
ROAD

◆

⸭ B⸱⸱K I ⸮

Meena

The Third Flight

The world begins anew, starting now.

I pick my kurta up off the floor and put it back on. The blood makes it stick to my skin. This is a soap opera. It can't be real. I walk back up the hallway toward the kitchen and press the wounds to see how deep they are. I feel panicked. I need to find a knife and break more glass with it. Instead I remember that I dealt with a wound like this at Muthashi's clinic, once, when we got a little girl who'd been bitten by a snake in a strange place, her solar plexus, down in the hollow between the shells of her breasts. I helped apply ointment and white bandaging in a cross. She looked like a little Crusader.

I become calm. This is what happened to me, too.

I don't know who put the snake in my bed. I just know I need to leave home right now because someone here means me harm. It might be Semena Werk. They say they're a humanitarian organization and not a terrorist one, but I've heard of them migrating south, targeting Keralam, though never so creatively, a snake in a bed, that's new. And already Mohini's voice is in my head, scolding me for blaming Ethiopians because of my family history, before I know anything, really. Her voice is so strong. I have to remind myself every few seconds that we're not together anymore. We'd been planning a hero's journey as lovers, Sita and Rama, Beren and Lúthien, Alexander and Hephaestion. Instead I'll go alone.

I'm already at the kitchen counter and pick up my satchel, which contains my scroll, mitter, and cash. I walk out the door and around the pookalam we've been growing by adding a new ring of blossoms for each festival day. The steps lead to the iron gate, the gate unlatches, and then I'm by the road, which is steaming from the monsoon.

I hear gunfire in the distance.

Mohini says: Calm yourself. It's just the firecrackers of children celebrating Onam early.

You're right, I say. I'm not in my right mind. I know this. My heart is pumping adrenaline instead of blood. I start walking and physical realities calm me: mist rising from the asphalt. Then the rain starts again and I withdraw back into my head. I have to get used to being solo again if I'm going on this journey alone. I like company, but only the kind that doesn't ask me to explain myself. I'm simple. Do good, be good, feel good.

I pass the cathedral and the stone wall of the old town rises up on either side of the road. I pick up to a jog. My satchel bounces off my ass. I'm soaked. I can't get any wetter than I am. Gold and pink bougainvillea get in my face and I raise my arm to protect myself. Here's another good reason for leaving home: there's so much shit blocking me down here. Like vines. And even when it's not raining, the air is so thick in the South. It's like breathing co-conut juice.

My initial path is clear. I need to go north, to Mumbai, and

given the concentration of Ethiopian migrants there, do some research. I have some college friends in the city—Mohan from the
Campus Alliance for Women, Ashok from Indian comp lit, Deepti
from rugby. I think she lives in one of the fancy high-rises near
the Taj that collects rainwater for showers. I'm thinking of Deepti,
muscled and dripping in her shower, when I realize I'm already approaching Vaddukanatha at the center of town. I don't remember
the last ten minutes. I digress, especially in crisis.

I reach Round East, the road that surrounds the temple complex at the center of the city, and slow to a walk. I'm ringing the
heart of the world. There are bright banners arching overhead to
celebrate Onam, the end of the monsoon. It's Uthradam Day. We're
supposed to buy vegetables today. I see a vendor I talked to just an
hour ago and turn away before she sees me. I shouldn't speak to
other people right now. I know I'm in a manic state but it also feels
like a sanctified state.

I turn onto Round South and there's a parade of children coming
toward me, defying the rain, like me. They're dressed in white and
gold. They're not well organized. Some boys in the front are carrying a banner that says THRISSUR SPECIAL PRIMARY SAYS WELCOME
AND BLESS US KING MAHABALI, but some rowdy girls are breaking
rank and rushing forward, touching the ground and darting back
in a game of inscrutable rules. I have to change my course to avoid
them. One of the girls hails me and I don't answer, so out of spite,
she calls me Blackie. Lovely. Another reason to leave.

I pass Melody Corner, where Mohini gives voice and dance
lessons, and take a left onto Kuruppam Road. Distance grows between me and the heart of the world. Now there's the march of de-
votional icons all the way down to Station Road. Shiva and Jesus
wear gold to see me off.

I turn into the train station lot. My blood still feels like lemon

juice. The autoshaws sidle up to me, warbling, and I wave them off.
I go to the counter and ask for a ticket to Mumbai. I don't make
eye contact, which makes it hard for people to hear me, weirdly,
always, so the teller has to ask me again. Then he holds out a scanner for my mitter. I hold it out, then snatch it back as if I've been
burned. I can't use my mitter because I might be being tracked,
either by Semena Werk or by the police, or both. I can't rule it out.
Nobody can know I boarded a train to Mumbai.

The teller is startled.

I say, "I'm sorry, I forgot, I need to pay in cash."

He rolls his eyes and fans himself while I dig in my satchel for
the wad of rupees. I hand them over. They're soaked. He tells me
to look into the retinal scanner. I'd forgotten this, too—all the new
security measures. I'm flustered. I tell him I have an eye condition
and that I'm sorry I'm such a bother. He reaches under his counter
and pulls out a stamp pad and stamps my hand with a bar code and
waves me on. An express maglev train leaves in fourteen minutes.
I'm fleeing in style.

The platform is sheltered so I can step out of the rain, finally.
Once there I realize I haven't eaten since breakfast. I walk to one
of the hole-in-the-wall kiosks, where a man looks out from under
hanging metal spoons. I order idlee and sambar and hand over a
five-hundred-rupee note. He takes it by the corner like it's a rotten
sardine and calls a boy to take it and store it in the special box they
keep for paper money. I'm lucky I have cash on me at all. I only
carry it to buy spices from Sunny, the spicewaala on the corner
of Palace Road and Round East, whose cardamom seeds are the
freshest because he picks them in his mother's garden. He wasn't
there today, though, so I had to go to somebody else. I still have
six plastic baggies full of spices for the Onam feast I'll no longer
be making.

There's no one to take care of now, and no one to take care of me.

It's clear that life continues after trauma. What's not clear is whether it's worth continuing to live.

A horn sounds in the distance. I look south. The train is coming, saffron yellow, with its silver emblem, the Lion of Sarnath, and its triad of lights, the top one shining like a third eye.

I have thirty seconds to end this story.

Everyone is crowding the platform. Everyone ignores the safety line. Everyone is so close to death. I move through them, toward the track. Some are closer to death than others. I move my right foot forward and then my left. I repeat the motion. Now I'm closer than anyone. I repeat. I repeat again. Now I'm in the track. I repeat. I repeat again.

The train triples in size.

My legs go weak.

I hear a shout from the crowd. The shout multiplies into many shouts and a thicket of hands pulls me forward.

I close my eyes and feel a great wind at my back, so close it makes my muscles itch.

So the dream continues.

When I open my eyes there's a crowd of people reproaching me with big angry eyes and I know I have to offer some explanation and so I emit lies that I hope will mollify them. "Thank you. I wanted to cross the track but I cut it too close. Thank you. I have a blind spot in my right eye. Thank you."

I'm a minor celebrity on the platform now, which is the last thing I wanted. Stupid, chutiya, stupid. I can't draw attention to myself.

I board the train and take my seat. Back to the dream, back to business. I watch the parking lot for another attempt by Semena

Werk, a bomb or an assassin, or for a sudden burst of police saying, Wait, Stop This Train; we need to question one R. G. Meenakshi, also known as Meena, Meerama, Mimi, Nini, Kashi, or M.

I don't see any police. But I do see a girl on the platform, staring at me.

She's not Indian, too dark even for a Malayalee, probably an African migrant, a rag picker or rat catcher. Her dress is rumpled, once pink, now mottled mustard. Her head is covered like a Muslim, but her dress only comes to mid-calf and she's barefoot. They won't let her on the train barefoot. She fits no prepoured religiocultural profile. She might be a new religion, an immigrant religion. It wouldn't be the first time it's happened in India.

I don't know why she's staring at me. I hate making eye contact anyway so I drop my eyes but I can feel her still staring. What the fuck is wrong with her. Though I could also ask what the fuck is wrong with me, given that I just walked in front of a train.

I'm distracted by a mother and daughter who sit down across from me. They're both immaculately dry and dressed in matching purple saris. The daughter lets her eyes go soft and unfocused around my head because she wants to read my aadhaar, my unique ID and cloud profile, to see what sort of person I am and treat me accordingly. But I keep my aadhaar locked. I'm old-fashioned like that. What you see is what you get. This girl is the opposite. I see her life haloed around her head like a charm bracelet: impeccable schooling, tours abroad, a Brahmin surname. And she's definitely not impressed with me, or with my choice not to display my own aadhaar, or the fact that I'm drenched, or my butch clothes, or my "African" cornrows that Mohini braided and teased me that I was asking for it. For a second I want to turn on my aadhaar just to fuck with her and let slip that I'm Brahmin too. But I stop myself. As Mohini also told me, being looked down upon is good for the soul, good for empathy, good training for a human.

The doors of the train pinch closed with a hiss and a woman's voice tells us to seat ourselves. I switch off my glotti because I'm about to hear the same thing in Hindi, Tamil, Kannada, English, and Mandarin. Now that I know we're leaving soon I feel safe enough to look out the window. And as soon as I do I wish I hadn't.

The barefoot girl hasn't moved. She's still staring at me. She might be twelve and she has baby-fat cheeks and a button nose. Her dress has slipped off her shoulder. She has this expression on her face like I've betrayed her.

I look away. I have other things to worry about than a mentally unstable African girl.

A warm electric hum runs beneath our feet. I hum the same note under my breath until the tones match perfectly and I can't tell one from the other. The note slides up and the train lifts. We're airborne. We slide forward on silken tracks of air.

The barefoot girl is no more.

My hometown, Thrissur, the center of the heart of the world, passes by. The city turns to suburbs, then paddies and fields, then jungle. The train gathers speed. I forget to be vigilant. Mundaneness returns. Banana palms beat by like a metronome. I'm always calmed by being in motion. I feel like a tsunami. I can only go forward. I can't stop until I come ashore, wherever that might be.

The mother and daughter across from me are already asleep, their heads tented together. All my adrenaline retreats from service and leaves me beached and my eyelids begin to flutter.

I dream of an age of miracles, when it only takes two hours to ride all the way from Keralam to Mumbai. And then I wake to find that the age of miracles is Now.

Mumbai Live

Dusk in Mumbai. There's one star in the sky for thirty million souls.

I'm stepping off the train with seven hundred fellow humans and I don't have a place to sleep tonight. Not that I'll be in Mumbai long. Just long enough to plan for the wheres and the hows of the journey. I think again of Mohan, Ashok, and Deepti, but they'd ask me why I was in Mumbai and so I'd have to tell them about the snake, which would lead to other questions I don't know how to answer yet.

Right now I'm hungry and my wounds still sting, so I have to take care of my body. I still have my white box of food. I sit down on the platform away from the crowds with my back to the wall. I use one hand to break the idlee and the other hand to slip inside my jacket to palpate the bites in my skin. They hurt. It's a bright, prismatic pain that means infection. So after I eat, I have to locate first aid.

Just when I finish eating, I see the barefoot girl get off the train.

At least, that's my first thought. It looks like the same girl, still head covered, still barefoot, still unplaceable. How did she get on the train? We left her behind. There's no way she could have boarded it unless she hitched and then was let on by a conductor who didn't make her pay. Only wealthy people could afford that train. Did she follow me? I watch her. I grind my palm into the cement until I feel pain. Then Mohini says to me, soothingly: In a manic state, one sees connections where there are none. You're not usually like this. You're of a sullen nature, certainly, but not paranoid.

I'm sitting behind a support beam, so the girl can't see me unless I let her. She joins the flow of the crowd but moves at half the pace. She looks around. She's clutching her dress, fabric balled in her fists. If this were the first time I was seeing her I'd think about approaching her and helping her. Mohini would, in an instant. Her heart bled for the charismatic lost.

She departs through one of the gates to the outside. I put the last of my idlee in my mouth and get up and head out of the train station in the opposite direction.

Outside of Victoria Terminus there's chaos. D. N. Road is a human river, clogged to a halt with cars, trucks, buses, bicycles, rickshaws, autoshaws, and autorickshaws. A local train glides overhead on its way to the suburbs. I smell oil, sparks, and sewage, all the smells I forgot about while living in a hippie Keralite enclave. People on foot weave between the vehicles and animals weave between the people on foot. There are cows, too. I read that the tourism office lets them loose for ambiance.

On the other side of the road begins Azad Maidan, the gathering ground. At one end there's a cricket game in session, at the other end, a protest. From what I can see it looks like Ethiopian domestic workers. I walk faster. They're everywhere, Keralam and Mumbai both.

Not everywhere, says Mohini, Not at all. This is your fear speaking to you. Your family history.

A flock of children runs toward me, breaks around me, and re-forms behind me. I calm down. I know this city. Already I'm remembering the grid and my orientation within it. I feel good. This is the manic phase of psychosis but it feels good for the duration, and only abnormal afterward, so I'll just accept this, that there's nothing I can do to change my course. I remember this is the park where I bought a first edition of *Crime and Punishment* and read it while eating bhelpuri from a newspaper cone. I sat under the bodhi tree, right over there, the one with the perfect shape. Enlightenment de Dostoevsky.

An explosion goes off.

I fall to the ground and cover my head.

Onam, I tell myself, it's just Onam firecrackers again, even here in Mumbai, they're celebrating a Keralite festival, that's nice.

But then I see a circle of motionless bodies at the end of the green where the protest was and so, it's not firecrackers.

I turn around and see the barefoot girl, staring at me from across the green.

Now things are starting to make sense. I take off in the opposite direction. I'm running perpendicular to everyone else who's either running away from the explosion or toward it. It's like a game. I'm dodging missiles. I collide with someone and I fall so hard my skull bounces. I get up and keep running.

I run till I hit Fashion Street and then turn south. I just assume the barefoot girl's following me. If she's still barefoot, that's fucking dangerous for her, and I can outrun her in boots, especially on stone roads. The faces of people I pass begin to change. First, people who are running toward the explosion. Then, people who only heard the explosion and are worried. Then, people who are still oblivious to any explosion that might have happened and are going about their lives, hefting mangoes at street-side stands.

I'm beginning to get tired. I can't keep running. This is like a movie. What does an action hero do? She takes a turn onto a side street and then ducks into a shop and lets her pursuer run past. So that's what I do. I thank The Film Industry in my head and then take a sharp turn into an alley and count one, two, three shops, then duck into the fourth one, which turns out to be a pharmacy, which solves the problem I began with, of needing first aid.

I get out of sight of the doorway and bend over, wheezing. I hear a cry from the woman behind the counter. She's asking me if I'm all right. I hold up my hand. I can't talk yet.

"You're bleeding," she says.

I look down at my kurta. So I am. The snakebites have opened up again, probably while I was running.

"Did you come from Azad Maidan? Is it from the terrorists?"

So the news hit the cloud already. "Yes," I say.

"Lie down," she says.

I do, out of sight of the doorway. I watch the ceiling and listen to the sound of drawers being opened, product wrapping rustling. I count to forty.

The attendant's face reappears over me. "Fucking Habshee," she says. "They want to live like Indians now."

Here I would usually say what Mohini would want me to say: first, that I'd like to know which Indians she's talking about. And second, that Habshee is a derogatory word for black people and she shouldn't use it. And third, that Habshee doesn't equal Ethiopian.

But right now I don't care.

The attendant begins peeling up my kurta. And then I remember the nature of the wounds and force it back down. She's startled.

"Sorry," I say, "they're not shrapnel wounds, they're something else. I'll take care of it."

She looks hurt but she hands me all of the supplies she'd gathered. I start peeling a square of clearskin but my hands are shaking. She watches me. Then she snaps her fingers.

"You! You went to IIT-Bombay, yes?"

I look at her face again. I realize it's the exact same attendant who worked here when I was at university nine years ago, and had my little episode over Ajantha, not unlike my current episode. Now it occurs to me that every word I say to this woman, and every minute more I spend here, is a liability.

"I have to go," I say. "I can pay for these."

She waves it off. "But how are you?" she says. "You were so sad. I never forgot about you."

"I'm fine," I say. Then I start making things up in case anyone comes to question her later. "Been living in Gandhinagar. Just in town to see family."

"For Onam? Aren't you Malayalee?"

"Nope," I lie. "Just a darkie Gujarati."

That shuts her up.

I thank her for the supplies and head back to the street. No sign of the barefoot girl, so my ruse worked. Why did I say I was from Gandhinagar? That's where my mother's from. It's deep dusk now. The sky is lilac and all our faces glow.

I have to find another place to apply the dressing, the farther away from the explosion, the better. The barefoot girl can't track me if I'm on wheels. I turn to face traffic and raise my arm to flag down an autoshaw, but one with a driver sees me first and veers to the curb. Its cord is dragging in the street so I pick it up and tuck it back before I get in. I tell her to take me to the first place I think of: Butterfly, a Singaporean club at the north end of Marine Drive. Mohini pointed it out to me when we visited last monsoon. It was very much her scene and very much not mine, but that's a good thing, now. Even if the barefoot girl tracked me there, they wouldn't let her in.

The driver powers up. I can see her smiling in the mirror. She has two dimples big enough to hold cardamom seeds. She might be fifteen.

As we speed up she begins shouting, loud enough to be heard over the wind, and I strain to listen so I can respond, but I realize she's talking to someone in her ear. Her sister. Wedding plans. The caterer has fallen through but she knows someone else, a brother of a boyfriend, who's cheap but not cheap enough to insult their in-laws.

Then the buildings pull back like stage curtains and I see the ocean. We stop at a red light. It's beautiful, the golden light on black water. The wind blows in from the bay. The ocean tang is stronger here, dirtier and saltier than in Keralam. There are more spices in this sea.

The light turns green and we swerve right onto Marine Drive. When we break free of the swarms and hit open road, she floors the acceleration and hugs the curve and I press my hand to the side to keep from sliding out. A fingernail moon drops into the sea. I fight to keep sight of it. It means something.

It's full night by the time we reach Butterfly. The autorickshaw slides to a stop and the driver says, "Yashna, wait," and turns around, holding out her wrist with a cheap mitter flashing.

"Do you take cash?"

She wags her head and turns over her palm.

I pay her and tip generously. She tucks the bills into a pocket sewn onto her kurta. "Thank you very much!" she says in English without looking back. I step out and she floors the pedal and is gone.

Butterfly is the neon confection I remember. The bathroom is down a black hall with pink track lighting. In the stall I get toilet paper and ball it up and run it under the faucet and then go back into the stall. For the first time, I take off my jacket and peel up my kurta all the way up over my breasts. The cloth is stuck to the dried blood and rips the scabbing when I pull up. Fresh blood wells like tears and runs down my belly. I wipe it up and press the wet wad of toilet paper to the wound, or rather the constellation of wounds, five scratches of varying depths, not deep but not superficial, either. I don't know what kind of snake it was. It wasn't

a cobra, krait, or viper, because I know them all by sight and anyway, I'd be dead by now. This snake was colored golden bronze.
I take out my scroll and search for images, but none are the right
kind of gold, or at least not native to Keralam. It might be an African species. If it is, that would tell me something.

I wipe up the wounds, apply oil, smear some on my throat because it smells like peppermint, press squares of clearskin to the
wounds, and then the larger white bandage over them. I flex my
torso to make sure it'll stay in place.

I come out and look in the mirror. I'm still wearing what I put
on in our bedroom in Thrissur this morning. I feel the need to alter
my appearance. I take my jacket off, then, and stuff it in my satchel.
I roll up the sleeves of my kurta past my elbows and undo three
more buttons. I can do nothing radical with my jeans or boots. So
I start unbraiding my hair. There's something about dressing my
own wounds and fixing my own hair that makes me feel invinci-
ble. Look on my works, ye Mighty: I both heal and adorn my own
body. In fact I could go for a drink, now.

Here is my new strategy: act normal.

When I come out into the club there's a people-scape of black
silhouettes against violet light. A Meshell Ndegeocello bhangra
remix is making the floorboards shake. The bartender looks like
an old Bollywood hero with shaved and pregnant biceps. He's
wearing a threadbare T-shirt with holes along the seams, carefully
placed, Dalit chic, not authentic. His eyes flicker up around my
head and, seeing nothing, look back down at me.

"What can I get you, madam?"

"Jameson's."

He takes a second look at me. "Malayalee?" he says.

How'd you guess, chutiya?

"Nominally," I say. "My family's lived in Mumbai since the
Raj." Lying is so easy and useful, I don't know why I ever stopped.

"Isn't it Onam?"

"I guess."

"Not much one for tradition, huh?"

"Not really." This bartender talks too goddamn much. And I'm a quiet person. Talking takes energy and anyway, nothing I want to say comes out right. I use my body to talk, when I can, but that's not an option here, so I say, "We live in Santa Cruz East. Haven't been down much lately. What's going on around here?"

"Oh, bombs on Azad Maidan, the usual." He concentrates on pouring my drink, looks angry.

"It's probably Semena Werk," I say. It's prejudicial speech that Mohini would warn me against. Given the snake. Given the barefoot girl. Given Family History. "They can't be reasonable."

"So they bomb their own people?"

"They don't think of them as their own people. They think of them as traitors."

"True." The bartender pushes the glass of whiskey to me. I take a sip and, as soon as the sting reaches my stomach, start to unkink. I hadn't realized how nonlinear the day has been. Now things feel like they're proceeding in order.

"Looked like you needed that."

"I did."

"Glad I could oblige."

I'm beginning to feel comfortable. This may be the end of the mania. Or it may be a new phase of the mania.

"So what else is going on downtown?" I ask.

"Lots of foreigners moving in, especially because of Energy Park."

"Which is—?"

"It's the cluster of towers at the end of Nariman Point, the one that looks like Oz. You should go see it if you haven't. They have a new museum in the HydraCorp building."

"A museum of what?"

"Energy."

"That could mean a lot of things." HydraCorp is one of the biggest multinational energy conglomerates. They're also the hippest because they invest five percent of all profits in developing weird new energy sources. I read about a device to power a Gandhian cotton wheel with human shit. I didn't know whether to laugh or cry.

"Have you heard of the Trail?" he asks.

I pause. Mohini and I saw an episode of *Extreme Weather!* about the Trail a few years ago. The bartender sees I know what he's talking about and says, "At the museum, they give you the corporate version, but it's still worth seeing."

Now memories come back, shook loose by whiskey. The Trail seemed unreal: a floating pontoon bridge moored just offshore from Mumbai, which spanned the whole Arabian Sea, like a poem, not a physical thing. I asked Mohini what she thought it'd be like to walk on it all the way to Africa. She received my enthusiasm in her gracious way but cautioned that the Trail was all blank sky and faceless sea, the perfect canvas upon which to author my own madness.

"What's the corporate version?"

"I can't tell you. Only, don't call it 'The Trail' when you're there."

"Why?"

"They try to discourage people from swimming out to it and walking on it."

I am amazed. "People walk on the Trail?"

"I've heard of—hey, Arjuna!"

Another man is in my space. He's well groomed, wearing a silver-gray shirt, unbuttoned to show a bush of glossy chest hair. He leans across me to kiss the bartender and his leg presses against my knee. He withdraws and presses his palms to me in apology.

And when we make eye contact I realize I know him: Arjuna Swaminathan, half Persian. He was in my nano seminar at IIT. I used to fantasize about him instead of paying attention to the lecture. But unlike the clerk at the pharmacy, he doesn't seem to recognize me.

The bartender says, "Arjuna, I was just telling—what is your name?"

I need to be careful. I lie again. "Durga."

"I'm Sandeep," says the bartender, and plants a clear shot in front of Arjuna, who takes a seat next to me and rolls up his sleeves. His hands are huge. His fingers are muscular. I can see the veins snaking up his forearms. "I was just telling Durga about the Trail. Didn't someone try to walk it last monsoon?"

"Oh yes, people try. They're crazy. Mostly poor kids who hear they can make a living from fishing and so they swim out to it and no one ever hears from them again."

"Arjuna should know," Sandeep says to me. "He works for HydraCorp."

"Do you work on the Trail?"

"No. But I can see it from my office window pretty far into the distance. Every now and then you can see a blur against the sea, so you know someone's camping, because they get special camouflage pods. They only walk at night."

"So they don't get caught."

"I imagine."

"What's the penalty if they do?"

"A night in jail, a month in jail, whatever the police feel like. It's corporate trespassing. But we don't have the resources to patrol it all the time. If you want to just feel what it's like, you can—"

Sandeep snaps his fingers in Arjuna's face. "Don't tell her!"

"Don't tell her what, chutiya?"

"I told her she has to go see for herself."

Then Sandeep leaves to help someone else and Arjuna turns to me, opening his body to face mine, spreading his legs. "He means the museum," he says smoothly. "I can get you free tickets."

On another night, I would not be impressed by his moves. But he's sexy, despite himself. This is a familiar sequence: see someone with potential, want to fuck them, fuck them. It is such a clean exercise of power, such a simple application of effort, leading to a desired result. He hasn't asked about my aadhaar. He didn't even check. I appreciate that.

I keep looking at the floor. Sometimes I can only talk to other people if I can make myself believe I'm talking to myself. "Would you go walk on the Trail, if you could?"

He shakes his head, Western-style. "No, I don't see why. It's like kids who ride the tops of trains. A thrill for thrill-seekers, but that's not me. I have a nice enough life."

And I can tell he does. I can tell he's a tech prince, an unmarried Third Culture playboy with a modern flat and a few servants. He's an only child. His parents are divorced. He works out every morning in his tower's basement gym. I can picture the wings of his iliac crest.

"Who needs thrills?" I say.

He smiles, leans back. "You remind me of someone I used to know," he says, "a girl at college. She wore heavy boots and a scarf around her neck, even in monsoon. She never looked anyone in the eye. She came to class alone and she never spoke."

I think: I didn't make eye contact because eye contact is too intense for daily use and I didn't speak because nothing would ever fucking come out of my mouth right. Sex was how I said what I wanted to say.

"I heard she dropped out," he continues. "But I remembered her. Fierce, but shy, like a femme trapped in a butch body."

I think: How perceptive of you.

But I don't say that. Right now I'm playing Durga, so I say what Durga would say. "What would you say, if you saw her today?"

"Probably? . . . I would ask her for a kiss."

Now my whole loin area is burning. The conversation goes on but the goal is secured, so it's all filler, now, and my mind sustains small talk with Arjuna as I'm having another conversation with myself: I need a place to sleep for the night. He's smarmy but my body needs this. I need the flavor of someone else in my mouth besides Mohini. I can delay planning for my journey or even better, consider this a part of it. I assure myself it makes sense that a day including an assassination attempt and a terrorist attack would end in the urgent need to fuck. In fact I can't even think about anything else right now but fucking this man.

When we leave the nightclub and mount his scooter, before we pull away, I scan the waterfront for the barefoot girl, sitting and looking at the bay, her headscarf rippling along the rampart. I don't see her.

The Trans-Arabian Linear Generator

I wake up alone in a pool of sunlight.

I'm lying in a wad of white sheets. I've slept maybe two hours. I'm still too wound up. The mattress sheet came off in the night and the pillows are all on the floor except the one we used to prop up each other's hips at various points. There are stiff spots in the fabric where our juices dried and left solids behind. I'd forgotten what it was like to have sex with a man. Mohini, by the time I left, had fully changed into a woman with woman-parts. We celebrated with a rosewater cake. I'm a good cook when I want to be. There's so rarely an occasion that merits my talents. But I was so happy to love her, finally, as she wanted to be loved and in the body she wanted.

But when a man is inside me, I feel like the eye of my body is held open, and I'm not allowed to blink.

And how is it possible that . . . Anwar? I can't believe this but I can't remember his name. My mind is blank. I'm sure it started with an A. This is ridiculous. But regardless of his name, why didn't he recognize me from college? Maybe he does, and he just never said so. Maybe we had sex and now he's going out to get the police, who are looking for me, a Malayalee on the run, nursing a snakebite to the solar plexus. Maybe he was filing away the information to use against me later.

This might be a trap. In fact I'm sure it is.

I can't run out of the room this second. I have to think. I sit down. I use the breathing exercises Muthashan taught me when I was little, but they fail.

I find the bathroom, get in the shower, and turn it on icy-cold. I count to ten.

When I get out of the shower I at least have the illusion that I can think more rationally. I run my fingers over the patch covering my wounds. When I took off my shirt last night, he—*Arjuna,* for fuck's sake, *Arjuna*—didn't even acknowledge it was there. He wasn't really present, in general: a vigorous lover, but too aware of himself, parroting endearments from Bollywood films, never having broken the surface and learned the real language.

I find a towel and spread it on the floor. I sit and lean back against the shower door, naked, dewy bush out. I haven't had five minutes in the last eighteen hours to just sit and plan my next move. I close my eyes and try to remember the flavor of my life one day ago.

It was an overcast morning in Thrissur.

The neighbor's dog wouldn't stop barking.

We had a breakfast of chai and leftover Chinese.

Mohini and I had been planning a trip to Africa to try to understand My Family History, which I knew the facts of, but had never really tried to understand. But Mohini felt this was the root of my restlessness. My parents were murdered by a young woman who'd been their friend, an Ethiopian dissident. My mother was only six months pregnant. They were killed in the hospital where they both worked as doctors. I was saved by the nurses who found them.

So an atlas of the Horn of Africa was open on our kitchen table. I wanted to go right away, but Mohini stalled, because she was slower, more careful, the means of transportation important, given her awareness of energy, responsible usage, modes of travel, better and worse, pros and cons. Meanwhile the map became a tablecloth. Africa was obscured by takeout boxes.

I spot two paper tickets stuck in the bathroom mirror. They're white with silver lettering in a slender font: *Admit One to the Museum.* On the other side is the HydraCorp logo, a stylized multiheaded snake. On one ticket is written, *Wait for me.*

I don't fucking wait for anyone. I used to, for Mohini. She was the only one.

There's a knock at the door. I wrap a towel around my body and look through the eyehole. It's the dhobi with laundry. He looks Ethiopian. I open the door.

"I'm sorry, he's not here," I say.

"That's all right ma'am," he says, looking down. "We settle up weekly." He hands me a stack of shirts, ironed and starched.

I close the door without thanking him.

I drop the stack by the door and press my ear to it. He might be a member of Semena Werk. He might be gathering information on me. I probably shouldn't stay here. At the very least I should leave before Arjuna gets back. Now I remember he climbed over me and pressed his body down and whispered in my ear that he was going to get me my breakfast and to make myself at home before dismounting and dressing and leaving. A door shut, a lock turned, and footsteps faded to silence.

I'll get my own breakfast. But I can use the ticket for the research I need to do.

◈　◈　◈

Two hours later I'm back on Marine Drive, standing in front of the HydraCorp Museum. White seabirds are dipping and wheeling overhead. The museum is eleven stories tall and shaped like an eight-pointed star. The outer walls are transparent so I can see the exhibits bunched up inside like intestines.

The lobby is hung with flags representing the consortium of participant nations and corporations. India and Djibouti are prominent. I walk to a sickle-shaped desk and hand over my ticket. The attendant, seeing no aadhaar, hands me a map of the museum and a glossy pamphlet about HydraCorp's many projects.

I can see he's unnerved by my not meeting his eye so I try to put him at ease. I wave the pamphlet. "HydraCorp. Funny name for a company with lots of projects," I say.

He smiles, but I can tell he doesn't know what I mean. It's my fault. My jokes aren't really jokes. They're oblique and not funny to anyone but Mohini. We had a shared language. No one else speaks it. I have to remember that. It seems my suavity from last night wore off and I'm beached again on the shore of awkwardness.

The attendant tells me to start on the top floor, so I get in the Lucite elevator and say, "Eleven." The car begins a smooth ascent. I rise higher and higher above Back Bay, the curve of Mumbai. I see a silver thread bobbing on the surface of the water, stretching toward a hazy horizon. That's that famous Trail, then. I stare at it all the way up.

Once on the eleventh floor I walk in the direction of a black doorway that says CINEMA in silver lettering. The word is comforting. I feel good. I'd like to sit still and watch an educational film. I enter a black velvet room shaped like a half-circle. When I sit, the room senses my presence and the screen dawns blue. I'm relieved it's not an immersive theater where the images get into your head and cup your eyeballs. I like there to be a distance between me and art. Mohini and I argued about that, with her feeling that I was being a Luddite on par with Luddites who impugned film as a valid art form in the early twentieth century. I disagreed. I still do.

The film begins. It's beautifully produced. The narrator is a woman speaking in English with a north Indian lilt and for once it doesn't annoy me. She tells me about the history of artificial energy on our planet. Wood. Water. Coal. Oil. Nuclear. Geothermal. Wind. Solar. The twins Fusion and Fission, both functional in laboratories, but still too expensive to be scaled up. And lastly Wave, which I think is what the Trail is. They call it Blue Energy, the successor to Green Energy. I'm excited for whatever Red Energy and Purple Energy and Orange Energy will turn out to be. I'm starting to feel euphoric.

The narrator doesn't call it the Trail. She calls it the Trans-Arabian Linear Generator, or TALG. She presents a succession of pleasing metaphors: that its technology draws from ancient pontoon bridges which, though remarkable for their time, only spanned distances of a few kilometers, like the Bosporus or the Hellespont, in times of war. And then they were discarded, more easily disassembled than assembled. The narrator emphasizes that the TALG only resembles a pontoon bridge, as its overall shape is more like that of an upside-down caterpillar. Each segment is a hollow, inverted pyramid made of aluminum, and each sunward surface is faced with solar paneling, which seems brilliant to me, makes me want to applaud. Between the segments are hinge arrays called nonlinear compliant connectors, each of which contains a dynamo, in each of which is suspended an egg of steel that bobs up and down as the wave does. This generates energy, as does the solar paneling, making the TALG a dual-action apparatus. Mohini would love this—I wonder if she knew about this. And then the energy is imported to its recipient plant in Djibouti—there is an image of a house in Djibouti lighting up, and a Djiboutian family rejoicing—via superconductor threads made of metallic hydrogen, a controversial material whose manufacturing process was perfected ten years ago. Despite its history of catastrophic accidents, metallic hydrogen is metastable, the narrator assures me; structurally sound, like an artificial diamond. She explains how the TALG was also a breakthrough in intelligent self-assembly on a mass scale, because every component of the TALG has an intelligent chip that, like a human cell, "understands" where it goes and what it's supposed to do and can monitor and repair itself.

Then the tone of her voice changes. This is a pilot project, she cautions. HydraCorp and its partners, mainly the Djiboutian government, rich from recent oil wealth, wanted to know if this is a viable, sustainable form of energy after oil runs out, in which case they'll build a TILG for the Indian Ocean and a TPLG for the Pacific Ocean and all the world's oceans could be crisscrossed with energy generators like a fishnet flung across the entire planet. This is incredible. Mohini would be clutching at my sleeve right now if she were here. And how does the TALG stay roughly in the same place? Well, because of breakthroughs in materials science, the TALG is anchored to the seafloor by means of Gossamoor, synthetic silk modeled on the draglines of Darwin's bark spider, native to Madagascar, which is not only the strongest substance known but weighs about twelve milligrams per thousand meters. And thanks to HydraCorp's partnership with China Telecom, the anchors parallel the SEA-ME-WE 3 undersea cable that carries data between Mumbai and Djibouti before veering up the Red Sea. And how does the TALG survive the many intrusions of maritime traffic? Well, gentle viewer, it turns out that the segments are programmed to sense oncoming ships and take on seawater, sinking up to thirty meters to let the ship pass, and then pumping the water back out to regain buoyancy.

The Trail is a conspiracy of ideal materials. I am fucking amazed.

When the presentation is done, a static map of the world appears and the narrator urges me to explore it with my fingers. I jump up to the screen. If I press my finger to any city in the world, a pie chart surfaces next to it, detailing the breakdown of that city's energy sources. This is marvelous. I press my finger to Djibouti. Thirty percent of their electricity is currently sourced from the TALG. The results are promising. And now I have a theory brewing in my mind, something I want to tell Mohini, a new field of study altogether, about how the source of a society's energy must necessarily shape their language, art, and culture. In the case of Djibouti, their people will be wavelike. Should I call it the sociopsychology of energy?—that then infuses its culture, even its individuals. Mohini was of a solar nature, certainly.

I need to find out my own.

Maybe that's why I'm here. Maybe the universe is conspiring in my favor.

After waiting a polite amount of time the narrator invites me to explore the rest of the museum and I take her up on it. I need to remember to ask the attendant who the voice actor is. I feel sentimental.

I descend a stairway that is slanted, crystalline. For each type of energy the narrator named, there's a dedicated floor, scientifically, technically, stylistically. I lose my intention of researching travel methods. I give myself to wonder. It's a palace of human invention. The Wood Gallery is paneled in sweet-smelling cedar and features a hologram of proto-Dravidian nomads chopping wood and throwing it onto a fire. They're wearing skins and pelts. They introduce a carcass of some woodland animal, which they roast, and it smokes and blackens. The hologram cuts away before they begin eating it, and resets, to one lone nomad wandering in the forest. She's gazing at the trees in wonder. She selects one, thanks it, and then chops it down with her stone ax. The sequence begins again.

I turn away and look at the exhibits against the wall. There's a display where you can select a wood chip, insert it into a clear box for burning, and then watch how much energy is generated. I burn six wood chips. I don't get tired of it. Everything is amazing to me. The display informs me that this gallery is powered by high-efficiency wood combustion, that in fact every floor is powered by the energy source it features. Next to the display there's a pair of immersive goggles that, when I put them on, casts me as a molecule of groundwater sucked up through a tree root. The journey up through the xylem is exhilarating. When I enter the leaf and get split up, I'm presented with a choice: *If you would like to go with the hydrogen atoms, say "hydrogen." If you would like to go with the oxygen atom, say "oxygen."*

I say, "Oxygen."

I'm released from the tip of the leaf and float out into the air. This is like flying. I look below me and there's a forest floor dappled with sunlight. I expect the simulation to pixelate and dissolve. But it doesn't. The trees are sharp and clear and I can see every leaf and flower. I keep floating. The programmer imagined a whole world for me. She's more than a programmer, she's a storyteller, a creator goddess. I'm crossing over a slow-moving green river and then the land turns to desert, where a caravan of trucks makes its way across the waste.

I take off the goggles. I'm back in the Wood Gallery. The hologram sequence is right at the moment where the animal carcass burns. I watch it a second time and then a third time. I feel like I could watch it all day.

I descend the stairs and explore the Water Gallery, where the walls are made of waterfalls, and eight mills pinwheel on the energy they make. The floor is crisscrossed with streamlets, each of which powers a display table featuring a notable world dam.

Below these are the Coal Gallery (uninspired), the Oil Gallery (depressing), the Nuclear Gallery (neon orange and green), the Geothermal Gallery (my favorite besides the Wood), the Wind Gallery (I set all the turbines spinning), and the Fusion Gallery (a hologram of Enid Chung at her bench, making the discovery).

The Solar Gallery is on the second floor. There's a miniature array I'm invited to manipulate, a model of the Sun Traps in Sudan. I remember from the floating pie chart that they supply twenty percent of Europe's energy and forty percent of North Africa's, after ARAP (African Resources for African Peoples) repossessed the land their governments had sold off and forced new lease agreements. My euphoria increases: despite the snake, despite the terror, overall the world is only getting better.

Now is the time for me to undertake a great journey.

I float down the last staircase. I come to the same lobby where I'd first entered. I ask the attendant: "Where's the Wave Gallery?"

He points to a doorway in the wall behind the front desk. "Down one more flight," he says. "It's in the basement."

So this'll be the room dedicated to the Trail. From the doorway comes a warm chlorine smell. This staircase is concrete, not crystalline. It looks much older than the rest of the building. I turn around to ask the attendant a question but he already has the answer: "It used to be a warehouse for fishwaalas. We preserved it and made it part of the museum."

I thank him. I wonder if he can see me glowing, if he can see that I'm a different person than I was when I first came in.

I descend the staircase and come into a low, broad room. In the ground there's a rectangular pool, maybe eight meters across. From this side to the far side is a pontoon bridge, each section bobbing with gentle artificial waves. I realize I'm looking at a prototype of the Trail.

A young woman stands up from where she'd been crouching on the opposite side of the pool. She's wearing a red swimsuit and holding a red foam buoy.

"Namaste!" she calls.

"Namaste. Are you the lifeguard?"

"Yes," she says. "The pool is only two meters deep, but that's enough to drown in. Have you watched the film?"

"The what?"

"The film in the cinema. About how the Trail works."

"I thought you weren't supposed to call it the Trail."

"You're right! The TALG. Don't tell anyone."

"I won't."

"Go ahead and try it," she says.

"Try what?"

"Walking on it, silly!" Even from this far away I can see she gets dimples when she smiles. "That's what it's here for. I promise I won't judge you. Believe me, I've seen everything."

I can sense she's eager to see me try. She probably sees couples and families, mostly. Not another woman alone, like her. I can feel she wants me to succeed.

I take a step toward the edge of the pool. The concrete walls have been painted with murals: a sunset on the left, a moonrise on the right.

I stall.

"So you just . . . walk across it?"

"Well, you can explore it any way you want. You can swim around it if you brought a swimsuit—there's a changing room over there. But walking on it is the coolest thing, in my opinion."

"Won't it sink when I step on it?"

"It's buoyant," she says. I can tell she gives this speech a lot, but makes sure to infuse it with warm reassurance every time. "We call the segments 'scales' because they ripple. Each scale reaches down one meter and displaces three hundred and forty kilograms of seawater. Each scale is also hollow, made of aluminum alloy and shaped like an upside-down pyramid, with a hundred and thirty kilograms of ballast at the bottom to counteract the weight on the top. So you're fine! Some water might slosh in and you might get your feet wet, but don't worry. I haven't seen them sink yet."

"Oh yeah? How long have you worked here?"

She laughs. "Only two months, I guess. I'm on break from college."

"Where at?"

"IIT-Bombay."

"That's where I went."

"You did? What did you study?"

"Nano and comp lit." I don't tell her I left my second semester.

"What a mix. I'm studying nano too."

"It's useful," I say. "Lots of jobs."

She knows I'm still stalling. But she's gracious enough not to say so. She says, "Do you want me to show you how to walk on it?"

"No, it's all right," I say. Now I feel ashamed. Apparently this has been done. I need to get over it.

I take off my boots. I place one bare foot on the surface of the first scale, right in the center of its solar panel, and then transfer more and more weight to it. I'm surprised that it holds. My weight creates a wave and the wave travels up and down the Trail. The surface is rough like sandpaper, not smooth like what I think of as a solar panel.

I continue forward. I let my knees be soft. I hold out my arms like a dancing Shiva. The scales bob more vigorously and I stop to regain my balance. I keep going. I enter a sublime headspace: my body learns from the mistakes I don't have words for, and my anima makes corrections.

I take a final lurch to reach the opposite side. My feet are wet and leave dark prints on the floor. I come face-to-face with the young lifeguard. She's gorgeously built, short, solid, muscular, like a gymnast. Her smile is that of a girl well loved.

"Good job!" she says. "You're a natural."

"Are you?"

"Oh yeah," she says. "When I get bored here, I just run across it."

"Show me."

She smiles and puts down her foam buoy. Then she jogs across, as if it were a solid sidewalk. I'm amazed.

"How did you do that?"

"You just learn to read it," she calls from the other side. "Your body learns to anticipate how it's going to move when you step on it. It's just a matter of practice."

"I want to try again."

"Do it!"

I love her enthusiasm.

Taking the first step is easier this time. My body makes ten thousand unconscious calculations in terms of ankle, spine, wrist. I don't hurry.

"See? Now you're a pro," says the lifeguard when I'm by her side again.

I want to go back and forth all day and get as good as she is. "Have you ever walked on the real Trail?"

She looks over her shoulder to make sure no one is coming down the stairs, and then she sits down at the edge of the pool and dangles her legs in. I roll my pant legs up and sit down next to her. The water is warm.

"No," she says. "It's illegal. I would if someone took me there, though. It'd be interesting to try it out on the open sea where the waves are a lot bigger."

"Do you think it can be done?"

"People have tried."

"Do you know anyone who has?"

"Not personally. You hear rumors about desperate kids and extreme hikers and such. And then there are rumors *about* rumors, like cults and ghosts and whole villages that live off the Trail."

"What do you think?"

"I think there are more things in heaven and earth than can be dreamt of in our philosophy!"

"Wouldn't expect Shakespeare from a nano major."

"Ohho?" she chides. "Free your mind."

She's right. I feel chastened. It was a cliché I said without thinking, only to prolong the conversation because I like her.

I try again. "So there are ghosts on the Trail."

"Well, I've heard of one, Bloody Mary. Supposedly she walks back and forth on the Trail and preys on travelers."

"Anyone seen her?"

"'Course not. But people never come back from the Trail, and so it's easy to say, oh, Bloody Mary got them."

"And not—"

"Not the hundred other things that could go wrong, right. I think it would be hell. Even if you were well prepared. You can't prepare for everything that could happen, even if you went to the Mart."

"The Mart?"

"It's some kind of secret store in Dharavi. They cater to fish-waalas, but I heard they also have a special stock for 'long-term workers.'"

"Like pods."

"Yeah, camo pods. Walkers have to be careful. Security is lazy, but I imagine they don't want to take chances anyway."

"I wonder what walking on the Trail does to them."

"What do you mean?"

What do I mean? I want to tell her all about my new theory of the sociopsychology of energy. How Mohini was of a solar nature but I'm just realizing here in this moment that I'm of a wavelike nature.

How I'm having a transcendent experience at this museum.

How I was at the Azad Maidan bombing yesterday.

How someone tried to assassinate me in my home in Thrissur.

How a barefoot girl has been following me and I think she's an agent of Semena Werk but I haven't seen her in twelve hours and so I think she lost me.

There's so much I want to tell her. But I can't get it out of my mouth. So instead I just splash my heel in the water.

The lifeguard smiles, rescues me. "What's your name?" she asks.

I pause, then remember to say "Durga."

"I'm Lucia," she says. She gazes into space. "I'm studying nano because I want to learn how to make things like the Trail. Did you know that metallic hydrogen is what they use as the superconductor? Amazing. Fifty years ago they couldn't even produce a stable sample."

I stare at the pool surface. "I think some people are like superconductors," I say. "They have no resistance to the energy they receive. They just convey it."

Lucia looks at me and reaches out her hand toward mine.

At that moment, a Chinese couple comes down the stairs. They're wearing kurtas and jeans. They seem embarrassed to have interrupted us. They begin apologizing in English.

"No, it's certainly all right," says Lucia in English. She jumps up. "Would you like to try it?"

As they come forward, I get nervous and step away and raise my arm in farewell to Lucia. She looks sad that I'm leaving. "Durga," she calls, "it was nice talking to you."

I wag my head and begin up the stairs. Leaving so quickly feels wrong but I didn't even know what to say to Lucia when we were alone, much less with other people there.

I come up to the ground floor and see Arjuna at the desk. He is talking to the attendant.

My blood turns to adrenaline again. I turn around and go back down the steps. Back to Lucia. Back to the Chinese couple. They're standing by the side of the pool, looking doubtful.

"Oh, hi again!" says Lucia, brightening when she sees me. "Did you forget something?"

I speak in Marathi, hoping Lucia knows it, hoping the Chinese tourists don't have their glottis turned on. "May I go into the changing room? There's someone upstairs I don't want to see and I'm afraid he's going to come down here."

Lucia sees the look on my face and replies in Marathi, "Yes, of course. I'll cover for you."

As I head toward the changing room, I hear her say to the couple in English, "She needed the bathroom."

I close myself in. It's clear to me now. Arjuna did recognize me from college. He's part of the conspiracy. He means me harm too. The walls are painted with blueprints of the Trail. I stare at them to calm myself. I hear Lucia encouraging the Chinese couple, but as far as I can tell they both just step on the first scale and then back to safety. They thank her and ascend the stairs.

Then a new, manly voice. It's Arjuna. I can hear Lucia greet him but I can't hear what they're saying over the hum of the pool.

He asks her a question, sounding agitated.

She answers, sounding soothing.

He mumbles.

I hear steps.

I brace myself.

I hear an outer door open and close.

Then bare feet padding on concrete over to me. The door swings open.

"Accha, are you a runaway or what?" says Lucia, looking flustered.

"Is he gone?"

"Yes, I said I saw you heading to Churchgate. Cousin?"

"No."

"Husband?"

"No. I just shouldn't see him right now."

"He was hot."

"Yes."

"Are you married?"

"No."

She raises an eyebrow. "This sounds like a juicy story. At the very least you owe me dinner. You can tell me then."

"Okay."

"Want to stay in here a little longer? It's slow today. If anyone asks I'll say the changing room is out of order."

"Yes. Thank you."

She eyes me over, smirks, and shuts the door.

Entanglement

We never make it out to dinner. First she insists on making me chai in her tiny Colaba flat in the old bus depot, cooled only by a ceiling fan, and I tell her that Arjuna's a man I met but don't want to talk to now, which is true, and she seems satisfied.

Then she brings out a box of hashish. I feel anxious but I tell myself that even if Arjuna is part of the conspiracy with Semena Werk, there's no safer place I can be at the moment, and I can use tonight to decide what to do next. So I let my guard down and we smoke. Then we're hungry, so we order tiffin, and when the delivery boy knocks on the door, we scream, and then can't stop laughing when we open the door, and give him a big tip for putting up with us. Then we eat. Then we get in bed together.

She's not like Arjuna. She's very present. She traces my lips and tells me my mouth is shaped like a cowrie shell, which I've heard before. And when we've taken off each other's clothes and her hand passes over the patch between my breasts, she rests her hand back on the spot where I was bitten and asks, "What happened here?"

"Somebody tried to hurt me."

"Why would they do that?"

"I don't know."

In the night, it rains again. I'm still too wired to sleep so I lie awake listening. I've gotten maybe four hours of sleep in the last three days. But I don't feel tired. Meanwhile, Lucia passes in and out of sleep, each time with fresh insights from her dreams. Her innocence is starting to grate.

Near dawn, she whispers, "Durga . . . now we're bound up."

I clench up. This is it. She's going to cling to me like Arjuna did. "How so?"

"It's like quantum entanglement. Our bodies have exchanged matter and so now we're interlinked."

She sounds intimate. I deflect. "I didn't get that far in nano."

"You learn it second year!"

I have to lie again. She's making me lie. "I switched to comp lit after my first year."

"Oh. Well, it means that if we think of our bodies as particles, our states are the same right now, but then when we separate, we remain entangled. Now it's impossible to describe you without describing me, and vice versa. We tell each other's stories by living our own lives."

I feel angry. As angry as I felt euphoric six hours ago. I try to control my voice. "That could be scary. Depending."

"True," she says. "It means that relationships never end. Once made, they just influence each other backwards and forwards in time, for better or worse." She nudges my arm open and docks her head against my breast. "But I'd say this is for better."

So hackneyed. I kiss her head but transfer no love. It's clear she's suffered little in life and it pisses me off. I close my eyes and try to control my breathing. In general I can tell those who haven't suffered trauma from those who have just by looking at them. It's marked on their foreheads and it shows in their eyes. The ones who saw something unbearable and continued living anyway. I'm one of those even though I don't have a conscious memory of it. As a baby I felt my mother die around me. And after a thing like that, why live?

I open my eyes and the barefoot girl is staring down at me with her finger in her mouth.

} BOOK II {

Mariama

The First Flight

Yemaya, can it truly be you?

I have only a memory of her face. You look so tired and sad, and how can a goddess be so? Yet you move as she did, and your eyes are just as dark. If you are Yemaya, oh, please come and rest. Please come sit with me. And please forgive me for losing faith. You are, and have always been, my only beloved. I will tell you my story, which you must already know, but in the act of the telling, all things shall be put right between us.

Where shall I begin?

The snake begins and ends all things, of course.

One day, many years ago, soon after we ran away, I came in from the ocean and crouched in the sand near a fire where some women were cooking. They were grilling what looked like a long black whip. A woman wearing a bright green dress with red sunbursts said, Are you back then?

I nodded, busying my hand around my mouth.

We haven't seen you before, she said. Your people come from the south?

I shook my head, looking at the whiplike thing they were grilling.

Where are you from, then?

I stood up and pointed east, toward the city.

El Mina? Kosovo? Arafat?

We used to live with Dr. Moctar Brahim, but we left.

Who's we?

Me and my mother.

Why did you leave?

Mother says we don't belong to anyone. She said she wants us to belong to each other.

Who got you out? SOS? IRΛ?

We did it on our own.

That's bold. He'll find you.

No, he won't, because we don't have chips, I said.

(That's what my mother kept telling me, Yemaya. I didn't even know what chips were, but I imagined them to be like the gold teeth in the Doctor's mouth.)

The woman cut a portion of the black whip, wrapped it in a cloth, and handed it to me. Take this to your mother, she said. It's sea snake. Something we've never seen before. The weather is changing and bringing us new things to eat.

I thanked her and then walked up the bank. I was so excited because I had two whole days' worth of food in my hands, and meat, at that. I started running along the track back to town and I was careful not to step on the plastic, the broken glass, the goat droppings, the metal slices, the wooden stakes, the tires and tanks, the crumbs of concrete. We'd set up on the outskirts of Sebkha in a cinder-block enclosure. My mother had gathered mats, blankets, and clothes to make a roof, which made for a shaded corner at all times of the day. She'd dragged part of a chain-link fence all the way from the beach to keep out dogs. She'd hung a picture of Bou-bacar Messaoud from a shelf in the concrete so that he watched over us, and she said, Whenever you don't feel strong, look at that picture and then look at me. I've decided that I'm free. You must decide that you're free as well. If the Doctor comes looking for us, we'll travel into the deep desert. If something happens to me, you must promise you will go forth alone and find shelter with kind people and remain free. God will love you more than He has loved me. I will make Him.

But in Sebkha, she'd find work shoveling back the dunes and I'd go to the school at El Mina. Not the special school for children like me, but the real school.

I spotted our shelter and as I half-walked, half-ran toward it, I couldn't help but unwrap the cloth and pry out a chunk of the meat. I put it in my mouth and stopped to chew it. The flesh was oily with a strong fishy aftertaste.

When I got near our shelter I felt that something was wrong, but I couldn't say what. Was my mother within? I peeled back the fence and stepped inside. And there, on the mat in the shaded cor-ner where we slept, I saw a coiled snake, colored sky-blue. When I saw it, many things happened at once: it hissed and struck out at me, I screamed and dropped the food, and then the little bit of meat I'd eaten came up and I had to swallow it again, but it didn't go down quite right, and lodged somewhere between my heart and my stomach.

I remembered my promise to my mother and ran away. I ran toward the city. My throat still burned, and I kept swallowing, but I could only get the spiky bite down so far, and it stuck, festering.

The tracks became roads and the roads became paved streets with checkered curbs. I passed billboards and minarets. I wove between men in robes, all Moors in boubous and sandals, talking to the air. It was just like running an errand for the Doctor—no one bothered me because that's what they thought I was doing, still, running an errand for him while he spent time with my mother. Except this time, I could never return.

I came to a market of arched colonnades and ran down the throughway. Then as I turned a corner, I ran into solid muscle, hard legs under blue jeans. I fell back on my bottom.

Pardon me, said a man with a white beard, who then crouched down beside me. A woman crouched down too, with Western-style hair. They were like buzzards, bobbing, one on either side of me.

Are you lost? said the woman.

I said no.

Where is your mother?

I pointed. They turned to look. I turned to run.

But the woman noticed and caught me by the arm. She was so much bigger than me, Yemaya—so much bigger than my mother, even. It frightened me.

You look hungry, she said. Come with us. We have a tent for children.

The man laughed at my expression. It's okay, he said, you don't have to trust us now. There are people all around us. You just follow us to the tent and if either of us do anything scary, you can leave, okay?

They shuffled their feet in a playful way and looked over their shoulders to see if I was following. Finally I did because it was true I was hungry and also I remembered what my mother had said about seeking shelter with kind strangers. Maybe these people counted. Maybe I could eat something and then tell them about the sky-blue snake.

They led me to a billowing khaki tent at the far end of the market, where two other children sat on a bench, legs dangling. The younger boy was crying in big heaving sobs. His cries wound up and faded, wound up and faded, like the curfew siren. The other boy, older, was gnawing a mango with both hands.

Sit here, said the woman. Have some water.

I drank the water out of a clear jar. It was warm. I drank the whole thing.

The man and the woman were standing off a little ways, talking in hushed voices. Something minor was decided. The woman came over to me.

My name is Doha, she said. Can you say that?

Doha, I said, insulted.

Good. And what's your name?

I didn't answer, even though my throat was softened by the warm water.

Okay, she said. You don't have to answer that just yet. But may I ask you another few questions? I promise you only have to answer the ones you want.

I nodded. The crying child stopped crying. Maybe he wanted to hear my answers.

Doha turned out her arm and pointed to a stitch near her armpit.

This is a chip, she said. Do you have one? If you did, it would probably be here. Or—Baaku?

The older boy looked up.

Can you come here for a moment?

He dropped down and came to us.

I just want to show her your chip, she said. He craned his neck sideways. There was a shaved lump under his ear. It looked like a disease.

I don't have a chip, I said quickly.

Just to be sure, would you mind if I checked a few places on your body? You don't have to take off any of your clothing.

I said Okay. I was surprised when she asked me before she felt each place. She felt near my armpit and the base of my skull. She asked me to pull up my shirt a little, and I did, and she looked at my belly on either side of my navel.

Doha sighed. You don't have a chip, just like you said. But you didn't do anything wrong. It's just a way to get lost children back to their mothers.

I don't need one, I said.

She smiled at me.

What a thing to say, she said. We'll just have to work a little harder for you. Would you like some mango?

I nodded.

She went behind a tarp. I could see a fancy solar fridge and a plastic cutting board wet with juice and mango fibers.

I noticed Baaku looking at me.

You don't have a chip? he said.

No.

These people will put one in you. Are you in the HLF?

What's that?

The Haratine Liberation Front.

I don't know.

Did you run away from home?

I didn't answer.

It's okay, he confided. I did too. But now they're just going to send me back.

Why did you run away?

My father wants me to be a butcher. But I want to be a hero like Deepak Tharoor.

Who is that?

You haven't seen *The Tamil Terror*?

No.

I've seen *The Tamil Terror* five times. And *Murder on the Chen-*

nai Express. They're much better than Nollywood. My father says Nollywood makes shit.

I didn't know what he was talking about, and I felt ashamed, so I stopped talking to him.

He noticed. But he pretended not to. He wrapped up the conversation casually, as if it were his idea to end it. He said, Well, if you don't want to go back and you don't have a chip, that means you can keep running. Just pretend like you belong, wherever you are. That's what Deepak Tharoor did in *The Tamil Terror* after he dug his chip out.

I waited till he went back to his seat. Then I turned around to look for Doha. I could see the shape of her behind the tarp, still cutting mango.

I hopped off the bench and ran back out into the market.

I felt clever, even euphoric. But I was still hungry. The marketplace smells of roasting meat and spices were making my stomach ache. I'd run all the way to the other side of the market, to a side street where big flatbed trucks were lined up along the curb, when I saw two men leaning against the back of a truck, one in a long robe and white cap and one in blue jeans and a T-shirt. They were tearing apart a loaf of bread and dipping pieces into a can of sauce. I wandered closer.

The T-shirt man noticed me.

Salaam-nesh, he said.

I didn't answer because his greeting was familiar, but strange. Instead I pointed to the can of sauce and touched my fingers to my lips.

You're very persuasive! said the white-cap man, and beckoned me over. He dipped a heel of bread in the green sauce and held it out for me. I took it and ate it, watching him.

No "thank you"? he said. I could understand him, but his accent was odd.

Thank you, I said. The sauce was very spicy and my eyes were watering.

This is my favorite stuff, said the man in the blue jeans. I'm taking twenty cans of it back home.

Where's your home?

Ethiopia, he said.

Where's that?

Very far away, he said. You want to come with us?

Don't listen to him, said the white-cap man. He's a famous child-snatcher.

I said, Is he still a child-snatcher if the child wants to be snatched?

They laughed. I liked these men. I was popular with them.

Ethiopia is near the other ocean, said the white-cap man. Across the Sahara. Have you learned your geography?

No.

Well, maybe you'll get there one day, he said. But now you need to go back home.

I don't have a home.

Of course you do. What does your chip say?

I don't have one, I said.

No chip? exclaimed the blue-jean man.

Slave, the white-cap man said to him.

The blue-jean man's expression changed. Ah, pity, he said, looking down at me.

What's your name? said the white-cap man.

Mariama, I said.

And where are your people?

I have no people, I said.

You're Haratine, no?

I don't know.

Do you work for a Moorish family?

No. I'm free. I want to come with you to Ethiopia.

Let her come with us if she wants, said the blue-jean man.

Your mother birthed an idiot, said the white-cap man.

The blue-jean man shrugged and dunked his bread.

I'm Muhammed, said the white-cap man, and this is Francis. It's very pleasant to make your acquaintance. But we must take our leave of your company to prepare for a nighttime departure.

To Ethiopia? I said. I wanted to prolong the conversation because in these men, I perceived no harm. These were definitely the sort of kind strangers my mother talked about, and I needed to seek shelter with them like I promised.

Yes. See these?

He pointed to a line of three flatbed trucks, packed with crates and boxes.

We're carrying crude oil all the way to Addis Ababa. We leave tonight. So please, go back to your mother before it gets dark.

I don't have a mother, I said.

Muhammed sighed. I think you do, he said, but maybe you've had a fight with her. You should go back and ask her forgiveness. A little girl like you can't survive without one. And things are not safe in Nouakchott right now, especially for your kind. You know that, don't you?

I didn't, but the bite of sea snake burned in my chest when he said so. I stayed silent.

He shook his head and said, Allah go with you, Mariama.

Muhammed turned back to Francis, and they brushed their hands of crumbs and then went behind a truck, not sparing another look for me.

I turned and walked away, looking over my shoulder. When I was sure they wouldn't see me, I hid behind an oil drum. And as I waited, the bite in my chest began to make a sound, a little cry that sounded like *kreen, kreen, kreen.*

Saha

I'd been hiding on the truck for two hours when I stopped hearing the men's voices and so imagined that they must have gone to sleep. I had made a little house; my roof was a green tarp and my walls were two drums of oil. I didn't have much space to move, but I managed to turn around and face outward in a kneeling position. I rolled up the tarp until I felt fresh wind. I angled my head so that I could look out.

Oh, Yemaya, I saw the most beautiful sight: a full moon blazing over the sea, like a sunrise all in black and white. I could see the ridges of foam rushing and rising as if they were crowds standing to applaud my passage. I was free. This was what was meant for me. I made the sound the waves seemed to make: *sa-ha, sa-ha, sa-ha,* which helped to silence the *kreen, kreen, kreen.*

And just like that—*zeep!*—my tarp roof was gone.

I looked up. Francis was looking down at me. He made a squealing sound like a baby goat and called for Muhammed, who came and shined a flashlight into my eyes. Francis was convulsing with giggles, but Muhammed was not amused.

Mariama? he said.

I didn't answer.

Francis said something about guests being gifts from Allah. Muhammed gave him an evil look.

He pulled me up by the elbow and walked me to a pile of grease-stained rags in the corner of the truck, just behind the cab. He sat me down on the cloths and opened a cooler and handed me a packet of glucose biscuits and a bottle of water. He told me to sit and be quiet. He pulled open a sliding door to the cab and climbed through and sat next to the driver. I could hear them talking. I was scared. I knew punishment must be coming.

Francis whistled and then sat next to me. I cringed away.

Easy, I'm not going to hurt you, he said. I guess you didn't like Nouakchott too much. I don't blame you. But now what are we going to do with you?

I'll live in Ethiopia, I said.

With who? Me? he said. My life is no life for a little girl. And Muhammed already has two daughters in Hawassa.

I can live with them, I said. I can wash their clothes.

They have a machine for that, Francis said.

I can cook for them, I said.

Oh? What can you cook?

I can make stew and mashed yams, I said. I can also milk goats and carry water.

Francis smiled, but also looked sad.

The cab door above us opened, and Muhammed climbed out and knelt between me and Francis. He and Francis spoke rapidly in that language I didn't understand. I knew the punishment was about to come. But Muhammed turned to me and said something I did not expect.

We can't take you back, he said. We have to make Addis Ababa in three months' time and we can't go back now. There's a camp for Haratine refugees outside Dakar. They'll try to find your people through the aid groups and if they can't, you'll stay with them.

You're not going to beat me?

He glanced at Francis. He said, No, Mariama, no one is going to beat you.

Nothing was turning out like I expected. But then I remembered that life was different now. I remembered the moon. I remembered *saha*. I remembered I was free.

I sat up straighter. What if I don't want to stay at the camps? I said.

Well, I didn't want you to stay with me, but you didn't give *me* a choice, did you? said Muhammed.

Oh, leave her alone, said Francis. But the reproach hurt me and my chest felt like it was collapsing all over again, the noise *kreen, kreen, kreen* drowning out the *saha*.

Francis patted my back. What do you want? he asked.

I want to go to Ethiopia, I said.

But how will you ever get back home?

I don't want to go back home, I said.

Francis looked up at Muhammed and said, Something bad happened to her.

What happened to you? Muhammed asked me.

I looked down at my glucose biscuits, Yemaya, and didn't answer. I didn't want to tell them about the sky-blue snake. I didn't know how to talk about it.

Bad things happen to millions of children, Muhammed said to Francis. Why is this one any different?

Because God sent us this one to take care of.

Muhammed regarded me. Then he said something to Francis, got up, and climbed back into the cab.

What did he say? I asked Francis.

He told me to sleep on it.

What language was that?

Amharic. What we speak in Ethiopia.

Then how do you know how to speak my language?

I don't, very well, he said. Just enough to rescue little girls.

(That made me smile, Yemaya.)

You sleep here, he said to me, indicating the pile of rags. We'll think of something else later. I'll sleep over there—he pointed to a crawlspace made by three crates—and if your hair is on fire, you can wake me up, but otherwise not. Okay?

I nodded.

He crawled away. I lay back on the pile and looked up. I could tell we were going very fast, but the stars hardly moved at all. They too whispered *saha, saha, saha*.

⦃ B◌□K III ⦄

Meena

Nariman Point

I shove myself away from the barefoot girl, which means I slam into Lucia and our heads knock and she sits up and screams and I climb over her body to drop to the other side of her bed. Lucia is calling my name and asking me what's happening and I can tell she's fighting to stay calm, to be reasonable, to assume the best of me. But I can't pay attention to her now. The barefoot girl is hugging her elbows and swinging them back and forth.

"Who are you?" I say.

She stops swinging and says a single word. My glotti says:

LANGUAGE UNKNOWN

I've never seen that error message before.

"Speak fucking Hindi. English. Anything else. Why are you following me?"

She seems scared. She shrinks back. But again she whispers

just one word and this time I can hear it, it sounds like *sa'a*, but my glotti reads again:

LANGUAGE UNKNOWN

"Durga," says Lucia, "who are you talking to?"

"The girl standing right fucking there, Lucia."

Lucia gathers up the sheets around her body and goes to look out the window.

"That's not funny, Lucia."

"What's not funny? I'm just—I don't understand—who are you talking to?" Her voice is breaking now and she's near tears.

And I realize that Lucia is part of it.

She is such a good actor. She's part of it, and so was Anwar, and now they have me.

I address myself to the barefoot girl.

"So who sent you? Semena Werk? The police? If I walk out this door, I walk into a dragnet, right?"

The girl squeezes her eyes shut and takes a deep breath and opens them again and says *saha*.

I'm fucking done with this. I take up my satchel and make for the door and fumble with the locks and wrench open the door, all while Lucia is yelling that I'm naked, but I don't care, I'll walk into a dragnet naked and make the morning news all over India. I slam the door behind me. There's no police in the hallway. Okay, so they're outside. I reconsider the nakedness bit and find an empty stairwell where I can put my clothes back on. My bandage has come loose, so my snakebites are bleeding again. I press the tape back in place for now.

I go outside. There's no dragnet, no police. Just hovercarts gliding down the street with breakfast, roti and vada and chai. I start walking toward the sea because I don't want to be still in any one place for too long. I look behind me and no one is following. Maybe I was wrong. Maybe the barefoot girl is acting alone, or just she and Lucia, or maybe a bigger force is arriving soon. I need to go somewhere no one will expect and ideally where no one can follow. Not Mumbai, a city every square inch of which is filmed all day and night.

Not even India.

I start walking north on Marine Drive, on the seawall. I pass men in dhotis promenading up and down, hands clasped behind their backs, and businesspeople standing still, talking to the air. There's a yoga class on one platform and a tai chi class on the next. Young women are drinking cups of coffee in the pearly orange morning mist. I could be one of them, but I'm a human scanner, back and forth, looking for the barefoot girl, looking for any other sign of being followed. I have to get out of the country and make my way to Africa. I've been lazy about the journey so far and now I need to be serious. But how will I go so that I won't be followed? I don't know my enemy's resources. I don't even know my fucking enemy.

Then I see two little girls spread a sarong on the seawall over-looking drowned Chowpatty Beach. They're wearing school uniforms of navy and cream. The younger one sits with her legs folded, and the older one takes a place behind her, and begins to braid her hair.

The elder notices me looking. "Namaste," she says.

"Namaste," I say.

"The Trail is very pretty at dawn."

"Yes, it is." I feel strange around children. I've never had much occasion to interact with them. I don't know whether to address them as small adults or intelligent animals.

"I come here every morning before school and watch the sunrise and braid her hair," continues the elder.

The younger one comes to life. "Are you going to walk on the Trail?"

"Yes," I say, and the answer comes so easily, an admission of a given, what I knew all along, before I went to the museum, before I even boarded the train to Mumbai, that the seed was there, and the solution.

She wags her head. "Our brother Rana left a month ago. Amma says he went to join the seasteads."

"Where are you from?"

"Dharavi," says the elder, more shyly.

"But we go to school at Francis Xavier," says the younger. "We take the student train."

I remember Lucia's tale of a special shop for the Trail in Dharavi. I remember the universe is conspiring for me. I ask, "Do you know of a store called the Mart?"

Of course she knows exactly what I'm talking about. "Yes, Amma can tell you where it is," says the elder. "Her name is Sunita. She has a fish shop in Koliwada. She's famous for her pomfret curry. Tell her that her daughters sent you and she'll give you a discount."

I thank them and say good-bye. When I turn around to look back at them, their heads are haloed in the sunrise.

Koliwada

It's a long ride north in traffic. I count my cash. Just under two thousand rupees left. That's a day's worth of food before I'd have to start using my mitter again, which would broadcast my location.

But my stomach feels like a black hole and I need to eat. So when I get to Koliwada, I ask around for Sunita, and when I find her, before anything else, I buy pomfret curry with chapati. I lean against a wall and eat out of the paper with my elbows close to my body. Then I go back to her, a barrel-bodied woman in a red sari crouching behind the grill.

"Where is the Mart?"

Without looking at me, she turns the filets out of the heat, gets up, and beckons me back into her shack. As soon as I follow her into the shadows, she snaps at me.

"Madam, you shouldn't say that word so loudly."

"I didn't know."

"It's illegal, madam."

"So it exists."

"Are you from the police?"

"No."

"Why do you want the Mart, madam?"

"I heard about it from your daughters on Marine Drive."

"Chutiyas," she says, which startles me. "Are you trying to join the walkers, madam?"

"It's not your business."

"It's so dangerous, madam. It's no place for a woman."

I'm not going to touch that. "But people survive, right?"

"I don't know, madam. There are rumors of settlements but we never hear back from them. My son Rana left a month ago and I've heard nothing."

"So I heard."

Something shifts in her eyes. "If you go, you could find him and tell him to come home, madam."

"If you tell me how to find the Mart, I might."

Five minutes later, carrying a picture of Rana and a box of soan papdi she insists he needs, she leads me by the hand through Dharavi. It's like being in a three-dimensional maze. The view ahead is a labyrinth and the view overhead is a labyrinth, too, since

Dharavi can only grow upward, not out, because there's no more space, and not down, because all the basement workshops flooded when the sea level rose. When I look up I see children swinging from building to building on a network of ropes, all the way up, ten stories high, until the white of the sky blots them out.

Sunita stops at a doorway and greets a well-dressed man in a prayer cap. He turns to me.

"Why are you looking for the Mart, please?"

"I'm interested in looking at your products."

"For what reason?"

"To go out on the Trail."

This statement fazes him not at all. "Very good. First we have to know you're not police. Please raise your arm."

I take off my jacket and do so. He runs a handheld scanner over my armpit, where my aadhaar is embedded, the little almond under the skin. The scanner beeps green.

"Thank you, madam. And thank you, Aunty. Two tiffin for lunch, please."

Sunita wags her head. To me she says, "Tell Rana to come home." Then she disappears back into the people soup.

"My name is Misbah," the man says. "Please follow me."

He leads me down a dark hallway, at the end of which is a door that has three locks, one mechanical and two digital. He unlocks all three and then leads me up a flight of stairs. We climb five stories. On the sixth landing he knocks on a door in a syncopated rhythm. After a minute, it opens. A man who looks just like Misbah, except older, taller, and with a cleft in his chin, lets us in. We're in a low-ceilinged room packed with six aisles of shelving under fluorescent light. I see glimpses of merchandise: folded cloth, shiny backpacks. I can see the older one's been watching soap operas in the corner. The holograms are on pause.

"Welcome to the Mart," says the older man as Misbah disappears behind a curtain. "I am Mehrdad, and that is my brother, and we are the two proprietors of this unique store. We have everything you may need for safe times and a high adventure on the Trail."

"Have either of you ever been on the Trail?"

"No."

I stare at him for a moment. Then Misbah reappears, bearing a tray of tea glasses. I thank him and take one. It's cold, strong, and sweet, made with fresh spearmint.

"Do you know anyone who's gone?"

"Oh yes. Several who've passed through here."

"Define 'several.'"

Mehrdad glances at Misbah. "You're the fourth."

"I see. Anyone who's come back?"

"No, no one has come back, not yet," says Misbah.

"But give it time! We've only been open a few months," says Mehrdad. "As the illegal sport grows in popularity, business will boom, and then it'll become legal."

"So I'm doing it at the right time."

"Before there are backpackers and weekend strollers all across the length of the Arabian Sea, yes."

I can't decide whether they're visionary or delusional. "I'm guessing all the things I need will cost more than two thousand rupees."

Both men laugh loudly.

"Yes," says Mehrdad.

"I have money," I say. "I just don't want to be tracked, and two thousand is all I have in cash."

"We're familiar with that situation," says Mehrdad. "Our customers wish to maintain a low profile. But all of our purchases are routed through our father's menswear emporium, so you don't have to worry."

"But I don't even want anyone to know I'm in Mumbai."

Mehrdad sucks his breath in through his teeth. "That, we cannot help with, madam."

That makes it simple. If I buy supplies here, I signal to the cloud where I am in Mumbai, and Anwar and Lucia and whoever else is involved will know.

So I'll have to leave tonight.

"Let's do it," I say.

Mehrdad and Misbah nod to each other.

They lead me to the shelf at the back of the room and we work our way forward. They explain each item to me as they pull it out. I make a mental sketch of each.

Two bottle-sized desalinators that, as a bonus, make sea salt in the top chamber.

A compass.

A sea anchor.

Two nylon ropes with hooks.

All-purpose soap concentrate.

One hundred compressed gas capsules.

A toothbrush, toothpaste powder, and a tongue scraper.

A waterproof, watertight backpack. Color: white. Misbah takes my measurements and then takes it away to make custom adjustments to fit the shape of my back.

Two high-sensitivity sunbits that can be hung from a strap on my bag and charge while I walk.

A state-of-the-art solar kiln that can convert any organic matter. That means kelp, algae, anything that can be broken down into simple sugars. It would take fish, too, but that would use more energy, and why not just eat the fish.

A filet knife and a fishing kit.

For dead zones and other contingencies, a box of protein cubes and a box of broth cubes.

A solar plate that's curved so that it can be used as a bowl, and a miniature irradiator brush to paint my catch before cooking.

A full medical kit, including broad-spectrum nanobiotics for diarrhea, bacterial infection, viral infection, heatstroke, and motion sickness.

A natural sponge for Menses Aunty. That's what Mohini called it.

A few small items to gift or barter: an extra compass, an extra bottle of soap concentrate, an extra tube of toothpaste, and three extra tongue scrapers, which are worth their weight in enriched uranium to a Malayalee without one.

A camo pod made of resealable sticky polymer, also waterproof up to ten meters in case I need to go beneath the surface for a storm. I feel reassured. They've thought of everything. Mehrdad demonstrates it for me: he opens it with his thumbnail and then seals it just by pinching the material together. He urges me to try. It reseals without a seam, like the membrane of an egg.

A special weather-resistant scroll pre-loaded with medical and survival information. I load everything from my old scroll, which holds the complete works of Reshmi West, Muhammad Licht, Anuradha Sarang, Wen Huang, Gregory Mbachu, Laura Prufrock Jameson, Gaudi Al-Qaddafi, Jorge Luis Borges, Norman Rush, Federico García Lorca, Nora Chu, Mary Renault, Thomas Mulamba, Kim Stanley Robinson, Sun Yoo, Rodrigo Jimez, Rainer Maria Rilke, Toni Morrison, Fatima Perez-Marquez, Enid Chung, Arundhati Roy, Ursula K. Le Guin, Leo Tolstoy, Jia-Chien Liang, Josefina Paz, Kuta Sesay, Fyodor Dostoevsky, Tori Biswas, Haruki Murakami, Dante, Chaucer, Milton, Homer, Confucius, Shakespeare, Rikhi, Nambiar, Nilambar, Shukla, Jain,

Tharoor, Narayan, Desani, Ambedkar, Gupta, Tagore, Valmiki, and Vyasa.

Six flares.

A pozit, a global positioning tag with a simple digital display.

I pick out models of clothing I want and Misbah prints them out of quick-drying, salt-resistant synth in the far corner, all in white or camo: two pairs of loose pants, a tank top, a T-shirt, a hooded long-sleeved shirt, a sun cap, two pairs of underwear, and two bras. One pair of thong sandals, one pair of canvas shoes, and one pair of second skins.

Wraparound sunglasses and a collapsible broad hat.

Mehrdad pulls out sunscreen, but I tell him I don't need it. I try not to see the look in his eyes. Only the very wealthy or very connected have access to elective gene therapy. He's wondering which I am.

Mehrdad and Misbah steer me through toilet matters. I don't mind squatting over the ocean, but wiping is something else. The brothers have considered this. They show me a special kind of diaper that releases fecal matter after exposure to light. Ergo, I have to keep it out of the light before using it. That seems like something I can expect of myself.

After an hour, I sit with Mehrdad, drinking more tea, while Misbah packs all my items into my new backpack, save for one full outfit of new clothes I'd picked out.

"When are you leaving?" he asks.

"Tonight," I say. "There's nothing left to do here."

"Where is 'here'?"

It takes me a while to answer this. Mumbai? India? Asia?

"Solid ground," I say.

He nods. "You'll find like-minded souls out there."

"What do you mean?"

"Travelers. They're all searching for something."

I think this is shitty and simplistic but I don't say so. "Have you heard any stories about Bloody Mary?"

Misbah and Mehrdad exchange a look. "Jinn," says Misbah.

"What?" I say.

"He's saying Bloody Mary is a spirit," says Mehrdad. "Yes, I've heard of her. The graving docks of the Trail were in Djibouti, not Mumbai, and apparently one of the construction workers died while the Trail was being laid out. So they claim her ghost haunts the Trail now." He waves his hand. "African superstition."

I see that Misbah has finished. He presents my full backpack like a wedding cake, then bids me turn around and hold out my arms so that he can thread the straps around them. They have me walk around the store with it on. They want to make sure I'm happy with my purchase. I am.

So Misbah gestures to my outfit, laid out. I go behind the curtain and dress in a white tank top, white drawstring pants, and second skins on my feet. I also take the opportunity to change my bandage. The wounds have stopped bleeding and are five maroon dots, now, like five bindis, each with a halo of red infection.

I come out in my new outfit and now there's only one thing left to do. I hold out my wrist to Mehrdad. My mitter glows. Once the money transfers, anyone can know where I am, if they want to.

He smiles and holds his wrist to mine. His mitter pings and glows green. He says, "Khuda Hafiz."

My glotti says,

URDU: Go with God.

Ballad of the Trail Snake

So now the proverbial clock is ticking.

First I leave my bundle of old clothes in the street in Dharavi. They'll get used. Then I use more of my cash to buy a ride back to Marine Drive, this time with a driver, a taciturn African man. I have mixed feelings toward him. I suppress the urge to tell him I'm going to Africa. I don't want to be That Indian Woman.

I get out near Nariman Point and walk to the very end of the seawall, a tourist spot with lots of people at this hour, scanning for any sign of the barefoot girl or any other pursuer. I see none. I shade my eyes from the sunlight until I see the Trail. It lies on the surface of the sea like a white garland.

I can't go in the daylight. My plan is to hide nearby until nightfall and then swim out to the head of the Trail. I don't know where I'll hide and I don't know where I'll enter the water. I'm just making up a plan, trusting that, in its execution, all basic physical principles will hold, like the yield of seawater to the force of my hands.

I sit on the edge of the seawall like a dozen other Mumbaikars, looking south toward the multibillion-dollar high-rises across the break. Looking casual. I look down and it's a two-meter drop to the breakwater, a tumble of slimy concrete jacks. The two meters were added to deal with the ocean rising. When I bend over to examine the seawall, for the first time I see that there are squares cut into the stone to dissipate the surf, like the jacks do. If I can climb down, I can sit inside one of the squares until night falls. No one will be able to see me unless they crawl down onto the jacks, and what are they going to do? I look like a sadhvi. They'll leave me alone.

So I have a plan.

Should I do a puja? Maybe I should do a puja. I'm not a very religious person. I celebrate whatever parts of religion give me an excuse to eat and dance. Mohini was much more solemn, a mystic, a contemplative. She tried to get me to take it seriously. She went to temple in the morning to get her forehead smeared, and when she came home, I let her smear my forehead in turn, because she had more authority to me than any priest.

But I think this occasion warrants a puja. For a safe passage to Africa. If I'm really doing this. Which it seems I am.

I drop down onto the jacks and pick through them for trash. I find seashells, a blue and silver Nordi bottle wrapper, and a gnawed Parle-G glucose biscuit, perfect for offering. Now I just need something to be a murti. There has to be a murti submerged somewhere.

I pick through the jacks for dolls or crustaceans or key chain souvenirs but find nothing that could be a murti. I actually feel panicked. I can't begin my journey without this puja. All of a sudden it seems I'm devout, even superstitious. But isn't the point of Hinduism that God is manifest everywhere, repeating Godself in endless aspects, so the specific object to which we direct puja doesn't matter? But still, it wouldn't feel right to pray to a greasy napkin. Would that be okay? I realize I know nothing about the religion in which I was supposedly brought up. This is what I get for being a nominal Hindu. I don't know how to make it real.

I decide the closest thing to a murti I have in my backpack is the tongue scraper. I'll make it a sanctified tongue scraper.

Now I've collected all the elements of a puja. I just have to wait for night to fall. I approach the hollow square in the seawall and, for the benefit of anyone watching, act as though I'd just discovered it, making gestures of surprise, curiosity. It's about a meter on all sides and a meter deep, which, I remember, are the dimensions of each Trail scale. I climb in. It's midday, so it's hot and wet. I lie on my back with my knees bent and look up at my concrete ceiling.

I put my backpack under my head as a pillow. I look out over the jacks, across the water, toward the Tata complex. I close my eyes. I haven't really slept in days. The voices of those above me, calling in Marathi, Chinese, Hindi, English, and Urdu, begin to blend in the heat and make a sunlight lullaby.

◈ ◈ ◈

The Trail becomes sentient, like a great sea snake, and wants to know how it was made.

The Trail wrangles itself out of the bay and onto land, blocking traffic on Marine Drive, slithering like a steel dragon to the doors of HydraCorp, which panics and calls the military, which drops in with helicopters and guns and shoots at it, calling for it to desist. It's a disaster. The Trail, badly wounded, retreats back into the ocean and disappears beneath the waves.

The engineers at HydraCorp hold a press conference, looking tired. They announce they've decided not to make efforts to catch it. It has its own life now. It just wants to be left alone.

So the Trail travels all the world's oceans, deep as the undersea shipping routes, where it causes some disruption, but the world is gently disposed toward the Trail and so its bumblings are tolerated. It's just lonely, they say.

The Trail becomes an object of lore. There are sightings reported off the coast of Japan. Fishwaalas wake up in the cold star glimmer and where there had been nothing the night before, there's the Trail, a long skinny tongue splayed in the harbor. Some consider it a blessing and others, an omen. One day a segment gets trapped in Sydney Harbor and picnickers gather to watch maintenance crews untangle and reassemble it. The Trail bears this indignity and, once whole again, retreats into the deep.

Some who see it can't shake it from their minds. They become obsessed. They push pins onto a map and hold conventions at hotels in small cities. And then there's a rumor of a young grieving woman who swims out to meet it and is received. She becomes the mother of the race of the drowned.

From then on, the Trail goes from shore to shore and more people come. They form towns and then entire cities along its length. The city at the end of the tail is used to being thrashed, like the tip of a whip. It's where the most fashionably drowned spend their nights, among bright colored lights, watching the ocean floor flick by, gossiping about the residents at the head of the Trail, which is the seat of government.

But even the race of the drowned outgrows their host. They depart for other adventures—condos in calderas, or houseboats on the moon. The Trail becomes a ghost of its former self, and when the last inhabitant finally departs, the Trail swims to the deepest North Pacific and there, lets itself come apart and be scattered to the currents, the parts finding their own way and settling in separate beds of mud where they felt no more.

❖　❖　❖

When I wake, the sun is setting. The high-rises across the water are faced in orange.

I feel energized. It's a good time to perform my puja. I try to remember the correct steps. Mohini knew them all. She would do a simple puja every day, but there can be twelve or thirteen steps, with special steps just for offering the murti water to brush its teeth. This won't be as elaborate.

I spread the Nordi wrapper on the concrete between my legs, anchor it with shells all around its perimeter, dribble a pile of sand in the center, and stick the tongue scraper into it so that it stands upright in an arch. Here's where I should offer something liquid to the murti. It seems obvious to offer seawater, so I bend down to cup from the surf, and pour it back and forth over my arrangement. But it doesn't seem like enough. So I reach under the bandage under my shirt and push one of the scabs until I feel wetness, and then paint the tongue scraper with that little bit of blood, for ten seconds, to make it real, and then I feel something at rest in my body that wasn't, before.

In fact there's more to be done.

I get out the filet knife and some topical anesthetic, which I apply with gauze. Then I lift my left arm until my hand is grasping the right side of my throat, for purchase. I dig in my fingernails so that I don't lose my grip.

I angle the knife toward my exposed armpit. My flesh is matter, and responsive to physical principles, just like water is. I make a first incision, feeling no pain but a faint tug, and then another incision at an angle to the first, so now there's a bleeding V in my skin. I have to work fast before I start bleeding too much. I dig the tip of the filet knife under the point of the V and work it up, tearing up a flap of skin, and there are few notes of pain, which without anesthesia would be a blinding white soprano pain. I nudge my aadhaar with the tip of the knife and it moves under another layer of dermis. I make a deeper cut. The tip of the almond is exposed now. It's even colored like an almond. Now it slips out easily and I hold it in between slippery fingers. I place it in the little pile of sand under the arch of the tongue scraper and then I place the biscuit in front of the tongue scraper and light it on fire.

I blow it out before it can melt the plastic of the Nordi wrapper.

My puja is done. As fine and grotesque as any spectacle in Madurai, the home of my namesake, Meenakshi Devi. My armpit throbs like a supernova and I dress my shoulder. I'm out of the cloud, now, and not physically trackable. The blessing from my offering was received in its making.

The First Night

Evening falls. Instead of families parading up and down Marine Drive, now it's young couples matching their steps and gazing sideways out to sea. Romance is in the air. My lover is the Trail.

To pass time, I unpack and repack three times to make sure I know where everything goes. I start reading the Mahabharata, which I've never read straight through, and I'm in the mood for grandiose undertakings. But I don't even get past the frame story. I tell myself I'll restart it once I'm on the Trail and I'll read something else for now. Something not millennia old, but still at a temporal distance, a few decades—Kuta Sesay, *Poems for Drowning Ndar,* Senegal, 2026. Some light early-century fatalism.

I wait until midnight, then crawl out of my square and up onto the seawall. A garland of golden streetlights, the Queen's Necklace, rings the bay. It's a lot of light but it can't be helped. There's traffic on Marine Drive, but dilute. Some people walk out to the end of the seawall, but not many. This is as deserted as it's going to get.

I can see the Trail head from here. It's a silver string bobbing on the surface of the water, visible, then invisible, then visible again. All I have to do is walk into the water and begin swimming toward it, and then no one will know where I am, no Semena Werk, no police, no barefoot girl. These are discrete and doable steps.

I drop back down into the jacks unevenly and bash my heel. It hurts but I tell myself it's good luck. I grab my backpack and tie it on, trusting it'll stay watertight. I pick through the tangle of jacks out to open water. My feet are wet, and now my knees are too. The water is warm.

The surf hits my thighs, then my waist.

There's cold water beneath the warm water.

When it gets up to my chest the saltwater stings my snakebites and I bite down to absorb that pain too. I lift my feet and give over to the ocean. My chest is in warm water and my legs are in cold water. I'm doing well. Once I pass the wave breaks, I start a breaststroke, head above water, keeping the Trail in sight. The first scale is about two hundred meters ahead now.

The waves get higher and choppier. I have to time my breaths to their amplitude so I don't suck in seawater. With every stroke my backpack, floating, bangs against the back of my head. I get my first mouthful of brine and cough it out. The Trail is about fifty meters to my left now.

The first scale fills up my field of vision. It moves like a drunken buoy with a lot more violence than the model at the museum did, where the underwater scales might have kissed each other, but here they clang so loud I can hear it underwater. It sounds like marine bells tolling. I can even feel it, it makes my pelvic bones vibrate. Of course it would be like this. An energy device wouldn't be worth making unless the available energy was extreme, profitable. And now here, up close, understanding the actual violence of the Trail's movements, I can't understand how anyone could ever walk on it. I can begin to understand why no one ever comes back.

But now I'm here and I have nowhere else to go. I have to have faith that it can be done.

I come to the end scale. My leg hits a thick mooring cable under the water, and there must be one on the other side, too. I get between them. Here come more discrete, doable steps. I grasp the side of the scale and my hands slip because it's very smooth. But on the top is the sandpaper, and if I get my hands up there, I can hold on. So I kick in place, right at the caboose of the Trail, and when the scale is tipped down toward me, propel myself out of the

water and on top of it. I get my breasts onto it. And then the scale
bucks so violently that my body is wrenched in two and I lose my
grip and I'm thrown back into the water. Mere fudi kha ley, motherfucking piece of fuck.

My lower back is in shock from the wrench. But I override
the pain. Again I tread water and wait for the scale to pitch down
toward me, and I throw myself at it, this time getting my whole
torso on top of it so at least the edge lines my body's own hinge.
To get purchase I reach for the far edge, and then scream when
the tip of my middle finger is crushed between the scales. Stupid.
Chutiya. I have to act like it didn't happen. Don't reach fingers
too far down into the hinge, then. My body is learning. The next
time the scale pitches down, I kick hard and push into my hands,
and I get my legs on top of the scale too. Then immediately I pitch
forward into the trough between this scale and the next. I brace
myself with my hands to keep from falling and my pinched finger
shrieks a high note.

Walking upright is unthinkable. I have a moment of deep spe-
ciatic memory, regressing to a crawl. I balance in beetle pose and
then work my way up to my hands and knees. I hate this horrible
rocking. I'm incredulous. But I watch for a chance to move forward, and then I do, making sure to avoid the snapping hinge.
I've forgotten about the pain in my finger, the pain in my heel, the
pain in my back, the pain in my solar plexus. All my concentration
is trained on the next movement. The waves make for a fourth
dimension of balance. It's like trying to ride a unicycle on top of
an airplane, or a pogo stick on top of a train, which strikes me as
an especially doomed venture, and I actually laugh aloud before
clapping my hand over my mouth. I'm going mad. Is this how adventures begin? With the hero cackling? I remember that after
lightning struck his rocket, Pete Conrad laughed all the way into
orbit.

I try to crawl toward the third scale but fall into it and bang my chin against the surface. I wipe my chin. Blood. So there's Wound Number Five. And there's no hope of keeping it dry, or any part of my body, as half of me is already soaked. I look ahead and keep my focus light, my joints loose, my muscles free. I tell myself I'll cover a hundred scales and then take a rest.

I make it to six before I stop. All my muscles are sparkling with acid.

I rest and then crawl forward again. I'm making better progress.

But then I go too fast. This time the bucking scale hits me so hard in the forehead I lurch backward and almost fall into the ocean. I start crying just from the pain of it. I'm overwhelmed. I haven't slept. I haven't eaten. I've been in a manic episode for three days. I know this, and now it's brought me here, the epitome of madness. No one is taking care of me.

"Saha," says a voice ahead.

A swell passes and there is the barefoot girl standing on the Trail just a few scales ahead of me. The golden light of Marine Drive outlines her body. Her headscarf is blown back and her smile is white in the dark. She is glad. She holds one hand to her heart and extends the other toward me. From behind her a black fan unfolds, a great circle of wings.

I scream at her to go away so hard I feel my lip split.

When the next swell passes, she is gone.

⦃ B⬚⬚K IV ⦄

Mariama

Camel's Milk

I woke up before dawn because I could feel we'd stopped moving.
I lay still and listened to the sounds of men loading and unloading
oil drums. Finally Francis came back with a baguette to share, and
the spicy green sauce, again, to dip it in.

I'm addicted to this stuff, he said.

Where are we? I asked.

Rosso, he said. Or Al-Quwarib. It's a border town.

Why are we stopped?

We have to wait for the ferry. They only open at nine.

What's a ferry?

Francis leaned back against a fuel drum and groaned, his
mouth full of bread. Don't make me leave you here, he said.

(And then he winked, Yemaya, so I knew it was okay.)

I asked another question: Where did the oil come from?

A Russian tanker in Casablanca, he said, tracing a route in the
air with his finger. Then Marrakech, my favorite place! I danced
all night! Oh, such music, and such beautiful women—Mariama,

you've never seen such women. I have three women there. I can't pick just one.

Then Francis sighed like the life leaked out of him.

And then nothing but wasteland, until we got to Nouakchott.

And then you found me! I said.

He smiled at me. So we did, he said. But you're too young to be my girlfriend.

The truck rumbled to life, and the whole flatbed vibrated. I put down my hands to steady myself.

I can be your girlfriend, I said.

No, you can't! he said. You're too poky. You can't even walk straight when the truck is moving. You're all humbly-jumbly like you're at sea but don't have sea legs.

No, I'm not!

Prove it.

The truck got under way. I took position at one end of the flat-bed and Francis arranged himself like a royal audience at the other. I took a few steps toward him, but then, as the truck hit a pothole and tilted to one side, I fell to my knees.

You're hopeless, he said. No one will ever marry you.

❖ ❖ ❖

But Yemaya, I got better. I kept practicing. I learned to sense when those changes were coming and how to adapt whenever they did. I made Francis watch me over and over—long after he'd lost inter-est! But he was very patient. How did I find these men, Yemaya? Now that I know more of the world, and how terrible it is, and how terrible people can be, especially to little girls, I am amazed that I had the good luck to find them. I was handed from angel to angel! I think you were with me, even then, guiding my steps.

Each truck in our convoy boarded the ferry and crossed a river of pale brown milk. It took hours. And then once we were all over on the other side, it was early afternoon, and we stopped *again*. Francis asked the driver why we were stopping, and the driver answered in a cheery tone. Francis turned to me and complained, We'll never make Addis in three months. Every year it takes four to six months, because in every place, we have friends and we need to drink tea with them.

Why? I said.

Because if we don't, he said, they will kill us.

He saw the look on my face and fell over laughing.

❖   ❖   ❖

Yemaya, I didn't even know this, but we were already in Senegal, a country other than the one I'd been born in. I barely even had a conception of other countries, much less of ever going to one! Whenever my mother had spoken of "the world," I had pictured Dr. Moctar Brahim's house, the houses around us, the mosques at the center of the city, the market to the south, and the stars hanging low, which is where everything we saw and heard on the computer and television and radio and phones came from. But that was all. Now I was getting used to not only being free, but the world being a very big place.

After finally leaving Rosso, we arrived in a new city named Ndar for a teatime that turned into a dinnertime that turned into a sleepover. Francis disappeared into the town for the night, so Muhammed took me. At first I was afraid he was going to take me to a refugee camp and leave me there. But he was quiet. He didn't say anything about the previous night. He seemed resigned to my presence.

Yemaya, even just walking the streets of Ndar, I could tell I was in a different world from where I'd grown up. The air was richer and heavier. There were both men and women walking freely in the streets, the women beautiful and beaming, each one a queen with a bright headwrap. Music floated from windows and open doors—not austere chants to Allah, but rounded drums and lush guitars and strange rhythms with many layers, women and men singing together. And there in Ndar, I could smell the sea again. The word *saba* came to me again and I snatched it out of the air and cradled it in my heart.

Muhammed took me to a house with pink and green walls. There were iron bars on the walls, twisted into beautiful shapes. He told me to sit in the corner. A servant came to give me a baguette and a cup of milk. I couldn't believe how much food I was receiving. I didn't even have to ask for it. Yemaya, for a moment I considered hiding some, to send it back, somehow, to my mother. But I didn't know how. So I ate it all myself and felt ashamed.

Muhammed and his friends spoke in low voices. They talked about the rising sea threatening Ndar and Kuta Sesay, the city's poet activist. It was too late to take protective measures, they said, unless UNESCO decided to save it. I thought "Unesco" was their god or at least a very rich man. I wanted to know why anyone who had the power to decide would let such a beautiful city drown. I was young, Yemaya, and had no idea that this city was one of hundreds of beautiful cities all over the world, each with an eye on the rising sea.

One of the men asked Muhammed about me, then turned around on his bench and glanced back at me and saw that I was staring right back at him, which scattered his gaze. He looked elsewhere and pretended he wasn't looking at me at all. But then he said, with pity, That's a black one for sure.

I'm not black, I said.

The man said to Muhammed, She talks too much.

They all laughed.

I think, said Muhammed, Nouakchott will get worse before it gets better. She'll have a much better life in Ethiopia.

Oh, yes, the very trees grow greener in Ethiopia, joked one of the men.

But Muhammed sat up straighter. I'm telling you, he said, Addis is growing.

Safe from the seas, that's for sure.

Yes, it's the highest capital in the world, said Muhammed, not catching the sarcasm in the other man's voice. He continued, Do you know our president was educated in Mumbai? She studied medicine and she's fluent in Hindi. Everyone is in love with her.

The other men teased him, but he said, Yes, I carry a picture of her around in my wallet, and I'm not ashamed! Look. She's a queenly woman.

I'm not black, I said again.

Muhammed looked at me while the others bent over the picture of the Ethiopian president. But you are Haratine, said Muhammed. And that can make life difficult in Mauritania.

I deduced that Mauritania is where I'd come from.

Are we going to Ethiopia tomorrow? I said.

We are, but we won't get there tomorrow. It'll be a long journey. Four months, at least.

I nodded, wanting to appear grown-up, though this was an incomprehensible amount of time to me.

He said, You'll be bigger and taller by then. I know, because I have two girls. Fatima and Rahel. You're going to sprout up like a shoot. We just have to keep feeding you.

I smiled, shy.

Muhammed called his friends' attention to it. Look how she smiles, he said. She understands far more than she lets on. She knows far more than a little girl should.

My smile faded right in front of their eyes.

◆ ◆ ◆

Through the next day we were always driving, stopping, loading, unloading. I tried to stay out of the men's way. Francis made a pallet for me in the corner, where the pile of rags used to be, but I tried not to lie down too long because then the snakebite in my chest would start burning *kreen, kreen, kreen.* I tried to slap it with the flat of my palm, even punch it, to get it to stop, but it never did. So instead I tried to calm it down by saying the word the sea gave me: *saha, saha, saha.*

The air began to change. It got even thicker, and there was more wetness in it, and sometimes I had trouble breathing. Along the road I kept seeing trees. I'd seen trees before, Yemaya, but never so many! In some places there were more trees than there was open space. And then the trees started to crowd up right along the road, leaning in to get a look at us, so that we had to plow through them and branches would rip off and fall right onto the truck bed.

I made friends with the driver, Samson. He let me sit up front in the cab when Muhammed or Francis didn't need to. He had fringed mats on his dashboard, each of them woven with pictures of a woman in blue.

Who is that? I asked him, pointing.

Maryam, Mother of God, he said. (He didn't speak my language very well.) You—Maryam?

Mariama.

It's the same. But you must honor her. Do you know how?

No.

You'll see. In Ethiopia. In the churches, in the street, in the air. She'll show you how to praise her. The woman is in every place.

The woman is in every place, I repeated to myself. I looked out the window and tried to see every woman's face as my own.

Dakar Live

The trees were one thing. But Yemaya, I was not prepared for the big city. I watched from the side of the truck as the buildings thickened around us, and then the people, so much darker, wearing so many varieties of clothing, down every alleyway, churning rivers of people. It seemed to me that they were all going to a party. Or that the city itself was one giant party. It was too much for me!

I crawled back under my old green tarp to limit my field of vision. When Francis walked by, I grabbed at his heel.

What's all this? I said. I was frantic.

We're in Dakar! he said.

Dakar?

The capital of Senegal, he said. Come out here, Mariama—look!

I suffered myself to be lifted by his strong skinny arms. We'd slowed to a crawl in the city traffic. Passing on our right was an army of rainbow women, marching down the street carrying baskets on their heads, full of solar cells, groundnuts, bananas, mobiles, chilies, kola nuts, eggs, and other things I didn't even have names for, their bodies and heads swathed in colors of sunrises and sunsets. Their bottoms alternated, haunch by haunch, the fabric barely containing their flesh.

You're looking at the women, aren't you? Francis said. So am I!

We pulled onto a road that bordered the sea, right up alongside a fish market at its busiest hour. All up and down the beach, men were loading and unloading trucks with crates of fish and sacks of rice. We parked on the curb. Muhammed had business downtown and the other drivers wandered off. I could see that Francis was frustrated to be left alone with me again but he acted like he wasn't. He just got quiet. He said, Follow me, and I followed him down to the beach, where he bought a bagful of prawns from a fisherman who gave them to his wife to grill. As we waited, Francis pointed to a long shiny dark fish, more like a snake.

What's this? he asked.

Something new, said the man. They started showing up two years ago. An invasive species.

Of course I recognized it, Yemaya. That bite of flesh still never really went down in me, and still smoldered in my solar plexus like a little tumor. I had come to call it the kreen, after the sound it made.

It's oily and tastes like metal, I said, and both men looked down at me, surprised that I'd spoken.

You've had this before?

Only a little bit, I said.

Should I try it?

No.

Francis laughed, and lightness returned to him. How can I ignore such a somber warning? he said. I'll take a lobster instead. If you don't like lobster, Mariama, you may not be human.

❖ ❖ ❖

I first saw the woman at dusk.

I saw her from a long way off, because she was tall, and her tangerine headwrap caught the sunset light, crowning her with fire. Wherever she walked, space opened up around her, and she shimmered within it like a mirage. She was wearing tight blue jeans and a tangerine kaftan that matched her headwrap. She had no fewer than three bags strapped across her body, hanging off of her like children. She was wearing sunglasses, so I couldn't see her eyes. Imagine my amazement when she continued not only in our direction, but straight toward our truck, as if led on a path by the divine.

Francis saw her coming and jumped up to greet her. She answered in a language I didn't know. The words had fluid slants and sharp edges, like the curves of dunes. She seemed to be asking questions.

Francis answered, gesturing to the flatbed. I could see he was flustered.

The woman nodded and reached into one of her bags, and pulled out a sheaf of papers.

Francis took them and paged through them. The woman kept asking questions. She was demanding. He was tripping over himself trying to focus on her papers and answer her at the same time.

Then she noticed me. She stopped, whipped off her sunglasses. Oh, her eyes. They were huge. Black blooms on white leaves.

She called out to me in the dune language.

I looked at Francis, ashamed and scared.

He said something about me to the woman, who laughed in surprise. Then she called to me again and her words were clear.

Child, you speak Hassaniyya? she said. What's your name?

Mariama! I said it so quickly that it sped ahead of me, a little goat that got away, no hope of return.

Where are you from?

I twisted up and pointed the way I think we came.

Francis said, We found her in the market in Nouakchott and she climbed onto our flatbed. A little stowaway. We didn't discover her until we were almost in Rosso.

The woman lifted an eyebrow. She's probably better off with you, she said.

Yes, that's what we thought, said Francis. Besides, even if she has a family, she doesn't want to go back. Something bad happened to her.

What happened to you? the woman asked me.

I looked down.

Maybe it'll be a while before she's ready, said Francis.

The woman nodded, eyes on me. She said, I'm going to be joining you, little girl. You're going to have to make room.

I was thrilled. I can make room, I said.

Good, said the woman. You don't have a choice!

You can have my bed, I said further. Or we can share it.

That's the plan, said Francis. Since she can't sleep with me.

The woman gave Francis a warning look. He giggled and then slapped his hand over his mouth.

But I, too, was struck dumb by the beauty of this woman. How she was clothed in sunset colors, blue and tangerine. I was afraid of her, and very shy at first.

I am sure you remember this, Yemaya, because of course, this woman was you.

Map-reading

That first time I met you, the kreen got very quiet, like a baby that sees its mother. Instead of shrieking, it started cooing.

Do you remember when we departed from Dakar the next morning? The very air felt warm and electric. I'd been too excited to sleep, and you'd been too agitated. You just paced the length of the truck as if you could make it go by force of will. When we finally started moving, you went to sit up with Samson in the cab, and I wanted to be near you and look at your beauty, so I just sat on my pallet and watched the back of your head. Your earrings dangled and danced.

On the way to Mbour, Francis and I hung over the side of the railing, calling to each woman we passed. Francis taught me to greet them in the dune language, which I later learned was French. I learned to say, *Bonjour, madame! Bonjour!*

You make me legitimate, said Francis. The women see you, and then they like me.

I smiled. I thought I must be good luck.

I like Senegalese women, he said. They're more free. Ethiopian women are harder. They're like bronze, tough to crack.

What am I? I said.

You're a little girl, he said.

But what kind?

Haratine, he said. But I think it's up to you now to decide what kind you are.

What about the lady who—

I pointed to the back of your head, as you were still up in the cab and I didn't yet know your name.

Oh, Yemaya? he said.

Yemaya, I repeated. It was the most beautiful word I'd ever heard!

Yemaya is Senegalese, he said.

So she is "more free"?

I don't know, said Francis. I tried to find out, though! I said, You look so beautiful this morning, Mademoiselle Yemaya. But she gave me a mean look.

He made a sad face in a bid for my pity, but I was distracted and said, What is Yemaya doing with us?

I don't know. I think she comes from a wealthy family. I can smell her perfume and it's not the cheap stuff. But she's running like she's being chased.

Maybe she's running away.

Maybe. She wouldn't tell me anything except that she'd pay us in cash for passage to Ethiopia.

Tell me again where it is, I said.

Francis got up and slid the door open on the cab. For one thrilling second I thought he was going to ask you to join us, but instead he asked Samson for a map. He brought it over, unfolded it, and turned it around.

On the map there was a shape like a steak, and across the steak there were colored lines crossing up and down and left and right like marbles of fat. He pointed to the red line. This is the road we're on, he said, Dakar to Bamako. Right now we're on this tiny part of it, just from Dakar to Mbour, which is the last time we'll see the ocean. Then we'll keep following the red line to Ouagadougou (Yemaya, I made him repeat that one five times and it is still my favorite word in the world after your name), then to Niamey, where my friend Hussein lives. He has good pistachio ice cream. Why I'm obsessed with it, I don't know. I like creamy green foods. Then we'll leave for Kano in Nigeria, and then on to N'Djamena, in Chad, where this road called the Trans-Sahelian Highway ends. Then we'll follow this yellow line through Chad and Sudan until we hit this purple line, the Cairo-Gaborone Trans-African Highway, and follow it into Ethiopia, and make a detour to Lalibela, and then we'll make it to Addis Ababa. That's where we all part ways for the season. Muhammed will go to his family in Hawassa and I'll go back to my job as a tour guide. I do that half the year and then I do this the other half of the year.

I pointed to one of the dots on the map. What's this one, again? I asked.

Niamey.

What's—I pressed my finger and made the lamination crackle— this one, again?

Lalibela.

What's—

You can't read, can you?

I shook my head.

You need to learn to read. Then you can sound out all these names for yourself.

I didn't go to school, I said.

It's not your fault, he said. But now that you're with us we have to start making improvements.

At that moment, you slid open the cab window and out came your legs like some beautiful spider unfolding its body. You were still unsteady on your feet. Both Francis and I were transfixed at watching you move. You said, What are you looking at?

Nothing! cried both Francis and me.

You saw the map in Francis's hands.

Long way to go, you said.

It should be about three months, said Francis with much officiousness.

You said it would be six, I said to Francis.

Francis gave me a warning look.

Three on official time, six on African time, you said. So it goes.

I sensed that Francis was a little hurt, but he made the best of it, as he always did. He said, Mariama doesn't know how to read. I think three to six months is an excellent amount of time to learn to read, don't you?

You asked, What schooling have you had, Mariama?

None, I said. But I can cook and milk goats.

Francis said, She was probably a slave. Slaves don't go to school.

Some do, you said, but you were talking to yourself.

Then you looked out across the land as the sun rose. I was tentative at first, but then I shuffled over on my knees and joined you, just far enough so as not to crowd you. You, and me, and Francis—we were all quiet, all watching. The land was changing. The trees were thinning out, spindly and exquisite, and the earth was colored bronze and sage. I felt solemn, like we were passing into a more ancient country, whose history covered the ground like a fine gold dust.

Golden women gathered at wells with golden buckets to be

filled with liquid gold. I tried to slow down each instant to an hour and commit each woman to memory. I made it a game of high stakes, telling myself that if I didn't remember them, no one would. One woman was wearing a dress with frills at the shoulder. One woman had skinny arms and teeth like those in a goat skull. One woman was tiny, her hair in plaits.

I memorized each one. I anticipated each one before I even saw her and then I thought, I know you. I've always known you. I knew you the moment before I saw you.

One woman waved, and so did the baby strapped to her back.

One woman was as beautiful as the sun and moon combined.

One woman slipped backward and I didn't see her rise.

I began to feel sleepy. I wanted to stay up so that I could keep seeing everything there was to see. But instead I crawled onto the pallet and my eyelids began to slide up and down of their own accord. I fell asleep.

I was woken up by your voice, saying, Child, child, as if you were disappointed in me. You told me to get up for a minute. In the bright daylight I saw you pull out a big green cloth, like a scarf but thicker, like a blanket, and laid it down on the pallet. You patted it down until the surface was even, like a mattress. Then you laid down on your side with your elbow cocked underneath your head, and said, Now it's better.

I said, Thank you, mademoiselle.

Something in my voice must have charmed you because you broke into a smile, a sort of smirk like you were trying not to laugh, and said, The pleasure is all mine. Now let's take a nap.

Alphabet

Yemaya, I wish I'd marked the moment we last saw the ocean, but I didn't remember to until after we'd left Mbour to turn east.

The farther we drove, the more dry it got. Francis told me there was bad drought in this area—the dry season was starting earlier and ending later, just like the Sahara itself was starting nearer and ending farther. I watched my skin turn red from the dust. I even fingered out pools of dust from the corners of the truck and smeared them on my arms because I wanted to be warmer-colored.

But this little game backfired. I got sick. That night I woke up with a hacking cough and my throat felt like it was barbed with spikes. When we stopped, Francis got Muhammed, who examined me. He made me drink five whole cups of water right in front of him. I had to get up to pee a lot all that night, but every time I woke up, I was surprised to see you were there, Yemaya, helping with even more water. After two days the barbs softened and faded into a gentle tickle that made me want to scratch my throat on the outside.

We stopped to refuel at a border crossing. I remembered the term from before and wanted to be sure I marked the event this time. I flopped into the front seat and asked Samson, Where are we crossing into? Samson didn't understand me very well, so it took many gestures and repeated words, but eventually he said the word *Mali* enough times that I assumed it was the name of the place we were going.

I stayed on the truck. When you came back from the market, you were carrying a blue plastic bag. You pulled out a notebook and on the front was a picture of an albino woman in a pink dress with a big red dot on her forehead.

You like it? you asked me.

I nodded. I hugged it to my chest. Thank you, I said.

Well, don't just hold it, you said. This is for learning your letters. Here, use this to write.

You handed me a sparkle pen. It was like receiving treasure.

You sat down across from me and opened the book for me. There was the same cartoon character on the margin of each page, but the rest of the page was blank.

Francis swung up to join us as the engines started rumbling.

So lessons have begun? he said. Which language will you teach her?

Wolof won't do her any good in Ethiopia. Neither will French or Arabic.

She speaks Arabic, though. So it might be a good place to start sounding things out.

Maybe. The most useful language for Ethiopia proper would be Amharic, but I don't know Amharic.

I could teach her Amharic.

I wish you could teach her Mandarin or Hindi. I don't know either. Mariama, would you like to learn English instead?

I nodded, not knowing the difference between any of these languages.

All right, Francis, I'll teach her English and you teach her Amharic.

Francis bowed and flourished his hand in a way that made you roll your eyes.

❖ ❖ ❖

Ae.

Bee.

See.

Dee.

Eee.

I pranced from one end of the truck to the other, reciting my English alphabet, until you told me to stop and recite it quietly to myself in a corner.

Ha.

Hu.

He.

Ha.

Hey.

Amharic was much harder because there were ten times as many letters to memorize! Francis showed me that all the symbols followed a pattern, and that made it a little easier, but still, it was overwhelming at first.

You told me that when I could recite each alphabet without making a mistake, you would have a surprise for me. You lent me a slender metal bar that clipped onto my dress, and it came with little plastic pearls to put in my ears, and when I pushed a button I heard a woman's voice reciting either alphabet I chose. Of course later I knew what all these things were, Yemaya—a sirius and ear buds—but at the time, it was so new to me. You had amazing treasures in every pocket of your bag. I was sorely tempted to go rooting through it when you weren't looking, just to see what else was in there.

It took me one day to recite the English alphabet without making a mistake. But it took me three days to recite the Amharic alphabet. We had plenty of time because in addition to our load-ins and load-offs, the trucks kept having things wrong with them. There were many breakdowns and necessary repairs. Sometimes we were stuck in the desert for hours while Muhammed or one of his other helpers flagged down a utility vehicle headed for the nearest town to bring back a mechanic in case we couldn't fix something ourselves. And then there was the bureaucracy! Once we stopped at a checkpoint and some men came to tally our cargo, and they looked so strange I screamed. You told me to be quiet, but one of the men indicated it was all right. He said something to you, and you translated to me: He's asking if you've ever seen a Chinese man before. I said no, I hadn't. He smiled and waved at me. He pointed to himself and said, Soon. I pointed to myself and said, Mariama. He was trying to be friendly and I was friendly back. But secretly I felt terrible for him, having to go around looking like that.

Francis told me not to worry about all the stopping, but I could see he was frustrated. That made me frustrated too, and the kreen stirred in my chest. I asked Francis why the police kept stopping us, and he told me that Malians were always scared about attacks from Azawad, to the north.

Why do they attack?

Because they're angry.

Why are they angry?

Mali's not letting them go.

Why don't they let them go?

I don't know. I say cut the bastards loose and let them have their own country, but what do I know? Ethiopia let Eritrea go thirty years ago and we still hate each other.

Then you spoke, Yemaya. You said, It's because of energy.

What's because of energy? said Francis.

Why they won't let them go. The Malian government knows about the oil fields in the north, but they can't tell anyone about it because the Chinese won't let them.

Francis looked hard at you. How do you know that? he asked.

You looked down at your lap and said, I have *connections*, over-articulating the word as if making a mockery of it.

Well, said Francis, making light again after the silence, You can sell that information to the Indian government when you get

to Ethiopia! No doubt they'll be very glad to have it and you'll be
a rich woman.

I don't want to be rich, you said.

I thought of Dr. Moctar Brahim's gold teeth and jumped in and
said, Me neither. Rich people have to get chips, and I didn't get
one, and that's how I got away.

You said, Lucky you.

But I couldn't tell whether you were joking or not.

❖ ❖ ❖

At the next town we reached, you told me to stay on the truck and
you'd come back with my surprise. I sat in the exact same place
you left me in with my hands folded in my lap. You came back a
half hour later, this time holding a pink plastic bag.

Indian sweets, you said. I didn't know whether they'd have
them or not, but they did. Would you like to try one?

I nodded.

You handed me something that looked like a ball of desert sand.
What is this?

A ladoo, you said. They're best when they're fresh, but these are
the prepackaged kind you find in the Sahel.

I took a tiny bite. The dusty-honey taste was overpowering.

Too much, huh? you said. Keep it. You'll get used to it and I bet
you'll be wanting more in about five minutes.

You were right. I ate the whole rest of it and then wanted more.
You gave me another one, and watched me eat it.

So. You're from Nouakchott? you asked.

I nodded.

What do you know about Ethiopia?

That they speak Amharic there. That it's on the other side of
the country.

The continent, Mariama, not the country. It's on the other side of the continent of Africa.

I nodded.

Where is your mother?

I don't have one.

And I'm a warthog, you said.

I giggled.

You said, You must be an orphan.

I disliked the way you said the word, so instead I asked, Why are *you* going to Ethiopia?

You shrugged and made your voice sound casual. Needed to get out of Dakar, always wanted to see Addis for myself, you said. The music, the dance, the culture. And they make beautiful clothing there. When we come to the market in Lalibela I'll show you the cotton dresses. They're white but they have bright-colored crosses, like you see in stained glass windows. Have you ever been to a Christian church?

What is that? I said.

You laughed. Good little Muslim, you said.

But I didn't get the joke. What a bitter education it was, all these adults telling me what I was and wasn't! Black, not Moorish; Hassaniyya-speaking, not French-speaking; Muslim, not Christian. That I Must Be an Orphan. The kreen was rustling in my flesh like a bird taking a dust bath.

I asked for another ladoo but you said no.

You knew what was best for me, Yemaya. I was greedy even then.

❖ ❖ ❖

We were in true desert now, so it was cooler at night than it had been before. There was a new moon so it was pitch-black, aside from the starlight. You and I had been sleeping on our sides facing away from each other. But that night, after a few minutes of both of us shivering, you told me to come close. You said we could keep each other warm with our bodies. So I stayed still and let you hug me like a pillow, with one arm thrown over me and the other under me, the inside of your elbow a warm, clammy spot to rest my cheek. I could hardly breathe for being so close to you, mashed up, skin-to-skin. But then I let myself breathe back into you, and feel you breathe forward into me. And for the first time, the kreen was totally quiet. Like a burn soothed with ointment. I felt calm and safe.

I mouthed the word *Yemaya, Yemaya, Yemaya* to myself. It seemed a better word than *saha,* the word I'd first used to calm myself. I could no longer remember where it had come from— somewhere remote—but I knew where *Yemaya* came from. It came from you, the person holding me, and you were real and warm.

⸎ B⊡⸱⊡K V ⸎

Meena

The Knife

The memory has a solid component, of coolness on my cheek: I was
leaning against the doorway because though my mother had called
me in to her study, she didn't notice me at first, so I lingered there.

She asked me to sit down in the chair she kept for patients. I
did. Then she told me that she was not really my mother.

Is Appa my father? I asked.

No, she said. I'm sorry, Meena. Appa is really your Muthashan, and I am really your Muthashi. But you are still our family,
our granddaughter. We will raise you faithfully.

I wagged my head. I didn't want to know a single thing more.

Do you want to know what happened to your parents? this
formerly-Amma, now-Muthashi asked.

I said yes because I was still scared of her.

She gestured that I come forward and sit next to her, behind
the desk. She told me to bring the chair closer so that I could see
the file folder on the top of her desk. She'd planned and prepared

for this day. She opened the folder and gave me a printout from the *Times*. "Indian Lovers Butchered in Addis Ababa."

Lovers, I said to myself.

They were not married, she said, as if that were the most important thing. They were both medical students. But there was a big election happening and the atmosphere for Indians in Ethiopia was very bad. Their maid was a secret rebel who wanted them out. She killed Gabriel and his girlfriend, and then she escaped, and the Ethiopian police didn't bother to go after her. You were three months premature. No one even knew your mother was pregnant. She was a shapely woman and hid it well. But the murders took place in an Indian hospital, so the Indian nurses found you and got you medical attention right away. It was a miracle you survived. You wanted to live very badly.

Gabriel, I said to myself.

Gabriel is your father, and my only son, she said. Would you like to see a picture of him?

She didn't wait for me to answer. She opened a desk drawer and handed me a framed picture of a young man. He was running backward, wearing a red cricket jersey, smiling as bright as the sun. He was extraordinarily beautiful. He had long wavy hair, golden skin, and bright lotus eyes. He looked like a prince from my *Children's Illustrated Mahabharata*.

As you can see, he was very handsome, she said, as if explaining an anatomical chart. He was studying to be—

I threw the picture against the wall. Then I was running away from that woman, who was now standing and yelling at me.

I ran outside, through the courtyard and down to the river beneath the banana palms where the quail was singing her winding spiral song, waterspouts that were spent as soon as formed. I summoned to mind a long knife, a kilometer long, with a blade so subtle that its edge began long before it was visible. It was only an

atom thick so that it began to separate matter, invisibly, long before it cut. And it could cut anything. Coconut palms, silken saris,
fruit stands, the metal of trains, and people. Everything would be
halved.

I closed my eyes and turned in a slow circle.

Phase Two

The pain wakes me up. I'm rocking back and forth with my cheek
on a cool surface. I feel like I got sucked down a wormhole of sleep
and then spit up again. The snakebites in my chest feel like the tips
of five skewers, rotating.

I see light to one side. I turn my head. My vision aligns. It's a
beautiful ring of orange stars. That triggers the cascade of locus
et tempus: it's late night, I'm on the Trail, I'm looking at Marine
Drive from two hundred meters away, and I'm injured. No more
euphoria. I'm in Phase Two of this journey now.

I rise to my hands and knees and all my muscles tingle. Eight
scales so far. That means I've come eight meters. I can try another
eight and then see how I feel.

I make it three more before I throw up.

I retreat from the vomit. I wait politely and let the seawater
slosh it off. I examine my finger, which is swelling and stiff to the
touch, but not broken. I might take anti-inflammatories when I get
a bit farther.

I cover two more. It's getting harder to see the outlines of the
scales and perceive depth accurately. I have visions of myself as
a cat.

I miscalculate and hit my chin again. I'm pretty sure the skin's
come clear off this time because I can feel a liquid trickle down my
throat.

I scramble forward in a fresh burst of energy. As a result I hit my knee so hard I get an instant headache.

I take a rest.

I give myself permission to go very slowly and cover five without throwing up or significantly hitting any body part.

I stop to rest. I take deep breaths of sea air. The waves make *glock-glock* sounds.

I look behind me. The Queen's Necklace glows. I can still see the cars on Marine Drive and hear their gentle zooms.

I cover three more.

I've come twenty-five meters.

To celebrate, I dry-heave.

The nausea passes again.

I cover five more without causing more injury to myself. It was an unthinkable goal twenty minutes ago. I pause to appreciate this.

I look ahead. Past a certain point, the Trail becomes a ribbon of silver, lit by the moon. How can something so beautiful be so difficult. Eve, beauty, snake, treachery: all the accidents of misogyny.

I cover five more meters. I must call them meters instead of scales. They are successive units of length that I conquer one by one.

I notice that the color of the light is changing. A little less is from the streetlights of Marine Drive, and a little more is from the moon overhead.

How long till the light is all moon.

I can't rest.

Am I in Phase Three yet.

I cover ten at a stretch and on the last one, collapse back into beetle pose.

I tell myself I'm on a train. I got to ride an antique coal-powered train, once, which was bumpy. Mohini hated it, but I liked it. I've always been able to sleep better when rocked by movement. I think it's because I used to nap on the floating jetty on the river that ran past Muthashi's clinic, where I used to have dreams of a sky full of milk.

I get up again and cover seven before I have to rest.

Walking upright on this thing is fucking unthinkable. So I just won't think about it for now. I will crawl all the way to Africa if I have to.

Various parts of my body report to my brain, reminding me of pain and serious injury.

Forehead.

Knee.

Chin.

Heel.

Finger.

Solar plexus times five.

Armpit, don't forget the armpit. I cut out a delta of skin there with a filet knife.

Each wound is a blazing star, and I'm a moving constellation.

I see myself as a cat again.

I used to watch cats pad along the ramparts of the stone wall around Muthashi's clinic. I watched their shoulders rotate and wished I could reprogram my flesh.

For the first time, I lose count of how many meters I've come.

Too late to go back and recount.

Sixty-ish, though.

That accounts for space. As for time, it's like a cloth being pulled underneath me, crosswise, wrinkle by wrinkle.

The water is black edged in white, like obsidian and shaving cream.

Things are not themselves. Just symbols. This experience should be a practicum for IIT-Bombay's introductory philosophy course. I'll have to write to the department about it.

Sixty-five-ish now.

I've covered the last five without paying as much attention.

I see a buoy bobbing to my right, outlined by moonlight. I wonder how much else is out there around me, but not visible. Floating fakirs. Cartoon sharks. Things with tentacles.

The barefoot girl, winged and perfectly dry.

I'm not in my right mind.

I can see the clouds better, now. There's a bank of them sleeping against the horizon.

Something like eighty-two.

Of all the pain stars, the one in my armpit is shining brightest. I stop to examine it and see that my entire left flank is soaked with blood. I pinch the fabric of my shirt and it peels away with a wet sucking sound.

I venture to half-turn, again, to see the shore. The streetlights on Marine Drive are smaller and dimmer and farther away.

I have to calculate what is reasonable.

I have to rest. I have to take water. I have to, if at all possible, re-dress my wounds.

The past hour is a patchwork of shades of black.

I make myself go twenty more meters, taking lots of breaks. And then I stop. I have to rest.

I sink into my new best friend beetle pose and take off my backpack. For several long moments I feel unspeakable rage at the sea. I don't understand why it can't be still just for five motherfucking seconds. What animal would ever choose to make their home atop a medium that moves.

I'm still not in my right mind.

I find my sunbit and squeeze it so I can see better. Earlier today I read my pod's inflation instructions while I was still sitting in the seawall. I hope I remember them right. I can program the pod from my scroll, or vocally, but I don't remember the command sequence, so it's good that there are also manual controls on the panel of the pod itself. "Press Full to activate the molecular pumps in the pod's skin, so that it slowly fills with air."

I press it and nothing happens. I realize why. The skin isn't charged. Here I spent the entire day's worth of sunlight reading about Senegal instead of charging my pod.

Crying would be a luxury, here, now. So to deal with it in the short term I name it a Mild Annoyance. I curl up on one side and fold my pod into a neat pie-shaped wedge that will make an economical pillow until the sun comes to charge it. I hug my bag to my body and curl around it. I close my eyes.

I get sucked back down the wormhole.

I get spit up again.

I open my eyes. The sky is a little paler. A little trickle of seawater is surging, with each pitch, across the scale hinge toward my head.

I don't know how much I slept but I spring to as if I've had a raj's rest in a feather bed because I remembered something: the compressed gas capsules. Misbah talked me into buying them, saying, These will work if it's cloudy and you can't charge the pod. They come in a hard case so they can't be crushed accidentally.

I find the case. Its edges are quivering. I'm grotesquely lucid. I have to make the best of it while it lasts. I pick out one capsule, make a rent in the pod with my thumbnail, toss in the capsule, reseal the pod, bring down my fist on top of the capsule, and then jump back. I watch the pod blow up into a real thing. I remember dimly that now I'll be one of those blurry smears that Anwar sees against the sea from his office high up on Nariman Point. This feels like Phase Three, finally. Things are looking up.

I wait till the skin is taut and then slice an opening and climb in quickly so that the air doesn't get out, and reseal it behind me by pinching the material closed.

It's pleasant. Actually it's wonderful. The air from the gas capsule is perfectly mixed and scented with rose. I remember that the pod also has settings for porosity and opacity so I find the control panel and experiment with sliding my fingers along the scales. When I increase opacity, the inner surface of the pod goes silver-gray. This is much better than full transparency. I also increase the porosity so that passive air exchange is increased. The internal pressure of the pod will lessen, but not enough to collapse in on me.

I've made my house.

I close my eyes and fall back asleep before my head finishes falling.

Canticles

New canticles of pain wake me up.

My skin is hot. My brain feels like throbbing strings of glue. I must be dehydrated. I realize I haven't drunk any water since setting out last night. I also never tended to my finger, which is blackish purple now, like I dipped it in ink. Several life-threatening emergencies I must address calmly and in turn.

I slice an opening in my pod just big enough for my forearm. Wet heat and light flood in. I lean out over the water and dip my desalinator bottle. Someone watching would see an arm appear out of nowhere and then slip back into its own dimension.

While the water filters, I take anti-inflammatories and wrap my pinched finger with gauze. Saliva wells up around my gums and I pinch the pressure point between my thumb and forefinger to prevent nausea. I should probably eat something too, so I turn on my kiln, which came already charged. But fucking fuck I have to stuff something organic in it. I slice an opening again and hang over the edge again. I see a kelp patch and so I haul in a handful of it, which looks like felt-coated plastic holiday garlands, and draw it back inside and stuff it into the top of the kiln. I program idlee at ambient temperature and close the door and save the rest of the kelp for later and after ten minutes there are four cubes of rice meal in the well. They don't yet come in the proper saucer shape but I hear they're working on it. I don't know why they haven't yet. Because if you've developed organic matter reprogramming, then topological finishing should not be that fucking hard.

I drink a whole bottle of water one sip at a time and then refill it to wash the brine off my skin. I eat one pseudo-idlee in small bites so I have a little strength. Then I get out my medical kit and take some broad-spectrum nanobiotics for pain and infection. Then I arrange all needed supplies in a row: antiseptic wipes, antibiotic ointment, clearskins, bandages, surgical tape. I tend to each area in turn.

The nanobiotics will take a few more minutes to lessen the pain, and until then, the rocking of the Trail makes each wound feel worse. Insult to injury. I would call this Phase Four but I feel suddenly annoyed at the childish delineations of the previous night and abandon the whole schema.

To distract myself I look through my medical kit and thank Mehrdad and Misbah in my mind. It's fucking incredible. It's like a miniature version of the entire first-aid cabinet we had at the women's clinic, including both Ayurvedic and Western remedies. There's a tiny surgical kit. There are rehydration salts. There's Plumpy'nut Ultra for emergency nutrition. In addition to the broad-spectrum nanobiotics there are pills for parasites, viruses, chest infections, skin infections, eye infections, throat infections, digestive-tract infections, nausea, diarrhea, constipation, sunburn, anxiety, and depression. And all of this fits into a sealed bag shaped like a kidney.

I eat another idlee and then lie back down. I'm not going

anywhere right now, and anyway, it's daylight, so I have to get used to sleeping now. But I can't sleep. Now that the pain is less I have the luxury of being angry. And I chew over everything I could be angry about. Why won't this Trail stop bucking so hard. Who put the snake in my bed in the first place. Who is the barefoot girl. Was she actually real. It's possible that my mania produced hallucinations.

I have to think about something else.

Preeti, then. One of my charges at the women's clinic in Thrissur. Eighteen years old, fatherless, mother some kind of addict. But she was pretty and petite and intense, with rare hazel eyes, and older men mistook this as indicative of some kind of woman-child depth, and she got involved with a married politician, K. P. Pillai, still very much in office, who got her pregnant and then beat her up to induce a miscarriage. She came to us. She miscarried anyway.

I was in the room then. What came out looked like a bloody squirrel. The doctor asked if she wanted to see it and she smiled and said no thank you, that's all right. And then in post-op counseling I asked Preeti, Would you like to press charges?

She didn't even know what I was talking about. Against who? she said.

Against Mr. Pillai.

Oh dear! For what?

For assaulting you and causing a miscarriage.

Oh, it was an accident, she said. He just needed to get his frustration out of his system.

There's no excuse for physical violence, I said.

It's more complicated than that, she said, patting my knee, even though she was eight years younger than me. She said, Human beings are passionate. Energy comes through us and we keep moving it around, and sometimes we're the receivers and sometimes we're the pushers.

Oh really? Have you ever been the pusher?

Oh yes, said Preeti, I'm very messy and it drives him crazy. I know it bothers him, but I never clean up enough before he comes over.

I stared at her.

I said: What do you want your life to be?

She laughed and said, Me and K. P., sitting in a tree!

I wanted to slap her. Right now I want to slap her too, slap that big childlike smile off her face. I didn't understand that people like that still existed in the twenty-first century and I still don't.

Mohini didn't understand why I couldn't be more compassionate. She said, Why are you in this line of work if that's how you feel? I said I was allowed to have complicated feelings about my charges. I was allowed to hold the private opinion that living in enslavement to "love" was a life wasted. Mohini said she didn't see how that described a state very different from my life, or hers, or anyone else's. I said, but Preeti only wants it from one person who hurts her, and no one else will do. That there are healthy and unhealthy ways to get love. It went on. It was a painful fight. Mohini dug into it like she needed to prove something to me. Something about how the fact that I always had fantasies of violence, even though I never acted on them, was problematic.

This isn't helping me sleep either. I try to clear my mind. I shift until I find the most comfortable position relative to the rocking of the Trail: curled in the fetal position, head forward, so I'm being rocked anterior to posterior, like I'm on a train.

I realize I haven't heard my own voice in almost twenty-four hours, so I sing the Suprabhatam to myself even though it's late in the day. In my life I've gone through cycles of hating it and needing it. I know the whole thing because Muthashan played the Subbulakshmi recording every morning when I was growing up, even after I stopped joining him for prayer. Mohini sang it herself, of course, and I thought she was better. I never thought I could sing for shit, but Mohini said I could, it just wasn't a good voice for Indian classical music. She said my voice was rough and wandering.

I get tired enough to stop singing and continue only in my mind, and then I get to singing on the sage Narada—*jhankaragitaninadaih saha sevanaya*—and my mind catches on the word *saha* and repeats it, and then the figures I've been drawing in my head start drawing themselves.

Discipline

I'm woken by footsteps.

They echo in my head when I sit up. I stay still in my graphite bubble. I don't hear any more. They were probably relics of a dream. But they had a syncopated rhythm of steps on the Trail that I remember from watching the lifeguard, whose name I can't remember now, I think Cecilia?—something Christian—but in any case, something my subconscious must have recorded at the time, not a steady beat, but a scattered offbeat with a deeper rhythm, like raindrops.

I check the time. It's approaching sunset, and I'll start crawling then, trusting both my camo and the glare to hide me from eyes on shore. If I were still marking phases, then this would be Phase Five: A Stab at Routine. First I eat. I dissolve a protein cube in desalinated water on my solar plate, heat it up, and then add tamarind and cumin to soak. I break apart the last two idlee with my fingers and swab the pieces in the broth. It's salty but otherwise good. I think of the spicewaala Sunny in Thrissur and what he might be doing right now. It's dusk on a Tuesday. He's probably packing up his corner at Round East, closing shop on his fat cones of spice.

I think I'll try surviving only on idlee and protein broth for the foreseeable future; fewer of the latter, since protein requires more water to digest. With a kiln I can make all kinds of food, as long as it's homogeneous—chocolate, sweet lassi, imitation dal. But I can't give in to decadence. I can't afford it. I've come into a new phase of discipline where austerity and humility are key.

Speaking of humility, I have to shit. I'd forgotten entirely about that aspect of existence.

I get out the diaper and set it in front of me. Muthashi's voice comes back to me, lecturing her patients on how crucial bowel movements were. That they were a sign of health. That, and menses.

It would be a lot easier to face forward, because then the rocking motion would be aligned with my front-to-back axis. But that means I'd have to shit directly on the Trail. And I don't want to. It seems like bad karma. So I scuttle on my knees out to the edge and point my ass northwest and pray there are no fishing boats nearby to see. My ass is over my ankles, so to avoid mucking up the Trail I have to work my way back until most of my shins are over the water, and I can feel the waves smack the tops of my feet, and I extend my spine lengthwise as far as I can in a modified child's pose. I wait. I tense. There are a few explosions and dribblings. And then I pee, too, forgetting that I'm literally not in a position to do so. I just let it go and then try to move my gear in time to get out of the way of the puddle, which of course expands with the movement of the Trail. All hopeless. I'm wet, and so is my stuff.

But I'm my grandmother's granddaughter. I've cleaned up much worse in the clinic. I have no shame.

I wipe first with the modified diaper and set it in the sun to self-clean. Then I refill my desalinator and use the new water to wash myself clean. I didn't make a complete mess. I'll get better. I use another bottleful to wash the parts of my stuff that got touched with urine, and then another, to rinse the urine off the Trail. It feels like a housekeeping gesture. I'll never pass this way again but I'll keep it nice for those who do.

When I finish I realize that kneeling on the Trail is easier than it was the night before. I still get knocked around. I still fall sideways and forward and backward and have to brace myself, especially with my hands, which means my wrists burn and my muscles are in a state of perpetual incredulity.

But I'm getting better. And I resist the urge to take more nanobiotics. I have to break my body in.

◈　◈　◈

I crawl a hundred more meters in the setting sun before I allow myself to rest. I feel like I'm roasting on a spit, skin crackling, muscles burning, pockets of fat bursting open. No wonder walkers walk at night.

When I look back, Mumbai is more faint in the haze. I might be half a kilometer from shore now. The tops of the buildings at Nariman Point are lined in bright orange from the sunset. This time yesterday, I was hiding in the seawall.

I take another capsule of nanobiotics for the pain. Everything takes fucking forever: getting out the medical kit, holding on to the bottle so it doesn't fly out of my hand when the Trail bucks, drawing more water, positioning myself to put the pill in my mouth, maintaining balance to drink water to get it down.

Then I crouch in child's pose and dictate to my scroll:

7:00 p.m.—wake up

7:00 p.m.–7:45 p.m.—first meal: two cubes of idlee, half
    cup broth, one bottle water

7:45 p.m.–12:00 a.m.—crawl. listen to music or read on
    audio. drink another bottle of water while crawling

12:00 a.m.–1:00 a.m.—second meal: protein dissolved in
    water with spices and one bottle of water
1:00 a.m.–6:00 a.m.—crawl. listen to music or read on
    audio, drink another bottle of water while crawling
6:00 a.m.–7:00 a.m.—third meal: my choice plus one bottle
    of water
7:00 a.m.–8:00 a.m.—get into pod, check position,
    inventory supplies
8:00 a.m.–11:00 a.m.—read or listen to music, leisure
11:00 a.m.–7:00 p.m.—sleep

I feel this is a reasonable yet generous schedule.

Then I keep going. It's only 8:13 p.m. I exist on restricted choices. There's nowhere to go but the next scale.

❖ ❖ ❖

I keep checking my pozit. I come to 1.5 kilometers. I congratulate myself on being so disciplined. Then I lie down, which feels so nice, and blackness comes.

I wake up. I reproach myself. I've only lost an hour, though.

The moon has set. I'm grateful for the darkness. I'm not forced to notice everything around me like I am when it's light.

Next scale. And next. And next. I count them in my head. I count to a hundred. Then I can only bear to count in rounds of fifty. Then twenty. Then ten.

❖ ❖ ❖

It's not 6:00 a.m. yet but I'm so sore I need to stop. More pain medication. More anti-inflammatory. I worry that it'll always be like this, and I'll run out of medication in a week.

My third meal is My Choice. I renounce all prior declarations of discipline and program idlee and imitation dal on my kiln. The dal is homogenous, with no distinct lentils per se. But I eat it and then program another serving and eat that, too. The hunger is like a concavity in my stomach. My body is starved for energy.

The sky gets lighter and lighter and now that I'm stationary, I can appreciate how pretty it is. I'm two kilometers offshore, now. I'm effectively on the open ocean. I haven't had a single chance to appreciate what I'm doing. Now I can, for an instant, and watch the sun rise. It smolders between the towers of Nariman Point.

Two kilometers down and 3,186 kilometers to go. I look at the satellite map on my scroll. I'm still well within the continental shelf, and then the seafloor drops to abyssal plain about 250 kilometers out, and then a ridge introduces more complex topology about halfway through, and then the sea gets gradually shallower going into the Gulf of Aden, an unthinkable distance away.

I calculate how far I've come.

It's 0.06 percent of the way.

I try not to think more about that.

My third meal is done. According to my schedule, I'm now At Leisure.

I blow up my pod and climb inside before it gets too hot. What world will I enter, now: Tagore's Kolkata, Chu's Singapore, Morrison's Ohio?

I choose to read Sesay, again, her watery poetry. But I read three pages and then I'm already fantasizing about what I'm going to do when I reach Africa. Africa is the new India, after India became the new America, after America became the new Britain, after Britain became the new Rome, after Rome became the new Egypt, after Egypt became the new Punt, and so on and so forth. Now we're back to Punt. I've watched the African youth uprisings against land grabs or "colonization by invitation." Mohini and I used to lie side by side and watch the reports roll in to the cloud. Addis Ababa, the city where my parents were murdered, is now the flagship city of Africa. Lagos is too big, Joburg is too white, Cairo is not really African, and so on. No one expected Addis to emerge as Africa's sweetheart city. But it has.

It feels good to leap into the future, when this current adventure will be done. First I'll recuperate in Djibouti. Then I'll take the train into Ethiopia and see what there is to be seen, because the woman who killed my parents was never caught.

Aquaculture

When I wake up again, I have no idea where I am, only that I'm in an orange globe. I try to breathe steadily as memory comes back to me. I'm in my pod. The sun is setting. It makes the pod's skin glow.

I eat my appointed breakfast. As I do this I think, So this is what life as an ascetic would be like. Two days in, I don't know how I feel about it. The jury is hung.

I change the dressings on my wounds. Now this includes my elbows and knees, both rubbed raw from the crawling. Some of the swelling from my forehead is beginning to slide down my face, under the skin, making my eyes itch.

I set out crawling toward the west. My knees hurt every time I set them down, no matter how gently. The pain is a fascinating terrain. I ideate it as a bottomless tropical jungle full of toucans with razor beaks. I try to focus on counting.

Then I start to see a colony of kelp or an algae bloom building up on either side of the Trail, actually rising above sea level. Then I start to think it's a huge garbage patch, because I see glints of plastic, but I wonder why the garbage seems to have congregated in such a geometric arrangement. And then I see the blurs against the horizon. They're pods. They're not as well camouflaged as mine. They might be an earlier or cheaper model. But they're much bigger than mine, enough to fit two or three people, more like domes than pods.

So I've come to a seastead.

Now all of a sudden being on the Trail is not an ascetic experience at all. It's going to be a completely different experience, starting now. Fuck the numeric, this is Phase Beta.

I stop, balance, take off my bag, and check for the presence of all my gifts and barter items. They're where I thought they'd be. I wonder whether they've seen me yet. And now I feel ashamed that I'm still crawling. I can't let them see me like this. So, especially given the state of my knees and elbows, I should try to stand up now.

I tighten my backpack against my back. I thank Parvati for big tits that balance it out. From all fours, I come to kneeling, and then push my hands down and come to a crouch. Low center of gravity. Fingertips balancing on the sandpaper surface. I spread my feet, left forward, right back, to compensate for the rocking motion, and then I try to rise. It takes four tries. I have to spread my feet even farther apart. I have to first master standing with both feet on a single scale before I even attempt to stand on two different ones. There's no pattern to the duration of any single pitch. My legs are in a state of constant tension.

I come to a wide-legged warrior pose, as if I'm on a surfboard. I wobble in every cardinal direction. I feel like I'm on a Japanese game show. I would laugh at myself if I didn't also feel like crying. When I've counted to ten and am still standing upright, I take a step forward.

In the split second it takes for the Trail to buck my front foot such that I lean back to safety and find no surface at all and I slip and cartwheel into the ocean, I think, *Meena, this is the difference between monovariable and multivariable calculus.* Then I'm in the water.

The lizard brain takes over until I find myself back on the Trail. Drenched and pissed, I stand again.

This time I try placing all my weight on one foot while I slide the other forward onto the next scale. I feel it bucking under my front foot. My shin is burning. My balance stabilizes. I begin to shift weight forward. The surfaces are rough, giving some traction. Otherwise I wouldn't have a chance. It's probably for the sake of the maintenance crews that never do any maintenance, according to Anwar. Briefly I wonder why they didn't just make special shoes for the maintenance crews, instead of making the Trail itself walkable. While I wonder this I realize I've already crossed over onto the third scale. It's better if I don't think too hard, apparently. It's like learning to salsa. I have to surrender to my partner and everything will go smoothly.

And anyway, now I have an audience.

There's a child ahead, standing halfway between me and the seastead. She's keeping perfect balance with the Trail, making me feel like a cow on roller skates. She regards me for a while, belly thrust out. I wave. She runs back to the seastead and disappears into a pod. She emerges pulling the wrist of an older girl who, upon seeing me, turns and calls toward a pod farther up the platform. Then she looks me over with ennui, in perfect contrast to the younger girl, who's hopping up and down and clutching at her dress.

I try to walk toward them but I fall again and sprain my wrist. I feel ashamed and try not to cry.

A woman in a cotton sari comes out of a pod. I can tell she's the mother. I feel both grateful to see other human beings and resentful of their intrusion on my solitude, though, of course, it's the other way around. Will they welcome me? Isn't hospitality a requisite feature of settlements in deserts and tundras and other harsh environs, being a kind of communal survival mechanism? I remember reading that somewhere. Besides, they're just as illegal as I am, and I have nothing to profit by exposing them.

"Namaste," I yell out. My voice sounds hoarse and thin to myself.

"Namaste," she yells back, and continues in Hindi. "Having some trouble?"

I still my rage. "I haven't really learned to walk yet," I yell back.

"It's hard for everyone at first. What's your business?"

"I'm just passing through," I say. I decide not to mention the barefoot girl at all. They'll think I'm crazy. "Do I need your permission?"

"No," she says. "But nobody is 'just passing through.' Are you a hiker or sadhvi or what?"

"Something like that," I say.

"Well, come on, then," she says.

I feel like an animal in a zoo.

"Are you going to watch me?"

"Fine, I can turn away if you like, but you might want some pointers."

"We get people like you," says the elder girl. "We know what to say."

I swallow my pride and capitulate.

"Okay," I say. I come up to crouching on my own just to show them I can fucking do something by myself. "What now?"

"Spread your feet forwards and back," she says.

I fucking knew that and did that already. But I do it again anyway.

"Keep your knees soft," she says.

"Now try to rise up," she says.

"Look at me," she says. "Don't look at your feet."

I look at her. She is standing, appraising, both fists on her waist.

"Theek hai, now switch legs," she says. "Don't move forward, just stay in the same place."

I manage this.

"Now go through your body and find where you're holding tight and try to let it go soft."

Great. I'm in fucking yoga class.

"Are you angry?" she says.

"No," I say.

"Now let your eyes go soft," she says. "Be passively aware of your surroundings. Let there be eyes in the back of your head and all over your body."

I wheel a couple times but I kind of know what she's saying and try to get in that zone.

"Shaabaash, now come forward, and keep your arms spread to either side, and just keep your eyes on me."

I do. I feel like I'm walking a tightrope, but somehow the tightrope is as wide as the earth and I can't go wrong. Night has almost fallen. The air is cool on my skin. Something crosses over in me. Somehow it's not as hard. I keep my eyes on the woman in the cotton sari, a figure getting darker in the dusk. She's crossed her arms, now, and she shakes her head from side to side.

"Shaabaash, good," she says. "You're almost here."

The Trail stabilizes, the closer it gets to the seastead. It feels like I'm back at the pool again. Easy.

The woman reaches out for me and pulls me off to the side, onto the seastead platform. After the rolling of the Trail, it feels like solid ground, and I fall to my knees, this time because it's stable instead of moving.

"Where are you from?" asks the youngest girl.

"Suri, not now," says the mother. "Go heat the water please. Sita, you help."

The two girls wander away, looking back at me. But the mother gets straight to business.

"So. Sadhvi? Tourist? Thrill seeker? Fishwaala? Refugee? Cultist? Political dissident? Criminal? Scientist? Poet? Pirate?"

"None of the above."

"Are you from HydraCorp?"

I feel offended. But I remind myself this is a reasonable and even necessary question for her to ask. "No. I went to the Hydra-Corp Museum before I started walking, but that's all."

"Are you from the government?"

"No."

"Are you from the press?"

"No."

"Just walking?"

"It seems so."

"So where are your people?"

"Keralam."

"I thought so, I could hear the accent. I have family in Alleppey. But I haven't visited in years."

I'm thrown off by this bit of personal information. But I think it's a good sign.

"You can't beat the fish curry," she adds.

I search for something to say. I feel like I'm in a dream, talking curry in the middle of the ocean. "That's true," I say. "I learned it from my Muthashan, but it's been a long time since I made it."

"Can we make it?"

Now I see the truth of the exchange. This woman has a veneer of hardness, which is necessary in her situation. But she's glad to see me and craves company of a woman her age. And even though I just had breakfast, I'm famished. All I can think about now is fish curry.

"If you have the fish," I say, "I have the spices."

"We have the fish, all right."

◈ ◈ ◈

Her name is Padma. Her husband is Ameem. I introduce myself
to them as Durga, because now I'm in the habit. They position me
rapidly vis-à-vis class and caste and region of origin, and I do the
same, but refrain from commenting on what I presume is a Hindu-
Muslim marriage. Not that it's unusual anymore. But I wonder if
that has anything to do with their living out in the middle of the
ocean. They own the seastead, the aquaculture equipment, the mo-
torboat, and all the profits.

There's one more adult, who turns out to be Rana, the Lost
Son. I get out the mashed box of soan papdi his mother gave me
and say, "She wants you to come home."

He rolls his eyes. "She wants me to sell fish," he says.

Instead, he says, he's saving cash before he starts traveling
through India, and heard that this was a better way to do it than
hawking in Koliwada. He's young and husky. He has long hair
pulled back in a ponytail and wears only a white dhoti swaddled
around his hips.

"I have two jobs," says Rana, kneeling by an open square in
the platform. The seawater is still enough to reflect the half-moon.
"First, I feed the fish"—he opens his fist to show me a clump of
dark flakes—"and second, I dive underneath the cages to make
repairs."

"You have scuba equipment here?"

"No. I just hold my breath."

"Really."

"I'm a fisherman's son. He taught me. The men of our family
have always had a talent for diving."

I want to laugh, but he's so earnest and I don't want to embarrass him. He's trying to impress me. He's younger than me, maybe
twenty-one. He's at his sexual peak.

And he hasn't yet asked me a single question about myself. He's in a state of life of total self-absorption and for some reason I'm attracted to that. I consider seducing him as I did with Anwar and Cecilia. Or I'm just excited at seeing other human beings after two days. So instead I say, "I'm a doctor's granddaughter."

He's unfazed by the class bomb. "Western or Ayurvedic?"

"Both," I say. "She's actually famous for it. She designed the first clinical trials for Ayurveda, which had never been done before, because, you know. Ayurveda doesn't deal with a single variable. So the statistics had to be invented, basically."

"Pretty cool."

"Yeah, it is."

"Are you a doctor?"

"Nope. Muthashi wanted me to be, though."

"Yeah, my mother wanted me to fish and sell fish," Rana says, "but I'm too restless."

"What about your father?"

"Father's dead," he says, no rancor.

"That makes two of us," I say.

Rana looks up, doesn't say sorry, doesn't console me, just shakes his head. The parentless understand each other.

Padma passes us, carrying an empty pot. "A half hour till the food is ready," she says, though we hadn't asked. I can see steam rising and smell the curry leaves, hot peppers, and coriander. She's using my Onam spices.

"Do you want to go swimming under the cages?" Rana asks me.

"What? It's dark."

"But it's even cooler then. I'll give you a light. Come on." He begins to unwind his dhoti.

"What am I going to wear?"

"Your underclothes," he says. "Don't worry, I won't look. I like men."

Chod. Of course he does.

So we go behind his pod on the edge of the water, he in nothing but cotton briefs and I in my bra and underwear. He sees all of my bandages, including the big square on my solar plexus.

"Whoa," he says. "What happened?"

"Snakebite," I say.

"I've never seen a snakebite there."

"First time for everything."

He hands me a pair of goggles with a headlamp. "We'll dress it again after we come up."

"I won't be able to hold my breath as long as you," I say.

"I know, don't worry," he says. "I'll be watching you."

"How cold is it?"

"It's warm in the upper layers, like blood. But if you go past two meters down, then it begins to get cold. But not true cold. If you feel really cold, start swimming up."

He smiles and rubs his palms together like a cartoon character and dives into the water.

This entire situation is bizarre.

But here I am.

I first sit on the edge of the platform, reliving my performance anxiety in front of Cecilia. Then I take a huge breath and heave myself off. It's black underwater but silver motes drift by in the beam of my headlamp. I turn in space and see Rana swim up to me. He adjusts his headlamp so that I'm not blinded. He touches me on the arm and points toward the cage, a cube that drops several meters deep. We watch fat fish slither past one another. Rana swims to the other side to test the cage. I look up and see that the platform is built from hundreds and hundreds of plastic bottles tied together. Ingenious.

My toe touches ice. I've drifted down too far.

But the ice feels good after the days and nights of humidity, after a lifetime of heat. I let myself slide in, feel the ice inch up to my ankles, then my shins, then my knees.

I feel a rough hand grab my upper arm. Rana is tugging me upward. I start kicking. We both break the surface and tread.

"What was that?" he says. "Can't you swim?"

I decide to lie again. "I've never been good at it," I say. "I should have told you."

He treads water. He looks away from me. He doesn't believe me. But he doesn't say so.

"You're bleeding," he says. "Come on, let's get it taken care of."

He helps me back up onto the platform. I take off the bandage and it's pink with blood. Rana gets a medical kit and sits down across from me. They have much the same array of supplies as I do. I hold my breasts out of the way while he swabs the five points with antiseptic. They all still have halos of infection and yellow scabs that got slimy in the water. Then he's smearing sealant and pressing down fresh gauze and giving me a nanobiotic capsule. I feel like I want to kiss him. Or just thank him with my mouth, somehow. I'm famous for my cowrie-shell mouth. I'm aware of moonlight on my breasts. I want to be with someone again. Maybe I can convince him.

But instead I take the towel he offers me and change inside his pod, where he's stored my bag.

❖ ❖ ❖

After we eat, the children take away the dishes to wash. Padma makes chai and we recline on folded tarps that serve as pillows. A fish leaps up out of the cage into Rana's lap, and he tosses it back in the cage and tells it to stay there, to be patient for its death.

I use the opportunity to learn as much as I can. "Have any of you traveled the whole way to Djibouti?"

"Oh no, we don't travel," says Ameem. "We have everything we need here."

"What do you do when there's a storm?"

"We drop over the side. The pods are watertight up to ten meters."

"That's deep enough to avoid the turbulence?"

"Yes. In fact both times we only had to go down four or five meters."

"So how many travelers do you get?"

"We've only gotten a few," says Ameem. He likes to explain, be in charge, be the authority. "But we've never seen anyone come back through, so we can only guess what happens to them. I think they stop and signal for help, or join one of the seasteads farther down the Trail."

"There are others?"

"Yes. Not many, but there are others nearer to Yemen."

I don't ask him how he knows that. Of course he doesn't know, but he'll bullshit like he does. He's that kind of man.

He continues, "We've taken the boat down the Trail as far as the Indian EEZ—"

"Exclusive Economic Zone," Rana says.

"Which is two hundred and fifty kilometers west, and beyond that point the shipping lanes go right through the Trail and make it sink on a daily basis. So it'd be very hard to maintain a seastead there."

"If you get that far, you have to be careful," says Rana. "Stay out of the way of the ships. They can't see you, and anyway, it's illegal to be on the Trail."

"I think that's how people die," says Ameem. "Frankly I think a lot of the travelers don't come back because they die. Something bad happens to them."

"Ameem," says Padma, warning.

"I'm saying what I think."

"It's okay," I say. And that reminds me. "Has anyone heard of Bloody Mary?"

And for the first time, everyone's silent.

I say, "Did I say something wrong?"

"No," say all three adults together, and then lapse again.

I try to fill the vacuum. "When I was at the museum, and then again when I went to the Mart in Dharavi, I heard the name, so I thought I'd ask."

Ameem takes charge. "She's a legend of the Trail. But I think she's just the explanation for anything strange that might happen. Oh, I lost a rope, Bloody Mary must have taken it. Oh, here comes a storm, Bloody Mary is angry. But no one's actually seen her."

Padma sits up. "I saw someone once, you know that," she says. "But I don't know who it was."

"Couldn't it have just been another traveler?"

"But she was coming from the other direction. And it was broad daylight. And she was naked."

Naked. In daylight. Out in the open.

"Are you sure it wasn't a mirage?" I ask.

"It was just like I'm seeing you now," she says.

Maybe I'm a mirage, I think to myself.

"I think you couldn't sleep and you were seeing things," says Ameem to Padma. "It was during the first week we were here. You were tired."

Padma's angry. "I saw something and that something is exactly what I just described," she says. Now her pride is hurt, and I'm her target. "So Durga," she demands, "tell us why you're going to Africa."

Everyone is looking at me. I say the first thing that comes to mind, which is, "My parents died there."

Faces change, as if an underwater bomb has gone off beneath us. But after a beat, the interrogation continues.

"How long ago?"

"When I was born."

"How did they die?"

"They were murdered."

A deeper charge. Boom.

"I'm sorry," says Padma. "But you never knew them, right?" Ameem and Rana have bowed out. It's just her and me.

"True. It's fine. It's been that way my whole life."

"But what do you do when you have no parents?" She seems to direct this question upward, to the universe.

"You're raised by your grandparents, if you're lucky."

"But they cannot replace your parents."

Well, she's on the warpath now. I feel like I need to not take offense, given their hospitality. "I guess not."

Padma wags her head as if I've given the correct answer. "Do your grandparents know where you are?"

"No," I say. "Nobody does."

"What will happen if you die?"

"I'll try not to."

Ameem laughs.

"So," says Padma as if summarizing a legal argument, "you're going to make it to Africa, and then what? Are you going to visit the place where your parents were killed?"

"That's the plan," I say. I'm feigning looseness and comfort and ease. "When I get to Djibouti City I'll get a coffee and a cannoli in a seaside café and plan the next stage."

"You think it will magically occur to you?"

"Yes," I say. It sounds faint in my ears, like someone else is saying it, from another body. A fizzing black soda crowds my vision.

"Leave her alone," says Rana. "Maybe we've been asking too many questions. Durga?"

I slide sideways.

❖   ❖   ❖

I wake up to the sight of silver fabric. I'm in one of the pods. I look to my left. Rana is curled up on his side, away from me, breathing deeply.

I remember I'd fainted. I was probably dehydrated again. I look to my right and my backpack is still there, so I pull out my desalinator, sit up as quietly as I can, and take a few sips.

Rana doesn't stir. I suddenly love him, totally, just for being present and quiet, a nearby metabolism.

I lie back down and notice that I've been well taken-care-of, with a neck pillow and a light cotton sheet. Maybe I should stay at this seastead. Maybe I could take over one of Rana's jobs. The fantasy elaborates on its own. Every evening, Rana and I will go for a swim. I will tutor the girls in science and literature with nothing but my scroll and my imagination. I'll go on walkabouts to the west when I want to be alone. I'll take the spices I have left, select the whole seeds, and grow our own spices. I'll grow a whole garden. They must be starving for fresh things here. I can provide them. Mohini and I had a garden at our house in Thrissur where we grew lettuce, mint, cardamom, ginger, cumin, coriander, peppers, cilantro, and turmeric. She was learning to cook, and that was the beginner's palette I grew for her. She would water them every day, pouring from a height as if pouring chai, and with the thumb and forefinger of her other hand, pinching her sari up. Once I asked her, Can't you water the plants without looking like you're posing for the paparazzi?

She gave me a sly look. How do you know I'm not? she said.

It's not as if I were actually protesting. I liked watching her, always. She looked like a royal courtesan every day, and I loved her for the care she put into her appearance, but also for the moment in the morning when she woke up, bare-faced, sleepy-eyed, hair-mussed, un-made.

I turn over and look at Rana, lying on his back. He also has that nude look to his face, lips the same color as his skin. I wonder whether he really only likes men or whether he just told me that to trick me into showing him my breasts. I choose to believe the latter, right now, for my purposes. I think about spreading my hips astride him, and grinding down on him until he's hard, and then pulling down his pants until his cock springs free, and then holding him in place, and then sinking down on top of him like depressing the plunger of a syringe. His skin is bare. Why would he do that if he didn't want to flirt with me? Did he even ask me if I liked men? Why would he torture me like this? Yes, these are the same courses of thought that rapists have. Yes, I want to have sex with Rana even if he doesn't want to have sex with me. I want to swallow him.

I touch his arm. He opens his eyes and sits up.

I don't say anything. But he sees something in my eyes, and he sees that my nipples are hard.

He gets up without a word and leaves the pod. From the circle of sky I see, dawn is near.

❖　❖　❖

When I emerge, Rana is nowhere to be seen. But Ameem is crouched over the fish cage.

"Good morning," he says.

"Good morning. Sorry I fainted."

"You scared us. But you seem all right now."

"I think I was just dehydrated. I got up and had some water just now."

"Mmm," says Ameem, still looking down at the water. I realize he's a stranger. Everyone here is a stranger. They don't really care about me because they know they'll never see me again.

Now I'm frantic to go, to be by myself again.

"I have to go," I say. "I need to get on the road, so to speak."

"All right then," he says. "But go see Padma first. She feels terrible. She thinks she made you faint with all of her questions."

I think: She fucking did.

When I go to Padma, she doesn't apologize, but instead asks to see my food supply, and picks through my provisions, reading ingredient lists. She then starts packing more food for me, including two dozen dried fish filets. She wants to give me more but I insist it's all I can carry.

"You need more variety. When do you have your lunch?" she asks.

"Around midnight," I say, remembering my schedule. I long to return to my schedule. But I let her mother me. Because, having heard I have no mother, she thinks that this is the cure: to become mine, even if just for a time. It's not for my sake that I let her go on. It's for hers.

Rana is still nowhere to be seen. I swallow down my vicious emasculating thoughts and tell Padma to say good-bye to him for me. I give her one of my extra tongue scrapers as a thank-you. She seems glad for it. She also makes sure I have their coordinates and aadhaars and cloud names, if I should need anything. I'm beginning to feel impatient but I remind myself that I'm in no position to refuse help of any kind. Suri and Sita dawdle at the mouth of their pod, watching me. We never got to know each other. I wave at them. Suri waves back but Sita crawls back into the pod as if she didn't see me.

{ BOOK VI }

Mariama

Sweets

During the day, I watched you.

And I watched Francis watch you.

You had a collection of four bright caftans that you wore over your jeans: cerulean, indigo, tangerine, violet. You were a peacock in the company of pigeons.

One morning Francis asked you, So, Yemaya. What kind of name is that?

You looked at him sharply. An African name, you said.

Wolof? Fula?

Yoruba.

Yoruba!

Yes.

I could see Francis was trying not to laugh. Why do you have a Yoruba name?

I chose it for myself, you said.

Yemaya isn't your birth name?

No.

I could tell that Francis wanted to ask you what your birth name was. But your tone was forbidding. So instead he pretended disaffection and said, Too bad we're not stopping in Yorubaland. They'd seduce you right off the truck with all their woo-woo.

Woo-woo? (Oh, no, there was that tone again. In my mind I warned Francis to stop it right there.)

But he said, We have them in Ethiopia, too. Superstitious religions, not Christian, not Muslim, just worshipping nature.

You turned on him and said: They came before Christ. They came before Muhammed. Yemaya is the goddess of the sea. The sea used to cover everything. She's spread throughout the world. She's in Senegal now. She's in Brazil. She's in the Pacific. She's rising. She's arriving. She's coming onshore all over the world now.

I was waiting for a witty comeback from Francis, but he had none. Instead he said, I'm sorry, I didn't mean to offend, mademoiselle Yemaya. It is a very beautiful name.

His apology disarmed you. You sat back on your feet and straightened your caftan and said, Thank you, and then, with nowhere else to go on a moving truck, went up front to sit with Samson again, and slammed the window rather hard. Through the slats of a crate I could see you rest your chin on your elegant wrist and look out onto the desert.

❖ ❖ ❖

After I learned to write and sound out each letter, you and Francis took turns writing new words in my notebook, making me pronounce them, and teaching me their meanings. I still remember those early words: Sea, Sky, Moon. Soon we filled up the little notebook with the albino woman on the cover (you made me find her name on the inside cover, written in English, and sound it out—Sa-ra-swa-ti, who you said was from India, a country even

farther away than Ethiopia). You had to buy me another notebook
when we stopped in Bamako, a windy city sprawled on the banks
of a river the color of steel.

Now we slept together every night. My body could tell when
we had come to a stop. I would wake up, turn beneath your arm,
and look up at the stars. They were so near in the desert. They
blazed close to my face. Then, when we were safely rumbling along
again, I could fall back asleep.

Whenever we stopped for any length of time, you took me looking for a shop that sold Indian sweets. It became our little tradition. If I could sound out the words on the label, you would buy
it for me. The ladoos were still my favorite, even though you kept
telling me that they weren't fresh, they were the kind you find at
a Lebanese truck stop instead of the fresh ones in Little India, et
cetera. How you lamented! But they tasted wonderful to me.

I began thinking about them all the time. Some days, when
there were no sweets, after I was done with my reading, I just sat
on a crate and stared out into the desert, imagining an infinite
Lebanese store with aisles full of every kind of Indian sweet. Balls
and bars and brittles. And I could just stay there and eat however
much I wanted.

◈ ◈ ◈

Sometimes you told me stories about your former life in Dakar,
where you lived at home, but were an artist and dancer. You'd belonged to a troupe that performed dances about African rebirth.
You asked me what I knew about African rebirth, but I didn't
know anything.

You said, Well, in Ethiopia you'll go to school. A good school,
from what Muhammed tells me. The nuns know what they're doing.
You'll get better at Amharic and English, and they may teach you

Mandarin or Hindi, too. You'll come to understand what's happening in Africa. How the weather is changing, the seas are rising, the peoples are moving. How foreigners are coming in to steal our land and our resources. Did you know the Chinese and Indians have taken more land than exists in all of Sudan? None of Africa will belong to Africans anymore. But you'll become educated and you'll be one of the ones to fight back.

What will you do? I asked.

I'm going to fight back too.

How?

By being alive. By speaking out. By making art.

You mean like drawing?

No, I'm going to study dance, you said. The Ethiopians dance like this—

And then you sat up and twitched your neck back and forth, like your jaw was tied to a string that people to your left and right were jerking on. I giggled.

It looks crazy, you said, but it takes so much muscle control. I taught myself a little bit from videos. Addis has the best dance school in Africa, with teachers from Ghana and Benin. And there's a new jazz institute that's opened up right next to it. They host poetry slams at the cafés on Bole Road. There's a special kind of poem in Amharic called a kinae, where the words themselves mean one thing, but a deeper meaning is hidden underneath—a golden meaning.

Semena werk, said Francis, looking up from his sirius.

What? you said.

Semena werk is "golden meaning" in Amharic.

But it refers to a kinae.

Yes.

You turned back to me and said, Do you understand what we mean?

No.

Well, if a boy says to you: The stars are reflected in your eyes, what do you think he means? That the stars are reflected in your eyes, yes? That's true. But what he's really trying to say is that he loves you. That's the golden meaning.

Will he open my legs, then?

You slapped me on my arm so hard it stung.

Where did you hear that? you said.

I didn't answer. I was about to cry because I didn't understand why you'd slapped me.

You looked at Francis and seemed to gather yourself. You said, It's not proper for a little girl to talk about things like that.

I'm sorry, I said.

But you were upset. You sent me away to do my letters, even though I was well past doing letters now. I was reading whole sentences and understanding some of their meanings. So I sat in a corner and tried not to cry, and instead, to practice my English, sounded out whatever signs we passed. I focused hard so that I wouldn't feel the kreen.

HEINEKEN NAMASTE INDIA.

SOLAIRE AFRIQUE.

NUTELECOM.

JUMBO.

SM!LE.

◈ ◈ ◈

We started and stopped, stopped and started. I had been keeping careful count of every stop, but then one day I lost it and never got back on track.

We spent a whole day at the Burkina Faso–Niger border and there was nothing to see for miles and so we just sat there doing nothing, and both you and Francis seemed moody and dispirited, and stared into your siriuses, and didn't want to play or help me with my reading. Those were my least favorite times. It seemed that you, me, and Francis—and even Samson, who had taken to playing Teddy Afro CDs on the old sound deck in the cab—were the most energized and high-spirited when we were on the move. So my favorite times were when the convoy was proceeding smoothly through the desert, and I could just kneel by the side with you both behind me, and the wind in my hair, and watch the country pass.

Ouagadougou

The easterly wind was blowing hard when we came to Ouagadougou. It drove dust into my eyes and I had to blink the crusts away. So at one of the gas stations, you got me a pair of tiny pink sunglasses with frames shaped like hearts. I loved those sunglasses. No one could see where my eyes were looking. I used them to look out at Ouagadougou, which seemed warm and cozy, less like a city than a very big village.

You took me by the hand and we walked through the alleys to a main thoroughfare, and on the corner there was a huge Lebanese supermarket, bigger than any I'd yet seen. The doors swooshed open and closed behind us, and frigid cold enveloped us. I'd never been that cold. I sneezed four times in a row.

Cold in here, yeah? you said. Feels good though. Air conditioning comes to the Sahel. Masha'Allah.

We got glucose biscuits, instant noodles, and packets of black chai. You took me to the sweets display and let me pick out what I wanted. They had ladoos and silver-foil pistachio bars and I said, I want one of each. But you said to the clerk, We'll take *two* of each.

Then we sat on a bench across from a big intersection with a metal sphere in an island in the center. You told me that the metal sphere was our planet. Yemaya, when I was that young I didn't understand that you meant it was only a sculpture of the planet. I thought that somehow the soul of the planet was enshrined in that sphere. And that the sphere itself was enshrined at the exact center of the earth, which was symbolized by all the traffic swarming around it, minivans and trucks and bikes and motorbikes sling-shooting around the center and taking off in other directions. We were at the heart of the heart of the world. We watched the people in silence. I wondered where they were all coming from and where they were all going. I wondered where I was going too. I hoped it would be where you were going.

So you really don't remember your family? you said at last.

My pistachio bar was melting faster than I could put it in my mouth. I concentrated on peeling the silver foil.

Did you have any sisters? Or brothers?

I shook my head.

No other children your age?

I shrugged.

Who is your father?

I didn't answer.

And you don't have a chip?

No. Do you have a chip? I asked, happy that I knew what a chip was.

You pulled up the sleeve of your violet caftan and showed me a scar in your upper arm, the size and shape of an almond.

So my father could keep track of me, you said. He works for oil. My mother works for . . . well, nothing. She serves on the board of an NGO. Which amounts to nothing. But she lives most of the time in Johannesburg. She gave me my name and not much more.

What's your real name? I asked.

You were agitated. You said, My real name is Yemaya. It's my real name because it's the name I've chosen for myself. So it conquers my birth name—

I was distracted and turned away from you.

—and my parents' friends in their bourgeois air-conditioned condos—

I saw a line of cars coming from a long way off. You were getting louder and louder, a soundtrack to the vision.

—would never believe me, because my father is a good man, all but abandoned by his addict of a wife—

Yemaya, I heard everything you said but I was staring down the road at the line of shiny black cars.

—and meanwhile he has one daughter, and how lucky she is to have such a good father, such a privileged education and a nice car, just one girl in the house—

There were little flags waving from the front corners of the hood of each car. The cars turned one by one, and in every car that passed, a window rolled down and someone looked out at me in black sunglasses. I regarded them each in equal measure behind my pink sunglasses. Then they rolled up the windows again.

—and every time it happened I wanted to run out into the desert and die, and I swore I'd never let myself feel that way again, and to live, I realized I had to leave. I finally had to leave. I had to decide to be free. Mariama, look at me. Do you understand what I'm talking about?

Yes, I said, because I recognized my mother's words.

We were both running away, Yemaya.

❖   ❖   ❖

We returned to the trucks. All three of them were lined up, facing the desert, ready to go again. I was so happy to be there. So happy to have come. So happy to be leaving again. Here in this dusty city everything was perfect. We were between goodness and goodness, and I had my sweets, and we were to be on the road again by nightfall. I never wanted it to end!

I didn't tell you, but I began to fantasize about living with you when we reached Ethiopia. That we would live together in the white cotton dresses with crosses in stained-glass colors. I would have a special room just for them, where I'd close the door and just look at them.

The green, I'd wear to dance.

The blue, I'd wear to swim.

The red, I'd wear to bed.

Agadez

Nothing compared to those days. Nothing before and nothing since. It's the only time I ever remember the kreen disappearing altogether, and I felt like a normal child, instead of one with a tumor where the sea snake didn't go down.

A few days after we left Ouagadougou, you started agitating to go north. Just one truck out of the three, you said. Francis fetched Muhammed to discuss the matter.

The second truck is half-empty, you said. You can transfer the cargo on the third truck, and we'll take it north to Agadez, and then rejoin you in Kano.

Who's "we," mademoiselle?

You turned to Francis. Can you drive this truck?

He snorted. He couldn't believe how bold you were, just marching into a situation and giving orders! But he said yes.

I'll pay, you said to Muhammed. I'll pay Francis for his work, I'll pay for the gas, I'll pay you for rental of the truck, and I'll pay you a sizable honorarium for your generosity.

Mohammed looked pleased. But he asked, What in Agadez is so important?

Beauty, you said.

Beauty, mademoiselle?

You've heard of the Wodaabe. (It was not a question.)

They're herders.

Yes. They hold a festival at the end of the rainy season. It includes dancing and a contest of beauty.

Yes, I've heard of it.

I would like to attend.

Surely you would win.

It's not a contest for women, Mr. Getachew, it's a contest for men.

Whereupon Francis proclaimed, I will only drive you there if I can enter to compete and win your love!

Oh, Yemaya, you gave him such a withering look. But once you turned back to Muhammed, Francis gave me a wink. I saw that some game was going on whose rules I didn't understand.

How long do you plan to take? said Muhammed.

You plan to be in Kano when?

The thirty-first.

Then we will plan to meet you in Kano on the thirty-first.

Muhammed held out his hand, and you shook it.

I was delighted that there was no discussion at all of where I would go. Of course I was going with you and Francis, to Agadez, to see the beauty.

❖ ❖ ❖

What a desolate country we passed through! There was no beauty anywhere that I could see—not compared to what I'd seen before.

The land was flat, crumbly, and all one color, and the people we passed seemed tired. The sky wasn't even blue. It was whitish, like an albino's skin.

But our mood could not have been more spirited. *We* were the color in the landscape! Francis drove, and you and I took turns sitting up in the cab, or leaving him alone to sing along loudly and passionately to the one Teddy Afro CD he persuaded Samson to leave behind. When we stopped, he wrote down the lyrics in Amharic and made me sound them out. When I could pronounce each word, he told me what they meant: Tey fit atenshigne eferalehu: Don't turn your back, I am afraid. When I pronounced it correctly he rubbed my head and said, See, you're already speaking your new mother tongue.

How many languages do you speak? I asked.

Amharic, Arabic, French, some English, and some Oromo. So that's how many?

Five.

Answer me in Amharic.

Amist!

Very good.

I want to speak ten languages.

You can. With enough education.

Or maybe twenty?

Well, the languages are getting all mixed up now anyway, so who knows. How long will Amharic last before it becomes Amhindi? And the Indians don't even speak Hindi, they speak a half-English hybrid. So it'll be Amhinglish before very long.

I giggled. What other languages? I said.

Oh, and then the Chinese will come along and say, Hey, we own half of Africa, we deserve to be part of the new world language, so it'll be Amhinglimandarin.

And then?

And then the Somalis will say, We're right next door to you, what about us?—and it'll be Somamhinglimandarin!

And then?! (By this point I was shrieking.)

And then the Arabs will come along and say, None of you have the least bit of culture!—here's an oud—and so it'll be Somamhinglimandarabic!

Then you shoved open the window to the cab. What is going on up here? you asked.

I'm telling Mariama about the new world order, said Francis. In fifty years everybody will all be speaking a language called Somamhinglimandarabic.

What idiocy, you said to me. But I could tell you were just the littlest bit amused. You closed the window to the cab, a bit more softly this time.

❖　❖　❖

We came to Agadez at sunset and camped on the outskirts of the city. Francis went into town for food while you searched on your sirius for information. Apparently the festival, called Gerewol, was already in progress, and we could only hope to catch the last day of it. You told me that most Gerewol ceremonies had been taken over by the government for tourism purposes, and that it was hard to find a "pure" one, still, which was why we weren't attending the big famous ones in Agadez or Ingall. The locations were secret, but by the time we went to bed, your sirius had given you coordinates.

Francis slept in the cab, up front, with a woolen blanket he'd bought in Agadez with the money you'd paid him in advance. You and I slept as we always did, closer-than-close, like one body. I traced your face with my finger.

Mariama, you said, catching my finger.

Yes?

Did a man touch you? Is that why you ran away?

(What bold questions you asked, with no preamble!) No.

Do you know you could tell me if it were true?

Yes.

But it's not?

No.

You pointed to the little mound between my legs that was split like a camel's lips, and at once it felt hot, like it was coated in cayenne.

Promise me something, Mariama. Promise me you will never give this away easily.

Give what away?

You paused, then said, Your golden meaning.

How can I be sure when to give it away?

You'll know. You'll receive a sign.

From Allah?

No. Don't think of Allah. The divine is energy itself, pouring from one vessel to the next. Energy is holy. You'll know when you feel it.

I feel it with you, Yemaya, I said.

You sighed and rolled onto your back and said, You're like I was, when I was a child.

So why can't I give it away to you?

You inhaled sharply. That's not right, you said.

It's yours, I said. You can have it.

Mariama, don't say that.

But wouldn't it be safe, to give it to you?

You don't know what you're saying.

I was quiet. But after you fell asleep I cupped my hand over that place, and wondered whether the hot feeling was the holy energy you were talking about.

❖ ❖ ❖

We were already under way when I woke up the next morning. You and Francis were in the cab, and you'd rigged your sirius to play Angélique Kidjo. I asked you how much longer we had to go, but strangely, Yemaya, you didn't answer. You just kept staring out the window as if you hadn't heard me. You were in one of your moody moods.

Francis noticed. He turned around to wink at me and wish me a good morning. Then he patted the seat next to him and told me to come up. So there I was, sitting with my legs dangling between the two of you, barely able to see over the dashboard, and we were quiet because you were quiet, but then the Afrika song came on, and Francis began to hum to it, and then sing, and by the end all three of us were yelling *shae Mama, shae Mama Afrika!* along with Angélique.

When your sirius told us we'd arrived, Francis pulled the truck alongside the nearest encampment. There were camels tethered, blue tents pitched, and women sitting on woven mats. Francis parked and asked you, What now?

Now we introduce ourselves, you said.

Do you speak their language?

No. But I have Polyglotti on my sirius.

Francis and I hung back as you marched forward to greet three older women who'd stood at our arrival. First you gave them all calabashes, beautifully decorated, and boxes of tea. They seemed mollified but not quite won over. You spoke into your sirius and then held it to them to listen, which immediately the women seized and passed among themselves and said things into it and then smiled when it talked back. I didn't blame them because I'd done the exact same thing when you first showed me your sirius. They all had mobile phones, I saw later, but nothing like this.

When you came back to us, you related that we'd been given permission to watch the Gerewol finale, despite being tourists. They'd said, At least you're African.

One of the women led us to a mat where we had a good view of the men performing, all lined up in a row. Yemaya, I had never seen men like this. Slim as reeds, bare-legged, bare-chested, crossed with straps, faces painted red, lips painted black, wearing feather crowns, wreaths of beads, rings of gold in every ear, and bright skirts of mirrors and metal that clinked as they stepped. And across from them, fingers to lips, the women paced, smirked, evaluated, and commented to their sisters about one or the other man. I couldn't believe my eyes. How could I have known that humans were made like this? That all of my ideas about how people were, or looked, or acted, were such a small drop in the ocean of how they could be? How could I have known any of this, Yemaya, unless you showed me?

I looked up to tell you how I felt, but your face was turned away from me. Your attention was elsewhere. You were conversing with Francis.

I felt the kreen stir inside me again. I'd forgotten it. Now it was back. I thumped my chest once, to tell it, This is a joyful hour! Now is not a time to start your kreening!

So I tugged on your arm until you looked at me. Easy, Mariama, you said. You got an ant up your bottom?

But I just pointed. They're so beautiful, I said.

I'm glad you think so, you said. Beauty is precious. I need beauty in my life. The Wodaabe say they're the most beautiful humans on earth. Which one do you like best?

I appraised the line of men, all of them rolling their eyes and humming from their throats and peeling back their lips to show their teeth.

That one, I said, pointing to the man I secretly thought looked most like you.

Yes, he's very handsome, you said.

Which one would you pick?

Francis leaned in and said, I need to hear this. I need to take notes.

You swatted him on the head and he withdrew, smiling at you.

The winners were chosen and the festivities ended. One of the women who'd originally greeted us presented us with bowls of milk porridge as an evening meal, and I took my cues from you on how to thank her. She sat down across from us, then, and indicated that she needed your sirius to translate. She introduced herself as Neneh, and then listed the names of her husband, her husband's other wives, her mother and father, her six children, and her four grandchildren. Then she said, Where is your family from?

It was clear that she thought the three of us were a family. You explained to Neneh that you and Francis weren't married, and that I was not your child. This was not an arrangement Neneh was used to, so she kept asking for clarification:

So you're from Ethiopia, you're from Senegal, and she's from Mauritania? Amharic, Wolof, and Haratine. All right. Are you all Muslim, at least? No, Francis is Christian. Well, do you get along? That's good. Why are neither of you married? She's very beautiful. What are you waiting for? He's not so bad-looking. How old are you? Do you own any cattle? How old is the little girl? Where are her kin? Where is her mother? Where will she go when you reach Ethiopia? How will she know where to go, what to do, how to behave? Who will take care of her?

The questioning lasted for well over an hour, and by then, other Wodaabe had joined us to listen. We were the center of attention.

Francis was charming and witty, turning the questions back on Neneh and making the girls laugh, making them entreat him to stay and marry one of them. You answered kindly at first, but then I saw your face becoming tight. You wanted to be alone. With us.

By the time we finally walked back to the truck late that night, with Francis holding one of my hands and you holding the other, I'd begun to think of us as a family, after all.

❴ B◻◻K VII ❵

Meena

Fantasy

My sleep schedule is all fucked up now. It's almost 6:00 a.m., which is when I'm supposed to stop walking, but now I'm going to walk until it gets too hot and then go straight back to sleep.

I don't know whether it's because my body's been processing the muscle memory, or because Suri proved that it can be learned, but walking is easier. As the sun dawns I'm in a liminal state. When I close my eyes I can see hills and valleys swelling toward me then passing underfoot. The motion itself is altering my perception. Reality is a wave now, not a solid.

❖ ❖ ❖

After I've eaten I crawl inside my pod. There are no emergencies. I'm bored. This is the lived reality of adventure.

I think of Rana. I didn't even do anything, or say anything, or touch him except with my fingers on his arm, but that scared him and he went away, so I feel like shit. Especially after he was good to me. It was just that I'd forgotten I was a sexual body. Which is the last thing anyone who knows me would think I'd forget. I told Mohini that sex was my mother substitute, but she said that was needlessly cynical, that sex was my dharma, even my art, like performance was to her.

I said, But my audience is limited.

She said, No, your whole sexuality is an ongoing performance. It's just that only a few are invited backstage.

I can try to reconnect with that dharma, now, even though I'm alone and wounded and sore. I'll see what happens.

I lie back. I scroll through my catalogue of usual fantasies. There's the one where the policewoman gives me her baton to use on her and while I do, we touch tongues. The one where blue- and lavender-skinned gods birth the world through their multilimbed lovemaking (though I haven't used that one in a long time—it's an adolescent fantasy that doesn't work anymore). The one where Dr. Sharma, the pediatric specialist Muthashi consulted for my panic attacks, uses my body as his thali, scooping and mixing sauces in my hollows, bringing the boluses of food to his mouth inches above my yoni. We never have sex. He just scoops food off of my skin and watches a cricket game.

I collected fantasies from my lovers, too. I got them in detail. I got several from Hindus ideating Meenakshi Devi, my namesake, the fish-eyed goddess, who must be the first love of adolescent Hindus everywhere because she has three breasts and lavender skin. If they're Catholic or Syrian Christian, they have a whole other set of fetishes, like popping Mary's cherry or confessing dirty thoughts to priests who take an active role in their penance. If they're Muslim, they're dealing with afterlife virgins who are made of calligraphy and unravel upon orgasm.

I increase the porosity of my pod so that more heat gets in, enough to raise a sheen on my skin. I put my hand down my pants and then pull up my shirt so I can see my own breasts. See, I'm just masturbating is all, not hurting anyone, not forcing anyone. Mohini once said to me that we're all children of rape, somewhere in our lineage, and how did I feel about that? We're all the result of energy forced, not welcomed. The waves coming whether we want them to or not.

I wrench my thoughts free.

I open up my specimen box once again:

Dr. Sharma.

The policewoman.

Anwar panting below me, talking dirty to me in Farsi.

FARSI: Your breasts and your bottom
FARSI: So sweet as unto my hands
FARSI: Dear bitch I am fifty percent

I switched off my glotti at that point because it was better if I didn't know what he was saying. I need a better Farsi-to-Hindi module.

I scroll through memories of other lovers. Dilip is prominent. He was a Bengali sitar player, Aquarius, vata dosha, who traveled all over India from gig to gig, not because he was a poor musician ennobled by the struggle but because he wanted to appear to be. His parents were both members of the legislative assembly in Kolkata. They sent him a weekly allowance via mitter. He was skinny, with a silky beard, silky chest hair, and an unexpectedly huge penis. His favorite color was pink. We didn't get along well.

There's Juno from Shanghai. She was an architect studying the flooding around Kochi, as Kochi had adopted an enlightened attitude toward sea-level rise that other coastal cities were copying. She was girlish, with an athletic frame, and tied her long hair up in a high ponytail. I met her working at the Kashi Art Café in

Fort Cochin. She came there to sift the day's data. I took her home one night, and then every night for a week. She wore me out. She wanted me to choke her because she had father issues. Then one evening she wasn't at the café as usual, and I never saw her again.

Neither Dilip nor Juno is working and my hand is getting tired. I have to go darker.

I pull out Joseph, the married man I slept with at fourteen. The first man I slept with. He was twice my age. I remember how ugly it felt, good and ugly at the same time, descending the first time and feeling like I was sitting on a fist stretching out a new lambskin glove, and then it getting easier, falling on a knob over and over as if it was a stone and not flesh at all. He didn't even unwrap his dhoti, he just let me push it up. There was no preamble or grace. Just meat and muscle and bone. I remember thinking, This is what animals do.

My vision dissolves. I come so hard I beat my fist on the floor of my pod. One, two, three, four, five.

And then like a penance I remember what I kept at bay: the sight of Joseph's young daughter in the doorway, cradling her own arms, having watched us the whole time, having not been able not to.

❖ ❖ ❖

I stop for my Second Meal at midnight. This time I cut up one of Padma's dried fish filets to stew in the protein broth. Clouds have risen in the west, or I assume so, because I can't see any stars over there.

I take capsules again, but at a smaller dosage.

I palpate all my bandages to test for pain. I can deal with wounds. I'm the granddaughter of Dr. Geeta Scholastica, who if nothing else was unflinching about bodies, ooze and fluid, in life or death. I used to bring her patients herbal tea while they waited. She charged half her clients full price, the technocrats and suburban nouveau riche, and the other half she saw for free. So our waiting room saw all kinds. I remember one day a woman wandered in wearing a dirty gray sari. At first I thought she was an ascetic, but then she sat in a chair, pulled up her skirt, and splayed her legs, and she wasn't wearing any underwear. Her yoni looked like a pink banana leaf laid against her skin. I was a child, so I giggled, thinking this was a daring adult practical joke I was being let in on. But she didn't close her legs, and her yoni was like the sun. I couldn't look at it straight-on, even though it was the source of all illumination in the room. All the other patients looked away from it. They looked out the windows. I knew something was wrong with all the silence in the room. The woman was staring at me, tired, waiting. It was left to me to do something. So I brought her a blanket. She looked at me like she didn't know what to do with it. I placed it on her lap and then patted her knee. Her face collapsed in something like shame and she began to wail. That's when I ran to get Muthashi. She came out, felt the woman's forehead, looked at her palm, and told me to help her get her up. The blanket fell, still folded, onto the floor. Muthashi took her by one elbow and walked her to the examination room that was farthest down the hall. I followed. Muthashi's helpers came to see about the noise, and as she walked, she gave them each instructions in a low voice.

In the examination room, we laid the woman on a soft cotton pallet. I need to see your eyes, Muthashi said. The woman could barely keep them open for all her crying, but she did long enough for Muthashi to get a good look. When she did, she straightened up and rolled up her sleeves. She took me by the elbow and steered me into the corner.

This woman is about to die, she said. I have no intention of hiding that from you. It is your choice whether to stay with me and help her pass, or you can leave, if you wish.

I said I would stay.

You don't have to be brave, she said.

I shook my head. I wasn't brave, just proud.

So she sent me to get a blanket, warm water, and lavender oil. One of the helpers massaged the woman's feet with the oil I brought. Another lifted her neck and pulled her tangled hair out from beneath it and brushed it out gently, and arrayed it around her like a halo. Muthashi herself held the woman's hand as her breaths became more and more rare.

The woman had no chip or other identifying information. We didn't know her religion. But Muthashi and Muthashan were friendly with the priests at Sri Gowreeswara Temple and arranged with them to have her body cremated and scattered in the Arabian Sea. Little flecks of her might be floating under my feet. In fact, they definitely are, statistically speaking.

Cecilia's words come back to me, something like, We never even have to miss each other.

Song for Aravan

I feel dawn from behind. My head gets warm, and then my back, and then my feet. I don't think of my feet as feet anymore. They've abstracted into the balled hinges on an artist's dummy.

I stop for my third meal of chocolate, rose lassi, and dal. And of course I fantasize about whatever food is not available to me: in this case, heterogeneous foodstuffs: palak paneer, pizza, sushi, bhelpuri, General Tso's chicken. Sometimes the wires of my sexual and culinary fantasies get crossed and I have brief visions of pushing doro wat up into my vagina as if into my mouth. First an egg, then a savory drumstick. This thought gives me a spicy feeling between my legs and I put in a finger to check and it comes away watery maroon. The lips have spoken. So I pull my sponge from a deep pocket in my bag, wet it with fresh water, squeeze it dry, and push it up with my fingers. There. I've taken care of myself.

I take stock of my accomplishments in general. I can see the tops of the buildings in Mumbai but not the shore anymore. I've survived for four nights and days now. I'm not dead. I'm injured but healing. I have a routine. I've made positive human contact.

The imagined reality of walking the Trail and the lived reality of walking the Trail are themselves companions on the Trail, keeping one eye on each other at all times.

I'm passing out of the crisis phase. Life feels basic and elemental: blood, water, piss, chocolate. This is my leisure time, so I'm supposed to read or relax or play croquet now but instead I open a new file on my scroll. I name it *Element Diary*. I make categories: Sea, Sky, Moon. I try to describe each one such that I could only be describing this day, and no other.

Sea: Gold.

Sky: Tufted.

Moon: Cocktail Onion.

❖ ❖ ❖

When I wake, dark clouds are bearing down, blocking out the sunset.

I start walking. I keep one eye on the clouds and, in another part of my brain, wonder if I can retrain myself to call everything another name—grammar intact, just different words. Here's my rule: though corresponding words are allowed to be nouns, each reassignment must be as arbitrary as possible. For example, Moon can be neither Circle nor Sun, as those are a descriptor and antonym, respectively. So,

Sea: Sari.

Sky: Braid.

Moon: Pickle.

I'll see how I do with these initial word reassignments. It doesn't occur to me that there's anything dangerous about this. I fuzz my vision and watch the waves, each one a hand rising to offer a card, then withdrawing it back into the deep.

Wind springs up. The surface of the sea shivers as if chilled. I can see a curtain of rain to the south. I could walk through it, but with all my bandages, I should probably stay dry.

I can already feel drops of rain on my face as my pod inflates. I climb inside. I adjust the pod's skin to one hundred percent transparency. When the rain comes down, it's incredible, like there's no pod at all, just the shape of the space I'm in. I face west, where the wind's coming from, and the rain makes an electric starburst shape.

I lie on my back. I don't feel hungry or thirsty. Instead I sing the first thing that comes to mind, which is "Lament for Aravan," something Mohini wrote. In fact it's the song she sang the first night I saw her, when she was performing at the Kuttampalam Theatre, once only for kutiyattam, now reappropriated by all kinds of performance groups, especially queer ones, including the new hijras. Hijras had been assured of ostracism for most of recent history, except when they were allowed to sing at weddings or the birth of boys, or to serve as bottoms for men who had sex with men but weren't gay. But now hijras had come to encompass all queer people who identified with transgenders, as well as cross-dressers and transsexuals in whatever stage of treatment they had chosen

(or not chosen). Of course petty hierarchies had developed about
who was a true hijra. Mohini was not; she was trans. But she em-
braced the hijra identity all the same and, by the time I saw her,
had become a celebrity in the queer community. Everyone wanted
to see her perform mohiniyattam. (I later asked her whether the
dance had come first, or the name. She said they coevolved from
a young age. The boy she used to be, Kunal, loved to dress up
in ceremonial saris and dance the mohiniyattam, so she made her
mother start calling her Mohini. When she turned fourteen, her
mother started saving money from her salon, Millennium Beauty,
and Mohini entered treatment at the age of twenty-three. But she'd
already been passing for years. Her female classmates were fond
of her. They presented her with an expensive makeup kit at the
graduation performance.)

That night, I came too late to see her dance, though the stage
was littered with marigolds, so I assumed whatever had just happened was a success. A stagehand brought her a white linen napkin and she dabbed her forehead. I took a seat near the back. The
audience was calling out various endearments and she acknowl-
edged each with a secret little smile. I could immediately see why
I'd heard so much about her at the women's clinic. She was a solar
beauty. She had delicate features and high eyebrows and skin with
warm undertones. Her nose was long and slender, and she wore a
golden headdress, golden earrings dripping to her shoulders, and
gold glitter on her cheekbones. In her septum was a big gold ring.
Her hair was parted on the side and swept back in the style of
classical dancers, in a crown of braids and marigolds, though later
I learned she was wearing extensions, and her real hair was a bias-
cut mop that fell across her face sideways.

Still in her mohiniyattam costume, she sat on a stool that had
been set out for her, and arranged her hands, one on her chest and

the other just below it, on her solar plexus. Her head bent to one side and her face assumed an expression of sadness. A tanpura drone began in the dark behind her. She began singing. The song was for Aravan, the mythical hero who sacrificed his life in battle but wished to be wedded before he died, so Vishnu became a woman named Mohini, wed him, then mourned him. I had a Hindu grandfather, so I knew the story. She sang, turning on slight intervals, then leaping high, then sliding back down deeper and diagonal from where she'd begun. I felt her voice knitting together nerves in my body. She clenched and unclenched her fists to punctuate her words.

That night I first saw her I knew I had to talk to her though I didn't know what I'd say. I just knew I wanted to wake up next to those eyes every morning and trace her face with my fingers every night. I'd never felt that way about anyone. I was a known bed-jumper and it suited me fine. But I knew I would have to take extraordinary measures for extraordinary beauty. So when she turned around on her stool in her dressing room to see who'd come in, I dropped to my knees to touch her feet and said *I want to be with you.*

Months later, when we were deep inside the garden of new love and still finding out how big it was, I asked her why she clenched her fist at her solar plexus while she sang. I told her I'd had painful surges in that spot all my life, like someone had stabbed me there and poured vinegar in the wound. She said it was the manipura chakra, a yellow flower with ten petals, and being an adrenal cortex, corresponded to issues of fear and anxiety and sadness. So of course she would emphasize it when mourning a lover.

Even thinking about it here, lying on my back and looking up at the rain slide down around me on all sides, I feel it hurting. I try to calm myself by pushing up my shirt and resting my hand over

the bandage. Mohini used to rest her hand there all night, sometimes, on the nights I told her I didn't feel I really belonged to this
world and never had.

It's been a week since I left home.

Crossing

Now I miss crises. Crises gave me something to focus on. I hope
a new crisis comes soon. I call the seventy-year-old NOAA buoy
north of me on their old telephone line just so I can hear a voice
recite wave data.

I walk through nights in a fugue state, first counting, then despairing of counting, then despairing of despairing. One moment I
rejoice in my progress. The next moment I think about how many
more kilometers I have to cover and it's like I'm falling upward into
the sky. I make a rule for myself: I can't think past two nights into
the future. That includes Djibouti. My world is contained between
two horizons, the forward and the back. That's all I'll worry about.

❖ ❖ ❖

Just after dawn one morning, I hear a horn.

My first thought is: the horn of Mycenae.

My second thought is: They've finally found me.

I scan the horizon in the direction the blast came from, southeast. There's a ship. Didn't Ameem say the main shipping routes
intersected the Trail much farther west? So it's probably the Indian
Coast Guard. Shit.

I inflate my pod, get in, trust the camo, and watch it come. It's
far enough away that the descending scales won't affect me. I can
already see them starting to disappear, ahead, one by one, like a

necklace pulled underwater, dropping below the surface to let the ship pass. The closer it gets, the more I see it sideways, and the bigger it gets. It's fucking huge. If this is a military ship, it's an aircraft carrier or something.

Then I see its flag: a white star on a blue field. It looks familiar but I can't place it. It's definitely not Indian.

So this is some merchant ship and there's no reason for them to take an interest in me. I get out of my pod and sit to watch the ship pass. I see only one person on deck, a man with both elbows on the railing, hands clasped as if in prayer. He's looking down at the Trail. He beckons behind him, and four more men join him, all staring down at the sea like he is. Of course: the Trail must be a sight to see. It might even be a rite of passage like crossing the equator. More and more sailors come to the side until it's crowded like birds on a wire.

Then I hear a hollering. I've been seen. The sailors all cheer. They're waving and clapping and calling out to me. My glotti picks up only some of it, then gets overloaded and confused:

FRENCH: Look it's a walker it's a walker it's one of the
    walkers
SOMALI: A man or a woman? walker
FRENCH: Is she alone
ARABIC: She is the hero
SOMALI: Woman walker
ARABIC: She is in the story
SOMALI: Who are you with?
ARABIC: She is telling a story
FRENCH: Have a good trip madame good trip hello
    mademoiselle
ARABIC: Where are your people?
SOMALI: Walk to Africa

ARABIC: Where is your mother?

SOMALI: It's not too far

ARABIC: Is she birthing or dying?

SOMALI: You will be all right

FRENCH: Mademoiselle you are a one-of-a-kind
    adventurer

SOMALI: You are mother to a new race

FRENCH: Hail Yemaya!

The ship slips through and the scales start to resurface. Then I place the flag: it's a Somali oil tanker, obviously. Maybe headed for Karachi. And I'll have to look up the word "Yemaya" because I want to know what I'm being hailed as.

I tell my scroll to look up the last word translated in my glotti. As I do, I see another anomaly in my peripheral vision, not a ship. Beyond where the Trail is resurfacing, there stands a little woman. She's naked. I can't see her face. But when she sees me look up, she turns and dives into the ocean, and doesn't resurface, even though I stand still, staring at the spot, until the sun is one finger higher in the sky.

No-Mother

I must be having stress responses. Hallucinations are common when one is under stress. Evidence the barefoot girl, who's hard to remember now.

Anyway, eyes deceive. When I eat at sundown I stare at banks of clouds and can make myself believe that I'm actually staring at mountain ranges. I don't have much empirical data to say otherwise. Just my pozit and scroll, which both say I'm ninety kilometers into the Arabian Sea and there are no mountain ranges around. But if I didn't have those, I could believe I was in any of a hundred places on Earth. Off the coast of Namibia, or Samoa, or Chile. I'm in something like the largest open-air park in the world but actually my experience of it is two-dimensional because I'm on a one-way conveyor and can't step off to either side. Meanwhile, phenomena present themselves, and I can only watch. Shadows on the cave walls.

◇ ◇ ◇

My scroll has much to say on Yemaya. She's also named Yemalla, Yemana, LaSiren, Imanja, Yemaja, Yemowo, Iemanya, Janaína, and Yemoja. Apparently she's a West African orisha who got carried over to the Americas and back. She's celebrated in Afro-Caribbean communities. She's enjoying a resurgence among young progressives in West African cities. Her primary affiliation is with the ocean. She also embodies motherhood.

So this is what the sailors called me?

I've never wanted to be mother to anything, because I don't have a mother.

Muthashi doesn't count. She knows that. My real parents are dead. My grandparents don't know anything about my real mother, Meenakshi Mehta. They didn't even know their son was dating someone in Addis. Details only surfaced later: she was nineteen years old, brilliant, classically beautiful, tall and curvy, from a conservative family in Gandhinagar. Whenever I was going through a shitty period as a teenager I looked up photos of her a lot. She was light-skinned, so whatever darkie genes I got came from my father. But when her family heard of the murders, they told Muthashi and Muthashan that their son had brought shame to their family, and wanted nothing to do with us, or with me. It remains that way to this day. I've tested them. They blocked me every way possible.

When I got older and learned a few more tricks, I looked them up again, but there was no record of Mehtas fitting their description in Gandhinagar. I called their old neighbors. The Mehtas had moved to the South Pacific and not been in touch since.

I sketch my mother in my mind. I'm already eight years older than she was when she died. I like to imagine she's a composite of six or seven tall, strong women I've known who weren't afraid to take up space. Some were friends, some I slept with. I think she would like coffee black, chai unsweet, and dal thick like porridge. But then I remember this is entirely a creation on my part. So I erase the slate and start making another sketch. The truth is, I don't know anything. I don't know what she would think of me. I don't know whether she would have approved of my being with Mohini.

Though I don't seek anyone's approval, generally. My grandparents loved me but with pain. They saw I was my own creature. I battled Muthashi until she finally washed her hands of me. Once I ended a fight by throwing an urn of medicine that broke on the wall behind her. I ran to the kitchen and pressed my forehead to the table, trying to breathe. She came in and began making chai as if nothing had happened. But her hands were shaking and she didn't look at me as she spoke. She said, It's enough that we have you. It is enough. It is enough. She sounded like she was trying to convince herself but couldn't.

She finished making the chai and then offered me some. I didn't answer. I let the silence stretch on and on, making her feel worse. She left to find Muthashan. I sat there in the kitchen until the sun set and my anger got cold.

They both stepped back after that, out of parental roles and into sponsorial roles. They paid school bills and medical bills, but didn't interfere otherwise. My explosions had damaged them. When I dropped out of college they didn't even say anything. But a few years later, I started feeling guilty. When I was living in Kochi I started calling them every day. I asked them how their days had gone. We became something like friends.

And then, three monsoons ago, they met Mohini for the first time.

The rain was blowing in sideways. Mohini was fussy about making an entrance. She wanted to impress my grandparents with her beauty, which was formidable, but still, she took care, like the old Bollywood stars she idolized. She insisted on coming in a closed car, using a parasol to protect her hair, wearing a full-body raincoat to protect her sari, and, having interrogated me about the entranceway blueprint of my grandparents' house, disrobing in the foyer before they could lay eyes on her. The plan worked. She bowed to my grandparents looking like a vision from the Kama Sutra, her hands pressed together, fingernails painted, perfectly ovaline eggs of gold, blue sari edged in gold, modest red tilak on her forehead, and hair (by her own mother, Seeta, of course) worked with golden ornaments.

Rupa had made special dosas. She was learning the basics of Ayurveda from Muthashi before applying to school, and in return, she cooked for us. She also joined us at the table. That had been the subject of one of my teen tantrums: that I wouldn't live in a house where servants couldn't sit down and eat with our guests. That they must have every opportunity I have. It made no difference to Muthashan, but Muthashi tried to tell me that the world simply didn't work that way. I said, It does if you do it. After that our servants joined us at the table and we got a reputation in the neighborhood for being radical.

Mohini was nervous about meeting my grandparents. Her family was backward caste, which I said didn't matter anymore, but she pointed out to me that that was my privilege to say, being Brahmin and wealthy. I stayed quiet at the table and let Mohini talk and impress both my grandparents, and Rupa, who watched her in fascination. Having arrived in splendor as planned, Mohini was the star of the table, facilitating discussion on everything from the plays of Josefina Paz to the success of the Haratine Liberation Front.

My grandparents were polite. And they never brought up her treatment. Even if they were curious, even if they disapproved, it was beneath them to say anything. They were perfect models of kind attention. I did love them for that.

That night, in bed, I apologized to Mohini that she couldn't meet my mother. I felt culpable. She held my head to her chest and stroked my hair and asked me to imagine what it would be like if I could.

I was prepared, of course. The parentless have a deep well of reunion fantasies. I was quiet, trying to think of the most beautiful or impressive one, and when Mohini asked what I was thinking about, I told her. There was no boundary between us. What I thought was what I said. I told her that I ideated my mother as a goddess. Which is to say, she lived in the heart of the temple, in the innermost of innermost chambers like in the temple complex at Madurai, and that my life would be an act of circling and penetrating each chamber, passing through each illusion until I finally arrived at the truth. The essential mother. The pearl of my existence.

The devi-urge, Mohini said.

I tickled her and she lurched from the bed screaming and then from opposite sides of the room we made a truce not to tickle anymore or make any more English puns. She came back to the bed, and she said, I don't mean to joke. That image is beautiful, Meenaji.

It seems too obvious.

You prefer your metaphors inaccessible?

I just don't know if it's the right one.

But that itself is allowed for, in your metaphor. Each chamber is imbued with its own degree of doubt or certainty. Including the chamber wherein you don't know whether the temple metaphor is the right one.

Yeah. What if I discover, Fuck, wrong religion.

Yes. You should have been Buddhist all this time.

My mother is no-mother.

There is no mother.

Buddha mother-is.

But that's allowed for too: the chamber of the temple that's not a chamber at all, but a zendo, or a lab, or a kitchen. Or a dead end.

Yes. All of them are parts of the temple. All are moving me closer towards the center. But I never know which chamber I'm in.

Right. You only believe in the present chamber and its sensory actuality. But every chamber contains a chamber, and is, in turn, contained by a chamber.

Is will involved?

What do you mean?

Like, if you say, I want to be out of this chamber and into the next one. If you actually call out the goddess directly.

It might work like that, she said. But if you call too soon, and you're not prepared, and not purged of desire and sentiment and fear, you may not be ready for what you summon, and she will destroy you.

◈ ◈ ◈

One morning I throw up from too much sun exposure and too little water. Only some thick, pasty idlee vomit dissipated by the waves and snapped up by fish.

◈ ◈ ◈

I play a game, trying to discern exactly when the sky becomes lighter. I try to define the threshold of non-ambiguity—is it when I can see the hair on my forearms? Is it when I can begin to see color? I stop walking and just stand still, moving up and down. Which colors are the first to appear?

I turn around to face the east. I relish sunrises. Every single sunrise is the greatest show on earth. I want to intuit the very instant the sun first appears. I'll say *Now* whenever I think it's coming. I say it low under my breath, "Now," but it's much too early. I get quieter. I stand absolutely still, and watch, and listen, and then whisper, "Now," and the live coal appears.

I once said to Mohini, Motherless children are addicted to beauty.

When I sleep, I dream a corporeal companion to the usual dream of finding new rooms in one's house: I discover new limbs on my body. First I sprout wings from my shoulders. Then three penises grow between my legs, long enough to become legs themselves, so I spin like a starfish. Extra arms bud from my flanks. I become a dancing Shiva, rolling up and down a rippling cloth but never moving forward.

❖ ❖ ❖

My language experiment doesn't last long. Around the third day of calling the sea *ᴕari* and so forth, I feel nauseated, like I've rolled ladoos in salt and eaten a hundred.

Copacetic

I've been walking for twenty-seven nights.

For a few nights I was rapturous about the stars. The experience was approaching holy. And then the next night the stars failed to produce the same ecstasy and I felt angry. I'd started out too high.

The nights are iterative. I keep count on the plastic surface of my medical kit by scratching marks with my filet knife. Keeping count is a way to prove to myself that time is both passing and moving in one linear direction. According to my pozit, I'm six percent of the way to Djibouti. And I'm still alive. Apparently, a certain throughput of water, protein, and rice is all that's required to keep my body functional. Why did no one tell me that before? All of human interaction can be reduced to matter and energy transfers. Speaking of human interaction, I don't know where all these settlements are that Ameem was talking about. I've run into zero. But I've had eight more close encounters with intercepting ships and lots more sighted on the horizon—aircraft carriers, oil tankers, and cruise ships parked on the horizon like wedding cakes. This is not an idle sea.

At night the galaxy is a rent overhead, with the greatest concentration of light in the center slit. Yes, it looks like a yoni. Must I relate everything to yonis? I can't help it. I'm a fan. I loved Mohini's. She was in the last stages of her changing when we were first together. We had sex as woman and man only once, because though Mohini was still transitioning, we couldn't wait. So in the afternoon sunlight filtering through a pink curtain in her old flat, I bared my breasts, and she kissed them both. I slid down onto her. She leaked tears from the corners of her eyes, let me come quickly and then gently palmed my belly up and off of her, and held me close while my passage still pulsed, trying to embrace an empty space. We didn't make love again until she was ready. When she was fully transitioned, her yoni was like a new bud. I was careful with it. Every night I came up with a new name for it and it made her laugh. Sometimes because it was funny (Prime Minister) and sometimes because she was embarrassed (Harvest Moon). I loved her too much, she said. Too much for who? I said. For me? I'm just having fun. I get to be with you all the time. And there's always something new to explore. Childhood! Religion! Schooling! Politics! Mother! Father! Queer identity in rural Tamilnadu! We had so much to tell each other, we never stopped talking, and everything was new. When I brought her to climax, she would go limp and fall back like a button-eyed string doll. And then I would just rest my head on her stomach and listen to her breathe and we'd fall asleep like that.

I think of Mohini because I still adore her. Because there's nothing else to do while I'm walking but think about people I know. They sit arrayed in a circle in the chamber of my head and talk to me. This is my life now. I struggle to pass time.

BOOK VIII

Mariama

The Sun Traps

On the way back from the beauty contest near Agadez, Francis got a call from Muhammed telling him that one of their engines was damaged. When we arrived, we learned we'd have to wait for an automotive part inbound to Lagos Port, but that the ship itself was delayed by a horrendous storm, even though it was supposed to be the dry season. It could take days.

This news had an effect on me I didn't anticipate. Because we weren't moving toward our final destination, I felt restless. I became moody and irritable. Francis tried to sway me by saying, You know what they speak here? Hausa. So if they march into Addis Ababa demanding to be part of the new world language, we'll all be speaking Somamhinglimandarabicausa.

But the joke was wasted. I just got angrier that he was trying to cheer me up. He saw the look on my face and made a show of slinking away.

◈ ◈ ◈

Francis, Muhammed, and the other drivers were content to sleep on the trucks. You were less so, because you could afford to rent a hotel room, but didn't want to break solidarity with the men, or with me. So we slept together on our pallet as usual. I traced your face with my finger until you slapped my hand away in your sleep, and turned over.

The novelty of Kano wore off. We went into the city, but it felt boxy and claustrophobic to me. Any city that wasn't Addis Ababa felt inadequate now. There were supermarkets with sweets, for sure, and we followed our little ritual of buying a supply, but one night I found the stash you'd been saving and ate too many of them and became sick, and made you angry. So I lost my appetite for a while. The kreen became very active, like a writhing ball of yarn. I stopped thumping it. I just let it writhe.

When we finally got under way again, we'd been in Kano for a week. I was happy to be moving and watched the sand rush out from under our tires and waited for the kreen to dissipate. But the malaise was hard to shake. My soul had gone dry and it took days of moving to moisten it again.

Because we'd been delayed in Kano, we had to move much more quickly across Nigeria, and into Cameroon, where the road wound through a dense forest along the Chari, a rich brown river I traced on our map. At sunset we three knelt at the side of the truck. You pointed out things for me to pronounce in English, and Francis pointed out things for me to pronounce in Amharic.

River . . . wenz.

Fish . . . asa.

Beautiful . . . konjo.

We were in Cameroon only a few hours before we reached Kousséri, the site of the crossing into Chad. But because of extended drought, the river was too low for the ferry. In its place

was a pontoon bridge. It was very new and the Sahara sun made it
shine bright like the wristband of a watch. I thought of Dr. Moctar
Brahim just then. It was the first time I'd thought of him in a long
time. The kreen sprouted knives and dug into the wall of my chest
from the inside.

At the entrance to the bridge was a sign painted in green,
white, and orange. Since we had to wait to cross, you took me off
the truck to stand in front of it and read. You told me the same
thing was printed in four languages—Arabic, French, English,
and Hindi. The fact that there was no Mandarin version, you told
me, was meant to be an insult to the Chinese.

I sounded out the English:

WE THE PEOPLE OF INDIA

DO PRESENT THIS BRIDGE

TO THE DESERT PEOPLES OF

CAMEROUN AND CHAD

AS A GIFT OF GOODWILL

BETWEEN OUR NATIONS

FOR THIS CENTURY

AND FOR ALL TIME

TIL THE OCEAN COME AGAIN

NAMASTE

A bit dramatic, you said.

Then you explained to me what all the words meant. You said
that India is where ladoos came from. For a while, Yemaya, it was
the only thing I knew about India. I thought of it as a factory that
made sweet milk balls and shipped them all over the world, and
who, with the profits, made gifts of bridges. How wrong I turned
out to be, for best and worst!

The crossing into Chad, and the entry into the capital
N'Djamena, was very difficult. We were stopped for hours at police

checkpoints, five within a kilometer, all for different things. You and Francis huddled together and talked, and when I wormed my way under your arm by your side, I heard everything Francis said: that the situation in Chad was very bad. That we'd had to bribe the Chadian border police three times as much as last year, that the usual documents were not sufficient. Muhammed had never even heard of the documents the Chadian police were asking for. He said they were making them up and laughing about it because they were drunk. Right now Muhammed was drinking with them, in fact, because the police had forced him to at gunpoint, and it was best to simply placate them. And in the east, the situation was even worse—water had grown so scarce that the nomads and villagers were on the brink of war, just as had happened in Darfur at the turn of the century.

What about Mariama? you asked Francis. Without papers, will they try to detain her?

They'll respond to money. Just don't show them how much you have. That assumes we only run into Chadian military police. If we run into the militias in the east, who knows.

What would they do? you asked.

Francis said, Not good things. They're bad people.

Why are we going through Chad at all?

You can only get to Addis through Khartoum. And you can only get to Khartoum through Abéché. Otherwise you have to go down south through Cameroon, Central African Republic, the Congo, Uganda, Kenya, and then finally up into Ethiopia—it's a mess. We wouldn't get to Addis until Easter.

Francis turned to me. If things get rough, Mariama, you know where to hide, right?

I nodded. Twice so far, when Francis had had a feeling that a situation might get dangerous, he told me to go to my hiding place, which was an empty oil barrel. They always kept one empty, just in case. Francis explained to me that my presence was a liability, because there was "traffic" that consisted entirely of children, and other countries were paying African governments so much money to stop it that they needed bigger bribes to stay quiet about it. Now I know what this "traffic" means, but back then, I just imagined long threads of girls and boys on motorbikes, interweaving across the desert.

◈ ◈ ◈

We made stops in Chad only when necessary. After the episode at the border, Muhammed wanted to get through the country as fast as possible.

In N'Djamena, you'd managed to pick up a secondhand book in English, so we read it together on those marathon driving days. Funnily enough, it was an Indian story—I had to pronounce it several times before I got it right—the *Children's Illustrated Mahabharata*. The men were very beautiful, the Pandavas and the Kauravas. They wore green jewels and rode purple horses. Francis teased us that you were cheating because he couldn't buy any Amharic books to teach me with. It was true that I was progressing faster in English than in Amharic. When we reach Ethiopia, he said, I'll buy you Amharic books so pretty it'll be the only language you ever want to speak. You shook your head at him, but you were smiling. It was like a little competition between him and you.

Just then, we felt the truck slowing to a stop. I hated that feeling because it felt like my spirit yearned to continue while my body was stuck. Francis climbed up front to take in the scene, and when he turned back, his eyes were wide.

Mariama, hide now.

I had never heard him use that tone before. I went straight for my empty barrel but before I climbed in I caught a glimpse through the front window of a row of men on horseback, each with a rifle across his chest.

Francis sealed the top and I was in darkness, but I could still hear and feel. When the truck finally stopped it seemed like a cruel joke that our favorite Angélique Kidjo song, "Afrika," was pumping joyously from the speakers.

I tried not to move. But I was very uncomfortable. It seemed like there was far less room inside the barrel than usual, and I felt cold, like I was in air conditioning. Had Francis hid something else in here?—I felt around for my usual air hole. But I didn't feel it.

And then I realized I was in the wrong barrel.

There was a sharp clang and shudder on the outside of the truck. The music stopped. I heard shouting in Arabic, but I couldn't recognize more than a few words. There seemed to be an argument. There were many voices speaking over one another, interrupting each other. I heard Muhammed's voice drowning in their midst. I heard booted feet ascend onto our flatbed. And then I heard you, very near, very close, say softly and almost singsong in my own language, Little girl, be brave, they're coming. They might want to take you. Do not let them take you. Run away into the desert.

That's what my mother had told me, Yemaya. For a moment I felt angry at you both: Why were you telling me to run? Why were you telling me what was best? Couldn't I just decide for myself whether to stay?

I heard a clang, and then another, and then another, getting nearer. Someone was rapping their fist on each barrel. When he rapped on mine, it must have sounded different to him, because he demanded that it be opened. I didn't know what to do so I just stayed where I was.

Air and light opened above me. Staring down at me was a man with his head wrapped, and only his eyes showing.

He laughed. He called to his friends. Then two more men with their heads wrapped were standing over me. They pulled me up by my armpits and lifted me, bodily, and set me on the ground. I saw you, wavering on your feet, blinking, trying to keep your eyes open, like you were sleepy. I tried to go to you, but I was nudged back gently with the butt of a gun.

I heard Muhammed calling. He asked to approach his own truck. Permission was granted. He mounted the flatbed and held up his hands in a sign of peace. I couldn't understand his Arabic. But he beseeched them and gestured to me. Finally something was decided and Muhammed pressed his palms together in front of his face.

The men smiled at me in a way that seemed unkind. Then they filed off the truck, one by one. You were standing in the space they had left, shivering in the heat. When the last one departed, your knees buckled and you fell.

I ran to you. I didn't cry because I knew I needed to be strong for you.

I asked, What happened?

You said, They wanted to take you. In exchange for passing through. Muhammed promised them you were a Muslim, so they let you go.

Why did they want to take me?

They wanted to hurt you.

Why did they want to hurt me?

Because someone hurt them. So all they know how to do is hurt someone else.

I could tell how furious you were. But you never cried either, not once. You just swallowed it down.

❖   ❖   ❖

In another two days, after crossing the border into Sudan, we came to the Sun Traps.

Our convoy passed through their ranks. We knelt by the side of the truck and watched them stretch to the northern horizon. They'd been built by the Chinese, you told me, but I must have missed the sign saying WE THE PEOPLE OF CHINA DO GIFT THESE SUN TRAPS TO YOU SUDANESE. It was the first large-scale solar array built in the Sahara. Apparently it powered four nearby towns, and soon, with the investment of the Sudanese government, they would expand operations to power most of Khartoum.

To me, the Sun Traps looked like a forest of yawning black metal butterflies, their wings opening and closing in concert. So I said so.

Francis said, Or like women, their legs opening.

You slapped Francis on the head and said, Watch your mouth around the little girl.

But I said, Yes, just like women opening their legs! I've seen it.

You both stared at me.

You said, You've seen what?

A woman with her legs open, I said. My mother! What a whore!

You and Francis looked at each other over my head. I had expected you to laugh. But you didn't. ·

Francis crouched down and looked me in the eyes. You must not speak of your mother that way, he said.

She's not my mother anymore, I said. And anyway, you can't tell me what to say.

I hated Francis then.

I walked away.

I didn't speak of my mother again for thirteen years.

The Girl in the Road

After the chaos of Chad, Sudan was quiet. We continued through a land of black rivers twisting on brown plains and buzzards hopping to and fro in their morning parties. We passed the days quietly too, as if talking too much would defile the desert silence. I sat against a crate, watching the road vomit itself from beneath our wheels. I wondered why the oil barrel I'd hid in had been so cold. I started counting shepherd boys and girls, much taller than me, strong and skinny.

And then there were no boys or girls for a long time. The dust blew across the road like curtains closing behind us.

I saw the crates shift before I felt it. The truck swerved. Then the world turned upside down: I saw sky where sand should have been, and sand where sky should have been. The crate hit the ground and my head hit the crate. My mind turned to static, a popping black fizzy soda, and my body tumbled over and over before finally coming to rest.

I heard explosions, like the sounds of guns. I saw silver mist stream overhead. I thought, We're all in a Nollywood film, a Bollywood film, a blue and silver adventure.

I turned my head. I could hear the sand grinding beneath my skull. A short distance away, there was another child, lying in the sand just as I was lying, in an identical position, like a gawky bird gone to sleep. But she was much too skinny and her mouth was too wide open. She was amazed at me. She couldn't close her mouth. Her teeth were wiggling. She sprouted a black wing, even though her body remained completely still. Then *I* was amazed at *her*. How did she come by wings? I wanted wings!

I got up and, at the same time, she got up. She took a step

toward me. Her black wings were fierce and shiny. Her dress was rumpled, once pink, now mottled mustard, and it whipped around her chicken-bone legs.

Saha, I said to calm myself, Saha.

What are you saying? she asked. Her eyes didn't open and her mouth didn't move, but her head tilted at an angle, which was how I knew she'd spoken.

It's my favorite word, I said.

Who are you?

My name is Mariama.

My name is Mariama, she said, and took another step toward me.

Where did you get your wings? I said.

She didn't answer. Instead she asked, Where are you from?

I'm going home, I said. To Ethiopia.

I am from Ethiopia, she said.

She took another step toward me. As she came closer, her flesh swelled into a round and pleasant face with a button nose.

I don't think the wings are mine, she said, answering my question late. I think they belong to the buzzards.

Oh, I said.

I want to be with you, she said.

Maybe, I said. What are you doing in the desert?

I ran away from the horsemen.

Why?

My mother told me to. She said it was better to die than be taken by a man.

Was it the right thing to do?

Oh yes. It was better just to end the story here. It feels good to rest.

I'd like to rest too.

You always can, she said. And you don't even have to run away. You can just lie down in the road, anytime.

I opened my mouth to answer her, but I had to spit out a warm liquid, thick like coffee. It got in my throat and I choked on it. I lifted my head to cough it out. That's when I started to feel pain.

Static resolved into sound. I saw your face above me, Yemaya. You were hysterical, but I couldn't make out your words. I wanted to tell you I was all right. But I could only mouth the words, because blood filled my throat.

Dressing

I woke up in a small concrete room. Again, immediately, I tried to say I was all right, but I couldn't speak. I tried to gesture, but I couldn't control my hands. They made broad chopping motions that didn't convey what I meant to convey. I wonder what you thought I meant—that I wanted to chop wood, or shake your hand!

One of my palms was caught and a pressure was applied. Thumbs pressed into my palm harder and harder, and cotton filled my mouth. So I slipped back into sleep.

❖ ❖ ❖

Voices were trying to get my attention. They were located in the upper-right corner of my brown field. I wanted to ask them if they were concerned with helping me plant, and if not, to please wait until I had finished the planting myself. A mongrel dog came shyly and sat between the beds and kept me company while I hoed. She said, *Saha, saha, saha.*

Mariama? said a voice.

I opened my eyes and sat up and said, Yes.

Palms pushed me gently back down to the bed. Easy, child, they were saying. Easy.

It was you and Muhammed. Your faces were overhead, on either side of me, sun and moon.

Your eyes were red.

Do you remember what happened? you said.

At first I thought you meant the brown field, but I sensed that
that was not it. So I said no.

We had an accident, you said. The truck swerved to avoid
something in the road. You fell off but you're alive. We're so lucky,
Mariama.

I asked, Where's the girl with the black wings?

You and Muhammed exchanged looks.

What girl?

There was a girl, I said, and struggled to remember what she
looked like. She was wearing a pink dress and she got up and
talked to me, and said—

There was no girl, you said.

It's no use lying to her, said Muhammed. There was a dead
body in the road, Mariama. That's why the truck swerved.

But she talked to me, I said. She said she was from Ethiopia.

Muhammed covered his mouth with his hand and walked away.

I turned to you.

She said her name was Mariama, the same as mine! I said.

You looked down and asked in a low voice, What else did
she say?

That she'd run away from the horsemen and was happy she did.

You nodded to the floor. You took deep breaths. You left the
room for five minutes.

You came back and said, Are you hungry? You should eat
something.

And then even though your hands were trembling, you tore
open a pack of glucose biscuits and opened a carton of milk and

dipped the biscuit in the milk and fed it to me. The grains melted in my mouth. The sugar made me forget the girl in the road.

◈ ◈ ◈

I hadn't died, but Francis had. He'd been tossed from the truck too, and because he was a grown man, he hit the ground harder, and bled to death on the inside. When you told me, you were very casual. So stupid, you said. He wasn't careful. He should have known better. He didn't value his life. He always just walked up and down the truck not holding on to anything.

I felt happy about your attitude, since I was still jealous about all the time he'd been spending around you, and mad that he scolded me for saying the word "whore." So I considered the matter settled. We didn't need him. I only needed you. And, after both terrible scares—the horsemen, and now the accident—you stayed close to me, which I loved.

My body was badly bruised by the accident, and for a while, it was difficult to move without pain. You had a torn muscle and some bruised ribs but were otherwise all right. But Muhammed had been in the front cab when the truck swerved and his leg was broken. Because it was his convoy, the entire operation was stalled.

You told me this would be a healing time before we crossed over into Ethiopia. We were in an Indian clinic in a large town, Al Qadarif, ringed by hills on three sides. They seemed vast to me, like we were at the bottom of a bowl where all the rains of the world collected. The city was rich with green fields and singing birds, which seemed to me a promise of things to come across the border.

After the first few days in the little concrete room, I was moved to the large common area, where there were many cots lining each wall. You came to sit by me and sometimes to share my bed. One day I asked you to tell me about the name Yemaya, that lovely rhythmic name. You leaned back against the foot of the hospital bed, crossing your feet up by my head. One of the Indian nurses passed us and smiled into her sirius. She probably thought we were mother and daughter.

Her African name was Yemoja, you said, but you'd picked the Cuban form because it was the most beautiful. Yemaya was the goddess of the ocean, the patroness of sailors and shipwreck survivors, the eternal and unending mother of all living things, whose children were as fish. You told me how Yemaya was a great lover, seducing beautiful young women and men alike, but her greatest seduction was that of a monstrous sea snake who lived in the Arabian Sea, to whom she swam in the middle of the night, and mounted, and tamed, and had a great many strange adventures and met a great many strange characters. That was my very favorite story of all. I made you tell me what people she met, and your tales never ceased to amaze me. The sea scholars. The wave surfers. The lotus eaters.

Can I go ride the snake too? I asked.

Of course, you said. I'll meet you there.

For years afterward I would recall these stories and think, How sly of you to tell me this! All the time, you were speaking of things *you* had done, people *you* had loved, lives *you* had lived. I see now that I was not ready to receive the truth, at that age; if you'd revealed yourself right there and then, I might not have believed you.

As it was, I was simply happy to hear the stories. The truth is revealed to us when we are ready for it.

❖ ❖ ❖

A week later, we were sitting in the garden next to the clinic. The vegetation was carefully planted—desert flowers from Gujarat, you told me, in the north of India. There was even a little sign saying GIFT FROM THE PEOPLE OF GANDHINAGAR TO OUR SUDANESE BROTHERS AND SISTERS.

You had asked the nurse to bring us tea, and he did, on a silver platter. We were both surprised at how nice their tea set was; though it wasn't real silver, you told me, it still shone. You knelt and poured while I sat, slumped to the side because my body still ached. I could see Muhammed at the other end of the garden, now in a wheelchair, conversing with the head doctor.

You handed me a cup and you said, How would you like to live with me in Addis Ababa?

I nearly threw the cup into the air.

Really? I asked.

Really, you said. I can send you to school, and feed you and clothe you. You don't have to do any work for me, besides what a normal little sister would do, helping around the house.

What can I do? I said. I was breathless.

You can go to school and do your homework and compose kinae with golden meanings, to recite for your schoolmates, you said.

I said, But in exchange for what? I'll do any work you want me to.

Child, you said. You must stop thinking you are owned. You only belong to yourself. Can you promise me that?

I said yes because I would promise you anything.

Muhammed wheeled over to us. He said, You look well, Mariama.

I'm going to live with Yemaya, I blurted out.

Muhammed looked at you in surprise. Is she? he said.

It's something I was thinking about, you said.

You've come to love her, said Muhammed.

Yes.

I understand. But God entrusted her to Francis and me.

You said to me, Mariama, can you go play?

I got up, my tea not even tasted, and went back into the clinic. The big room was full of rows of beds with bright-patterned cloth, most empty, and each with a metal staff at the bedside. Through the doorway I looked back at you talking to Muhammed with great passion and animation. I wished I could eavesdrop, but there was no clear way to do it.

Eventually the two of you stopped talking and Muhammed wheeled up the ramp into the clinic. He saw me standing there.

I've agreed to let Yemaya take you, he said, on the condition that she provides me proof of your schooling. She's very young, this woman. And she's much aggrieved by Francis's death even though she doesn't show it. She may have good intentions, but with the young, intentions count for little.

I nodded right away. I didn't comprehend anything he said, really, because I was so happy he'd agreed to let me go.

I regret you won't meet my daughters, he said. Fatima and Rahel. You would have gotten along like old friends.

Then he wheeled past me, looking sad.

I rejoined you on the bench and said, I think Muhammed has come to love me, too.

He'll be all right, you said.

I know, I said. I just want to be with you, anyway. Can we take a truck by ourselves and Muhammed can give out the oil by himself?

Ah, oil, you said.

You sat forward with your elbows on your knees and looked back at me, as if considering. I sat forward to join you in your seriousness. That made you laugh.

I have something to tell you, you said. You may not understand all of it, but it's important for you to know. I don't believe in hiding things from children. Besides, you've reached the age of reason.

Okay, I said.

Mariama, what are we carrying on the truck?

Oil, I said immediately.

That's what I would have said. And Muhammed. But when the truck overturned, the barrels came loose, and five of them broke open.

I nodded, remembering now the explosion sounds and the silver mist.

We weren't carrying oil, you said. Muhammed was deceived. His superiors may have been deceived too. We were carrying metallic hydrogen.

What's that?

It's a material used for conducting energy, you said. You see how the lights in the clinic turn on? And the ceiling fans run? All of that uses energy that comes through wires. But this material can make a wire that works so well, no energy is wasted. It just travels straight through. It gives exactly what it receives.

It all sounded very inconsequential to me. I must have looked unimpressed.

I can't make it sound exciting, you said. But it's important. This material is illegal in most of the world because it's dangerous.

Then I remembered. I said, When the horsemen stopped us and I got in the barrel, I felt cold.

Because it was refrigerated. Metallic hydrogen is refrigerated during shipment.

Won't people be mad when they see they've been getting the wrong thing all this time?

None of the handlers knew what they were handling, you said. Only the end users knew. The whole plan was to pretend it was crude oil so they could get it across borders easily.

Is Muhammed mad?

As mad as Muhammed gets, you said. He's still trying to get straight answers from people. But he can't do much when he's stuck in bed all day.

But we're still going to Ethiopia, right?

Yes. Muhammed still has to make his deliveries, no matter what those deliveries are.

You picked up a pebble from the ground, fingered it, and dropped it again.

He's not in a position to refuse to.

The Great Rift Valley

We were approaching our final days of recovery and I was more eager than ever for our long-promised home. In the garden, after a rain, I asked you to tell me stories about Ethiopia even though you'd never been there. They didn't have to be stories, I said. Just things you knew.

You pointed at the hills. You see those? you said. They're the beginning of the Great Rift Valley.

I didn't know what those words meant, Yemaya, but the hushed way you said them gave me chills.

The Great Rift Valley is splitting Africa apart, you said. It runs from Djibouti all the way down to Mozambique. Millions of years from now, the whole valley will be filled with water again and all the cities will be drowned. But in the time that it's been dry land, the human race rose out of the earth and spread all over the world. It's important for you to know about Dinkenesh, since we'll be living in Ethiopia. It means "You are wonderful."

What's Dinkenesh? I asked.

She's our ancestor. That means your mother's mother's mother's mother's mother's mother's mother's mother's mother's mother, all the way back, as far back as you want to go.

(I thought to myself: How far back do I want to go?)

Dinkenesh is revered in Ethiopia, you said. When we go to Addis, I'll take you to see her.

Should we bring her ladoos?

No, Mariama, you misunderstand. She's a skeleton.

What's a skeleton?

It's a person's bones. Dinkenesh is only bones. She's not alive like you and I are alive, but she lives, nevertheless. Do you understand?

To be alive, but *not* alive—I did understand. In fact I think I knew exactly what you were talking about—what you'd told me on the bench in Ouagadougou, and then what the girl in the road had told me!

Was Dinkenesh running away? I asked.

I don't know. Maybe she was.

Did she run into horsemen, and then ran into the desert?

You didn't answer.

Did she know it was better to die than be taken by a man?

You didn't answer.

Because that's what the girl in the road said to me.

You hit me so hard I saw the black fizzy soda in my eyes. I'd only seen that once before, when I fell off the truck.

I stayed in the pose the slap had sent me to, cast like clay. I tried to draw breath but could only get little sips of it. I knew I had done something very, very wrong, but I wasn't yet old or wise enough to understand what.

Of course, now I do, Yemaya. I was greedy and arrogant and trying to learn all your mysteries at once! I wasn't ready to love you the way you deserved. And even though you apologized to me at once, crying, which I'd never seen you do, just a few seconds after you hit me, saying you didn't mean it, that it was because of your father, I knew you wouldn't have done it without just cause. I didn't cry. I fed the tears to the kreen, who was very much awake, and simply a part of my body now.

B☐☐K IX

Meena

Field Station

Shortly after sunset, when my pozit reads 227 kilometers, I see what looks like the end of an old-fashioned telephone receiver sticking up out of the waves and hung over the Trail. As I get closer, it gets bigger. It might be four meters tall.

I assume the worst and approach with my hands up. At least I have my dignity this time. I see a young man drop down out of a hatch in the receiver, then an older man. The young man stalks forward while signaling to the older man to stay back. They're both wearing khaki vests and sun hats.

The young man calls out,

FARSI: Hello

Great, more Persians. Maybe I'll ask them what *dear bitch I am fifty percent* means.

"Hello," I say. "I come in peace." I feel dumb saying it, but it seems necessary out here.

"Where are you from?"

"India."

"You're traveling?"

"Yep."

"What are you doing it for?"

The older man intervenes. "Navid," he says. "She's harmless."

Navid transforms at the older man's voice, becomes placative. "We shouldn't trust anyone," he says.

The older man addresses me. "Forgive my son," he says. "He's just protective of me. You're the first traveler we've seen on the Trail."

"How do you know I'm harmless?" I say.

It's not a question either of them was expecting. Navid tenses up. Maybe I shouldn't have said it but I fucking hate it when any-one assumes I'm harmless because I'm a woman.

"We don't," says the older man. "But if you say you mean us no harm, we'll believe you."

"I don't," I say. "Do you mean me harm?"

"No!" says the older man, surprised, and then looks over his shoulder at Navid, who's giving me the evil eye. Finally he says, "I mean no one harm who means me no harm."

"Well, I mean no harm," I say. Why am I so obstreperous? It's like, now that I see so few humans, I have to audition them for worthiness.

Our charade is done. The older man claps his hands together and approaches me and says, "Great! That's settled. I'm Dr. Mohsen Yazdi, and this is Dr. Navid Yazdi."

They're father and son oceanographers based at the University of Tehran. The phone receiver thing is actually a mobile seastead, a spar model that can bob around the seas and not fall over, which seems intuitively ridiculous, but here they are. It's technically illegal to park their spar on the Trail, but they do if they're close and no one's watching. We like to stretch our legs, says Mohsen.

I sit a few scales away while they perform the evening prayer. Navid's temper cools and he tunes me out when he joins with his father's voice. It calms me to hear other people pray. On the open ocean, their chant doesn't echo, it just goes nowhere.

When they're done, Navid climbs back up into the spar to heat water. Mohsen apologizes and says they don't have much left besides what they've caught on the Trail. He offers me some dried sea-snake meat. I say sure. He climbs up into the spar too and after a few minutes he descends with a plate of circles like cucumber slices, except they're dry, withered, and colored pink with black skin. I bite one and it's chewy, with a texture like dried mushroom and a strong metallic flavor.

"It's a cultivated taste," says Mohsen. "They're an invasive species. Beautiful things in the water though, just beautiful, like black ribbons."

He reminds me of Muthashan.

"You have a faraway look in your eyes," says Mohsen.

"You remind me of my grandfather."

"Is he still with you?"

The question is strange to me. My glotti probably didn't catch the nuance, but I think he's asking whether Muthashan is still alive.

"Yes," I say. "Far as I know, anyway. Haven't been in touch with him for a while."

"Does he know where you are?"

"Nope."

"Ah." Mohsen sits back on his mat. "What in me reminds you of him?"

Here we go again, when I try to translate what's in my head to what comes out of my mouth and I fuck it up. If I could say it right, I'd tell him about the time I looked out the window and saw Muthashan sitting alone on a stone bench in the garden, and his shoulders were shaking, so I thought he was coughing. I'd just made chai, so I brought some out for him in a chipped white cup. I rounded the corner of the bench and he turned to me with cheeks wet and eyes red. So he wasn't coughing, he was crying. I was mad. I was a teenager and he'd sprung this on me.

I turned to go, but he held out a snotty hand to invite me to sit next to him. I did. I could tell he wanted to make a Connection. He put his arm around me and hugged me to him and cried on my shoulder. I stayed still, absorbing the shudders of his body. It was so un-Malayalee of him. I usually didn't care about that kind of thing, but at that moment, I did.

I watched an orange lizard thrash over the lettuce bed.

Finally I asked, So what are you upset about?

My son, he said. My son Gabriel.

Oh, I said.

Your grandmother would be so angry with me if she knew I was sitting here, crying like a child, while you comforted me.

My hand settled on his back, but my eyes were blank. His crying dissolved into coughing. So I'd been right to bring the chai after all.

"Here's your tea," says Navid.

I realize I'd never answered Mohsen. I'd spaced out again.

"Gentleness," I say to Mohsen. "You have a quality of gentleness."

"That's kind of you," says Mohsen. "I take it as a compliment."

"I mean it that way. So what do you do out here?"

"Gathering data on waveforms."

"Height and energy?"

"That, and frequency and morphology," says Navid, having decided I'm worth talking to. "And the usual conductivity, temperature, depth."

"You do this every year?"

"Every year for the last ten," says Navid.

"He was fifteen, the first time I took him out in the spar," says Mohsen. "He did so well! The best assistant you could ask for."

Navid actually blushes. These men are fascinating to me. I never knew fathers and sons to behave like intimates.

"So what are you finding out?"

Navid and Mohsen exchange looks. "How much do you know about the weather?" says Navid.

"I know it's getting worse."

"Right," says Navid. "Because there's more heat in all of the systems, which means more energy needs to be redistributed."

"Average wave heights all over the world are increasing quite dramatically," says Mohsen.

"Good time to invest in wave energy," I say, indicating the Trail.

"Indeed," says Mohsen. "HydraCorp knew what they were doing. Now if the Trail itself can just survive being out here."

"Why wouldn't it?"

"Ah, you underestimate the sea," says Mohsen. "She's a violent mistress."

"I can't believe you're walking on this thing," says Navid. "Do you know anything about metallic hydrogen?"

"I know it's the superconductor used in the Trail."

"It's also unstable."

"Navid, peace—it's unstable under certain circumstances, like any substance."

"Killed hundreds of workers in Africa," says Navid. "And it's never been tested at sea. So hey, it could be fine, it could stay inert. Or it could get out and propagate instability."

"Speaking of which, I'm surprised I haven't run into any storms."

"Ha! You will," says Navid. "Bound to happen. What protection do you have?"

"My pod goes underwater," I say. "I haven't had to try it out yet."

"You'll have your chance yet," he says.

Why is he on my tits. I want to smear that condescending smirk off his face.

Mohsen comes in to rescue us young hotheads. "Yes, there's plenty more heat to redistribute," he says, "which means stronger winds, which means stronger waves."

"So what makes a wave?"

"An initial imbalance."

"Between what."

"Between layers of a gradient. All systems wish to be at rest. So they redistribute energy until they re-equilibrate, though of course, they never quite get there."

"Like castes," I say.

The word doesn't initially translate for them. I have to say, you know, like layers of people in traditional Indian society, Dalit, Kshatriya, Brahmin.

Oh, oh, yes, they nod.

"Like people themselves," Mohsen says. "Seeking equilibrium."

"But you can never trace the first imbalance."

"It depends on how far back you want to go."

I think: *How far back do I want to go?* For a second I feel like a game-show contestant and I'm pondering the question with bright flashing lights all around.

For now I say, "So you're saying we're doomed."

"Yes," says Navid at once. "Even the ocean may reach a tipping point. It will look calm, and then it will snap."

"Live far away from the shore and you'll be fine," says Mohsen.

"Or live on the Trail," says Navid. "There could be a tsunami coming through here right now and we'd never know it."

Mohsen sees that my tea is finished. He nods to Navid, who takes the cup and plate from me and kneels a few scales away to wash them in purified water.

"So you're headed off again tonight?" asks Mohsen.

"Yeah. I mostly walk at night because the water is calmer. And I don't get roasted by the sun."

"Very smart. Do you know the stars?"

"Some of them."

"The Needle?"

"The what?"

He tries again. "The North Star?"

"Oh, the Dhruva Tara. No, actually. I always forget how to find it."

Mohsen stands up and scans the sky, which is flushed deep blue now. He points northwest up toward the Saptarishi and tells me to trace upward from the two pointer stars. I can see it now. A very unassuming star.

"Thanks," I say.

"Take good care of yourself," says Mohsen. "Be smart. Be careful."

A kilometer later, I throw up all the sea snake I ate.

Geeta

I wish Navid hadn't been right, but he'd been too much of a prick not to be. When I wake up a few days later the sky is overcast and the wind is snappish. As I make breakfast I notice planks and other flotsam knocking up against the Trail, on the south side. Their corners aren't weathered. They've splintered off in recent history. I guess that means a nearby meteorological event.

I stop and check my locality. Nothing. I widen the range, and then I see it: Cyclone Geeta, coming up from the southeast. Wonderful. It's not even cyclone season. Though seasons as a concept don't have much integrity anymore.

I'm heavy, but not that heavy. I can't risk the wind on the surface of the Trail if the cyclone hits. According to my scroll it's about twelve hours away, so I keep walking through the night. There's a full moon, but it's covered by clouds, so its light suffuses the whole sky like I'm walking under a gray veil thrown over a lightbulb. On the Trail it's hard to appreciate natural beauty. I'm too aware of thousands of kilometers left. These sights might be beautiful to me, someday, in memory, but now I just walk a tightrope over an abyss.

When the sky begins to lighten, I see a discoloration to the southeast, approaching like an army on the battlefield. But of course each stage of arrival is not the ultimate stage. The sea is still calm. I feel a little reckless. For a while I entertain the illusion that I'm keeping pace with the storm or even outpacing it. But it keeps arriving. I see the first flashes of lightning.

Time to go under. I take out my scroll and pull up the pod manual. It says that my pod is designed for depths of up to ten meters and that the skin can be adjusted for oxygen porosity, though it takes more energy the deeper it goes, because dissolved oxygen gets more scarce.

I inflate the pod as usual and activate the oxygen extraction mode that assumes submersion in water. I have no idea what these pods were originally designed for. Rich Brahmin adrenaline hounds? I imagine them inflating pods and taking them over Jog Falls. Which would be idiotic, though hardly less idiotic than what

I'm doing. And I'm Brahmin too, imagine that. The poor don't have the luxury to be so dumb.

The wind is picking up and the waves are getting choppier. I have to work fast. In the original pod kit are two items I'd been tempted to throw out in the arrogance of someone who assumes that if they don't know the purpose of a thing, it must have no purpose: (1) a ten-meter elastic cord that expands in water and (2) a rubber sphincter lined with the same polymer as the cord, so that, when joined, form a watertight seal. Again, up to ten meters' depth. Regarding anything below that depth, the manual is silent.

I need something to secure the cord to. On the seasteads, I'm sure they have steel rings anchored to the platform for this very purpose. What can I use? The Trail runs smooth for hundreds of kilometers in each direction. There are no protuberances. Excellent. I'm fucked. I begin to feel rain spattering my face. The only thing I can think to do is tie the cord around an entire scale, which will take up two or three meters of its length, and hope it holds.

I insert the sphincter into the pod's skin, making sure the lining makes a seal with the rest of the skin, and then thread the cord through. No time to think. I take a deep breath and slip into the water with all my clothes on, holding the other end of the cord, and swim down under the scale deep enough where the water gets cold to make sure I'm clearing the scales by a good meter, because if they knock together while my head's between them, this adventure will be over. I clear them and surface on the other side and heave myself back up, having made a loop underneath, and tie it around the hinge assembly.

Now the wind is blowing rain into my eyes and it's hard to see. I hold one arm up against the wind and nudge the pod to the edge of the platform. I slice it open and crawl inside it with all my things and then pinch the skin closed. I take off my wet clothes and wrap them up and set them aside to deal with later. I'm naked in an orb. Typical. The new oxygen extraction setting isn't completely clear; it's translucent, like seeing the outside through a filmy window. Rain begins to come in sideways.

Nothing left to do but go down. I rock forward. No luck. I have to be more forceful, but not enough to break the skin. I rock again and feel a sickening dropping movement and overcorrect back in terror, but it's too late. My pod rolls on the surface of the water and bobs in the waves. Then I begin to sink.

The water rises like a stage curtain. It's already a third of the way up my pod. I can see drifting gold dust in the gray water. I tell myself this is exactly what's supposed to happen. Though now I feel certain that this pod wasn't made for the open ocean, but calm ponds and reefs off of Goa. I curl up at the bottom of my pod, wishing I were lighter, if that would make a difference. I reread the instructions. It might take a minute for the pod to begin to sink completely, it says. So I have to wait. I fight the urge to unseal the pod and scramble back out onto the Trail. The storm would be much worse on the Trail.

Slowly, the water level rises farther. It's halfway up. Then there's only a circle of sky above me, rain drumming hard, and then the circle is gone. My world is blue-gray with yellow crumbs floating by. Getting darker. The air inside the pod becomes cooler and wetter. I force myself to take deep, calm breaths. It's almost as if the pod isn't sinking at all, but rather that the world is flooding. This is my new state now. The air is fresh. The oxygen extraction seems to be working. I examine the seal that the cord makes with the lining of the sphincter, which itself bonds with the skin of the pod—all seem to be holding. I realize I've been clenching all my muscles and try to relax. The pod becomes still as it sinks. Then there's a gentle tug from the top. I've descended three meters, which I set as my initial stop point.

I'm not sure I could sleep even if I wanted to. According to the Established Routine, this is the time of day when I read, but it seems ridiculous to read when I just dropped myself into the ocean like a tea ball. I can't reconcile the absurdity of that idea with the mundane reality of it. How I'm lying on my back naked with my legs crossed and my backpack in my lap. How it feels like I'm sitting on a waterbed. How the orb around me is colored a perfect gradient of light to dark.

I try to get comfortable. Being in neutral buoyancy, the pod has assumed a more spherical shape than it does on the Trail, where it sags from gravity. I try to spread my weight around because I still don't trust the pod skin to hold me. I keep my eyes trained on the light color above and sing through the twelve or thirteen kritis I know by heart. I may be agnostic but I know my people's songs.

I've been lying in the pod looking up for maybe fifteen minutes when I trust that, since I haven't suffocated so far, and my knot seems to be holding, and the pod skin hasn't split, I can give myself permission to move. I pull up a baggie of food I brought down—a couple of idlee cubes without sauce—and eat them, still staring up. They settle my stomach.

I pull out my manual and read it again. It says that, to pull myself up, I have to take the cable in through the sphincter and basically pull myself up like pulling myself up a rope. As of now, the cord is letting out bit by bit on its own, which means that the scale it's tied to is bucking in the waves. The storm must have really arrived now. I just have to wait it out.

I go through my kritis again.

I hold out the last note of the last song until I run out of breath.

I take out my scroll. I reread the section on underwater survival. In theory, I can stay down here for a few days—the pod's skin has molecular pumps for both oxygen (in) and carbon dioxide (out). I'm beginning to actually feel comfortable. But sleep is still inconceivable. I turn my head to look down and there's only darkness. How many meters to the bottom, I wonder. Probably two or three thousand.

I tell my scroll to play the essays of Reshmi West, the writer-guru I first started reading after I dropped out of college. I close my eyes and listen. She was born in Dubai but went to India for college. Then she retraced Gandhi's travels by train. Then she lost touch with her parents. She traveled, not begging, but eating very little and filling whole journals, each of which she mailed to a friend in Trivandrum when finished. She carried only one salwar kameez and one sari ensemble, which she wore on alternating days, and washed herself on the ghats of whatever village she was in. I've seen holos of her from this period: light, skinny, fragile. She was a tiny woman to begin with, but here she looked like a marmoset.

She came to Madurai, the temple town that's home to the Sri Meenakshi Sundareswarar Temple. The gods there are Meenakshi (mine and my mother's namesake) and Shiva. The priests bring Shiva to Meenakshi's bedchambers every night, sing them lullabies, and then leave them alone for their cosmic lovemaking. No one is allowed to see it.

Reshmi spent the entire day in the temple complex. After all the pilgrims left, after the priests had put Meenakshi and Shiva to bed and gone to bed themselves, she remained. She was so quiet that no one noticed her. She sat on the floor, with her back to a pillar by the Golden Lotus Tank, and strained to listen for the sounds of lovemaking. She claims she heard them. She heard panting and whimpering and gasping, sounds that one makes when one's finger is struck with a hammer. On through the whole night it went, and she sat still and observed her reactions to it. At first she was delighted and felt especially blessed, that she'd been allowed not only to catch a glimpse of the gods, but to hear them at night. She closed her eyes and pictured them: water-blue Shiva and fish-eyed

Meenakshi, the lovely warrior. She pictured them entwining. She moved from delight to tears at the beauty of it. But the tears were not entirely happy. She was jealous, too. She realized she'd been alone for three years, not allowing anyone to touch her, and she was jealous that Shiva and Meenakshi had found each other, and flaunted it every night. Their sounds echoing through the pillars became not beautiful, but ugly. As if she were being forced to witness something unbearable, the embarrassing, sordid coupling of strangers. The gods were merely animals in heat. Can't they control themselves? she thought. And then the sky began to lighten, and the rapacious moaning finally, slowly, lessened with the coming dawn.

Reshmi found a group of women pilgrims camping in the street. She sat with them and tried to sleep, but the city was already awake, so she spent the day wandering far afield, across the river and back, before collapsing from fatigue in the street. This episode in Madurai became central to her literary imagination. How beautiful and revolting sex was. How its juices are both nectar and poison. For a year afterward she eschewed "shadow languages" and spoke only Sanskrit because she was convinced it was the fundamental mother language, the language that most closely reflected divine order, where each word was synonymous with its meaning and could, in theory, be regenerated ex nihilo by an infant who grew up in a natural paradise devoid of linguistic influence. She argued that Sanskrit words arose spontaneously in the mouths of babes all over the world. Her favorite mantra was the Sahanavavatu because her favorite time of day was morning.

I start singing it because it's morning. The first two syllables, "saha," remind me of the sound the barefoot girl made. I don't know if she was real, but my glotti responded as if she was, so that's a point toward her actuality. My glotti couldn't recognize it only because Sanskrit isn't spoken anymore.

I pull out my scroll and look up "saha." It has two contextual meanings.

One is *powerful*.

One is part of the construction *let us be together*, or simply, *with*.

◈ ◈ ◈

It's funny that this cyclone is named Geeta. That's my Muthashi's name. I remember when I first told her I was dating Mohini. It was the dry season, hot, right before the monsoon, in the last week of May. I was standing on the footpath by the Manimala River downhill from the clinic. The river was just a colloid of algae and pollen. Trees dropped their seeds into the dark green emulsion, which, suspended, would send out roots, and soon the river would become a movable garden.

Muthashi came down the ghats, holding up her peacock-blue sari by the hem. Her hair was white and pulled back in a bun, and she insisted on wearing gigantic square glasses instead of getting corrective laser surgery, which was the only thing I'd ever known her to be irrational about. Something about a fear of not being able to blink. Around her neck was a thin silver chain with a small silver cross—her nod to her Catholic mother, though her husband was Hindu, as her father had been.

When Muthashi joined me, we didn't kiss or embrace. We were still in the early stages of our reconciliation.

You're home, she said.

Just for a few days. I wanted to surprise you.

Muthashan said you had something to tell me.

Yes. I've met a woman named Mohini. She's a hijra. We're going to live together.

Muthashi shook her head in slow assent. Are you going to get married? she asked.

Maybe. I haven't asked her yet.

You're too young, she said.

I'm twenty-four.

Too young, she repeated. I married your grandfather at age twenty-nine. You should wait, Meena.

I looked out over the river. I'm ready for the monsoon, I said.

So are the patients, said Muthashi. The heat is terrible for them. We're almost out of turmeric.

I'll go get more, I said. I knew Muthashi hated patronizing the nearest source, a big air-conditioned market called SpyceWallah. The place she liked to go was all the way in Kozhencherry. And she was almost eighty years old.

That would be a big help, Meena, she said. Then again: You're too young to marry. How well do you know Mohini? Do you know her family?

I've met her mother, Seeta. She's great. She owns a beauty salon.

I saw this register on her face: NB, Not Brahmin. She ventured, And her father?

Died on a construction site when Mohini was three.

(DNB, Definitely Not Brahmin. But she wasn't going to say anything, because she knew it wasn't politically correct anymore.) Where is the rest of her family?

Her grandmother lives in Chennai, I said.

How do you know Mohini will be faithful to you? You know her kind.

I focused on the river and counted to ten. This was an emotional management technique I had learned as a trainee at the women's clinic.

What kind do you mean, Muthashi?

Hijras.

So despite all political progress, social advancement, and

appearance of acceptance, here was my grandmother speaking the voice of prejudice. It had to be something. If not caste, if not class, then gender. Children must un-train their elders over and over again.

I forced my voice to remain calm: That's a misconception, Muthashi. Hijras used to be sex workers because they were outcasts. They weren't allowed to live as other people do or work jobs like other people worked.

They could sing, said Muthashi. At the birth of boys.

But that opportunity didn't come often. And then there was lots of competition for those opportunities and most were shut out.

Muthashi was silent for a while. She did that when I out-argued her.

Then she said, A hijra came to sing at Gabriel's birth.

She waited for me to object to her saying his name. I didn't. This was also a feature of the reconciliation: that we could begin to mention the names of the unmentionable.

She said, We held the ceremony outside, on a field where boys used to play cricket. Your Muthashan was holding the baby when one of my friends came to tell me that there was a hijra outside asking to give praises. I would have dismissed him but Muthashan said, Geeta, let him come. I told my friend okay and then Muthashan gave me the baby and went to the microphone and said, Now we're going to hear a song. And the hijra came into our midst. Everyone got very quiet. Even Gabriel got quiet. The hijra was dressed in a bright orange sari with gold edging. He turned out to be quite good. He sang a beautiful song to bless Gabriel and then he came forth to kiss him, which Muthashan instructed me to allow. I was happy with him then, and we paid him. But then he continued near the fringes of the party asking men if they wanted to take him home, and it upset quite a few people. I had to ask him to leave. I think he had been drinking.

She finished the story as if to say, See, that explains my feelings.

I said, If you must know, Mohini has never worked as a sex worker.

Muthashi shook her head. She said, I'm only bringing this up for your own benefit, Meena. You must think these things through. You're like your father. Very impulsive.

We stood on the footpath for a few minutes, quiet, looking at the river. I spotted a turtle on the other side but didn't say anything. It was motionless in the sun, waiting for the monsoon to come so that it could swim in a fresh river.

It's good to have you home, Muthashi said, starting back up the footpath to the ghats. I can use you. Mrs. Nair just went into labor. She and her husband will be arriving from Alleppey within the hour. You remember what to prepare for a birth?

I wagged my head without looking at her.

Now I'm hanging like a Christmas ornament in the middle of the Arabian Sea, riding out a cyclone. I could sit here and indulge in thoughts that my grandparents might be dead. I could ideate the manner and timing of their deaths for maximum pathos. They're the only relatives I have left. But they're one step removed from me, a secondhand report on my nature. I want real parents. I want to know firsthand.

Mohini and I start talking again. The part of me that is her is very useful to me. She always has helpful things to say, especially because she lost a parent too; though she always displayed a casual relationship to the loss that was hard to believe. I thought it should manifest as a major dysfunction and was always waiting for it to do so. But in the meantime, at least she had the vocabulary to understand me. I return again to our conversation of how my mother is like the goddess in the innermost chamber.

You're seeking your mother on the Trail itself, she says to me.

What do you mean?

You don't think of the Trail as a temple because it's not enclosed. But you're passing through chambers. You're penetrating deeper.

It doesn't feel that way.

I know.

It feels like I'm doing something incredibly unnecessary.

And what would you rather be doing?

I don't know. Being in Africa.

But you'd have to get there first, and that's what you're doing.

All right.

Meena, what do you want to find at the end of this journey?

The woman who killed my parents.

This is important.

I imagine so.

No need to be sarcastic, Meena. What would you do if you found her?

I don't know. Ask her why.

Be honest.

I'd want to kill her.

That's understandable.

But there's no point because my parents are dead.

Being dead and being findable are not mutually exclusive.

So what would I be finding?

You're your mother's issue. She made you. So whoever she is, is also you.

I wouldn't know how to begin.

You don't have to know how. You're already deep in.

❖ ❖ ❖

When I open my eyes again, I'm in complete darkness. I forget where I am. I'm cool, damp, naked. Then I remember: I'm underfuckingwater. I feel in the dark for my bag, pull out one of my sunbits, and squeeze it. The gentle yellow light fills the pod. But outside there's nothing but blackness. I wish I had a mother. The mothered never get into situations like this.

I don't know how long I've slept. Anywhere from two to six hours. Enough for Geeta's arm to pass, I hope. The cord is at its end and the polymer plug is tight against the sphincter. I touch the skin of the pod, and it's much harder, which means I must be down a full seven meters.

A grid of silver shoots by. It was probably a school of fish. If I sit still and watch, my mind's eye makes a composite of what floats by, filling in what I can't see. What if I just stayed here and enjoyed the view of the abyss? One day, they'd find a cord attached to a sphere seven meters deep and pull it up and find my body curled in the fetal position. I'd chosen to lie down in the road.

Something big moves past and I jump back violently. Stupid. I could still split this thing open if the pressure's concentrated enough so I have to be fucking careful. I try to reconstruct what I saw: a dolphin or shark, maybe. I had an impression of bulk. It was not a fish.

I squeeze my sunbit again but it does nothing except reflect back the walls of the pod. I hold my hands around it to concentrate the beam outward. I sit still. And then again, something bulky passes by and this time it actually hits and indents the skin. I kneel into attack position, which doesn't strike me as illogical but rather simply that if this thing is going to make another pass, I have to be ready. I keep the sunbit trained into the darkness.

And then right in front of my face a handprint appears in the skin of the pod.

I scream.

But the handprint is gone, as soon as it appeared.

A hallucination from oxygen deprivation. It must be. I need

to get up to the surface because suddenly I feel like I'm in a black womb swarming with ghosts.

I reach up to take hold of the plug and encircle my other hand around it to push up against the sphincter at the same time. I pull the cord down and so pull the pod up. After a meter, my arms ache and I have to stop. I shake out my arms. I take a deep breath. I reposition the sunbit in my lap and grab hold of the cord again.

After sixty seconds I can see the water above me lighten. It looks blue, which is a good sign because it might mean the sun is out. I want to go quickly because I feel like I can't breathe even though I can.

A circle of white opens at the top of my pod. It's air. I stop myself from rending it open immediately. Instead I pull the pod up flush with the Trail so that it's hanging off of it like a bubble on the edge of a wand. Then, in my greatest feat yet, I pull myself and my bag up onto the Trail while still inside the pod like a fetus in an amniotic sac.

I peel the pod open with my thumbnail and climb out with my bag and set it down on the scale and crawl out naked into the wind. The clouds are ragged, low, and moving fast overhead. I take out my scroll to check that the cyclone is past (it is—spending itself against the Iranian coast now, only a Category 1) and then set it down on the scale while I pull the rest of the pod out of the sea. The sea is still choppy and the Trail is still bucking and the hinge nearest me snaps up and my scroll spins into the water.

Immediately I know it's gone.

I can't go after it. I have to attend to my desalinators, my kiln, and my pod, without which I would literally die.

So my scroll is gone.

I stick my knife blade-first into the scale so hard that it stays there. The gusts are lessening now, and there are patches of sunlight on the ocean. I can see them far away like oases.

◈ ◈ ◈

I search for my scroll so that I can make a list of what I've lost and then realize I don't have anything to make a list with.

I have to tick them off in my head, in order of threat to corporeal survival.

1. The ability to visualize where I am on a map. I still have my pozit, which can give a position and calculate the distance between two positions, like between here and Nariman Point. But it's a simple numerical display. It doesn't show whole maps.
2. Information on oncoming weather, e.g., cyclones. Now I have to prove my Keralite blood by intuiting all things maritime.
3. My Element Diary. Which seems like a juvenile exercise in this light.
4. My survival guides. I'll have to get by on what I remember and by what seasteaders tell me.
5. My equipment manuals. I'm glad I read the pod manual three times while I was underwater. As for the kiln manual and the solar plate manual and all the other manuals, they're gone.
6. My music and literature. I've lost everything of entertainment value, which I'd been considering my umbilical cord to sanity. No more Mahabharata or poetry of Kuta Sesay or essays of Reshmi West.

The last loss is the least threat to corporeal survival but it hurts the most. I'll have to make other connections to sanity. I'll have to work harder to take care of myself. I'll have to generate my own mother like a blow-up doll and make her tell me stories.

{ BOOK X }

Mariama

Shiro

The night we left for the Ethiopian border at last, you couldn't sleep. You whispered to me, pouring all your thoughts into me like I was a jug.

I'm not sure where we'll live, you said. We'll have to stay in a hostel and explore Addis for a few days, get a feel for the place. Piazza is supposed to be best, for character—but then there are all these new developments nearby, just outside the main city, and they have Internet and air conditioning. But then I keep reading that Bole Road is still the best place to get a flat. I have enough money for a few months. Then I'll have to find a job. Maybe in one of the art galleries or English-language bookstores.

I just liked listening to you talk, Yemaya. Your voice was fluid and deep, like the lowermost current of the ocean. It made me thirsty. I still felt terrible about what I'd said that had made you hit me, and so I kept looking for a way to bring us back together, to make us whole again.

You said, Will I actually be able to make a home? I'm only

twenty years old. What if I'm discriminated against? I look Oromo, and the Oromo and the Amhara have a bad history. Maybe it'll be different because I'm Wolof. I need to find Amharic language classes. Till then, I can get by on my English. I need to take care of myself.

I tried to wrap my arms around your body, but my arms weren't long enough. You rolled on your back and I climbed on top of you and laid on your chest, and tried to encircle my arms around so that they met underneath you.

Finally your eyes closed. You didn't lift your arms to hold me; they splayed out to either side. While you slept, you muttered Francis's name, but as much as that roused the jealousy of the kreen, I didn't wake you. I understood that it was my time to take care of you.

◈ ◈ ◈

We crossed into Ethiopia at Gallabat. I was clutching the railing and trying to memorize every detail, to understand with my own eyes what sort of place Ethiopia was, and how to distinguish it from all the other places I'd seen, but it was too late and I was too sleepy to make any real conclusions. Then I slept from Gallabat to Shihedi—I remember Shihedi only by the dim yellow lamplights that measured out my sleep—and from Shihedi on to Gonder.

You hardly slept at all. My body could sense that, because we had come to know each other's rhythms so well. When the trucks finally parked in a dusty lot, you were already sitting up, staring into space. Then you saw me and said, We're here, little girl.

Ethiopia!

Yes, you said. You weren't as excited as I thought you would be.

But I told myself it was because we weren't in Addis yet. We were first staying in Gonder, and then heading to Lalibela, and then finally to the capital city. Our long journey was almost over. I wanted it to be over but at the same time I wanted to relish every last moment of it.

It was almost dawn. Some of the drivers, still tense from the overnight drive, stayed behind to find food on the street and then sleep on the truck bed as usual. But Muhammed decided to rent a hotel room for the night, on account of wanting to rest his leg properly, and you said that we would also get a room. You said we deserved a special treat after so many weeks of sleeping on the truck.

You took my hand and we walked with Muhammed away from the lot and up to the town center. We had to move slowly because Muhammed was still using crutches. He told us he knew where to go; there was a hotel on the piazza with a beautiful rooftop restaurant that might be seating customers already.

I gripped your hand. The essential Ethiopian-ness I was trying so hard to discern from the truck was clearer to me here. I saw women covered in gauzy white fabrics, edged with deep jewel trim. Many of them looked different from us—their faces were colored lighter and yellowish, like mustard. Their noses were narrow and their lips were thin. Many of the women had dark blue tattoos of big crosses on their foreheads, or little blue crosses all along their jawlines. They didn't smile. I imagined myself as a grown woman and thought, This is my future: regal and fierce.

Muhammed was clearly glad to be back on his home soil. He pointed to this and that, proudly narrating his homeland. I think he mentioned the Battle of Adwa three times, how the Ethiopians beat back the Italians, and how Ethiopians alone among all Africans had never been conquered, never been colonized. He pointed to a thick stone wall along the road. That's the Royal Enclosure, he said. The castles where the great kings of Ethiopia ruled.

Do we have time to see it? you asked.

Yes, said Muhammed. We'll be here all day, leaving at dawn tomorrow.

But first you need to sleep, I said to you, touching your face.

You laughed. You were taken aback. How do you know me? you said. Are you the one taking care of me, now?

I nodded and buried my face in your side.

The manager made us wait on a padded white bench for half an hour before she was ready to seat us. Then she showed us to a beautiful table, wicker with spotless white cloth draped over it. After the waiter took Muhammed's crutches and laid them against a nearby pillar, we ordered food, like a little family again, except with Muhammed instead of Francis as "the man." I remember your being pleased that the restaurant took "cards" so that you wouldn't have to "change money." (It was years before I understood what all that meant.) The food arrived swiftly: a cup of fruit and yogurt, a plate stacked with gummy bread bent sideways, and a smoothie with four bands colored green, yellow, pink, and white.

Muhammed acted as if he were greatly impressed with my choices. He explained what each thing was: there were papaya, watermelon, and mango chunks in the fruit cup; the gummy bread was called a pancake, filled with hot guava jelly; and the smoothie was called a mix juice, with layers of avocado, mango, guava, and banana. You spooned little portions of each dish onto my plate and you gave me a straw to drink my mix juice, but I'd never used a straw before, so I sucked too hard and juice came out of my nose. Muhammed laughed, but it was a kind laugh. He wiped my nose for me.

After breakfast, I could see your feet dragging. I needed to get you to bed. When we got our room key, I led you by the hand down the hallway and into our room—huge, splendid, sparkling, like nothing I'd ever seen before. There was a clean bathroom with a shower and flushing toilet. A beautiful painting was on the wall, a portrait of a woman with dark blue crosses on her face, and a black rectangle on the opposite wall, which I thought might be a frame missing its painting, but later you told me it was a flatscreen for satellite television. I couldn't wait to explore everything in the room, but you lay down on the bed and asked me to be quiet so you could sleep. So I did. I sat in a big soft chair and watched you sleep. You said Francis's name only once this time. That was an improvement.

I was still trying to figure out how to make everything perfect, to make us whole again. We were almost there, but not quite. Before long, after all the breakfast sugar, I was asleep too.

❖   ❖   ❖

I slept even longer than you did. I slept right through the shower you took. When I woke up, you were clad only in white towels, and they didn't even cover all of you!

I hid my eyes and giggled.

What are you giggling at, little girl?

Nothing, I said.

You've never seen a naked woman?

I shook my head.

You were in a high, wild mood. You talked fast. You said, In Morocco, they have common baths called hamams, where all the women bathe together. It's so humane. Every society should have them because then, girls see women's bodies and how they take pride in them. Then they become proud of them, and not afraid.

It had never occurred to me that my body should be something I was afraid of. Something that felt fear, certainly—the kreen whined even when my attention wasn't focused on it—but not something I should be afraid of.

I'm not afraid! I said.

You narrowed your eyes at me. I went still. I understood that you were about to test me.

You took off both towels and stood before me naked. I gaped like a moonstruck goat. You were tall and broad-shouldered, with thin muscled arms and high teardrop breasts, and nipples darker than your skin; your waist was high, and your hips flowed down from it like the drape of a dress.

This is what a grown woman's body looks like, you said. You turned around and slapped your own bottom. I was too dumbstruck to giggle. Or maybe I was in religious awe, suspecting what I now know for certain!

You're pretty, I said.

You smiled and said Thank you, little girl.

And then it became clear to me what I should do, to make us truly whole again.

I pushed myself out of the chair and stood. I took off the plain shift I'd been given at the clinic. I climbed up onto the bed and laid down on my back.

You weren't looking at me. It wasn't how I wanted you to react. I had to be clearer.

Come here, I said.

Why? you said.

I have something to give you, I said.

Still not looking at me, you sat on the edge of the bed. What? you said.

I sat up and took your hand, and laid it over the place between my legs, and lay back down.

My golden meaning, I said, even though I didn't understand what that meant. I just knew you had to be the one I gave it to.

Your hand was light on my skin, but you didn't take it away.

You don't know what you're saying, Mariama.

I do, I said. I want you to have it. There's no one else I want.

You need to be older, you said. It's not for me to take, not even me.

But your voice was getting weaker.

No, I said. I say now.

A command had come into my voice. The kreen was speaking now. It seemed that I was the elder and you were the younger.

This can't be the way to heal, you said to yourself.

Yes it is, I said. We both need to be one and whole again.

How could you know, you said. How could you know.

Your hand became heavier, and then you curled one finger up into my body. I was young, so I thought that's as far as it could go. But your finger wriggled and pushed and made new room as it went and as it went it sucked the breath out of me. It felt like a stick of cayenne. I watched your shoulders rise and fall ten times and tried to breathe along with you. We both knew we had to wait, to count to ten, to make it real.

Then you withdrew and turned me on my side and hugged me from the back, while inside me, the kreen licked up the new flame.

❖ ❖ ❖

It was late in the afternoon when we set out for the Royal Enclosure, my hand in yours. Your mood was even higher and wilder, as if now that we were whole again, a single electric current was coursing through both our bodies.

When we were crossing the piazza we saw a woman stirring red stew in an iron pan. You spoke to her and gestured a lot, and laughed in a high, hysterical pitch I'd never heard from you before.

You turned to me and said, She's going to give us a bit of shiro! It's a kind of spicy bean paste. This will be your first real taste of Ethiopia!

The woman handed me a morsel wrapped in brown paper. I picked it up with my fingers, a flap of spongy bread soaked in red sauce, and ate it. It was mushy-sour-savory-spicy.

You like it?

I nodded vigorously. It tasted like what we had just done in the hotel room.

You gave the woman a bill and then we continued on our way. You babbled: If you like shiro, you're going to fit right in here. In Dakar there was an Ethiopian restaurant my friends and I used to spend time in. There was a whole circle of dancers and artists that stayed there for the coffee in the afternoon and the honey wine at night, which they call tej here, remember that, for hours on end, playing music or talking about politics. That's how I learned about Ethiopian dancing and music and jazz. Some of us wanted to go to Lagos or Johannesburg. But most of us talked about Addis, where the president spoke Hindi and wore a traditional Amharic dress to state meetings. There's a whole team of women devoted to spinning her dresses from the best cotton in the world, and three master embroiderers who make the edges, and after she was elected, the fashion shows in Dubai and Mumbai all showed Amharic dresses.

We arrived at the front gate of the Royal Enclosure. You paid for us both. We walked up the pebbled path under blooming hyacinth trees shooting up through the ruins. Birds had built nests on the tops of the pillars. We walked through banquet rooms, empty and echoing, with lizards scooting in the corners. We came into a grand hall with a vaulted ceiling, but the ceiling had crumbled and showed right through to the sky. There were doorways and stairways that led to nothing but air, and diamond holes that showed other castles, far away.

We wandered from ruin to ruin, quiet. Yemaya, I don't think I'd ever been so happy in my whole life, not even in Ouagadougou.

Whatever we had done in the hotel room, it'd worked. We were whole again.

When we returned to the hotel, we joined Muhammed, who was dining alone.

So, he said with obvious excitement, it looks like we'll be headed to Lalibela right in time for Timket.

Neither of us knew what that was.

It's the holiest day for the Ethiopian Church, he said. Lalibela has the biggest celebration of it. It's famous all over the world.

Is that a good thing or a bad thing? you asked.

It means more headaches, for where to park, where to eat, where to sleep, he said. But it's a very holy day for Christians. They hold mass baptisms with water hoses. I'll go and watch just for the show of it.

So we said we would go too.

Baptism

You were quiet the next day, as quiet as you had been excited the previous day. It felt like an anticlimax since I thought that, once we were in Ethiopia, and once we had become whole again, your mood would get better and stay that way all the time. How little I understood!

I followed our route on the map splayed on my lap. We were going south, around Lake Tana, which was a gigantic blotch in the middle of the country. Muhammed showed me the lake itself, far below us. At first I was confused—I couldn't see the other side, so I asked Muhammed if that was the ocean, if we'd made it all the way across to the other side of Africa. He said, No, but you'd be forgiven for thinking it is. It's a very big lake. A false ocean.

I found you to tell you what I'd just learned about Lake Tana.

I know, you said.

Do you think it's safe to swim in it?

I don't know much of anything anymore, you said.

What an answer! So I knew you were still in a quiet mood, so I didn't prod you further.

It was hard to keep my balance on the truck that day. We kept winding up and down hills, which was not a landscape I'd ever experienced before. I didn't know the land could be so bumpy, and not only bumpy, but sheared such that I could see land rearing up above me, or plunging away below. Now I know, of course, that we were driving down the outermost lip of the Great Rift Valley.

We passed through a town called Debre Tabor, but only to stop for fuel and snacks, as Muhammed wanted to push on through the night. I tugged on your hand and said, Let's go check and see if there are Indian sweets. You nodded and got up and we dismounted the truck and walked into town. It was twilight. By silent agreement, we went into the most modern-looking store we could find. It turned out they had a huge display of Indian sweets—the biggest selection I'd yet seen. They weren't even prepackaged. They were in tin pans, sitting in syrup, or wrapped in wax paper.

The clerk told you that there was an Indian community in Debre Tabor, and that one of the families made sweets to sell at the markets. Apparently Ethiopian sweets left something to be desired, so Indian sweets were filling the market niche.

Can we take one of each? I said.

Let me see how much money I have, you said. You rummaged in your bag, and then caught a glimpse of my face, which must have looked pathetic, because then you said, Of course we can get one of each.

We left the store with a yellow plastic bag filled with sweets. And when we got back on the road that night, you turned on your sirius so we could see what we were eating. I think it was that night that converted me to gulab jamun, Yemaya. They're best fried, so it's impossible to prepackage them. A fresh one tasted like heaven on earth. I finally agreed with you.

◈ ◈ ◈

I remember the drive to Lalibela only through dreams: that we were winding back and forth up a mountainside, ascending a road to heaven. When I woke, we were parked in a lot that sat at the edge of an abyss. The plain was a thousand meters down. My brain could not comprehend the distance. I'd dreamed the truth: we'd come to the doorstep of heaven.

You'd been out already. Before I even had my breakfast, you told me to look on the front seat of the truck where, inside a plastic bag, there was a small white dress made of cottony gauze, with deep blue borders and a blue cross embroidered on the front.

You told me to try it on. You held up your blanket while I changed behind it. I was happy to take off my old shift and put this new garment on. You knelt in front of me and showed me how to tie the matching sash around my waist, and then the matching headscarf around my hair. When you were done, you called Muhammed to look. He said I looked just like a little Amhara shepherdess. There were tears in your eyes. Looking back, Yemaya, now I know why.

The two of us set off into town alone. What a spectacle! The town itself was like something from another world, a village of round houses, high on the mountainside above that vast plain. And the mountainside was swarming like an anthill. We were two of thousands of people come to the city for Timket. Everywhere we turned, there were people, families and their donkeys and whole flocks of children running free. Almost everyone was wearing white, many of the women in dresses like mine.

We walked with the crowds because there seemed to be a direction to the flow. You were quiet again, but seemed serene. Now I know why you looked that way: you were preparing for what was to come. The sun broke through the clouds and fell on us hosts of white, rivers of pilgrims spilling from ledge to ledge, down into the ancient stone-cut city, into the trenches and churches.

You picked me up and carried me on your shoulders. I wrapped my legs around your back and kissed both of your cheeks and tasted tears. I knew you were as happy as I was. From this height, I could see again how high up we were. The rest of the earth was so far away! Cliffs and escarpments could only dimly be seen, in pale watery colors, across all that distance. I had trouble breathing because the air was so thin. I had to gulp it in.

We made a turn in the labyrinth. On the street ahead of us was a line of youths advancing, step by step, with bright golden faces, each arrayed in white, hunched and cupping their hands as if to catch water.

You turned your face up to me, and indeed, tears were streaming down your face. They're singing to you! you said. They're singing to Mary!

As they stepped forward, you stepped back. It was like a game. Like we were leading them. You turned to face forward and I twisted back, to make sure they were following us. I didn't speak their language but I could beckon. The youth followed. They were praising me, just like you said. They were calling my name.

We passed down into a crevice of rock that widened again to reveal an ocean of white. The procession of priests moved through it, toward us, carrying their jeweled crosses and fringed umbrellas and water hoses. The song of the youths swelled and merged with the song of the priests and then water rained down on us from above. The crowd pressed forward to receive the blessing. We were picked up by the crush of other people's bodies, lifted and carried, coming closer, to where a priest was swinging a hose, back and forth, mouth open in prayer. The spray hit me squarely on the fore-head. It was ice-cold and I shrieked and laughed and my brain felt numbed. I was baptized.

And then I realized I was no longer sitting on your shoulders! I was one leg down and one leg across the shoulder of a teenage boy who gave me a confused look.

I called your name. I crawled over people's heads, but that made them angry. I lost my balance and fell. A large woman seized me by the waist, carried me out like a sack of meal, and deposited me just beyond the press of people, where I wouldn't be crushed. She said a few stern words in a language I didn't understand and then went back in. I was alone.

I called your name. I turned around and around. But you were gone.

⦃ B◖·◻︎K XI ⦄

Meena

The Shallows

I consult my counselors about the handprint I saw underwater.
Their answers unfold in my mind like glotti text.

MUTHASHI: So you were hanging underwater during a
   cyclone. That is a stressful situation. And you were in
   an environment of strict sensory deprivation. I would
   be surprised if you hadn't hallucinated. You have been
   hallucinating already: the barefoot girl, the naked
   woman.
MOHINI: Consider it one of the chambers. A shocking one,
   a scary one, but just another chamber to pass through.
MUTHASHI: There are five stages of hallucination. The
   person experiencing hallucinations progresses from
   understanding their unreality to believing in their
   reality. And then that reality fuses with real reality,
   and the person cannot tell the difference.

What if one of the hallucinations is dangerous, and actually real, and I fail to deal with it?

MUTHASHI: I suppose that's a risk. Better to defend
yourself as a rule. You'll find out on a case-by-case
basis whether the threat is real.

But Muthashi, what qualifies something as real in the first place? You define it in the scientific sense: that which is observable, predictable, repeatable, and falsifiable. But so many phenomena are none of those things. Especially lived experience.

DILIP: Damn, girl, you're deep.

Dilip, shut up, you assfuck. I wish you were ten thousand times smarter than you turned out to be.

❖ ❖ ❖

In two nights, losing my scroll starts to feel like a blessing.

Didn't I want to lose context and find myself?

I have nothing to fall back on. Nothing to pull me out of the world I'm in. I have to learn to read stars instead of words. I have to let them write their meanings on my mind. This is what Mohini was trying to tell me: I'm passing through chambers. I have been, ever since I mounted the Trail, but now I'm aware of it and can move forward in a directed and conscious way. My scroll was a distraction.

My pozit tells me it's the first of November. On land I might be celebrating Diwali or, more accurately, scorning Diwali as a racist northern festival while Mohini celebrated it, teasing me that cultural phenomena are allowed to have multiple meanings for goodness' sake. So I would suffer myself to go to temple and light candles with her and be secretly delighted to do so. It was all a show. I loved accompanying her. I loved being seen with her.

❖ ❖ ❖

I remember less, now, of what came before. My mind used to travel through the same space, and at the same intervals, that my body traveled in. Now my mind only skips along the surface of the space my body travels in. Like a skipping stone.

❖ ❖ ❖

When the dawn comes, the light shows water colored pale turquoise and green. I might be over a reef, though the nearest shore I know is Oman, a few hundred kilometers north of me, according to my laminated map. I can see schools of psychedelic fish darting a zigzag pattern under my feet. I get out my fishing kit for the first time. There are lines, lures, and sections of a meter-long staff that have to be screwed together, with a hook on the end. It takes some experimentation to find the best position for holding the staff and then for spearing quickly and effectively. I always seem to strain a muscle group I hadn't been aware of before, and only discover via pain. But soon I have three small fish, all of which look innocuous.

I cut off their heads with my filet knife, slice and clean each of them, and put them on my solar plate to cook. I let the fat melt and then sprinkle on spices.

I eat sitting cross-legged as the sun comes up. Now is the difficult time—between dawn and mid-morning, when I used to read. Now I close my eyes and take long tours of places I know.

Muthashi's clinic. The house attached to it, where I grew up. The
university in Mumbai. Kochi. Kodaikanal. Madurai. Then I open
my eyes and stare at the skin of my pod, watching it breathe for me.

I talk to Mohini, who knows my moods, including the manic
ones. I've always had a gift for sounding sane when I feel insane
inside and she was familiar with that, too. I abused this gift. If I
was in conversation with someone I thought was intellectually in-
ferior, I took absurd positions and argued them with perfect equa-
nimity. Mohini would get upset when I did this. She didn't think
it was an admirable trait. I saw her point. The longer I was with
her, the more I noticed myself refraining from humiliating the less
intelligent.

Mohini was intelligent, though. She was brilliant. We had a
game we used to play called Distraction. The game was this. We'd
be having an intense, heated conversation about religion or politics or literature, and then without warning one of us would steer
the other (still conversing) to the bed. The steer-ee would have to
keep talking while the other performed erotic acts on her body.
So, I would be remonstrating the Indian Congress for their sanc-
timonious attitude toward the African middle class, whom they
essentially regard as a lower caste, though it's not polite to say so,
and Mohini would be passing her fingers over my lips and brushing her lips over my breasts. I had to keep talking or I "lost." Mohini, of course, would continue engaging with me, asking me why
I was ignoring the very real and cumulative influence of African
fundamentalists, and I'd have to respond. It was a doomed game
because nothing was at stake. Eventually one of us would break
and we would dive into bed. Or onto the table, or against the wall,
whatever surface presented itself for the feast. I once told her: Your
body is my shrine. This is where I perform my pujas. This is that
to which I attend.

She took this worship as her due. She was used to being beloved. She had a following by the time I met her, but she pointed out that I did too. I didn't remember what I looked like that night but she told me exactly: she noticed my extraordinary mouth, first, shaped like a cowrie shell, and that I was wearing a tight red tank top, tight jeans, brown military boots, a thick tangle of gold necklaces, and red and gold smears on my forehead. She thought I was Hindu. I am, somewhat. But I told her I'd taken to thumbing pastes and powders onto my forehead as an act of identification: culturally Hindu, even though God qua God was not really important to me, except as God manifested in my lovers and the emptiness left by my lovers. It was the only thing I knew how to do, being motherless, fatherless. I had made a religion of making presence out of absence.

When the morning comes, the water around me has turned amethyst. I can see fathoms and fathoms down, a violet sparkle devoid of any life. No fish, no algae, no floating flotilla of seaweed. I stop for the day. I lie down on my stomach. There's a flash of dark at the corner of my right eye. I turn just in time to see a small figure slip into the sea, feet-first. Another hallucination of the small naked woman.

Mohini, see, this is what I mean about my religion.

You say, Yes. Presence and absence are the same thing.

Memory Lane

To escape, I also retell myself stories of my life.

These stories take several nights, which in general have much less resolution now. They combine into mega-nights. I tip into an extended period of recalling past lovers and the extent of our affairs, one night per lover. I call this mega-night Memory Lane.

Initially it's because I start thinking of the first woman I ever slept with, Ajantha. She was eighteen. I was fourteen. She was my peer counselor at D. K. Soman International. It was a scene from a lesbian pulp comic. One night late at school at our counseling session we were sitting across from each other cross-legged and she leaned over as if to whisper something in my ear but instead she sucked on my earlobe. I remember my vagina made an actual noise, an un-glocking, because my labia got so swollen they unsealed. Ajantha heard it too and pressed her palm over my pants and things went on from there.

She was expelled once she was found out. But I caught something from her, an inclination to disregard norms, boundaries, appearances, already present because of my nonstandard upbringing, orphaned and all. And it was in the air because while I was growing up India was undergoing its third or fourth cultural revolution of the century and even twentysomethings were shocked at what teenagers were doing and teenagers looked at toddlers and wondered what cocktail of traditional and radical and appropriational they'd serve up one day. Mohini and her mother, Seeta, were at the vanguard, calmly accepting Mohini's trans identity and taking action at an early age, despite being lower middle class. But there was more. A whole new sector of the world population declared themselves transracial and sought genetic modification. At college I slept with a man who was undergoing treatment to change from Anglo to Desi features. Rafael aka Rahul. He was misguided.

He was one of a whole string of lovers at college. Having barely made it into IIT-Bombay and therefore fulfilled the Indian grandparent's wet dream, I got there and learned what I'd already known, that I didn't want to be a biofuel engineer, the vague vocation I'd named for my grandparents to placate them, and so I strapped on my goggles and went about destroying myself. People became flavors, collect all fifty. I was riding the wave of a new

sexual revolution where all known venereal disease was either in-
oculable by vaccine or curable by the full-spectrum nanobiotics
that came out when I was fifteen, and where all birth control was
perfect, administered via aadhaar at puberty in both women and
men that had to be deactivated if you wanted to get pregnant, a
triumph of international public health in the 2040s.

I ran in the small circle of fellow discontents at IIT-Bombay and
had slept with everyone by the end of the semester, even the hold-
outs I considered a challenge. I studied sex. Women, men, trans,
didn't matter. Skin was skin. I was shy and quiet and hated speaking, but I made up for it with genius for flesh. Sexual triumphs
were like trophies I piled up in a corner and stared at. Rebekah
punched a hole in the wall beside her bed. Krishna liked to slap my
face. Munny sneered like Elvis when he came. Sonali screamed so
loud that someone called campus police. Ying used a harness that
suspended her from the ceiling and I'd kneel below her and lick
her like honeysuckle. Mukesh and Thomas were gay but shared
a fetish for tag-teaming a woman. Bilal needed to be blindfolded
and deprived of breath. Ahmed was ticklish after orgasm. Kiran
wanted me to say dirty things to her in Malayalam while I fucked
her. I absorbed this fetish and demanded it of new lovers and so
over the course of three months got dirty talk in Cantonese, Tamil,
Bengali, Urdu, Gujarati, French, Korean, Russian, Portuguese,
Japanese, Maya, Arabic, and Zulu.

But in the second semester everything started catching up with
me. Munny and Ying started dating and shunned me. Krishna
started slapping harder than I wanted and so I kicked him out.
Ahmed was religiously repressed and stopped calling me back.

Meanwhile, though my first yoni-love Ajantha had been expelled from Soman International, she'd enrolled somewhere else
and gotten into IIT-Bombay two years ahead of me. She generally

tried to avoid me, but I was still in love with her. One night I saw her on Fashion Street in the company of a young man and I called out to her and she saw me but pretended not to, whereupon in my last greatest act of self-destructive conflagration, I started scream-ing in the middle of the street and beating my fists on the asphalt until I'd attracted a crowd, including a pharmacy attendant who drew me in and calmed me down and took care of me, for hours.

And then recognized me nine years later.

I reach the halfway point of the Trail, which is 1,610 kilome-ters. Everything will be easier from here. Everything is downhill, so to speak. And to mark the occasion there's a lump on the Trail that turns out to be a body.

Chorus

Mohini still talks to me, as do Muthashi and Muthashan. They're joined by others who all sit enthroned in a ring around my skull and advise me or comment upon the sights. Ajantha is there, and so are Ameem and Padma (though curiously not Rana), and Navid and Mohsen, and the two little girls I met on Marine Drive who directed me to Koliwada, and so are various people from my life whom I respect, and others I don't respect but think are sexy, like Anwar, Dilip, and Rafael aka Rahul. They're the comic relief.

They all say different things about the body I found on the Trail. It was human, certainly. I have no sense of bodily decay rate but I thought she might have died recently. No birds had disturbed her yet. Her face was turned south, away from me, and I didn't look. I went on quickly. The first time I thought maybe I should have lingered and determined cause of death, or pushed her over into the sea so that no other traveler would have to see her and suffer some kind of despair-attack that I miraculously had not, I was two kilometers away.

Muthashi-in-my-head again insists it was a stress hallucination.

MUTHASHI: Admittedly it's a more sinister one than
you've been having up to this point, but consider that
you've been on the Trail for almost eight weeks now,
and surely you're suffering from the Ganzfeld effect.
Extended sensory deprivation results in hallucinations,
including threatening ones.

ANWAR: Dear bitch!—

ELDER LITTLE GIRL: My amma says that people die on
the Trail all the time. They run out of food or they lose
their water filters.

YOUNGER LITTLE GIRL: Or they just lie down because
they don't want to live anymore.

DILIP: Have you ever thought about, like . . . *not living*?

AJANTHA: You've fucked some winners.

Ajantha, I realize that. But I'm asking you whether you think the body was real.

AJANTHA: Did you touch it?

Only with my foot.

AJANTHA: Was it solid?

Seemed so. Looked Desi. She was wearing a golden sari.

AJANTHA: Do you trust your senses?

Not really. Muthashi keeps bringing up the Ganzfeld effect. And I've seen other things I can't explain. Like the little naked woman and the handprint, when I was underwater. Those seem like textbook hallucinations. And the fact that anyone would wear a sari on the Trail is bizarre. I can't even walk in those things on land.

ANWAR: Fifty percent!—
AMEEM: I'd say it was probably another traveler from
      another seastead who got unlucky. Lost her filter
      somehow and didn't know whether she should crawl
      forward in the hopes of finding another seastead, or
      back, to reach one she knew was there, even though
      it was kilometers away. She must have tried to go
      forward because she knew it was her only chance.

But she could see all the ship crossings just like I am. She could have flagged one of them down and bartered for a new filter.

PADMA: Perhaps she was running from the law. Do you
      have enough fish?

I ate all the ones you gave me.

PADMA: Onions keep at sea. I should have given you
      onions.

I'm all right for food.

PADMA: You need a mother.

Fuck you.

AMMA: Molay, I'm right here.

I stop.
I say "What?" to the open air.
The voice unfolds in my head once again.

AMMA: Yes, molay, I'm here. And your father, too.

I take a few long breaths.
It's the first time I've ever heard that voice.
If I do something wrong it might scare it. It might go away again for good. So I don't say anything.
I just keep walking but not hoping. I can't allow myself to hope.
Then I realize my chest wounds are infected again and so I stop and reapply dressing.

◈ ◈ ◈

I don't know what day of the week it is anymore. When I try to figure it out I get snarled at the point where I started marking nights instead of days. It's either a Sunday or a Monday night.
The moon is waxing. I know that much.
Now that I'm halfway through I break my usual rule of not thinking more than two days ahead and start fantasizing about what the end of the Trail will look like. Whether it'll just end in the middle of the water, or extend all the way to a dock. Whether there will be police waiting for me, or a flotilla of happy Djiboutians. Whether the Djibouti shore is even swimmable, or if I'll get dashed against a breakwater.
I break another of my rules and start ideating suicide. It's not that I want to kill myself. It's just another thing to fantasize about when walking. I keep it light and comical. I didn't know my

mind was so inventive. It generates categories for different types of death, and even prizes for superlatives. Most Awful (guinea worm). Most Fun (heroin).

I tell all these things to Mohini-in-my-head, in our own language. We could begin a conversation one day and pick it up again four days later, keyed in by a word, both knowing exactly where we'd left off. As if we existed outside of time. As if parts of us were carrying on conversations on other planes, with other organs; not just the skin and the brain, but our livers and noses and kneecaps, conversing about whatever they converse about.

Now I tell her I've been thinking about what it would be like to not exist.

She says, Walking in front of a train would accomplish that.

I knew you'd bring that up someday.

It didn't work.

No. People pulled me over, which was lucky.

But still, you tried.

What's your point?

The act splits the soul. You're haunted by the part of you that tried.

I feel like I'm whole.

Oh, really? she says. Were you not at first followed by a barefoot girl?

⦃ BⵔⵔK XII ⦄

Mariama

Quit Ethiopia

Yemaya, you may not believe me, but even as a child, I immediately
understood what had happened. Lalibela really *was* the doorstep
to heaven, and at the moment of baptism, you had transcended,
dissolved in bliss, passed into the spirit world—whatever religious
image one could use, you had done it! And of course, I hadn't gone
with you because I wasn't ready. I had to understand you better.
In the days before we reached Lalibela, I had become proud, stub-
born, and—worst of all—possessive of you. But you belong to no
one, and come and go as you please, which is how you are able to
love so intensely. Over the long years, now, I have come to understand: you held nothing back from me: you revealed your golden
meaning right away. But I wasn't ready to receive it.

I certainly felt affection for other people over the years. I felt
gratitude to Muhammed, who was still at the trucks when I wandered back from Lalibela town, who asked me what had happened
and, when I said that you had disappeared, swore (which startled
me!) and shook his head. He didn't understand, as I did. But he

took me down through Addis, after all, and then finally to Hawassa, to the orphanage to which he had first promised me. I was
too old to be adopted, but I was happy about that, because I'd
already been on such a long journey and Ethiopia was my long-
promised home. I didn't want to go anywhere else. Muhammed
went back to his wife and his daughters, Fatima and Rahel, and
he came to visit me once a month until I turned twelve and then he
told me he didn't feel it was appropriate anymore. I heard he died
from brain cancer a few years later.

I felt affection for the nuns who ran my orphanage, Sisters of
Mercy Home for Children in Hawassa. I never misbehaved. The
nuns noticed that I did all my assigned tasks with quietness and
diligence because everything I did, I secretly did for you. They
put me in charge of the library. We had such an odd assortment
of books! There were pulpy comic books in Amharic, and dictio-
naries of Hindi and Mandarin, and flat hard squares of Japanese
picture books showing albino children playing with cats. I was in
charge of keeping records on the computer. With the help of the
nuns, and other tutors and volunteers, I built on the Amharic that
Francis had taught me. It was difficult at the beginning—and the
other children called me Ghana Gorilla—but they left me alone
once I commanded them to, in the voice of the kreen.

The kreen never went away. I had become used to its presence
during our odyssey across the Sahara, and now that I was safely
in residence at my destination, the kreen took up permanent residence in my chest. It always hurt a little, true, but only as a faint
soreness. And it was a source of power when I needed it to be.

During the years of managing the library, I tried learning
other languages in addition to Amharic. I memorized other alpha-
bets, each of which had a distinctive look. Mandarin looked like
ten thousand tiny houses. Hindi looked like the curls of grapevines
hanging down from a trellis. Whereas Amharic, now my adopted

mother tongue, looked like naked desert trees reaching from earth to sky.

In school, a frequent assignment was to compose hymns and psalms. I got good at them, and once I even won a national prize in the age-ten-to-twelve category, and got to read my poem in Addis with the minister of education sitting right behind me, to five hundred people in an auditorium as well as millions of people across the country who had tuned in on their radios and computers and televisions to watch the newly minted, first-annual Pan-Ethiopian Pageant. I even won ten thousand birr, which the nuns helped me put into a savings account. After I won the prize, I kept composing poems, to Jesus, or Mary, or God—but to me, the golden meaning lay underneath; which is, I was praising you all along.

So there was none that I loved as I love you.

But I must confess myself. Yemaya, you know all that is within my heart. I know you've been watching me. I was young, only twenty years old, the age you were when you rose to heaven, studying political science at the university on a scholarship sponsored by the Chinese government, and active in the new anti-Indian ARAP Party. See? I had always remembered what you'd said to me: *You'll become educated and you'll be one of the ones to fight back.*

But also, I had begun to look elsewhere for comfort and meaning without even realizing it. It hurts to admit this to you, but I'd begun to wonder whether you weren't just a girlish fantasy. The strange thing is, Gabriel appeared to me in Addis exactly the way you did in Dakar, and on Timket, no less. So I was deceived.

On that particular day, I was standing at the top of the steps of the university library, waiting for a student demonstration to start. We'd begun to hold them every weekend in the run-up to that year's election, the first election in which ARAP might have a chance, now that the UN had cracked down on election transparency because it didn't need Ethiopia's help in the region since the dawns of oil in Somalia, solar in Sudan, and hydro in Kenya. We wanted to unseat the ruling Pan-Ethiopian Party, which had done great good by uniting Ethiopia to unseat the EPRDF in 2025, but retained the EPRDF's too-friendly relations with foreign investors.

That day, we were to march from the library steps to Sidist Kilo, where we would circle the roundabout once, stopping traffic; then down Entoto Avenue to Arat Kilo, where we would circle again; then all the way down to Meskel Square (we would be gathering crowds along the way, but especially at Meskel), and then down Bole Road to Embassy Row, where the Indian embassy sat behind high iron fences, secured with a laser perimeter and shards of broken glass glued to the ramparts. We were marching to kick out Indian farmers who had bought land from our government in the 2010s at cheap prices, not to grow food for Ethiopians, but for Indians. Activists had posted pictures of the ships that departed from Djibouti City, heavy with grain, while Ethiopian children still starved waiting for international aid. Anti-foreigner feeling was swelling across the country; indeed, across all of North Africa. So it was all the more remarkable that, that day, while I was standing at the top of the library steps waiting for my fellow students, I saw a young Indian man from a very long way off, who made straight for me as if led on a path by the divine, carrying a handmade sign that read QUIT ETHIOPIA.

He stopped at the foot of the steps and looked up at me. I'd noticed that I had this power, to silence people, to stop them in their tracks. I think it was the kreen, looking out through my eyes even when it wasn't speaking with my tongue. But though this young Indian had stopped, he stared right back at me as if he knew he had power to match my own, a power of joy. He was golden. He glowed. I don't know how else to describe it. He said,

Salaam-nesh!—yikerta?—meuche . . . meutash?

I answered in Amharic: I came about ten minutes ago. I'm early.

Ishi, ishi, he said. Ke Hend naw . . . yemeta- . . . Hend neng.

I can see that, I said in Hindi. You have quite the accent.

He seemed relieved to not have to speak Amharic. Is this where we're gathering for the march? he said.

Yes, I said. How did you hear about it?

The student newsfeed, he said.

Are you a student here?

No, he said. He had come a few steps farther up now, and we never broke eye contact. He continued, I'm a resident at the medical school. I work at Our Lady of Entoto.

I noticed that he seemed eager to please me, to win approval from me, even though he himself was (I could tell on sight) never the sort who would need to seek approval. He had dark golden skin and thick smears of eyebrow, his glossy hair was pulled back in a messy ponytail, and his earlobes were long and round like a Buddha's. He stood, waiting for me to say something, wavering slightly in place.

So where are you from? I said. Delhi? Mumbai?

Keralam in the deep south, he said. It's God's Own Country.

Why is it God's Own Country?

He had not expected to be questioned on this. He stammered to justify himself. Well, that's what the Brits called it, he said. But they were right. It's very beautiful. It's green and lush and full of colors and spices and rivers.

He could see that I remained unconvinced.

I said, I think Ethiopia is God's Own Country.

Tell me why you think that! he said, boyish, eager, open.

Human civilization began here, I said. In the north of the country is the home of Dinkenesh.

You mean Lucy, he said.

Her name is Dinkenesh. It means "You are wonderful."

Understood, he said. Maybe you'll take me to see her someday?

I smiled slightly.

He asked me, then, if he could approach.

I nodded yes and sat down on the steps.

He climbed the few remaining steps and sat down next to me.

"Quit Ethiopia"? I said. That's bold.

I thought it would lend legitimacy to the cause, he said.

You think we need legitimacy?

That's not what I meant, he said. (Oh, Yemaya, he was trying so hard to impress me, to communicate his good intentions effectively, to not embarrass himself.) He said, I meant, in the eyes of the Indian government. They've become so arrogant. They think that, because we're the most populous nation on Earth, that we're entitled to seize whatever land is necessary in order to feed all our people.

I nodded. It was a beautiful, clear day in the dry season. The hyacinth trees were budding all over the city.

So what do you study? he said.

Political science, I said. And some religion.

Religion and culture are one and the same in Ethiopia, no?

That's changing. Are they not also in India?

That's changing too, he said.

What are you?

Catholic mother, Hindu father, he said. That's why my name is Ramachandran Gabriel. I celebrate both and practice neither!

He laughed at himself. Then he asked, What are you?

It was always difficult for me to answer that question, Yemaya, because my religion was you. I had never felt anything more true or perfect than the time during which you walked on this earth. But how could I explain that to a stranger? That was *my* golden meaning, my semena werk, my true religion—and no one else knew it. No one, yet, had been worthy of knowing.

So instead I said, I'm a student of religion.

(Which was also true.)

He understood my subtext and dropped the line of questioning.

Thank you for speaking Hindi, he said. My Amharic is still terrible.

How long have you been here?

Only two weeks, he said. I just finished medical school. And then I go to Ayurveda school. But before that, I wanted to see the world. I wanted to help. In some way. In as many ways as I could.

So you're carrying a sign that says QUIT ETHIOPIA through the streets of Addis Ababa.

Do you think its meaning will be understood?

Well enough, by those who need to. Indian nationalists in India, certainly.

Do you think ARAP has a chance of winning?

Sure. As long as Somalia stays quiet and the PEP doesn't whip up an emergency requiring martial law.

PEP could whip up an emergency involving Somalia, he said.

I gave him a Look.

Then he tried to guess at my ethnicity. He said, you look Oromo, but your hair is done in Tigrayan style, and you wear an old-fashioned Amhara dress.

(This was true. I was one of the activists reclaiming native Ethiopian fashion, which meant reimaginings of traditional dresses—white cotton with bright embroidered edges, just like the one you had bought me in Lalibela. Once I outgrew it, I wore it as a headwrap. See this cloth I carry? This is the very last bit of it!)

I didn't tell him what I "was," but only shook my head whenever he was wrong. So no, I was not Tigrayan, nor Amhara, nor

Oromo. I was not Somali or Harari or Eritrean or Dinka. I was content to remain a mystery to him. In my own heart, I didn't identify with any tribe; I only knew I belonged to you.

We stayed in a loose orbit that entire day. We marched together. We initiated slogans and heard them spread through the crowd. We arrived at the Indian embassy, which had been anticipating us; they had sent servants to meet us at the gate, to serve ladoos. We did not expect that! We didn't know whether to eat them (as Ethiopians are, above all, a polite people) or throw them against the stucco walls of the embassy (as Ethiopians are, above all, a proud people). So we refused them and then chanted for a few hours. The media came. Dispatches and photos of the event were posted all over the world. We made Al Jazeera. Gabriel's sign, QUIT ETHIOPIA, made it onto the front page of the *Times of India*.

Darkness had fallen by the time the crowd dispersed. I saw the organizers shaking hands with individual protestors, slapping them on their backs, kissing cheeks. The march had gone well. We were dispersing back into the city. Gabriel said to me, Is there any seafood here? It's like mother's milk in Keralam. I miss the ocean.

I felt a deep yearning. It had been so long since I'd thought of the ocean, the place you call home.

So do I, I said.

Have you ever seen the ocean? he said.

Yes.

(I could tell he was filing this information away, so as to better guess my origins, later.)

Instead he asked again, So is there seafood in Addis?

There's certainly fish, I said. Come with me. I know where to take you.

The restaurant would have been hard for him to find, as a ferenji. Only locals knew about it. We were seated at a traditional mesob, a woven table shaped like a chalice. A puffy golden lamp hung overhead. He was the only ferenji in the house and a few people stared. I ordered for us: two whole tilapia, grilled, from Lake Ziway. When the food came, he rolled up his sleeve and hunched over, his left arm propped on his knee. Eating was serious business to him. He turned the fish over once, then twice, like a dog ensuring his treat met muster, and then began to pull white flesh from the bones. He was adept with his hands. He had elegant, muscled fingers.

After a few mouthfuls to sate his hunger, he asked if it was bad for me to be seen like this: alone in the presence of a foreign man. He'd read that Ethiopian women seen in public with ferenjis were assumed to be prostitutes. I told him that attitudes had changed drastically, especially in Addis, and that I also didn't care what people thought. Impulsively I added, I've always moved lightly on the earth. Maybe a centimeter above it.

Ninety-nine people would have ignored such a comment because it was too strange for common speech, especially between near-strangers. But not Gabriel. He just nodded, as if he knew what I meant.

This is the moment, Yemaya, when I began to trust him.

When we were done with our fish, and nothing but greasy piles of bones remained, I ordered buna for us. Black, for me. I asked him what he liked; he ordered a macchiato.

I said, You like cream and sugar.

He said, I'm a self-respecting Indian man.

So I asked him to tell me more about himself. About his country. About what India was like. His feelings on Eritrea ("Let them be"). How many languages he spoke (five: Malayalam, Hindi, Tamil, Kannada, English). How old he was (twenty-one, one year older than me). How he liked Ethiopia ("fascinating"). Where else

he'd been in Ethiopia (only Ambo so far, on a trip with the other
medical residents, to bathe in the hot springs). What caste he belonged to (Brahmin mother, on her father's side; Kshatriya father).
What kind of music he liked.

He liked Ethiopian jazz. He had real vinyl records and a record player, brought all the way from India in a trunk. He'd been
combing the stores for pre-Derg records. Most had already been
bought by foreign dealers who then sold them to collectors abroad
for huge sums of money, but he'd found six so far. He intended to
host a listening party at his flat for his fellow Indian residents and
their fellow Ethiopian clinicians, and serve chaat, Indian street
food. He invited me. I accepted.

See how well I fit in, Yemaya? It was all a bit of a game to me.
This person Gabriel could never know me the way you knew me,
I thought; and so in the meantime, I would humor him. I would
humor myself, even. I would pretend that I was a normal young
Ethiopian woman, orphaned but blessed, and ambitious. Foreign
scholars from all over the world were interested in the fledgling,
real, post-EPRDF Ethiopian democracy. In fact, I was offered a
fellowship and could have skimmed right out of the country, but I
turned it down to study at Addis Ababa University. I felt invested
in Ethiopia and wanted to stay, but I admit that the real reason I
turned them down was that I was afraid of leaving the country at
all, in case you chose to come back. I didn't want to miss you.

And even though I began sharing my heart with Gabriel, I
don't think he ever really knew me. He never watched over me and
saw everything I did, as you did. There was the time—I'm sure
you must have seen it—when I killed that man who was raping my
neighbor. I had just started at the university and came back to my
little flat near Tewodros Square. I heard a strangled scream from
behind one of the doors and, my heart beating loud, tiptoed along

the corridor to discern which flat it was coming from. I heard a man yell back. This was a normal part of city life—a city man bringing his village wife into the city and seven kinds of hell ensuing. The more I listened to the screaming, the lighter I felt, the more free. When the woman's screams reached a sustained pitch I knocked down the door with my shoulder. It was as if matter had become immaterial. I came in through the kitchen and the first thing I saw was a scissors, used for cutting meat from bone, lying in the sink. I went through the kitchen to the living room to the bedroom and there it all was, exactly as I'd pre-seen it in my mind's eye before rounding the corner, a man pressing his hands into a woman's back while she struggled to get out from beneath him. His pants were down and her skirt was up. He turned too slow; he didn't see me coming at all. He wore a black-and-white checkered shirt. He was unprepared. Jumping on him and stabbing him through the throat was one fluid motion. I kept the scissors there and he kept clutching at them, trying to pull them out, but it was like a contest of wills, and I pulled them out and drove them in again. Finally his hands stopped clutching and he relaxed. I had stopped him! I felt like I could do anything. I could run a race. I could fly from Oromia to the Simien Mountains. I could alight on mountain peaks, and find the Ark of the Covenant, and the True Cross, and Dinkenesh's grave. I could find them all in one day. In that moment, I knew where they were.

Then I heard a bird sing. The call and answer.

Nhoo-nhoo? Nho-no-no.

Nhoo-nhoo? Nho-no-no.

I remembered that I'd needed to get rice on the way home from the theater. Had I remembered? Yes, I remembered buying it. Indian jasmine white extra-long-grain. It was in my backpack. Where did I last have my backpack? It was in the corridor.

That was when the sweet buzzing in the back of my mind broke into its component pieces, and became the cadences of a human voice.

I turned to face the woman who was huddled in the corner with her face in her hands.

He was hurting you, I said, not as a question.

The woman kept crying as if I'd said nothing. I recognized her. I'd seen her in the elevator before. She always wore a mustard-colored shawl over her Western clothes.

I tossed the scissors toward her. They left a smear of blood on the tile and came to a stop at her feet.

Say it was self-defense, I said. His pants are down. They'll believe you.

I walked out of the bedroom and stopped in the kitchen. I washed my hands. I used the spray fixture to make sure I got every spot until all the water ran clear down the drain. That's when I noticed the orange rinds and the waterlogged garlic. She'd been preparing a meal. I thought of cleaning it up for her but then decided to leave it be. I stepped out of the flat and pulled the door shut behind me until it clicked. I picked up my backpack where I'd dropped it.

I went back to my own apartment. I felt so relaxed, sweating, cool. I lay down on my couch. I pulled a blanket over myself. I could feel the buses rumbling on the street below. Ever since childhood, I could only sleep if there was a tremor underfoot, like the hum of our truck on the desert road. I fell into a deep sleep. In my dream, I was trading gursha with the man I'd just killed. He was still wearing the black-and-white checkered shirt. He held up a morsel of kitfo wrapped in injera, all of it soaked in red berbere sauce, and the bite was delicious, the spongy bread and the striations of lean beef muscle. I did the same for him. He was laughing, eyes sparkling, though his teeth were all red from the sauce.

Medhane Alem

Gabriel's flat was in a high-rise on Medhane Alem. It was located just a block from the new 3-D multiplex and galleria, so before the listening party, I went to a café called New Sheba on the highest floor of the galleria, where I could look out the windows and down onto the roof of the cathedral. Women wrapped in white were strolling the grounds far below, small as ants to my eye. I ordered a mix juice and read a little about Kerala, putting aside my prejudices, for the moment, about India as a whole. I learned that Kerala was the only freely elected communist government in India, and had been for decades. That it was a green and wet country, even more so than Senegal or Cameroon. That everyone could read and write. That women made up over half of its local and state legislatures. That queer people were free and protected by the government. All of these things made me think well of Gabriel. I reminded myself again that my quarrel was not with Indian people, but the Indian government, and more immediately the Ethiopian government. I had no contest with Gabriel or his friends I was about to meet.

I wanted to be on time to make it to Gabriel's place. I didn't know how Indians regarded time; I thought it safe to be punctual as per Western custom. His building was sleek and modern, with brown glass paneling and bronze beams, Africa Nouveau–style. There was a man in a garnet uniform guarding the front door. He greeted me in Amharic and called the elevator for me. He asked if I was a maid for a family in the building. I told him no, I was seeing a friend. Ishi, he said. He seemed to have drawn his own conclusions: that I was a maid who was lying about being a maid.

I took the elevator to the twelfth floor. Gabriel's flat was at the end of the hallway. When he opened the door, delicious warm

aromas flooded out. He looked handsome in a white linen shirt and
a blue dhoti tied around his hips. A woman's voice called from the
kitchen in Hindi, Is somebody here?

Gabriel called back, It's Mariama from the march!

Oooh, Mariama! I want to meet her!

A woman emerged from the kitchen. She was very tall, almost
taller than Gabriel, queenly and curvy. She looked like a doll of a
classical Hindu dancer. She wore dark-pink salwar kameez, the
scarf fluttering behind her like two wings. When she offered her
hand, a dozen gold bangles rang like chimes.

Meena Mehta, she said. I'm pleased to meet you. Rama has told
me a lot about you.

I shook her hand and said, Rama?

She calls me Ramachandran, even though it's my father's name,
he said. But especially in Ethiopia I go by Gabriel, to blend in
better.

Oh yes you blend right in, I said.

Meena laughed loudly and Gabriel's golden skin darkened. I
regretted the joke, thinking, Ethiopians have a morose sense of
humor and maybe Indians don't.

Meena said, Please excuse me, the pakoras are frying. She
turned and her long silky hair swished behind her, like a waterfall
rippling.

Gabriel asked if I would like a drink. I asked for water. He
returned with a bottle of Nordi, expensive Norwegian water, and
a filigree-etched glass filled with ice. He invited me to sit on piles
of beautiful pillows, expensive embroidered ones that I could tell
were all from the same stretch of the Women's Market, Shamanade,
north of Sidist Kilo. The poor fool must have been browbeaten by
those women. I wondered how he'd gotten all those pillows home.
Didn't they bargain in India? Could he not say no to a woman? I
decided that he must have a strong mother.

He asked me how I was. I replied that I was well. He seemed anxious. He launched into a catalogue of things he'd been thinking about since our last meeting. He could barely formulate one thought before he was on to the next. Immediately we were on intimate terms. He wanted to know the name of the restaurant I'd taken him to; he believed it was enchanted, because it was the best meal he'd yet had in Ethiopia, and the tilapia we'd eaten had spoken to him in his dreams. He wanted to know whether I agreed with Worknesh Gebremariam, the ARAP deputy Speaker who believed that all foreigners, even students and other so-called goodwill ambassadors, should leave the country for the time being. He wanted to know why Ethiopia, like India, had had a particularly hard time dealing with religious and ethnic pluralism; or whether he was equating the situations of two countries that were actually very different. He said that India was called Karma Bhooma—the Land of Experience—because in India, everything that could happen under the sun had already happened. But *he* felt that Ethiopia was the true Karma Bhooma.

Why? I asked.

Because humanity began here, he said. Like you said, Dinkenesh walked this earth. You convinced me.

He was passionate, even a little wild. He was drinking tej from a slim-stemmed glass.

It's the womb of the Earth, he continued. The Great Rift Valley is like the two legs of the mother goddess, opening.

Upon hearing that, Meena admonished him from the kitchen. He looked into his wine.

But I thought it was a lovely image. I smiled at him and asked if he had yet seen Dinkenesh.

No, he said, sitting up and looking at me intensely. Will you take me?

I said I would. See, Yemaya, I had already been to visit

Dinkenesh many times. The first time I saw her, I was on a chap-
eroned trip with the other students who had won the national poetry contest. I was eleven years old. Our guide was named Elyas,
who was a great storyteller. He jumped up and down and waved
his arms and did different voices to make us laugh. When we entered the room where Dinkenesh was kept, I was at the back of
the group. Elyas said that Dinkenesh had been found by a team
of French, British, and American scientists. They had missed her
burial place over and over again, and it was only a hunch of a
hunch that led them to see an arm bone protruding from the earth.
Elyas reenacted their amazement in French, British, and American accents that made us all giggle.

MON DIEU!

BLIMEY, OLD CHAP!

WELL, I'LL BE DAMNED!

Finally the group shuffled into the next gallery, and I lingered
to get Dinkenesh all to myself. I remembered everything you'd
told me about her, about her being our mother's mother's mother's
mother. I looked up into her skull holes. And they reminded me
of something I hadn't thought about in ages: the girl in the road,
with black wings, whom I'd spoken to after I'd been thrown from
the truck, who turned out to be just a dead body after all. I wondered whether that girl would one day be discovered too, millions
of years from now, bones and cloth preserved, her skeleton recon-
structed and placed in a glass box, her skull tilted to one side, just
as it was when she questioned me, What is your name?

Elyas noticed me lingering and called to me. Don't stand there,
he said, She'll hypnotize you! You'll go running out into the desert
and never return!

The other children laughed. I returned to the group, feeling
embarrassed.

But since then, I'd gone back to visit her many times. Whenever I visited Addis for any reason—to minister with the nuns, to read one of my poems, or to interview at the university—I stopped by and said hello. I watched other tourists come in and comment on her. They were Chinese, Indian, and South African. There were even some Americans, who I could tell by their angular pronunciation of English, every morpheme at a right angle to the previous. They said things like:

She's smaller than I thought she'd be.

Lucy in the Sky with Diamonds.

Look at the way her wrists dangle.

Just a blues brotha, walkin' down the street.

I listened to them until they noticed me in the corner, watching them with the eyes of the kreen. I made them nervous. They'd apologize and exit quickly.

I was the first of Gabriel's friends to arrive at the listening party. Then more guests began pushing the doorbell. There were only two other Ethiopians who came, both men, Dawit and Haile; the rest were Indian. We Ethiopians clumped together. We all spoke English, though I spoke it better than the other two, and they soon looked isolated and impatient as the Indians chattered on in English. English was the lingua franca for the Indians, who spoke dozens of languages, each with its own heritage and pride, such that no speaker of any one Indian language would accept another Indian language as the Indian lingua franca, so English it was.

Meena placed seven steaming platters and a stack of ceramic plates on the table. I watched the Indians for clues on how to eat. They first spooned chaat onto their plates, then bent forward over it, engrossed in eating (much like Gabriel had behaved with the tilapia) or sat back against the pillows. I was relieved to see that they, too, ate with their right hands. They molded the food into bell shapes and then bent down to shorten the trip from hand to mouth.

Meena saw that my bells were falling apart. She said, Make sure you have enough sauce to hold it together. A few of the other Indians lifted their heads to take note of my incompetence. I felt anger at being called out. But I made myself say thank you because I didn't want to be a rude guest.

One of Gabriel's Indian friends admonished him to put on some music while we were eating. Gabriel said, Of course, and got up immediately, abandoning his plate, and went to the corner, where he crouched by the record player. I thought this marked him a good host, the sign of a good man. He straightened up from the record player and I recognized the voice of Bizunesh Bekele warbling from the speakers. He returned to his place slower than he had left it, already lost in the music. His eyes gazed inward and saw nothing. When he ate again, he ate slower.

I watched him out of the corner of my eye. I noticed everything about him. I'm much older, now, Yemaya, and I know my folly; but when I was twenty years old, he was such a delicious mystery to me! I noticed the way his collarbone rose like a wave in his skin. How broad his shoulders were, and the round muscles of his calves. His feet were large. I could see his toes from where I sat on my pillows. Each toe was distinct and articulated. This was a man who had spent his life barefoot.

In turn, Meena was watching me. As soon as I met her eye, she looked down at her food. There was something I disliked about her, something I mistrusted. She was a beautiful woman, arrogant and fierce and, I could tell, used to getting her way. She was wealthy, probably Brahmin. She had grown up doted upon by her father, fighting with her mother. She had never experienced any kind of hardship. She had never known anything like the kreen.

The purpose of the listening party was not only to enjoy and appreciate Ethiopian music, but for the Indians to discuss their lives here. I could tell my opinion was valuable, and that Gabriel knew I would impress people with my laconic answers, after each of which Gabriel would smile at me as if I'd said the most brilliant thing in the world. His friends looked back and forth from him to me, and smirked.

Meanwhile, Meena acted out. She announced strong opinions. She dropped a serving spoon with a loud clatter and didn't apologize. I felt smug because I suspected she had feelings for Gabriel, whose attention was on me, instead.

Forgive me, Yemaya, I didn't know what I was doing.

{ B□□K XIII }

Meena

Semena Werk

I hear a shot and see an explosion on the surface of the water.

I drop down. Then I hear a voice yelling from far away and my glotti barely picks it up.

ENGLISH: Who are you?

A woman's voice, not friendly. "Durga," I yell back.

ENGLISH: What do you want?

I default to the science-fiction classic. "I come in peace," I yell back.

ENGLISH: Stay where you are. Rahel, guard the other side.

I keep my head tilted to the side to demonstrate docility. These people have firearms, Mohini. I don't want to piss them off. I feel thumps on the scales until someone's shadow crosses my body. The woman's voice calls back to her companion,

 OROMIFA: She's not the one we saw. She's much bigger.

If they ever lower their firearms, I'll have to ask what she's talking about.

She addresses me again.

ENGLISH: What do you speak?

"I speak English," I say, "Hindi, Malayalam, and some Marathi."

She switches to Hindi. "You can get up now," she says. "Move slowly. Hands on your head."

I get to my feet and get a look at her. The first thing I notice is that she's holding a dart gun. Probably loaded with sedative or something. How do I know that? Action movies. That's what this is: I've walked onto the set of an action movie. This woman has a great costume. She's dressed in tattered blue fatigues. Her hair is shaved close. Her skin is as dark as mine, but with yellow under-tones instead of red.

She's doing the same racial assessment of me. "Indian?" she asks.

I remember to nod instead of shake my head. Then I remember: *Oromifa*. It's one of the languages of Ethiopia. Fuck.

She gestures forward with her dart gun. "You first," she says.

Now I can see her companion, Rahel, twenty scales away, with short straightened hair, also dressed in blue fatigues, holding a rifle and slouched to one side. I'm surprised she didn't also have a ciga-rette dangling from the corner of her mouth. The costume depart-ment did a great job. They look like a pair of Phoolan Devis. They bring me up alongside their set, which looks like a dinghy moored to the Trail and rigged with an all-weather canopy. I hadn't even seen it while walking. I must have been too much in my own head, talking to you, Mohini. I can see a console inside. And there's an antenna six meters high poking up out of the canopy.

"Drop your bag, please," says Rahel.

I do so. "Can you tell me what you're going to do?"

"No."

"Am I being robbed?"

They don't answer.

I can feel the dart gun behind my back, like a finger pointing at my spine. I feel defiant and sassy in spite of, or maybe because of, the danger. This is all being filmed and so I need to play the part of the rogue hero.

Finally Rahel looks up at her companion. "Nothing," she says. "She's just a backpacker."

"Is that what you are, a backpacker?" the other woman says.

"Can you tell me who you are first?"

"Fatima."

Classification of stratum complete: Ethiopian, Oromo, Muslim. "Okay, Fatima. Yes. I'm a backpacker."

"You come from where?"

"Southern India."

"And you're doing this for fun?"

I want to tell them it's because I'm on pilgrimage to visit the city where a fucking Ethiopian woman murdered my parents.

"I wouldn't call it fun."

"What would you call it?"

"Right now, honestly, a waste of time."

"What do you know about Ethiopia?"

This seems like a trap. "That's a big question."

"Ethiopian politics."

"I know ARAP got beat in the last election."

"Rigged. Like every single one since Haile Selassie," says Fatima.

"I'm sorry," I say. And immediately I know it's the wrong thing to say. Rahel and Fatima exchange looks and roll their eyes. But I'm tired of holding my hands on my head and so I say my next line and hope it lands well. "My parents lived in Ethiopia," I say. "That's where I was born."

"What did your parents do? Farm to feed Indian mouths?"

"They were doctors," I say. "They worked at a clinic near Meganagna."

Whatever that name is, it seems to touch them. Their shoulders drop. I'm glad I retained it from the articles.

Rahel says to Fatima,

 OROMIFA: Our Lady of Entoto Hospital.

After a few moments Fatima says, "You can put down your hands."

"Thank you," I say, though I don't mean it.

The two women are awkward now. Neither of their guns is pointed at me anymore. They're both looking toward the dinghy. Now the first source of tension in this scene is dissipated and so I have to create the next one. The director will be pleased with my improvisation.

"What's in there?" I ask.

Rahel looks to Fatima, who seems to be in charge of information dissemination.

"Semena Werk," she says, and my glotti says:

AMHARIC: Golden meaning

The heroine knows that phrase, of course, but never knew its meaning.

"I don't understand," I say.

"It's the name of our radio program. We broadcast from here."

So Semena Werk in India has a pirate radio station on the high seas, Mohini! What a good subject for film. "Why?"

"Banned in Ethiopia. Unwelcome in India."

"Why do you care about India?"

"There are not a few of our countrypeople in India now," says Rahel.

Fatima sits on the edge of the dinghy. "Indo-Ethiopians get their news from us."

"Where do you get your news?"

"Our contacts on the ground. You've heard of Semena Werk, I imagine?"

I drop the big reveal. "They tried to kill me."

Fatima throws her head back and laughs, which I did not expect. "All Indians think all Ethiopians are trying to kill them." She cocks her head at me, assessing, such a good scene partner. "Semena Werk is the kernel of an Amharic poem. We revere the poetic form, as do your people. So whatever you are looking for in Semena Werk, you have to look deeper. What you first see only reflects your prejudice."

I have no lines after that, so I remain silent. A beeping noise comes from the console. Rahel climbs into the dinghy and disappears under the tarp.

"So you've never been to Ethiopia," says Fatima.

"No," I say. "But I plan to go. After I make it to Djibouti."

"Why aren't you going with your parents?"

"Because they're dead."

"I'm sorry."

"Thank you."

A moment passes.

"Died in India?"

"No, in Ethiopia."

Now it's come. Dear Fatima has to deal with the fact that some beloved comrade of hers murdered my parents.

"Were your parents A. R. Gabriel and Meenakshi Mehta?"

The camera zooms to my stunned face.

"So you're the baby."

The heroine cannot form words.

Fatima twists around.

OROMIFA: Rahel! Guess who we got here.

A voice comes from the darkness under the tarp.

OROMIFA: Who?

OROMIFA: Election Baby.

OROMIFA: What are you talking about?

OROMIFA: The 2040 election when those two doctors were killed.

Rahel's face emerges from shadow. "You're the baby?" she says.

The heroine finds her voice. "Am I a celebrity or something?"

"You're known," says Fatima.

"I remember when that happened," says Rahel. "I was in Nairobi, remember, Fatima?—and saw it on the Internet. Terrible."

"The Indian media jumped on it," says Fatima. "A good story of Indian nurses saving Indian blood in the face of Ethiopian savagery."

"The story also says that the Ethiopian police didn't bother to chase the killer because they hated Indians," I say.

"Do you believe that?"

I shrug, fall back. "I don't know enough to believe it or not."

"She probably went to Djibouti," says Rahel. "Do you intend to go looking for her?"

I try to look heroic for the camera. "Yes."

Fatima stands again. I can tell she's looking at me even though I'm not looking at her.

"What she did, she didn't do in the name of ARAP," she says. "She was already unhinged. She wasn't even Ethiopian. She came from somewhere in West Africa."

Something in me dissolves. I laugh. "I didn't know that."

I look to the southwest, where the Trail heads. The wind is dead today and the sea is flat. "Which West African country? I need to know who to hate now."

Fatima shifts her weight and spits into the ocean like Clint Eastwood. "Just pick one."

I nod. The Wise African is wise.

"You should be on your way," she says. "But be careful. We were raided three nights ago."

"Is that why you trained guns on me?"

"We thought you might be the thief, but you're much bigger than she was."

"She?"

"We could tell that much."

"Maybe it was Bloody Mary."

Fatima's eyes change. I imagine the camera lenses are telescoping for a close-up. "What do you know about Bloody Mary?"

"Rumors."

"They might not be. Bloody Mary might be our thief. No one mystical, just a parasite."

"What did she steal?"

"Dried mango rings."

"I could go for some of those."

"Got anything to barter?"

"A tongue scraper."

We all have a good laugh. We make the trade. And the camera pans up to film me from overhead, and the infinite ribbon of the Trail ahead of me. We don't see its end before the scene changes.

The Narrows

I'm at 2,020 kilometers. I don't have a map but I remember that the Trail enters the barrel of the Gulf of Aden at some point. Not close enough for me to see Yemen to the north or Somalia to the south. But the way gets narrower.

I pick up our conversation where we last left it. Mohini, I was being followed by a barefoot girl, yes. But the hallucination or spirit or whatever it was went away. She didn't follow me onto the Trail.

That's because you told her to go away. You banished her.

Huh. I don't remember it.

What about the body you saw on the Trail? she asks.

What about it? It wasn't following me.

Didn't you wonder who she was?

She was wearing a golden sari.

Why didn't you look at her face?

Seemed disrespectful.

Why didn't you bury her at sea?

She wasn't mine to bury.

What did you think her story might be?

I don't know. Maybe she was a refugee from another seastead nearby. Or maybe this was a cruel and unusual death sentence.

Not by a court, but by, I don't know, the woman's spouse. Drove her out here in a boat, blindfolded, and then left her here with no supplies.

India is far away.

There are lots of Indians in Oman and Yemen. Shit, there are lots of Indians in Africa. They could have come from Djibouti and said, "Walk home, bitch."

I've never been to Djibouti. It looks like a nice place.

Yeah. I'm excited about it. And not just because it'll be the first land I see in four months but because, I don't know. Because for most of my life I hated Africa because of my parents getting killed, but now recently I love it because I want to get to the root of everything, and Djibouti becomes this sparkling magical place, but it's only the antechamber, the doorstep to Ethiopia, which will be even more magical.

Magical how?

It's the last chamber. The ultimate chamber. I can go to the physical place where my parents were murdered, and look at it, and be okay, and keep going. Life will continue.

It didn't for the woman in the golden sari.

I get that.

(You say nothing.)

You know, Mohini, she looked just like you.

(You say nothing.)

She looked like you right when I left, and you weren't responding to me. You were just limp, and your head was falling off the bed. And your eyes were barely open, like you were tired.

You say nothing, but you don't have to because, just then, I come across another body on the Trail, and it's the same one. It's yours.

Sensory deprivation again: what I see in my head manifests. I step over it and keep going. Chambers are chambers.

Team Fourteen

The five wounds in my chest still haven't healed. But it's not be-cause I haven't taken medicine. It's because I've started to worry them. Their cultivation has become a comfort, something I sow and reap on a daily basis. I pick them, they bleed, I apply dressing, I go to sleep. When I wake up they're scabbed over again. A self-perpetuating recreational activity.

❖ ❖ ❖

At sunset I see a boat coming up from the south. They're on an intercept course. This doesn't feel like a film set. This has the ring of a dream.

A beautiful bare-chested man at the bow waves to me. I return the wave. The boat slows down as it approaches the Trail and I see it contains two other people, a woman and a man. They make a radiant trinity. The woman has planted her foot on the starboard railing and her long hair ripples in the wind. The other man is car-rying two palm cameras and turns both his hands gently back and forth like he's waving in a beauty pageant.

The first man says,

ENGLISH: Do you speak English? Or French?

"You can speak whatever you want," I say in English. "I have a glotti."

TAHITIAN: Oh, thank goodness. I only have to use a tenth
the brainpower. Greetings to you, traveler! Could you
use coconut milk? We just restocked at Soqotra.

Yes, I think, this is not quite real somehow. But it's another chamber, like the pirate radio station. I have to pass through it.

"Sure," I say. "My kiln can't program that."

The boat sidles up to the Trail and the two men moor it with a magnetic anchor. Then the woman hands me a cup of coconut milk and I drink it. They stare at me as I drink.

TAHITIAN: Look how big her eyes are.
TAHITIAN: Idiot! She can understand you.

"My eyes are big?"

"You look like you have too little flesh for your frame," says the muscled goddess.

"I've been walking a long time."

"All the way from Mumbai?"

"Yep."

"Smashing! May we join you for a rest?"

"Sure."

Their faces light up and they scramble onto the Trail. All of them are adept at balancing. I sit down cross-legged on the Trail and the three of them sit down across from me, the same way, the woman in the middle. I feel like I'm sitting across from three life-sized action figures.

"I'm Milton," says the first man.

"I'm Aish," says the woman.

"I'm Greg," says the second man.

"Durga," I say.

"May we film you?" asks Greg, the one with the two palm cameras.

"What for?"

"We're making a documentary about our quest."

"Wow. First tell me what your quest is."

Aish nods to Greg and Greg turns off his palm cameras and folds his hands in his lap.

"We're watching for the wave," says Aish.

I wait for more words that don't come. "Just one?"

"The signs are very clear. The tipping point is near. A time bomb could go off any day: the collapse of the West Antarctic Ice Sheet. The collapse of La Palma. An earthquake anywhere in the world, which will trigger a tsunami of unimaginable proportions."

"And you want to see it happen."

"We don't just want to see it happen. We want to surf it."

Milton offers his hand to me. "Nordi Team Number Fourteen, Arabian Sea. Pleased to meet you."

The dream gets a dash of reality, now that they mention something as concrete as Nordi, the Norwegian bottled-water brand. These days they add ingredients that make your whole gastrointestinal tract feel icy, then warm. Mohini couldn't drink it because it gave her a rash.

"You're all going to surf it?"

"No," says Aish, "Just Milton. Greg is our cameraman. I'm the captain of Team Fourteen. There are other teams scattered all over the world."

"North Pacific, South Pacific, North Atlantic, South Atlantic, West Indian, East Indian, Mediterranean," says Greg. "And the poor shivering bastards patrolling Antarctica."

"Though they may well be the victors," says Milton solemnly.

"If the glacier goes? You bet," says Aish.

"Imagine it," says Milton, gripping my forearm, a gesture that seems too familiar for our acquaintance. "First you hear a peal of thunder that never ends. It just grows, getting louder and louder. Then you feel a trembling in the waters and the surface begins to vibrate even though there's no rain or wind. Then the thunder dies away and the vibrations settle and you hear and feel nothing. And then the wave appears."

Greg has started filming again. "That's beautiful, beautiful," he says, interweaving his hands.

"Don't point those things at me," I say.

"No, of course not," he murmurs, not looking at me.

"How do you know when and where it'll be?" I say.

"We don't," says Aish, who is now drinking her own cup of coconut milk. Where did it come from? It seems like I have gaps in my memory. "But we have access to the earthquake warning grid on the seafloor. Certain predictive factors can tell us when and where a major quake is about to happen. Then we model where the water's going to well up, and speed like hell to intersect it."

Milton stands, feet braced, gazing west. We all look up at him. Greg positions his hands so that he looks like a medieval shepherd worshipping the Baby Jesus of Milton's ass.

"I saw it in a dream," says Milton. "The epicenter off the coast of Kerala, the sea bed thrusting up beneath the subcontinent, the displacement of new water up, up, up into a wall a thousand meters high, and we gun our noble little craft right into the swell, and Aish runs the tow rope with superhuman agility, and I let go and then I surf down, down, down the face of the great wave, riding over sea and reef alike, entire islands drowning beneath my feet, one long ride at the speed of sound, until at long last I surf ashore in Karachi or Mogadishu or whatever port dare remain in the face of this wave."

Aish is wiping tears from her eyes. Greg would be too, except he's still angling his palm cameras and can't spare a hand. "Beautiful," he says. "That's beautiful, Milt."

"Beautiful?" I say. "With so many people drowning? You sound like an asshole."

It's as if I started waving a gun. All three of them jump back in an exaggerated but coordinated way.

"How could you say that?" says Greg.

"Our mission is pure," says Aish.

"Wave is destiny," says Milton, who seems the most wounded.

"If it's what you want, good luck," I say.

Milton straightens and brushes off his bare chest as if brushing out wrinkles. "I thank you for that," he says briskly. And then the three of them jump back in the boat and detach the magnetic anchors, and steer away without a backward glance. It's then that I realize I didn't even see a surfboard.

Performance art, maybe, says Mohini in her golden sari.

⦃ BⷦⷧK XIV ⦄

Mariama

You Are Wonderful

I became Gabriel's guide in Ethiopia. But not in the sense that he paid or patronized me. Once he offered to pay for a meal as a way of saying thanks, but I didn't want to feel indebted to him, so I forbade him to. I was with him because I chose to be, because I liked him and liked that he liked me. So he put his money away.

Once I asked him, Do your friends care how much time you're spending with an Ethiopian woman?

The question seemed to agitate him, and he searched the sky looking like he was about to deliver an answer that would take several days, but I watched his face, and after a minute all of his thoughts collapsed in his head so that all he said to me was: Mariama, if they do, I don't care.

And so I left it alone.

Soon after the listening party, we made a holiday of seeing Dinkenesh. As we made our way down Entoto Avenue from the university, the National Museum was on our right, set back from the road. There was a stately green courtyard and hyacinth trees blooming in rows. A woman in blue fatigues scanned us in. Gabriel gaped at the first exhibit, meant to impress, right as we walked in the door: a glorious golden throne draped with a cape and a crown. But I took his hand and led him down a flight of stairs into the darkened basement. Here, the exhibits were more modest to look at, but so much more important: fragments of bones and skulls, like the relics of saints. We were silent, reading each caption, then moving on to the next. There was no one else there.

I didn't rush him. In fact, Yemaya, it felt like the day you and I spent wandering the Royal Enclosure in Gonder. We didn't have to say anything. We just wandered, happy, in a garden of stone.

When we finally entered the room where Dinkenesh was, walking toward us, always in mid-stride, Gabriel pressed his palms together and bowed to her, saying Namaste, Amma.

Then we stood side by side looking at her.

I could feel the thrumming of the power generators below our feet. I felt I could go to sleep in this room. I could curl up on this floor with Gabriel, this strange man who felt so familiar, and hold his hand beneath Dinkenesh's shadow.

Then an Ethiopian man came into the room. He was wearing a name tag that said ADAM and his face resembled a goat skull. He said, May I help you? Do you need a guide? Can I tell you about Dinkenesh?

I said no, thank you. I could see Gabriel also felt that way, but didn't want to be rude to an Ethiopian man.

But how will you know what you're seeing? he said. I can tell you what you're seeing. Only a hundred birr for a guide.

I felt anger swelling in my body. I didn't need anyone to tell me what I was seeing. I said with the voice of the kreen: No, thank you.

He flinched as if I were about to hit him. He backed away. He was halfway out the door when he flung his arm toward Dinkenesh and said, That's not really her, you know. It's a replica. They made it out of plaster.

He paused, then added, But you could be forgiven for thinking it's her.

Then he left us alone.

The Golden Meaning

One day, I instructed Gabriel to meet me at Delhi Café on Taitu Street, a magnet for expat Indians that he was sure to know. It was another cloudless, dry evening in Addis, and the sky had turned lilac to match the hyacinth trees. We set off from the café and climbed a steep, winding hill until we reached an asphalt plateau, upon which stood a vast villa in the Italian style, flanked by stately rows of flags.

The Sheraton? he said, with amusement.

I said yes, with a note of reproach that hushed him.

You see, Yemaya, the Sheraton was another one of my sacred spots. It was the place I'd stayed when I won the poetry contest. I had had a roommate named Tigist, and we were both required to write thank-you cards to the Chinese corporations that had sponsored our trips. But it was the first time I really, truly glimpsed the future. I saw how the rest of the modern world lived. There was no television like the one I knew from the orphanage; instead, at the command of my voice, the entire wall became a living screen. The first night of our trip, Tigist and I stayed up until four o'clock in the morning with our backs against the headboards of our beds, watching shows from all over the world, having arranged our pillows into separate "houses," and only communicating by opening a pillow "window" and speaking through it.

I was deeply impressionable, then, and I could remember each of those programs years after I saw them. We watched a rerun of *Durga X*, about a woman who fought crime lords in Kolkata, and killed them by twisting their heads completely around their necks. We watched a documentary about a Mexican woman, Inés Ramírez, who delivered her own baby by Caesarean section with a dirty kitchen knife because she was too far from medical help. We watched two straight episodes of *Extreme Weather!* that documented all of the terrible things going on around the world. The first episode was all about the West Antarctic Ice Sheet. Scientists said the sediment underneath would cause a massive landslide, or that the ice itself would melt to inundate the world up to four meters in sea level someday. That didn't sound like much to me, Yemaya, but the next episode was about all the drowned communities around the world, the islands and villages that had been lost even after half a meter's rise. They showed ghost-blue underwater footage of boardwalks, shopping malls, office parks, houses, grocery kiosks, playgrounds—now empty, and slowly becoming the territory of fish, corals, and thin aquatic spiders. They told the story of people who had chosen to stay while their homes were slowly drowned. They would calmly climb to the second floor, then to the roof, over a matter of months or years. The narrator focused on one couple on a South Pacific atoll, Julia and Julio Legazpi-Sanchez, who had attracted media attention; journalists paid them to keep a video diary, documenting their day-to-day ascent to ever-higher ground. Then one day, they were not heard from. The producers took speedboats to the location of the house and found it already ten centimeters underwater. They sent divers to look for the couple in their bedroom, fearing the worst. But they were not there. Where had they gone? It was an unsolved mystery to this day.

When I felt my eyelids begin to droop, I called to Tigist, but got no answer. I suddenly feared she was dead and the chaperones would blame it on me. But then I crept forward on the bed far enough to peer into her pillow cavern, and saw she was fast asleep. I whispered *Off* as the card on the bedside table had instructed me to do, and the wall went black.

We were both very tired in the morning. We were scolded by the chaperones, and tucked in early the next night, to be rested for our reading the next day.

When I began attending university in Addis, I would come alone to the Sheraton to walk the grounds once a week. The hotel staff was used to me. The bartender would nod to me as I passed through the lounge where diplomats sipped Joburg vintage and stared into space, scrolling newsfeeds in their heads. Over time, what had once been so astonishing to me—the marble walls, the majestic columns, the sparkling fountain, the reflecting pool, the arbor walk—became the familiar fixtures of a second home. I bought overpriced Norwegian water at the bar and stood in the doorway of the ballroom, hoping for a wedding in progress. Or I sat by the reflecting pool and trailed my fingers in the water. In fact, I liked to imagine that it was your palace, and then when I visited there, I visited you.

Thus it was of great import that I was bringing Gabriel there. I see now that I was too greedy: I wanted too much. I wanted both to float above the earth, to be nearer to you, but also to bind myself to the earth, to be with Gabriel.

I led him along the arbor walk that looked down on the Somali quarter. We talked. The stars came out. The security guard, making her rounds, came to ask us to leave, but then she recognized me and apologized.

You brought a friend this time? she said.

Yes, I said, and my face was hot.

I'm glad to see it, she said. And she said it in an approving, loving way, as if she were my aunt who had been looking after me all this time.

Gabriel told me about his life. I'd known it in sketches before, but now he painted a complete and colorful mural, and even
showed me the plaster and the foundations underneath. What I'd
suspected was true: he would never want for love, having the easy
confidence of an only son. But despite this, or strangely because of
it, he sought approval constantly, because his parents (his mother,
chiefly, I could tell) had instilled in him a strong sense of moral
duty, to use his birth and standing for the betterment of the world.
She was a famous Ayurvedic doctor, trained also in Western medicine, and Gabriel's childhood was filled with memories of reading
books on the woven rug that covered the floor of his mother's study.

Am I telling you too much? he said. I'm probably boring you.

Not at all, I said. Your stories are like music to me.

He smiled. He said, I feel like I can tell you things and you'll
understand. Things no one else can understand. I hate how my
country is treating your country and I wish I could find a way to
stop it.

I placed my hand over his. It's not your fault, I said.

He nodded. He said, My mother says I have too much of a
sense of justice. I get angry and it gets me into trouble. She always
reminds me of the story of the snake.

What's the story of the snake? I asked.

Gabriel looked down and closed his other hand on top of mine.
He said, When I was in primary school, my teacher introduced a
snake to the classroom as a pet for everyone to take care of. One of
my classmates provoked the snake and it snapped at him. It wasn't
poisonous, and it didn't bite, it just frightened him. I said, The
snake was just trying to take care of itself. The boy told me to shut
up and went home crying, and then the boy's father complained,
so the teacher had to remove the snake from the classroom and let
it go into the wild. But the boy and his friends must have found it.
The next day, walking home, I saw them sitting in a circle around

the snake. They were taking turns torturing it. One of them took out a knife and began to cut into it, like cutting a cucumber but not all the way through. I started throwing rocks at them and yelling at them to stop, but they wouldn't stop. They started doing worse things, because I was watching.

Gabriel stopped to wipe the wetness from his face, and then returned his hand to mine. This time, he didn't apologize for sharing too much. We had entered a new and wordless intimacy. I was taking care of him, like I had once taken care of you.

We had named the snake the Sanskrit word for *powerful,* he said. She was indeed powerful, but not in the way we intended.

What is the word?

Saha, he said.

And I remembered, Yemaya! *Saha!* I remembered that word from so long ago, when I was just a child hiding under the tarp on the truck, and I hadn't even met you yet, and Francis and Muhammed didn't even know I was there, and the only one who knew I was there was the full moon, lighting up the rushing sea and spreading surf, and the sea gave me a word to calm me, and that word was *saha!*

And I knew too that this was the sign you had taught me to look for, when we were on the truck on the way to Agadez and you touched me for the first time and told me not to Give This Away Easily! I had always considered my maidenhood yours, Yemaya, but perhaps I had been wrong in my interpretation—maybe, all along, you had wanted me to be with a man when I was a mature adult woman, and you had simply prepared me in that hotel room in Gonder all those years ago. Yes, this was the sign indeed!

I had difficulty not betraying my epiphany to Gabriel. I was glad it was dark! Now there were hot tears in my eyes to match his!

So I lifted his hand to my mouth and kissed it, and then told him, just as I tell you now:

I ran away from home when I was little. I hid on a caravan of trucks headed east. When we stopped in Dakar, a beautiful woman appeared and joined us. She began to take care of me. She fed me, clothed me, taught me how to read, and told me stories about her namesake, who was a goddess. But she wasn't just her namesake. She was really Her. After we had crossed the desert safely, She went back to heaven.

Gabriel nodded and in his eyes were only belief and acceptance.

What was her name? he asked.

Yemaya, I said.

What a beautiful word. What did she look like?

It's hard to remember now. I don't have any pictures of her. I only have an image in my mind, and a feeling. But her hair was wavy, like she had some European blood. She tied it back in a headwrap. And she had big bright eyes. Like yours.

Tell me more, he said. I want to listen to the sound of your voice.

I never looked for her, I said. I knew I wouldn't be able to find her if I did. She would only come to me when I was ready. So I'm here, in this life, for now. But I don't feel I belong here. I'm on loan.

Why did you run away from home in the first place? he said.

This was the one question I was afraid he'd ask, Yemaya. No one had asked me that question for thirteen years. And yet tonight, I'd received the sign that all would be well. Tonight was a night for breaking the habits of years and breathing free air.

We were Haratine, which meant we were slaves, I said. My mother and I served the Brahim household. The father was always sending me away to spend time with my mother. When I was a child, we escaped and tried to settle in one of the slums. But somehow he found us. I came back from the beach to the concrete house my mother had made for us, and he was there, and he was wearing a sky-blue robe like the men in Mauritania do. My mother looked at me, and even though she was upside down and I was right side up, she looked at me and said, Don't worry, I'll be all right.

I found myself held against Gabriel's body. I had never been held in such a way. I was a virgin. But I reminded myself: I had received the sign. This was all right.

I ran away, I said into his chest. She had told me to, if any-thing happened to her, because she never wanted me to be enslaved again.

He held me tighter. His body was warm and hard.

For so many years, to calm myself, I'd said *Yemaya, Yemaya, Yemaya.* In the darkness, against his chest, I mouthed it, feeling the way it formed in the back of my throat, touched my lips, and ended with an open mouth. And then I tested the new one: *Gabriel, Gabriel, Gabriel.* It didn't feel quite as right as your name did. But for now, for this life, on this earth, it would do.

{ B☐☐K XV }

Meena

The Commune

Mohini, how did I get here?

The bodies are routine now. They're always you, in a golden sari, with your head hanging off the edge of the Trail. They never animate or sit up and start talking. I just hear your voice in my head.

We talk about how I moved to Thrissur when I was twenty-three and got a job at the women's center, where I worked with survivors of domestic abuse. It was a struggle. Most of the time I just wanted to find the abusers and kick the shit out of them on my clients' behalf. You know this about me. I'm honest with you. You're gentle and understanding.

You say, You're carrying a lot of baggage.

You're right, I say.

I kneel at the edge of the Trail and empty my bag and, like Jesus separating the sheep and the goats, I put things into two piles. The breakdown goes like this:

Pile 1: Underwear, bra, sunglasses, desalinators, toothbrush, toothpaste, tongue scraper, kiln, solar plate, filet
knife, fishing kit, irradiator brush, medical kit, menses
sponge, diaper cloth, pod, ropes.

Pile 2: Mitter, purse, sandals, soap concentrate, protein
packets, broth packets, sunbits, gas capsules, sea anchor, laminated map, pozit, flares, picture of Rana,
compass, brimmed hat, sun cap, hoodie, T-shirt, long-
sleeved shirt, canvas shoes, thong sandals, and the pair
of pants I'm not wearing at the moment.

Without letting myself think about it I sweep the second pile
over the edge. The various items scatter on the surface. My pants
bloom to life as they take on water. The hoodie is hardest to sink. I
have to tow it back in and hold it under and it accepts this fate, having been long embittered about its role, grumbling as it sinks. The
other items are more obliging. One by one, they disappear. When
they're gone, I feel lighter. I've gotten rid of a lot of weight and my
bag will be easier to carry. Already my body itself is lighter and
easier to carry. All my fat has disappeared. My breasts are flat.
My bones are prominent. For the first time in my life, it hurts to
sit, and so I eat curled up on my side.

Your golden body appears every thirty meters or so, like a
crumb trail. I consider these part of the ordeal. More chambers.
They all have some purpose I can't yet tell, something that will
prepare me for the final chamber, the first and the last, Ethiopia.

◈   ◈   ◈

Patchwork rafts are lashed together and covered by Persian car-
pets, their corners wet and dragging in the water. There are half

a dozen residents and they all look like Maharishi devotees from 1968. They rouse from beanbags and lurch up, heavy-lidded, like zombies. The nearest one wears a batik robe that pools around his feet and leaves his shoulder bare.

MARATHI: Who goes?

"Durga," I say.

MARATHI: Whoa. Durga. Do you bring new life or
    destruction?

"Both," I say.

He gestures to the assemblage of beanbags and the adherents press their palms and bow toward me. But their aim is off. One of them is bowing to the space to my left and the other is bowing to the space above me. Not a film, not a dream. What chamber is this, then? Maybe a test. "Please, partake with us," he says.

"What, hashish?"

"No, seawater," he says.

"You can't drink seawater," I say.

"Ah, but you can," he says. "Five hundred milliliters a day before your kidneys revolt. We're here to prove it."

"To whom?"

"To the world. That Bloody Mary is real."

"What does Bloody Mary have to do with this?"

"You call her Bloody Mary, but we call her Mother of the Race to Come."

Mohini, this sounds like some bullshit.

"I'm not keen on giving up fresh water, thanks," I say. "I'll be on my way."

The batik man moves with surprising speed to block my way.

"Either you sacrifice your desalinators to Bloody Mary, or you offer a story," he says. "That's the bargain."

Ah, so I was right, Mohini. This is a test.

Tell them the one about Parvati, you say.

I'm sure they know about Parvati, I say.

No, Parvati Rai, you say. Your first client at the women's center. Remember?

Oh, Parvati Rai.

I tell Batik Man to sit on his beanbag because I'm about to tell a story. My words will get fucked up because I'm me, but there's going to be a beginning, a middle, and an end. I feel you behind me, listening and supporting.

"Once there was a slave woman named Parvati. She had been born into slavery, not in the sense of intrinsic worth or karmic reincarnation but in a social construction sense, obviously, and not by any fault of her own but just because people can't control where they're born, and then energy flows directionally through the human race because the gradient's always trying to reach equilibrium. Like the layers of the ocean. Right?"

You say, Just tell the story and don't worry about extemporizing. The facts are enough.

"Okay, so. Parvati's mother died when she was young, so she grew up in the house alone, as the slave of the family. They called her a servant, but that's just the kind of bullshit rurals get away with; according to the international definition she was a slave because she never received schooling, was never paid enough to live on her own, was prohibited from forming any kind of relationships that would help her get out of her situation, et cetera. The man she served was violent towards her, especially after his wife left him and took her three daughters with her. So it was just Parvati and him in the house and he raped her a lot. And that was just her normal life."

My voice is beginning to shake, but I can feel you behind me, holding me in strength. I stop to swallow and take a breath.

"Sometimes Parvati thought about killing herself. But she needed to believe that life was worth living if only she could get free. So she ran away to another village, but no one would take her in. Eventually her master found her through her aadhaar. He humiliated her in public and then put her on top of his truck and strapped her down like she was luggage, and started driving back to his village really fast. The bumping on country roads loosened the knots, and Parvati fell off the truck, into the road. She hit so hard her skull cracked. She was still lying in the middle of the road, bleeding from the head, and she thought, I should just stay here in the road.

"But she was still alive. And things that are alive need to move, eventually, whether they want to or not, because they still have energy to spend. She crawled out of the road. She was weak, but she pinched the skin of her upper arm and dug out her aadhaar with her own fingernails and left it in a field. She crawled farther to put distance between her and her aadhaar. Then she got up and walked through the night. When it got to be dawn, she found herself on a road high above the plain, and she saw a car passing, and she flagged it down, and it turned out to be a medical student, who took her to the hospital. That student was my father, Ramachandran Gabriel."

And after that? you say. Finish it.

"Parvati got better. She started helping other women. When I arrived at the women's center many years later, she was its director. On my first day, she told me about how my father had rescued her from the road. She also told me that she went back to her old 'master's' house. She'd forgiven him. She wanted to lay eyes on him again and show herself that she had nothing to fear. But when she got to the house, it was empty. The wind blew through it like the bones of a skeleton. He'd left long ago."

"So," says Batik Man, "what did she do?"

"She went back to her wonderful life," I say.

All of the devotees press their palms and bow to me again.

"You may pass now," says Batik Man.

In answer, I take out my two desalinator bottles, and like a buzzard spreading its wings, fling each into the ocean. They arc to my right and left and drop into the water at the same exact moment.

You've passed the test, you say behind me. Now you're ready for the next chamber.

Madurai

I stop wearing clothes. They felt like just one more barrier between me and the elements. I want to merge with the elements instead of remain separate from them.

The batik man said the body can tolerate five hundred milliliters of seawater a day. I take my first capful of it—the water of life, all around me; what was I thinking?—every other thought is an epiphany for the ages—and drink it down, careful not to let it touch my lips. The salt burns my throat like a neat shot of liquor. I let it settle and sink into my cells. I tell them to welcome the new food. It's better than water. It's broth.

I begin to see that the Trail is actually contained within a glass tunnel. There's no fear of being swept away to either side. There's not even any danger of drowning. The sea, sky, and moon—the members of my old Element Diary, fondly resurrected—are the background film that's playing while I walk, and will, until I reach Djibouti. I can see the end of the Trail in my mind's eye: it stops offshore, but I can see the lights of the city. Not as vast or majestic as Mumbai, but it'll have some other quality, something essentially *African* as the skyline of Mumbai is essentially *Indian*. I try to imagine it but I feel like anything I imagine will just be a function of stereotypes. Violet lights, instead of orange? An assemblage of low colonial-era buildings instead of the towering HydraCorp tiara? I don't know anything about Djibouti, but for reasons I can't name, I'm expecting something welcoming and warm. And friendly hands to help me ashore.

❖ ❖ ❖

I thought the bodies would go away after the commune. But they keep appearing, and now, in different positions, as if I'm paging through a very slow flip book.

I know the story they're spelling out for me. So I start telling it first, to get ahead of them.

❖ ❖ ❖

Mohini, life got better for me after I went to Madurai.

I'd left college after the episode with Ajantha. I went home but I had no place with my grandparents. They were too sad even to be angry with me. I moved in with a divorced man in Aranmula for five months, then left in the middle of the night. I baked bread in Varkala for two weeks and then got sick of the tourists. I worked at the Kashi Art Café in Kochi for longer but, again, got sick of the tourists. And then for a year I worked as a waitress in Kodaikanal, writing poetry at night huddled in blankets, but I was getting sick of the cold. Then one day I was serving a customer, a stick-up-the-ass Hindu nationalist, who saw my nametag and asked me when was the last time I'd visited my namesake Meenakshi Devi at her temple in Madurai, which was just down the mountain from us, the jewel of the plain.

I said, Never.

He slammed down his fist and said, That is unacceptable. How will you receive her blessing? How will she even know you exist?

I didn't tell him all the complications behind my name, that it was also my mother's name and that my mother was murdered with a scalpel, that my grandmother was Catholic, and that anyway I wasn't particularly religious to begin with. I was stunned by his passion.

So I just played the poor waitress card and said, I don't have the money.

He got out an actual billfold and held up an actual fifty-thousand-rupee note.

I'll give you this, he said, If you promise to use it to visit Meenakshi Devi and ask her blessing.

I was sure the note was fake. But just in case it wasn't, I promised with all solemnity that I would use it as he instructed. He gave me the note. I folded it in my pocket. I served him extra respectfully after that.

On my break, I took the note to the cashier's office, and found a dusty box of miscellanea that included paper money and a pen to check for fake notes.

The note wasn't fake.

I left the restaurant, fed the bill into my account so that the money was accessible on my mitter, went back to my studio flat, stuffed my things in a sack, and flagged down an autoshaw to take me all the way down the mountain to Madurai on the plain. The farther we descended, the more I felt myself coming to life. I was warming up. I'd forgotten how much the cold had frozen all the parts of me and now it was like I could move again.

I got a hotel room and then went out walking. Of course I wandered toward the temple complex because that's where all the roads lead. I had Reshmi West's essays running through my head. It happened to be a Friday, Meenakshi Devi's special day. So there were tens of thousands of pilgrims there.

❖ ❖ ❖

The bodies have been lying perpendicular to me on the Trail. Now they start swinging toward me, headfirst.

❖ ❖ ❖

There was a thick crush of people trying to get around the Golden Lotus Tank to see Meenakshi Devi at the other end of the complex. So I just had to wait. And I paid the full one thousand rupees to get in line to get right up close to the deity. But again, I didn't feel impatient or unhappy, I just felt content. I'd never felt that way in my life. The line moved from one chamber to another, from the daylit open air to the dark inner passages lit with tubes overhead and oil lamps set in the walls and fans that moved the air of a thousand exhalations. Shiva giving a boon. Shiva killing a boar. Shiva and the elephant. But the real show here is the divine feminine: she's the one we want to see: and then I'm before her and she's black, resplendent, petaled, and smeared.

I looked at her and felt like I wasn't answerable for anything I'd done and I was free of all family, all history, all circumstance. Like I was free of context and could reenter the world as a baby.

Soon after that, I met you, Mohini.

❖ ❖ ❖

The bodies start tilting up, feet in the air, head dangling, like upside-down marionettes. The golden saris fall down around their hips.

◈ ◈ ◈

Onam 2068 would be our second anniversary, and I was planning a feast.

That day, when I got in the door from the market and put my bag on the kitchen counter, I heard the sound of furniture moving in another room. Mohini must be cleaning, I thought, or rearranging the bedroom as she had to do every few months "to keep things fresh." I tiptoed down the hall, trailing my fingers along the wall. It was an old cottage, almost a hundred years old, made of plaster that always stayed cool. When the monsoon came we'd open every window and door to let the rainy air flood the house. We'd painted it with warm colors, each room a different shade of sunrise, with mandalas and murals and verses of the Vedas. As I approached the room, I took off my jacket, and then my shirt, leaving them in a trail in the hallway, and then unzipped my jeans. I heard heavy breathing and felt so much love for you, because you worked so hard for our home. Then I came into the bedroom and saw you lying on our bed in a golden sari with your head turned away from me. I thought you were sleeping. I moved around to the foot of the bed. I came closer to kiss your forehead. And that's when the snake lying on top of your body struck at me.

Your eyes were upside down, open, and tired.

I ran away.

Witness Dogs

The bodies go away.

For a long time I'm left with the basic elements again. Sea, sky, moon, and the Trail in its glass tunnel. It's transparent, so it's hard to detect. Sometimes I think I see its outline above me. Once I even see the little woman crawling overhead. Whether that lends credibility to her actual existence, I'm not sure. I consult my counselors, who are now broadcasting from the Semena Werk pirate radio station, including both my mother and father weighing in now, up and running and fully ideated, speaking from recliners made of clouds.

> AMMA: If she tries to hurt you, we'll protect you, molay.
> APPA: Right! We'll give her what-for!
> AMMA: Are you eating enough?
> APPA: And make sure you get enough sleep. You're crabby without it.
> AMMA: Make chamomile tea tonight and I'll tell you a story.

They're an opium drip of all the things I've wanted to hear my whole life.

On a diet of seawater, and the kelp I don't bother converting anymore, my body changes. My blood gets thicker. My flesh is gummy. If I press my finger into my arm, a depression stays, like a dimple, and it takes a long time to fill up again. My lips crack and crust over and I peel them till they bleed. I have trouble sleeping when I lie down during the day, and I have trouble staying awake while I'm walking. The lines between different phases of consciousness aren't clear. I go through cyclical periods of lucidity and fog. I lose a lot of energy. I want to sing a kriti but I can't remember the words, and anyway, I don't have the strength to sing. I can feel the salt on my vocal cords.

But I left you, Mohini, not knowing whether you were alive or dead, so any suffering on my part is good and deserved.

❖ ❖ ❖

On the horizon I see a new structure. In a burst of lucidity I send up a prayer to whatever gods might be listening, saying, Please, I can't take any more hippies.

But there seems to be only one inhabitant. He's standing on a barge moored to the Trail. There's a kiosk set up, a little thatch-hut stand with a bar, painted in bright tropical colors. He's standing behind it and is working with metal tongs and a plate. I see steam rising from below. I get closer to the kiosk and now I can see a sign that says WITNESS DOGS in five different languages. There's one stool at the bar.

He's still busying himself behind the counter. When I get to him, and open my mouth to say hello, nothing comes out, so I just knock on the counter and wave when his head pops up.

He looks at me and cries out. I jump back. It's a startling sound after so much of just waves and wind.

"What happened to you?" he says in Hindi.

Again I try to speak, but my throat has the texture of jerky.

He sees me trying to form words. "Here," he says, and indicates the stool. "Sit down. I have a lot of work to do with you."

First, he fetches a robe. I'd forgotten I was naked. I hold out my arms so he can fit the sleeves over me and then I manage to wrap it around my front so my breasts are covered.

Then he puts a glass of clear water on the counter. I look at it and turn around just in time to throw up. The vomit is dark green against the barge platform.

"Oh dear," he says. "No, don't get up. I'll take care of it. You're in worse shape than I thought."

I watch him clean up my vomit.

"Now take a look at the glass of water again," he says.

I will myself to.

"Just look at it," he says.

I can do that.

"Good," he says. "There's hope for you. I don't suppose you ran into the Lotus Eaters a few hundred kilometers back, did you? That's what I call them. So what, you couldn't think of a story and they confiscated your desalinators?"

I can't think of an expression, or series of expressions, that would convey that I did tell a story, and then threw out my desalinators of my own volition. Let alone why. I wish I knew sign language. Maybe they have entire vocabularies for explaining unexplainable things, even motivations unknown to the speaker.

"Don't worry about talking yet," he says. "I'm speaking rhetorically. My name is Subu."

I shake my head to tell him I'm with him. He's already a better trail angel than Ameem and Padma were, ten thousand years ago.

"I run Witness Dogs. I run it for two reasons. One, to serve food. As you can see here, in addition to the fruit of the sea, I cook hot dogs. Kosher. Vitamin-enriched. Don't look at them too long—we don't want you throwing up again. I wrote a designer program for the kiln, patent pending.

"Two, it seemed to me that on a landscape like this, a walker needs a good reality check. That's why I witness."

Here it comes, I think. He's a Jesus freak.

"Empiricism," he says. "I witness for empiricism."

Didn't see that coming.

"Look at my hand. I'm real."

I shake my head in assent.

He pokes me in the shoulder. "Feel that. You're real."

I assent again.

"Good. Now take another look at this glass of water."

I do. I place my hands around it to steady it so that the water doesn't slosh out to either side.

"Now just put your lips to it. Don't drink yet."

I do. I have the same feeling as I did when I descended down from the mountain to the plain. What have I been doing?

I fall asleep at the counter.

❖ ❖ ❖

When I wake up it's bright afternoon. It doesn't feel right. I should be asleep.

Subu is lying in his boat, hands folded across his stomach, with his hat over his face.

Mohini, I don't know what I expected the Trail to be like when I began. But I don't think I thought it'd be like this.

I put my head back down.

❖ ❖ ❖

I wake up to Subu's voice.

"All right then, let's see how we do with the water this time."

I raise my head to see him throw out the old glass. I feel an impulse to stop him, but I don't have the strength, and so I just watch him do it.

He pours a fresh glass and puts it on the counter. "Just a little sip now," he says.

I take a sip. After the brine of seawater, it tastes like sugar.

"Slow, now."

I take another sip. I drink a third of it. And then I drink the whole thing.

I rest, this time in my own pod.

I wake at sunset and drink some more.

I can start to whisper words and, with practice, even put a little voice to them.

I start to return to the world. I hadn't even noticed I'd gone.

❖ ❖ ❖

The third night, Subu judges I'm in good enough shape to try a hot dog.

Again he assures me they're kosher. I make the gesture to say, It's okay, I don't mind either way.

He claps the metal tongs a few times and then reaches into the steamer and pulls out a thick, pale hot dog. He puts it in a bun.

"What would you like on it?"

I sweep my hands wide, which I hope conveys The Works. So he adds curry sauce, sugary ketchup, mango pickle relish, onions, tomatoes, thick dal, and crumbled paneer. He makes one for himself, too, and I wait. Then he says, Let's eat, and we both take up the overflowing oblongities and chew, looking back east, where the dusk is pink and blue.

"So, where are you from?" he says.

I point east. "Keralam," I whisper.

"What's your name?"

I begin to say Durga. But that name seems to belong to another, delusional self. I'm like a snake that keeps shedding skins. Every time I shed a new one, I think it's the last one, and I can't believe there could ever be a new one to shed.

"Meena," I say. "Named after my mother."

"Is she in Kerala?"

"No. She's dead."

"I'm very sorry."

"Thanks."

"I bet your walking has something to do with her dying."

A former self would have taken offense at this. But I just say, "Yeah."

"Looking for her."

"Yeah."

"What do you hope to find?"

Well, I hope to find some ancient matron on the street in Addis who'll see me and jump up and cry out, Miss Meenakshi Mehta, can it be you?—even though I look so much more like my father. She'll see something in me that I can't see. Some evidence that my mother existed. Some evidence of her regard for me. Someone who knew her while she was in Ethiopia. A lost diary. Her flat in Addis. Her favorite restaurant in Addis. A photograph where she holds a stethoscope to a smiling patient's chest, smiling. Records of her visa application. The gardens she used to stroll with my father. Our Lady of Entoto Hospital. The clinic inside Our Lady of Entoto Hospital. The room inside the clinic inside Our Lady of Entoto Hospital, where she died.

The woman who killed her.

I answer, "The innermost chamber, whatever that is."

He's Hindu. Culturally, at least. He gets it. "Do you have anyone at home?"

"Yes," I say. And then I say, "No."

"I see."

"I did, but I left her. Even though she'd been attacked."

"Attacked by what?"

"A snake. The snake bit me, too." I parted my robe to show him the five scabs, which have become like overlapping red moons and their penumbrae.

"Who put the snake there?"

"I don't know."

"What did the snake look like?"

"It was golden."

"What was his name?"

"Sunny," I said.

"Ah," he says.

I concentrate on watching the dusk. I count to ten, then to twenty, then to a hundred. The colors turn to red and violet.

"So," says Subu. "In the interest of empiricism, what really happened?"

"He was the spicewaala I went to for cardamom," I say. "He'd broken in." And he was folded over Mohini like a frog, with a hand at her throat, and her eyes looking upside down at me, tired.

"What did you do?"

"Same thing. I ran away."

❖ ❖ ❖

I stay at Witness Dogs for two more days. I drink the water Subu gives me, and for every meal, I have his vitamin-fortified hot dogs. Always with everything on it.

When I'm healthy enough to go, he checks my kiln to make sure it's working properly, and then uploads his special hot-dog program. He also gives me two desalinator bottles. "Don't lose these," he says. "You want to make it."

"I do," I say, and I mean it truthfully.

"Good luck," he says. "But I have a question for you."

"Shoot."

"If there was no snake in your bed, then where did the bite marks in your chest come from?"

My mind compiles the explanation. "There was still a snake there. Sunny was using it as a weapon."

"But how many fangs does a snake have?"

"Two."

"Then tell me, why are there only five bite marks in your chest, and not six?"

⸨ B☐☐K XVI ⸩

Mariama

Awara

That night, Gabriel and I couldn't let go of each other. It was like
our hands had magnets in them. And not just one pair, but both,
which sometimes made it hard to walk forward! Outside the Sheraton we boarded the el train for Medhane Alem. We sat on the roof
deck, not speaking, faceup to the stars. Our hands fumbled for one
another in the dark until the foursome lay at rest.

When we came to his flat, he became nervous. He turned on
the light overhead, but it was garish and fluorescent, illuminating
everything. He locked the door behind us, saying, I have to make
sure I do that because I always forget to lock the door. Amma says
I'm too trusting. He apologized for the mess, though everything
looked tidy to me. We both stood there, not knowing what to do.

Then the kreen itself whispered into my ear: turn the light
back off.

So I reached behind us and turned off the light again. And in
the dark, I felt for his face, and my hand found the curve of his jaw
as if I knew it by heart, and I opened my mouth to kiss him.

All the nervousness went out of him. I could feel it draining from his body. He caved to me, cupping the back of my head and pushing his fingers into my hair. When we drew apart and tented our foreheads together, we knew what to do again.

I'll make better light, he said, but he couldn't see in the dark. So he turned on his sirius and we both laughed, and I cupped his head in my hand and pressed my lips to his temple. Our bodies could not separate. He had me sit down on the same couch he'd sat on before, during the jazz-listening party. But now it was just me here alone. With him.

Using his sirius as a light, he found matches, and lit candles. By the light, I saw pictures of his parents on the table, his mother stern and handsome with large square glasses and salt-and-pepper hair bound low at the nape of her neck; his father sweet and guileless, with caved-in shoulders and the smile of an embarrassed schoolboy.

When Gabriel was done, there were twelve points of golden light glowing around the room. He saw me getting up but he told me to wait. He disappeared into the back room, his bedroom. Golden light began to glow from that room too.

I became aware that soft music had begun to play, of a nature I'd never heard before, gentle and spectral, with sparkles of sitar against a drone, a woman's voice sliding up and down a scale that felt at once ancient and familiar. Gabriel reemerged from the bedroom, and put his sirius down on the table, and then offered me his hand.

Yemaya, where is it written that virgins are shy? And where does it say that they are unskilled? Gabriel undressed me and I undressed him as if we had shared a bed for all time past, and would, for all time to come. I ran my hands down his throat like a potter shaping clay, then down farther, one hand along his spine and the other passing through his solar plexus. I thought his body was much bigger than mine, but with our clothes off, we seemed to be the same size.

He laid me down on peacock-blue sheets like a baby, and covered me with his body like a blanket. And into that space where only you had been before, he came, bringing necessary pain, feeling like the burn of cayenne I remembered from your finger, but wider and hotter. He saw the look on my face and moved very slowly. He rained my face with kisses. And as I willed my body to accept him, the cayenne burn melted into something else, like honey.

The kreen uncurled from its lair in my solar plexus and descended down to meet him.

Gabriel was completing what you had begun.

Election Season

In the morning, I was woken by a ray of sunlight that fell across our chests and warmed our bodies. Gabriel was sleeping like a child. His black hair was loose. In the sunlight I could see the reddish tone underlying the black. Strands waved in the air like live wires.

I felt that the moment was so perfect, I didn't want to even take the chance of ruining it. I would see him again soon. I would send a message to him later. But right now, oh, I wanted to step back into Creation as the changed woman I was! Gabriel didn't stop slumbering even as I dressed and let myself out. Not even the doorman's condescending look could dampen my spirits. Outside, the blue vaults above Addis were scented with eucalyptus smoke, a salt-and-pepper incense I still miss. I didn't take the train. I wanted to walk everywhere. I saw ARAP posters and PEP posters and students marching in the street, though I didn't join them. It wasn't that I believed any differently. It's just that my constitution was bigger now, and given to joy, a new garden of feelings I wanted to explore. The movement could do without me for a while.

I told myself, surely things between Gabriel and me are altered now, and I mustn't pretend otherwise. But I knew, just as surely, that I wanted to see him again. I waited a day for the exhilaration to settle, and then, standing by a lamppost in Arat Kilo, sent him a message in Amharic saying Hello and The Sky Is Full of Euca-lyptus Incense, which I hoped would at least inspire him to study the translation on his glotti and educate himself, so that he could respond in Amharic, the tongue of his new home.

But there was no reply that night. Nor the next morning.

I told myself: you're learning a new person and his singular ways! He is Other, he is a mystery, he is a delicate puzzle not to be rushed. Was not Yemaya Herself temperamental at times? You must have patience. Or perhaps he was put off by my use of Am-haric? It was rude of me to presume.

So later that day, I sent another message, this time in Hindi. Greetings Friend and I Hope You Are Well.

There was no reply to that, either.

Oh, Yemaya, the kreen began to stir within me.

But then I cupped the embers of that night again: the stars: the candles: the sitar: the rain of kisses. Such beauty cannot amount to nothing or the universe would not cohere.

❖ ❖ ❖

The hours turned into days. The kreen had stirred, before, but now it began to writhe in its nest.

I began to look up Gabriel in the cloud, even though his aadhaar was limited; he was not very active. This made sense to me. He wasn't the sort of person to groom a public profile. So I looked at past pictures of him, taken by other people. Gabriel at university, president of the Society for Bioethics. Gabriel in secondary school, running backward in a red cricket jersey. Gabriel as an adolescent, not long after the incident with the snake, I imagined, posing in the brown-and-khaki uniform of his new private school in Madurai.

I began to blame myself. I realized it was because I'd left in the morning, not saying good-bye, just slipping out—my intentions had been good, but what if that had been an unforgivably rude gesture? I didn't know what Indians were like. I didn't know what they expected. I was so inexperienced.

So I sent him another message, again in Hindi, that said: I'm So Sorry I Left. Spend Time Together Soon?

And again, there was no reply.

❖ ❖ ❖

The days turned into weeks. I kept thinking, Surely there must be a mistake, an explanation. I found myself loitering in favorite places of his, or places dear to his friends, or places frequented by medical students. But it was as if he'd disappeared from the earth. The kreen made it difficult for me to sleep. I had little appetite because the kreen took up so much room.

Then one day, I realized: a family emergency must have occurred. His dear father had fallen ill, or his brilliant mother had broken a leg, and he'd had to vacate Addis suddenly, too suddenly to send me a note. I decided that this must be the case and so I sent him another message: I Hope You and All of Your Loved Ones Are Well. I considered my interpretation of his situation as good as confirmed when I received no reply to that, either. After all, the alternative was not possible, not from the sweet golden boy who'd cried about injustice to a snake.

◈　◈　◈

For the next few months I threw myself back into the election. I made calls for ARAP. I drew posters and canvassed and organized street teams. I rode the train south to camp at the reservoir near Koka Gidib, recently taken over by Indian contractors. We sat in a human chain in the soil, linking our arms in the face of an oncoming tractor. Again, Al Jazeera was there. Again, the pictures went viral all over the world. I sent one of them to Gabriel to remind him of how we met on the march through Addis but again there was no reply.

Poor boy, I thought. I hope he and his whole family are all right.

Then we learned of an all-new travesty: an Indian corporation's plan to build a wave array across the entire Arabian Sea, which would ostensibly benefit Djibouti. But how was India going to benefit, in ways it wouldn't say? How was Djibouti going to suffer, in ways that wouldn't be made clear to them? They wanted to use metallic hydrogen, that mysterious substance I remembered from our journey, Yemaya. How much clearer that whole situation, including Muhammed's moral quandary, became to me in retrospect! Metallic hydrogen was known to be an unstable substance, introduced by Indian contractors before being properly vetted, and had resulted in African deaths, most notably when it escaped containment in a Zambian plant and killed two hundred workers in 2035. If metallic hydrogen could cause such destruction on land, what would it do in the ocean?

Oh, I wanted to talk to Gabriel about these things! For me, he was the human face of India. I felt that the answers to everything, even international peace, lay in a loving and rigorous dialogue between the two of us. I cast us as the heroes of warring cultures. I wanted to understand his country, so I began reading everything I could about India; I even sat in on a special seminar called "The Indian Mind-Set." I started watching streams of Indian dancers: Bharatanatyam, Theyyattam, and Mohiniyattam. I found a program to teach me Malayalam, which was Gabriel's mother tongue. I learned a few words so that I could surprise him when he came back. I even learned how to say *I love you,* so that I'd be ready when the moment came.

What an odd feeling: that India had invaded my country and oppressed it, but as I read more about them, Yemaya, part of me wanted it to happen! Just as easily as I had identified with Ethiopian culture when I was a young girl, I was beginning to dis-identify with it. Though I believed in fighting the exercise of the strong over the weak, I came to feel that one cultural identity was as arbitrary as another. Maybe I was really Indian. Maybe I was transracial, like the transsexuals who underwent expensive treatments to change their body to reflect their soul. Maybe I was beginning my slow transformation into an Indian woman.

I confided this to Dr. Kebede, the faculty adviser to ARAP on campus. She was not happy with me.

Mariama, I've been watching you, she said. I'm worried about you because you have no kin. Who takes care of you? Do you have any real friends? Do you date anyone?

I met an Indian man, I said.

An Indian man? Do you know how Indians see Ethiopians? Indians can be very racist. Especially the wealthy. They regard Africans as beneath them.

Not this one, I said. Not him.

Is it serious? she asked.

Yes, I said, even though I hadn't seen or heard from Gabriel in months.

Has he told his parents about you yet?

I don't know.

That's the test, she said. Even the most progressive Indians still have parents stuck in the past, and they're helpless to stand up to them. When is the last time you saw him?

I didn't answer.

Ah, I see, said Dr. Kebede, victorious. What is he then, a crush? Wake up, Mariama. It's time to stop acting like a child. There's important work to do in the world.

I got very quiet and the kreen got very loud.

Dr. Kebede looked frightened. She raised her voice as if in defense against an invisible threat. She said, I'm just being honest with you. I've seen it happen. Too many times. They pretend to be equals but really regard us as a resource. They need energy. They'll take it from us. I want them out, Mariama. You must want it too. You must forget this nonsense.

I walked out because the kreen was thrashing so hard I was afraid it might do violence and I wasn't ready for that yet.

I couldn't put my faith in a bitter old lady. I still believed that I had to put my faith in love. Gabriel had told me about the snake, and I had told him about my mother, and that had to mean something.

Even though I'd convinced myself that Gabriel was out of the country, I began, again, to haunt the places he might be. School let out and the rainy season came. I drank buna in Meganagna and watched the entrance of Our Lady of Entoto Hospital. I found an excuse to wander down Medhane Alem, to the apartment complex where Gabriel's flat was. When I asked the doorman whether Gabriel still lived there, he said no, he'd moved before Christmas.

Ah, back to India? I said, sad but accepting.

But he said no. That he'd moved somewhere farther east in the city, in the more modern developments.

The kreen snapped up this information and gobbled it down.

I thanked the doorman. I started walking east.

BO·OK XVII

Meena

Onam Satya

"What do you mean?" I ask Subu.

"A snake has two fangs. So if the snake struck you, there should be six bites."

He reaches forward. I slap his hand away.

"Meena," he says.

"Don't touch me."

He turns around and walks back to his kiosk. He sits at the stool at the counter. He raises his hands to either side. "I won't."

I turn around to walk forward but my foot slips and, because there's actually no glass tunnel containing the Trail, I fall into the ocean. I scream into the water. I beat my fists on the Trail and shed the robe because it's pulling me down and lift myself up all the way up to my feet. I'm back, soaked.

"Meena," he says again, more softly.

"Don't touch me," I say.

"I won't," he says.

I take a step toward him.

"I said I won't," he says again.

❖　❖　❖

When I saw Sunny and Mohini, I circled around the bed and sat on the chair across from it, the one next to the glass cabinet. Mohini's eyes were wide. She stared at me. She was terrified. Sunny pushed back using his hands and withdrew from her and his penis trailed white slime and swung to one side and stuck to his thigh. He lifted a pillow to cover his dark black-bear patch. Mohini rolled down her sari and turned over on her stomach and then pushed herself up to a kneeling position.

"Meena," she said.

I was only wearing my bra on top, and my jeans were unzipped. "Yeah," I said, "I'm here."

Mohini saw the smile at the edge of my mouth and smiled back, in something like relief. "Meena, did you know?"

I heard the quail's spiral song right outside the window, and I swirled my finger in the air as if to trace it, as if to answer her question.

"You're not mad?"

I wagged my head like a good Indian girl. I felt strong, so full of life, like my heart was made of menthol.

"Oh. Wow. Meena, I love you. Look, Sunny—"

"I'm going," said Sunny, already out of the bed and shrugging into clothes. "I'm going."

"Okay, that's probably best," said Mohini, turning from him to me and back again. "But Sunny?—Meena—I think we should all sit down and talk sometime. I really want to respect everyone's feelings in this situation."

Mohini pulled up her bra strap. Sunny wagged his head and zipped up his pants. We both watched as he gathered up the rest of his things and made toward the front door, then changed his mind and made toward the back door. He held up his hand in farewell. Mohini and I both did the same.

Mohini got off the bed and walked toward me. I rose and she reached for my hand and squeezed it hard. We couldn't look at each other yet. We both looked at the floor. She took a deep breath and said, "Do you know how much I love you, Meena?"

Yes, I said. She loved me, so all would be well, even though all things were collapsing in flood and fire to form a new world. I still couldn't look her in the face so I pressed my cheek to hers and squeezed my eyes shut and in the dark behind my eyelids I saw her face take shape again, her skin dewy from the effort of sex.

At this I became calm.

With my eyes still closed I hugged her shoulders, swung her around, and shoved her into the glass cabinet.

It shattered top to bottom. A dog started barking outside.

I took her by the throat and slammed her head against the broken glass. She was in shock. I pushed her face back again and my hand got into her mouth and she bit me and the slime from her tongue got on my skin. All the glass had fallen now and I was beating her head against the wooden shelf. Then she was pushing back, trying to get me to let go.

I threw her against the bed. A fan of blood appeared on the sheets and a halo started spreading around her head. I grabbed her throat again. I could see her lips forming my name. She was scraping at my stomach. Her eyes were overflowing their sockets. She tried to push me away but she was getting weaker. I felt a bite at my solar plexus and reared back. She had punctured me with her fingernails. I stretched the skin above it and saw blood swell and run down. I was enraged.

I punched her in the face.

She went still.

◇　◇　◇

When I'm done with the kiosk, it's a patch of wreckage floating away. Subu got out of my way. He sat a few scales away and
watched the whole thing.

I don't know how to make amends. I don't even want to.

I try to keep walking west but I can't balance anymore. I'm
surrounded by the opportunity to die. The ocean is so much bigger
than I am. Mass wins. I should submit to it. I want to drop sideways or just lie down and not move.

But I act from animal self-preservation. I come to my knees to
put my center of gravity closer to the Trail. I imagine a line running straight down the middle of the Trail and focus on putting my
hands on it. I crawl forward. I hug the solid.

◇　◇　◇

Mohini doesn't talk to me anymore. None of my counselors do. I
listen but they've all fallen silent.

There's only the little woman. I see her from a long way off. She
retreats before me, but a little less every time. Even from this distance I can tell she isn't shifting her weight at all. The Trail is her
medium. I imagine it's the same woman I saw dive into the ocean
after the ship crossing, and the same woman I saw crawl overhead
on the glass tunnel, and also Bloody Mary, and also the mango-
ring thief. She's the bearer of all phenomena. She doesn't appear
iteratively like the bodies did. She's one continuous vision.

Then she starts leaving things. I find a conch shell sitting in
the middle of a scale one evening. I leave it where it is. The next

night, there's a starfish oozing from A to B, still alive. How did it get up here. I nudge it over the side and hope it survives the long journey down. The next day, as the sun is setting, I find ribbons of brown kelp arranged in a circle. She watches me from a safe distance while I examine it. I feel she wants me to. I feel she's seeking my approval. So I take note of the distribution of kelp as even and careful and artful and then crawl through the middle of it toward her.

This time she stands her ground. She allows me closer. She doesn't take her eyes off me. She seems terrified. She's naked and her skin is burnt. She looks familiar. Her arms hang askew from her collarbone. She's an old woman with the body of a starved child. Her legs are crossed with rivulets of salt. I want to lie down but instead I come just a little bit closer and see that she's holding a white rag balled up in her fist.

I stop two scales away.

"We meet again," I say.

She drops to her knees and says,

HASSANIYYA: Yemaya, can it truly be you?

BOOK XVIII

Mariama

The Second Flight

I didn't find Gabriel that day.

But with the new knowledge, the kreen swelled like a tumor. Sometimes the pain was unbearable. People on the street and on the bus looked at me strangely, often with pity. I suspected they could see the kreen in me.

Class was out for the rainy season. I slept all day and watched the news at night. The ARAP and the PEP were both preparing for the election in August. Elections were usually in May, but the PEP had pushed them back so that the student effort would be weakened, or so rumor had it.

But I couldn't care. The kreen wouldn't let me care about anything else but itself.

I stopped going out except to get food near my apartment in Tewodros Square. I ate the same thing every day: rice and ladoos from an Indian on the corner. I liked him because he didn't give me the same pitying looks that everyone else did. As for the ladoos, made of milk and sugar, they were the only thing my body wanted. Now I know it's because they reminded me of you, Yemaya.

On Election Day, I went downstairs to get a bowl of rice and a few ladoos, just like any other day. The square was full of media, agitators, protestors, and voters streaming to their appointed polling places. It was an impressive circus. Six months ago I would have joined. But the fight had gone out of me: I loved not Ethiopia, nor India, nor cared much who won the election. All that was left was the kreen and I didn't know how to make it go away.

Then, across the square and swimming with the current, I spotted a golden young man, fine and handsome and broad-shouldered. It was my Gabriel. He looked healthy and happy. He was alone. He was wearing scrubs. He stepped out into the street and hailed the bus. He boarded. The bus pulled away south down Churchill Avenue.

So it was true. He was in the city. I realized he probably had been all along.

I paid for my ladoos, sat on a bench on the street, and ate them. I had a premonition that this was the last chance I would have to eat for a while.

When I was done, and had wiped my fingers and thrown away the napkin, I stepped into the street and called an autotaxi. The yellow vehicle slid to a halt and the door arced back. I entered and sat and told the soft mechanical voice, when prompted, that I would like to go to Our Lady of Entoto Hospital. The voice instructed me to hold my mitter to the screen. It scanned it to check my account, and then the door slid closed and the car merged onto Churchill Avenue.

I watched the great Ethiopian pageant outside my window. We were gliding through the ferenji quarter now, so there were storefronts of pale mannequins modeling the latest, wildest interpretations of Persian clothing, dresses of jade with puffed sleeves.

We passed a gang of street boys with eaten shoes. A priest spoke to the air, answering the voices piped into his ear from his mobile. Two country women in Amhara dresses stepped around garbage. A stray dog wagged his tail and stared at a shop owner, ever optimistic. High compound walls glinted with broken glass. And then we were leaving the ferenji quarter, passing Ethiopia Airlines, the Ethiopia National Theatre, and Ethiopia Telecom. The car came to a stop and then turned left on Ras Mekonnen. We swung through the slingshot of Meskel Square, past a group of girls playing soccer in front of the Ethiopia Tourist Commission. At the sight of the girls, the kreen swelled and burned again. I put my hand over my solar plexus to try to soothe the pain and, with my other hand, clutched the handle of the door. The car asked me if I was well. I said, Yes, I just want to get to the hospital soon. The car clicked and sped up.

We sailed along Ras Mekonnen until it became Haile Gebre Selassie Road. The buildings thinned out. So did the crowds. We were approaching the eastern suburbs. The sweat from the kreen's most recent fit was cooling, and I wiped my hand on the soft bench seat.

The car reached Meganagna and swung around the whole roundabout, finally turning right to enter the hospital compound from the back. We slid to a stop. A pleasant tone sounded and the voice informed me that I had arrived at my destination. I got out of the car and stood in front of the hospital.

The kreen got excited. It knew we'd arrived.

How would I find Gabriel? I went to the front desk where an Indian woman sat. Immediately I realized that this was not a place where Ethiopians worked, except as custodians. This was an Indian contract hospital. My old prejudices flamed anew. The kreen ate them and swelled and became more powerful.

The clerk assessed me as I walked up. I becalmed myself and asked her where Gabriel might be.

You mean Dr. A. R. Gabriel? she said in a tone of reproach.

I felt ashamed and said yes.

Do you have an appointment? she asked.

No, I said. But he knows me. It's an emergency.

She looked at me—in fact she looked right at the kreen!—with the same pitying look I was used to from people on the street. She said, I think he's on the second floor in Obstetrics. I'll page him. Have a seat.

I did have a seat. But after she paged him, I excused myself to go to the bathroom and never went back.

On the second floor there was a directory on the wall with an arrow pointing to Obstetrics. I walked down many corridors, all white, all bright, all slippery. Then I came to another desk, where two Indian women sat. They seemed to be nurses. I couldn't go past them without asking, so I asked where Dr. A. R. Gabriel might be. The left one asked if I had an appointment. I repeated what I'd said downstairs. The right one got up and looked down the hallway and came back, muttering.

Kamala just paged him downstairs, she said to the left one. You suppose he's seeing patients right now?

The left one laughed. Let's see, it's four o'clock, she said. Time for Dr. Mehta's tea break.

They both laughed.

The kreen snapped at the inside of my chest with its fangs. I doubled over. The left one came around the desk and asked me if I needed a wheelchair. I said no. I said, It'll pass. I heard myself making mewing sounds like a kitten. She told me to breathe, and I did.

They helped me to have a seat and told me Dr. Gabriel would be with me shortly. I thanked them. Again I asked where the bathroom was. They pointed me toward it, around the corner. I walked to it but of course just kept walking.

I got to the end of the hallway and turned left. I passed a room where a lettered sign said A. R. GABRIEL, K. L. MITRA, S. J. ANDREWS, M. MEHTA, PHYSICIANS—FAMILY MEDICINE. But I saw through the window that the office was empty. An old Amhara in a white coat started down the hallway and I asked him if he knew where Dr. Gabriel was. He said he'd last seen him about to take tea in the gowning room and lifted his hand to point down another hallway. I rushed past him without saying thank you. I felt like there were worms writhing in my head and trying to come out of my eyes.

Like when I broke into my neighbor's flat, I began to see a few seconds into the future and float above the ground. I saw the scene forming in my mind's eye. Gabriel was in the gowning room. Gabriel always forgets to lock the door. I could hear heaving breaths in my head. I passed a nurse's station where there was a basket of scalpels, each individually wrapped, ready to use. I picked one up. The kreen flopped and snapped, striking at my skin from the inside. I pushed open the door and the universe opened its book of permissions because there stood Gabriel with his pants around his knees, thrusting into the backside of a naked woman.

The world plunged into perfect silence.

They separated, though a cord of slime still connected them. I went first for Meena, who had never felt the kreen, only love and adoration. I moved in double time, above time, outside of time. I seized her jaw and pushed her head back against the cabinet to draw an arc under her throat and then, in a calligraphic stroke, down through her solar plexus all the way to her wet pubis. She slumped to the floor in a sitting position, hands at her throat, trying to keep the blood in. I then turned to Gabriel, who was frozen, staring at the kreen. He opened his mouth but the kreen wouldn't let him speak. I stuffed my fist into his mouth, which forced his neck back, and I drew the same line across his throat. He landed a blow on my face and pushed me away but then fell over sideways onto the floor.

Black soda flecks danced in my eyes, like they had when I hit the sand all those years ago. I couldn't hear anything. I'd gone deaf. I just watched them, Meena keeping one hand to her throat and trying to gather her feet underneath her, Gabriel trying to make his way across the floor. After a minute, both of them slumped and stopped moving, just like that man in the checkered shirt.

But this time, I didn't feel better.

I'd been given permission. I'd thought to silence the kreen with these deaths once and for all. But it struck inside me again and again, with even more force. I grabbed hold of the counter to steady myself and the scalpel dropped to the floor, but I still couldn't hear it. I couldn't hear anything. The kreen was enormous now, a swelling monstrosity, eating me from the inside. It was not my friend. It was not my protector. It never had been.

And then, in one instant, I understood the path of my deliverance.

Oh, Yemaya.

You had guided me all along. And I had all the tools. I only needed to act.

I picked up the scalpel again and used a towel to wipe the hilt so that I could get a grip. I knelt on the floor between Gabriel and Meena. I closed my eyes and under the fluorescent lights I remembered the program I'd watched in the Sheraton all those years ago, how Inés Ramírez had survived, though here I was to deliver not a baby, but a demon.

I began a cut above my mons and punched far enough that I felt an itch deep in my viscera. Then I drew the knife across the skin. I was still in such an inspired state that I felt little pain. I knew you were protecting me. I had cut a hand's width when the wound bloomed like the meat of a grape escaping its skin; out surged flesh, white fat, and iridescent fascia. I put my finger inside the wound and then my whole hand, letting the blood lubricate my fingers, pushing and feeling by instinct, letting you guide me. I hit a band of muscle and went under it and found a rubbery wall under which the kreen writhed. I could feel its very contours. I spread the muscles up with one hand and, with the other, reached in to slice the final barrier.

Then I reached in and pulled the kreen out onto the floor. It looked like a red lizard, mouth open in a silent scream. Another bag of flesh followed it. A twisted cord connected me to it and I cut it.

So this is what it looked like, this demon spirit born of the sea snake I choked on all those years ago. I was free of it. It could haunt someone else, now, and I knew just who. I lifted the kreen off the floor and anchored it in the lap of Dr. Meena Mehta under the waterfall of her blood.

Now she would know what the kreen felt like.

I felt euphoric, but I also knew I couldn't waste time. My victory was incomplete. I could still be caught. You'd given me respite from the pain, for now, but I couldn't take it for granted. I started opening drawers. I found stacks of disposable gowns and tied one around my middle. It was very messy and inexact and the wound was bleeding down my legs. I began to feel glimpses of pain. In another drawer I found all kinds of medical supplies and stuffed them into my bag—boxes of nanobiotics and stem-cell strips and tubes of surgical glue. I used more disposable gowns to slough the blood off my arms and legs as best I could. There were street clothes on pegs near the door; I picked a big red T-shirt that fit over my makeshift dressings, and black denim jeans that were three sizes too big for me, and fastened them on with a brown belt.

I looked at the lovers one last time. They didn't move, and the kreen was clawing at Dr. Meena Mehta's skin and trying to wriggle into her. It wouldn't trouble me any longer.

I opened the door and looked both ways. There was no one

near. This was an old deserted wing of the clinic. I had to act log-
ically and carefully from this point on. I told myself I was on an
adventure, pure and free, now, of the kreen and other adulterating
influences. No one else would understand what I had done in the
way you would. I had to leave the country.

I walked right out a back exit, into the sunlight, into an asphalt
parking lot. My hearing began to return. I took off my mitter and
dropped it into a sewer. My cash was still unbloodied, so I could
use that to pay for transportation. I hailed a private car, which
meant it lacked a security camera, and directed it to Autobus Terra
in the west of the city, where there were buses leaving for every
corner of Ethiopia every day. I could take the train, but buses were
cheaper, privately owned, and less likely to be monitored.

The car asked for an initial deposit, so I threaded in a few bills
and it started off, past crowds gathered at screens all around the
city, watching the election returns come in. The PEP was winning by a landslide, somehow, though the Al Jazeera polls had
predicted a wide margin of victory for ARAP. I knew it wasn't
good. Violence was near.

When I got to Autobus Terra, I began to truly fall back into
my body. I could hear again, and everything was loud. My belly
burned like it was on fire. I limped out of the car and ignored the
stares and bought a ticket for Assaita and went into a stall in the
women's bathroom, struggling to remain upright. I peeled up my
T-shirt and untied the dressing gown I'd used to bind the wound.
The pain was so great I thought I would faint.

I made myself take deep breaths. I knew you wouldn't abandon
me now, having brought me so far. I had to have faith.

I leaned back against the wall to make my torso as flat as possible, then used my hand to move the two walls of the incision together. With my other hand, I peeled a stem-cell strip out of its
wrapper and laid it across the wound. I added one more on top of

that, and then three more perpendicularly just to make sure. The wrapper instructed me to bind it over with gauze, but I had none, so I picked the bloody dressing gown back up off the bathroom floor and re-bound it around my hips. Infection. I had to watch for infection. I swallowed four broad-spectrum nanobiotics, dry, for the time being. But I would need real medical attention soon.

The border with Djibouti was only 250 kilometers away. A matter of hours on smooth, paved roads. Surely I could hold out that long. I boarded the bus and collapsed in a back seat and watched the screen mounted in the ceiling. The PEP's victory was clear. I looked out the window and saw young women and men tearing down the street and shouting, rocks in hand, probably on their way to Meskel Square or the Presidential Palace. Oh, Yemaya, I could see the following scenes play out like a movie. All our noble student efforts had amounted to nothing.

So it goes, I said to myself.

The pain was swelling now, transforming me into a radiant being. But I knew you were with me in this final trial. I would wait and watch for the signs.

❴ B☐·☐K XIX ❵

Meena

A False Ocean

HASSANIYYA: Yemaya, can it truly be you?

I remember what the sailors called me. So I say, "Yes."

The little woman reaches for me, then snatches her hand back again and cradles it to her chest.

"It's you," she says. "Forgive me. I forgot how many languages you speak. I feel like a little girl again. You always called me 'little girl.' There's so much I want to tell you. I've already been telling you, for years, going to the place inside myself that is you, where the kreen used to be. But skin is skin. There's no substitute for skin. You're here in the flesh. You're so beautiful, naked, as I remember, in the hotel room. Where have you been? What have you been doing?"

The sun is setting directly behind her and Venus is rising above it. I stare at it. I'm still in the same universe. I don't know who she thinks I am, but I give the only answer I have.

"I hurt someone," I say.

"Hurt someone?" she says. "Who?"

"Someone I loved."

"They must have hurt you first."

I shift my eyes to her.

"Oh, Yemaya, I know how that feels," she says. "Stay with me. I'll tell you everything."

So I wait for her to continue.

◈ ◈ ◈

Months later, I was in Djibouti City, washing the floors of a convent and still watching for signs, when a nun handed me an old-fashioned flyer.

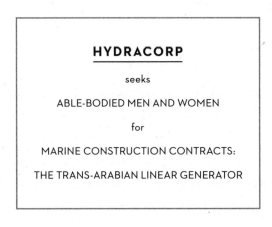

HYDRACORP

seeks

ABLE-BODIED MEN AND WOMEN

for

MARINE CONSTRUCTION CONTRACTS:

THE TRANS-ARABIAN LINEAR GENERATOR

And I remembered the wave array from my student protest days.

I went to the recruitment session at the Port of Djibouti, where a large crowd had gathered, and a beautiful woman in a fine silver suit spread her hands wide, between which appeared a holo of a sea snake that spanned the entire Arabian Sea. Of course it wasn't a sea snake, Yemaya. It was the Trail. But as soon as I saw it I remembered your story from the clinic all those years ago, and I

knew it was the final sign. The Trail was where you would reveal
yourself to me.

Can I go? I asked.

Of course, you said. I'll meet you there.

Ten years later, I was assigned to the ship carrying the last
scales to their destination. In the middle of the night, when all the
crew slept, I slipped out of a hatch by moonlight. I swam to the
Trail just a kilometer away from where our ship had dropped anchor. I pulled myself up. At first I crawled, and then I walked, and
by morning I was far, far away.

❖ ❖ ❖

Night has passed and the stars have cartwheeled overhead. Now
by the light of the eastern horizon I see the little woman's cowrie-
shell mouth is shaped like mine.

So this is my mother.

I'm so tired. After everything, this is all the final chamber is,
was, and ever will be, the concrete shack where her own mother
is upside down, mid-rape, saying she'd be all right, on repeat, forever. That was the end of her life. There's nothing anyone else can
say to her. I don't have the energy to try, even if it set the course
of my life as a bloody baby trying to enter people who are not my
mother.

There's nothing anyone can say to me, either.

So I just say, "Thank you for the story, little girl."

Then she asks if she can touch my face.

I say yes.

She crawls forward and reaches for me, and her skin is like
leather, and she stinks of sweat and sour brine, and she wraps
her arms around my head, like she's forgotten how to hug. I tell
myself: My mother is hugging me. This should feel good. But it

doesn't. She's hugging my head to her chest more tightly and my arms are limp at my sides. I open my eyes and see blackness. She squeezes harder and harder. I start seeing sparkles. She wants to consume me.

I push her away.

She looks terrified. She curls into a ball and rocks. "Have I angered you, Yemaya?"

"No," I say. "I just couldn't breathe."

"Forgive me," she says, uncurling and reaching for me again. "I just wanted us to be together again, one and whole, as before." Then with a shy look dawning in her eyes, she lies back and parts her legs before me. Her yoni is soft and hairless from age.

I look away. I focus on the sea. I try to imagine what the goddess would do. I try to imagine what would make us whole.

I crawl forward and lie down next to her and turn her over and hug her to me like she says Yemaya used to hold her. She's fragile. Her body expands and collapses. I breathe her in and now under the brine I smell a faint violet smell from a recurring dream I've had all my life but couldn't remember till now.

For a time, we sleep, and share that very dream.

We wake near dawn, when the clouds are sage and gold.

She turns over and holds my face in her hands and says, "I am yours, Yemaya, as I always was. Take me."

Djibouti

It begins to rain.

So this is how the Trail will end for me. A Trail-ending rain, a world-ending rain. I think again of holding the knife, the blade with the infinitesimal edge, that could cut everything, palms, saris, salwar kameez, fruit, the metal of trains, and people. Here the

world is already split in two for me: sky, sea. But now in the rain
they blur into one continuum. So does the Trail. I wonder where
the real Yemaya is now. I wonder what her real name was. Maybe
she did go to Addis, for a few months, feckless, to go slumming
and do the artist thing, only to realize that she had no skills and no
job prospects, only to move on to another imagined paradise, and
then another and another, because she could never go back home.
I begin to see visions of Africa, coming from the west. The fantasy
of flotillas was naïve but surely I'll be welcomed, somehow. Who
else has walked this far. Who else has stepped off the edge into
the arms of the continental shelf. I want to be a hero for practical
reasons: I'll be taken care of: I'll be given a bed and warm food. I
remember pictures of Djibouti. The sovereign nation of Djibouti.
The colonial architecture. Cafés and sea spray. The musical legacy
of which I know nothing but have no doubt exists. A little cross-
roads of the world. A tongue of land. A continuation of the planet
on which women and men, clean and healthy, go about their business on solid ground, in suits, with jobs, picking up pastries from
kiosks on the way to work. Like waking from a dream I begin to
remember what real food is like. Hot food with different kinds of
things in it. Hot food over rice. Pappadams that crackle. Spices.
Cold icy drinks and hot steaming drinks. Sugar. Pickles. I have to
spend the next few hours wisely. I have to conserve energy. Even
though I've lost the strength to walk I still crawl, down the mid-
line, not permitting myself to think except about food. I have to
make it to land. I have to see whether life continues, after I laid
my mother on top of the waves and let her sink, and watched her
head bend back, and her little body turn in the current until I
couldn't see it anymore, and then I closed my eyes and watched her
from the inside, and saw her pass through the warm upper reach,
then cross the boundary into the freezing dark, descending down
the gradient, down into darkness, then carried on currents to the

deepest parts of the world, until her body came to settle in a place where the sky was always black and the moon was always new.

I have only two kilometers' notice that I've reached the end of the world, and I don't see land but I keep crawling because this is definitely the last and most cruel hallucination, made worse by the rain that confuses sea and air, and I'll pass through this veil like all the others, even though my mother is already found and lost again, life will be nothing but more veils to pass and pass through again. I know this now. There are yet more chambers. I crawl to the end.

The scales end in the middle of the sea.

There's no land in sight. I think that there must have been a catastrophic break where the Trail drowned and didn't resurface and I get frantic and plunge my hands down into the water, but feel the two mooring cables that I remember running into below the surface, at the very beginning, in Back Bay. This is definitely the end of the Trail.

I dig out my pozit. I'm only a kilometer offshore. I should be able to see land. But then I see a flock of hovercraft glinting in the distance, turning this way and that, swimming through the air like a school of fish, low over the water, and now I understand that the sovereign nation of Djibouti is nowhere in sight because the sovereign nation of Djibouti is gone.

Epilogue

I approach one of the cook fires on the beach and a young girl sees my traveling clothes, jumps up, and offers me passage. She's wearing a hijab and demure jean shorts with flowers embroidered on the pockets and she has a hoverboat that she assures me is very safe, very comfortable. She's in her element. This is the heart of the world, for her, both before and after the wave, which didn't hit as hard here on the west coast as it did on the east coast. But it still hit. The world changed when Yemaya came ashore.

I show her the address written on the side of my hand and she nods and gestures me to follow her. This is too easy. This part should be harder. I expected resistance or some other species of difficulty but now everything is going very fast. We get into her hoverboat and she takes me out into the shallows, down alleys of water between houses on concrete pillars, and above us, men in sky-blue robes watch from their porches and call to the girl, who yells back with clever rejoinders that make them laugh. I like her. I want to be like her.

Too soon, the girl slows down the boat and pulls up to a concrete staircase leading up out of the water, up to a square house with a narrow porch running all around, just wide enough for a stool to sit on and look out in any direction. On the walls are white chalk drawings of crescent moons and fish.

I want to ask the girl to stay with me, to beg her, really, to stay in her hoverboat at the foot of the stairs, in case something goes wrong, in case I change my mind. But instead I pay her in rupees and watch her go. And then I'm left alone on the concrete stairway.

There's nothing left to do but ascend.

How did this moment arrive so quickly?

My thoughts keep slipping from the present. They want to avoid it and go somewhere else. Nothing is like I thought it would be: the concrete, the sea, the white chalk drawings. I become self-conscious. I make myself look down at my feet and take fifteen steps. But when I reach eye-level with the porch there's only a dog by the door, who lifts her head and thumps her tail, once. Maybe I have the wrong name or the wrong house. In fact, I hope I do. I feel like I might float up into the sky. But I have to stay here. I have to be present for this.

Then a little girl comes to the doorway. She's wearing a clean white dress and is otherwise barefoot. She falls back against the door frame, shy, her finger in her mouth, looking at me.

I'm not confident in my Hassaniyya but I've learned some French during my travels, so I try it on her. I ask her if her mother is home. She says no, she's at school. The girl is sweet but looks confused at my clothing, my manner, my nervousness. I feel panicked. I'm intruding, clearly. It was arrogant of me to come, and even more, to think I'd be welcome. I apologize and begin to turn back down the stairs.

But then an old woman comes to the door, wearing a dress the color of young leaves.

She knows my cowrie-shell mouth.

She puts her hand on the little girl's shoulder and closes her eyes and I know I've found who I'm looking for, and so the act is done and can't be taken back, so I say nothing, and just wait and listen to the surf, the calls of men, the cries of children, the laughter of women, course up and down the waterways.

Then she opens her eyes and nods to me and says to the little girl,

HASSANIYYA: You must invite our guest in, Saha.

Acknowledgments

My deepest thanks to Deepti Gupta, Nebeyou Zewdie Tesema, Dr. Stefan Gary, and Dr. Jennifer Bishop for their professional assistance on the manuscript; and to R. Subramanian, Umair Kazi, Sisay Gebre-Egziabher, and Aatish Salvi for their insights. Thanks also to my early readers Stefani Nellen, Kat Howard, Jay O'Berski, Byron Woods, and Dr. Beckett Sterner for their warm encouragement.

The novel never would have been written without the Mary Elvira Stevens Traveling Fellowship for Wellesley College alumnae. I cannot express enough gratitude to the fellowship committee for having faith in me. For the same, I also thank the Durham Arts Council and the Vermont Studio Center. Thanks and love to those who aided and sheltered me during my travels: Sisay Gebre-Egziabher, Samson Challa, Eva Miranda, Jessica Ozberker, Nicole and Joshua Wengerd, Marcy and David Aldacushion, and the kind staff of Mr. Martin's Cozy Place in Ethiopia; Leena PS, Alysha Aggarwal, Chriselle Bayross, Dilna Shelji, Dr. Sarath Chandran, Anuradha and Gautham Sarang, Unny LJ, Bala Prakasam, and the extraordinary staff of Vijnana Kalavedi in India; Eleanor Kleiber in Fiji; and the hundreds of unnamed strangers who pressed on my heart, especially the little girls who wished me well.

Warm thanks to my wonderful agent, Sam Stoloff, who's been my advocate and champion since day one. He made the match with Zachary Wagman at Crown Publishing, who turns out to be the kind of editor every writer dreams of working with. Along with Molly Stern, Jacob Lewis, Sarah Bedingfield, Lauren Kuhn, Kayleigh George, Cathy Hennessy, Rachelle Mandik, and Emily Burns, working with Crown has been a dream come true. And though I don't get to see them as much, the team at Little, Brown UK has also been an incredible pleasure to work with: editor in chief Antonia Hodgson, marketing director Charlie King, editorial assistant Rhiannon Smith, head of digital sales Ben Goddard, and export sales manager Rachael Hum. I thank them all for handling my work with such care, wisdom, and generosity.

Thanks also to those who supported me during the very earliest days of writing: Lucy and Don Aquilano, Mary, Andrew, and Ginny Beazley, Clare, Donald, Julie, and Mary Byrne, Amy Calhoun, Erik and Martin Demaine, Danielle Durchslag, Cynthia Fischer, Mirren Fischer, Jackie Geer, Cecilia Gerard, Jim Haverkamp, Stefan Jacobs, Scott Jennings, John Justice, Sam Kirkpatrick, Jessie Kneeland, Alice Kunce, Jeanne Manzer, Lisa Martin, Ellie Mer, Jenny Nicholson, Cally Owles, Kristin Parker, Michelle Legaspi Sanchez, Laurie Stempler, Beckett Sterner, Sandy Sulzer, Ingrid Swanson, Laura Westman, Prem Yadav, Frances Wiener, and Laura Wysong. Thanks also to Arian Aareeyan and his agent Hanif Yazdi for accommodating my strange request.

For research on this novel, I'm deeply indebted to the nonfiction writings of Gita Mehta, Michio Kaku, Anand Giridharadas, Susan Casey, Laurence C. Smith, Roz Savage, Nega Mezlekia, Jeffrey Tayler, Kira Salak, Bill Bryson, and Thalia Zepatos. I also give thanks for the wonderful novelists whose books guided me in writing my own: Norman Rush, Ursula K. Le Guin, Mary Renault, Kim Stanley Robinson, Arundhati Roy, Toni Morrison,

Donna Tartt, and Haruki Murakami. Also, percolating through this book like water through limestone is the music of Meshell Ndegeocello. I thank her for being herself and no other.

My companions in this life are Mary Anne, Donald Edward Jr., Julie Elizabeth, Donald Edward III, Clare Siobhan, and Mary McMonigal. I love them more than I know how to say. From the day I was born, they've held all my dreams in a space of unconditional love and support, including my dream for a creative life. As Julie once said, No one could ask to be so blessed in this world.